THE POLYGRAPHER

DOHN JAGSTER

authorHOUSE®

AuthorHouse™
1663 Liberty Drive
Bloomington, IN 47403
www.authorhouse.com
Phone: 1 (800) 839-8640

Published by AuthorHouse 03/10/2016

ISBN: 978-1-5049-8501-7 (sc)
ISBN: 978-1-5049-8500-0 (hc)
ISBN: 978-1-5049-8502-4 (e)

Library of Congress Control Number: 2016904126

Print information available on the last page.

CHAPTER 1

He measured five foot eleven from the tip of his toes to the top of his head—and six foot even from the tip of his toes to the roof of his hump. Yes, Al was a hunchback who daily prayed for the soul of his recently departed mother and thanked her for not terminating him, her less-than-perfect son, and thereby giving him the life he so richly deserved. When she found out the male child she was carrying was deformed—and most certainly would never be physically normal—she'd steadfastly refused to give in to her husband's demands; she carried the child full term and delivered a healthy baby boy—a baby boy with a hump. His mother routinely fretted about her son, believing that he would be tormented, picked on, ridiculed, and maybe even physically abused as he aged, but contrary to her bleak expectations, none of these worst-case scenarios ever materialized. In fact, to a large extent, Al's hump was more of an asset than a liability. People bent over backward to give him a break, and they always gave him the benefit of the doubt when really important decisions were in the offing. Al was certainly no intellectual giant, but he basically skated through college, receiving his bachelor's and then master's degree in business administration in record time and with pretty good grades. He'd always believed a number of his professors had cut him some slack because of his deformity; they felt bad for him and thought he deserved a break. In retrospect, he appreciated their kindness, but it was unnecessary—the material wasn't all that difficult. After graduating near the top of his class, he looked around for a career with a bit of excitement and maybe some travel; he wanted to meet interesting people—and exciting women. Al was anything but a loner, and his hump never slowed him down; the world was his oyster, at least according to the class valedictorian. Contrary to what one might think, women weren't turned off by his hump.

In fact, some thought it quite exotic, but most just ignored it as they might disregard a disproportionately large nose or a bucolic, down-home southern accent. In many respects, Al was quite good-looking: he had an athletic, muscular body with not an ounce of fat. He had a kind, appealing face, bushy eyebrows that picturesquely frame the bluest of blue eyes, and a quizzical smile that seemed to say, "I see you—stop peeking at my hump." By any measurable standard, Al was a decent sort of chap, and if he were forced to identify one character flaw, it would be that he loved *things*; he loved acquiring things. And to buy things, he needed money. Yes, Al loved money and what it could do for those he cared about, but more importantly he loved money for what it could do for Al.

Al spent most of the summer casting here and then there, looking for that dream job. And while he had several offers, none appealed to him. He could afford to be picky, since his mother had left him a large nest egg; she'd never gotten over her fear that his handicap might somehow impede his success or derail his journey through life. After he'd spent a few months looking, a friend told him that Central Intelligence was recruiting. If he was interested, he should bring three copies of his résumé to the Tyson's Corner Holiday Inn around nine the following day. When asked, his friend replied no, he wasn't interested in being a super-snoop—he was enlisting in the army and hoped to be accepted into Officer's Candidate School and be commissioned a second lieutenant in a year or two. Al had never considered the military, knowing he'd automatically be medically disqualified. "No humps allowed … talk about discrimination. Atten-hump! No, not my bag, anyway. Too much discipline—just shut up and do what you're told. No, definitely not for me," he said as he smiled to himself a rather grim, self-deprecating smile.

At the Holiday Inn the following day, Al dropped off his rather lean résumé, had a few cordial words with an Agency rep, and then departed disappointed that the interview wasn't more extensive. He said to himself, *This will be a complete waste of time, a dead loss.* A few days later, however, he received a letter in the mail advising him to show up in five days' time for a preliminary interview at CIA HQ, just outside McLean in northern Virginia. He'd have to sign in at the security checkpoint and get a temporary visitor's badge, but everything would be organized up front, and there would be no problems entering the Agency compound. It was all there in black and white. Al ticked off a few boxes to accept the invite and returned it in the stamped, self-addressed envelope. He was excited; working for the country's premier clandestine service seemed very interesting, and what would his friends think? Most of his friends already had jobs—mostly entry-level jobs in business administration—but he, Al, might walk in the footsteps of, yes, James Bond, the most famous spy ever. *How very radical*, thought Al. The fact that James was British and worked for MI-5—or was it MI-6?—was just a minor technicality that Al chose to ignore; his imagination ran rampant.

Al was up at the crack of dawn, multitasking. *How to dress? What to wear? What not to wear?* All these questions and others raced through his mind as he brushed his teeth and ran the shower until it got too hot. Al knew Agency employees were notoriously tasteless dressers. How he knew that, he couldn't say, but he knew, so he picked out a plain, solid-gray shirt and gray slacks. Navy sports coat and brown shoes—no tie or T-shirt. It was November, so this ensemble would do nicely; an overcoat would not be necessary. All of Al's shirts were tailored to fit snugly over his hump, and as humps went, his was not too large. But it was large enough to cause a curvature of the spine, so when walking, Al looked as though he were searching for loose change. As Al's spine allowed little vertical movement, he used his powerful neck muscles to look ahead or to the left or right. While looking up was not impossible, it was very difficult and could only be done in short bursts. If Al could stand up straight, which he couldn't, he'd be well over six feet tall—quite imposing.

Al passed through CIA security without a hitch; he got a temporary visitor's badge that neatly clipped onto his lapel, well above the waist as required. He was permitted to wander the original headquarters buildings with no escort—and got lost a couple of times. He eventually found his interviewer in a small cubicle crammed with a largish computer workstation, a printer, several shelves of books, and two chairs—one for visitors, presumably. From the placement of the visitor's chair, it looked as if it had been recently dragged in from another cubicle. The room size didn't impress Al; he'd figured he'd be interviewed in a plush office with the interviewer seated behind a large mahogany desk with the walls lined with photos of previous directors, maybe an American flag at attention in one corner, and the pervasive odor of freshly brewed coffee. Al also figured he'd be seated in a plush, burgundy leather chair and sipping coffee from fine English china, but that was not to be. The interviewer welcomed Al with a less-than-convincing handshake and then, with the wave of a hand, invited him to sit. Al had to keep his long legs tucked under his chair or risk knocking his feet against the interviewer's feet, which protruded well beyond the center of the cubicle. Al noticed that his interviewer was seated in a rather grand, real-estate-hogging chair with arms—certainly not appropriate for an office this size. He was offered neither coffee nor tea.

His interviewer introduced himself as John. He was about forty, of medium build and medium height, clean shaven, and mostly bald. He had dark horn-rimmed glasses and a very kind, open face—not an angle to be seen. He wore light brown cords that were wrinkled and didn't fit, brown leather shoes that needed a shine, and a gray shirt similar to the one Al was wearing—and it too needed pressing.

"Well, Al," he began. It appeared that he couldn't take his eyes off Al's hump. Al tried to look composed and confident—leaning forward, head slightly down, eyes straight ahead and glued to the face of the interviewer who, all of a sudden, seemed to explode with one unrelated question after another. Al could only figuratively weave and bob, countering with a series of disjointed answers to disjointed questions. He hoped his responses were intelligible, but he suspected they weren't.

The reason I'm here? ... Why do I want to work for the Agency, the CIA? ... Do I like to travel? ... Why? ... Why? ... Why?

Al was ill at ease and was never given enough time to wrap his brain around a question, parse it, and assemble a meaningful, cogent response. Therefore, none of his responses were internally checked for reasonableness, accuracy, or even common sense. Like the questions, the answers just gushed. One question, one answer; no time to just get to know John, no time to think, and certainly no insight into what he might be qualified to do at the Agency. Al could only assume his résumé had been read, but it was nowhere to be seen, though it might have been lying somewhere on John's untidy coffee-stained desk.

"Well, you know, John, I want to spice up my life, add some adventure, see the world, meet interesting people, and even serve my country. I'm still young; you understand. I'm sure you do. Challenging also, yes. The job must be challenging and require hard work and ... maybe even long hours, at least to start with. I'll relocate if necessary, but I prefer the DC area; this is my home … Yes, I did fairly well in college—a master's degree, pretty good grades." On and on it went, for just short of an hour. It was like an impromptu test with John launching clay pigeons and Al attempting to shoot them down with a peashooter.

John appeared to be listening, though he took no notes, but Al could see in his eyes that he'd hardly heard a word he said. Al figured John had heard all this before and was maybe even a tiny bit bored with the whole process, just wanting to get the interview over with, maybe even looking forward to a late breakfast or early lunch. As the cubicles were so small, anyone on the other sides of the partitions could hear everything, and Al hoped that anyone eavesdropping didn't think him too immature, too boring, or utterly too uninteresting.

Any time John managed to pull his eyes off the hump and tried to pay attention and strike up a meaningful dialogue, his eyes, as if drawn by a magnet, would slowing and irrevocably drift back to that mass on Al's back, and any connection between them, however tentative, was lost. John was clearly mesmerized by the hump.

John had to make an assessment of Al and recommend or not recommend his employment with the CIA. In the short space of fifty minutes, John had to figure out if Al was worth investing time and money in and if Al not only had the educational credentials but would live the lifestyle of a future Agency employee. The decision to recommend or not recommend was not usually very difficult for John. He had learned very early that not recommending would most certainly result in a barrage of questions from every which way asking for analysis, justification, and rationale. And from experience John had learned that his initial responses to those questions about his recommendation would be deemed unacceptable—either too brief or too tiresome—and the back and forth would go on for weeks, sometimes even longer. So only in the most egregious cases would John give a thumbs-down. He'd leave the weeding out to others, others who enjoyed weeding and didn't lose any sleep over yanking out a dandelion or two.

Al was quite sanguine about the entire process; if he didn't get the job, it would be disappointing, but there would be plenty of other opportunities. After several more innocuous questions from John and a very general synopsis of what he could expect as an Agency employee, the interviewer began to lose focus again and began to slightly stutter, or was it stammer? Al had him: an offer was in the bag, and it was his to turn down. The hump had worked its magic again, better than a best friend or rich uncle. No way would a less-than-perfect recommendation be forthcoming. For John a poor recommendation would be shameful, disgraceful. He would accuse himself of bias, bias against a deformity, and Al knew full well that the Agency prided itself on hiring the handicapped, who usually excelled at their work and rapidly integrated into the Agency lifestyle and mind-set.

"Well." John now seemed unnerved to the point of distraction. He looked at the floor as he spoke and fidgeted with his wedding band, passing it from one finger to another, even occasionally dropping and then retrieving it. Things started to wind down; Al could see that John was running out of steam. Then came a minute or two of silence, enough silence for Al to contemplate working day in and day out in a tiny little blue-paneled cubicle. *Maybe*, he thought, *the work will make up for the crappy digs.*

"Well, Al, here's the straight scoop. With your education and motivation, in my opinion you're made for the CIA, and I'll unconditionally recommend you be immediately mainstreamed. Let me cover a few more basics, things you can look forward to. There's an extensive up-front training program. It's a doddle—you'll have no problems. Security will also check you out, and you'll also have to take a polygraph. I won't tell you it's just a formality—it's not. The Agency just wants to make sure you have no skeletons—you know, dead bodies in your backyard. If you fail your poly or are found unsuitable for any reason, you'll probably be cut loose. We're only concerned with major issues, things that you could be blackmailed for or that would somehow prevent you from doing your job. That wouldn't be good for you or us. Oh, Al, a suggestion: don't go to the library and read up on polys. It'll just confuse you and might even skew your responses, and your examiner might think you're trying to be clever—you know, trying to outfox the fox or, worse, screw with the Agency. Not a good scenario—for you, I mean. Finally, remember the polygraph is a machine. It only measures perspiration, respiration, and blood pressure. Don't try to beat the machine. If you have issues, work with your polygrapher; he's there to get you through the examination. He's not there to see you get eliminated as a candidate for employment. In a way, if you fail, he fails.

"Any questions, Al?"

Without waiting for Al to respond, John rose and proceeded to the door, a heavy-duty steel door with a complex locking mechanism, a door that always seemed to be unlocked.

Al got the impression John would be glad to see the back of him. Together they walked to the door, and there they shook hands. John almost patted Al on the back but caught himself in the nick of time. John pointed Al in the right direction. As Al advanced down the hallway, he could feel a set of eyes burning a hole in his hump. He put his right hand high in the air, waved, and then gave his hump a gentle, cursory pat.

A few weeks later, Al was again up quite early and on his way to a different Agency site for his first poly. He was looking forward to it. He had nothing to lose—if he didn't qualify and get the job, he could still enjoy 007 in the pictures. He didn't really need this job; something else would turn up, and he could afford to enjoy the experience, almost be arrogant about it, though not ostentatiously arrogant. Even if he did pass this time, he'd heard Agency employees had to pass their polys every seven or eight years or lose their clearances and most likely their jobs and the benefits that came with Agency employment. Rumor had it that Agency wages were on the order of 25 percent higher than comparable jobs not requiring high-level security clearances. Job satisfaction was reputed to be high because the work, by and large, was not only challenging but very interesting and directly related to national security and protecting the homeland. So many things were running through Al's head that morning that in a blur he was in his car and off to his future.

Al checked in with a receptionist who confirmed his appointment and verified his identity. All was in order. He took a seat along with about twenty others who were, he assumed, also there for polygraph testing; all looked young, some too young to vote. A TV was showing a mundane video about the purpose of the polygraph, what it was meant to accomplish, and how the interviewee was to interact with the polygraph and the polygrapher. One by one, interviewees were greeted and led off. Men greeted men, and women greeted women, all very cordial, all smiling as though to say, *No problem.* Al figured one or two had secrets they wished not to share, but if that were the case they should have stayed home, though maybe, for whatever reason, they had to show up. Al started to get a bit nervous; he wished his polygrapher would show up. Finally, a quarter of an hour later, a middle-aged man in brown jacket and black tie appeared, introduced himself, and led Al to a small office with a very clean, very tidy desk. On the desk was a keyboard, a bulky monitor, and a thin manila folder probably containing Al's résumé and university transcripts. A rather large but not very imposing gold nameplate was located precisely in the middle of the visitor's side of the desk. It simply read "Jim"—no last name, just "Jim"—in black mixed-case letters.

"Sit down, Al. My name's Jim, and my friends call me Jim, not James and certainly not Jimmy or Jimbo, just plain Jim."

Jim chuckled, obviously thinking he was being amusing. Al reciprocated but only halfheartedly. To Al's thinking Jim would be very difficult to consistently describe. Yes, middle aged, rather rotund, and short, with no facial hair whatsoever—including no eyebrows and no eyelashes—and no glasses. One thing Al noticed straightaway: Jim's face didn't match his rotund shape. He had the face of a very skinny man with close-set eyes; a small, pointy nose; thin lips; no chin to speak of; little ears; and sunken cheeks. It was as if he was Mr. Potato Head and some children had put together a face designed to mesmerize and distract. Once the observer was distracted, the kids would fly in and slyly replace a nose or a chin. Jim's face seemed to morph from minute from minute.

Yes, thought Al, *it would be impossible to pick this guy out of a lineup. He ought to rob banks ... hmm, more money, and I do love money.*

Al sat in a large, soft, light blue leather chair facing straight ahead at a wall. He swiveled his chair in order to face Jim, but the chair only swiveled so far, and Al sat staring over Jim's right shoulder. In order for Al to make eye contact, insofar as it was possible, he had to sit on an angle and rotate his head fifteen degrees to the right. To Al, Jim looked a bit on the weary side; maybe he'd had a hard week.

"Well, Al, let's get straight to the point." Jim spoke loudly, like a first sergeant, almost shouting, almost startling Al to attention, which would have been quite impossible. Unlike John at CIA HQ, Jim didn't seem fazed by Al's hump; in fact he didn't look much at Al or his hump and instead spoke into space like some well-oiled Roman orator playing to the Senate. "I'm not much for small talk, and you didn't show up for us to become pals, did you? Usually, anyone sitting where you're seated has had a background investigation. We call it a BI—yep, Bravo India.

Background investigations are not only expensive but time consuming, so the Agency's new approach for potential new hires is to ensure that they pass their poly and then do the BI. If the background findings or your poly are the least bit questionable, an offer of employment will most likely not be forthcoming, but if your poly and background investigation are okay, then you'll probably be offered a job. Mind you, you'll start off pretty damn low on the totem pole, but as I like to say, a job's a job. So you need to ask yourself if there's anything in your history that might preclude you from working at the Agency, anything that might put you in a vulnerable position, like a serious crime, alcoholism, drug abuse, a serious unnatural predilection, major financial issues, questionable friends from a foreign country, close ties to journalists. All these are of great concern to the Agency. Now, we're not saying you have to be squeaky clean. We can usually work around onetime, minor crimes, a bad driving record, juvenile offenses, et cetera. Now, if you're not sure if something is major, we need to talk. Bring it to the surface, but please just don't bury it because I'll find out—one way or the other I will find out, and you'll suffer the consequences. One more thing, Al: no lying. No fucking lying. Try and throw me a curve ball, and I'll throw you a screwball. I'll see you get screwed right out the door, and it'll all be documented in your personal file, and you'll never work for any government organization, not if you live to be a hundred."

"Get my drift, Al? If the answer to any of those questions is yes, you might be better off just getting up and dragging your sorry ass out of here, because I'll find out. I will find out, and that's a promise, and you'll have wasted your time and my time, and that's not good, and I will not be a happy camper."

"Did you say journalists, Jim, like in reporters? Why? I can understand your other examples, but I always thought reporters helped sustain democracy and the American way of life."

"Well, Al, it's like this. We here at the Agency consider ourselves to be silent warriors—the less publicity the better. We kind of like to get the job done on the sly, and we usually do, and we don't want any recognition or unnecessary hoopla. We have to repeat that old saw over and over—no hoopla—but those bastards at the *Post* and the *Times* just don't get the message. Why? Because reporters consider themselves to be watchdogs, out there protecting democracy, motherhood, and apple pie. No matter how hard they try, they just can't keep their goddamned mouths shut. I don't know, Al. In a nutshell, we just consider them to be blabbermouths. Their mantra is to just get the story at any cost, no matter who gets hurt, no matter what Agency resource gets compromised. Just get the story, print it, let the chips fall where they may, and then move on. Yep, move on. They don't want to hang around and clean up the blood, literally. They just love putting the screws to the *CIA*, and they don't mind naming names." When Jim had said "CIA", he'd emphasized it the way some people did when speaking of God, respectful for fear of eternal damnation. "I swear they really do dislike us, Al, and for the life of me I can't figure out why. So, take my advice—stay away from journalists, and if you do have friends who work in the media keep your employment record to yourself, because if they ever do find out that you work for the Agency, you will become a source to be mined, not a friend."

Al suspected that Jim would have been very pleased if he had left, right then, refused his poly, but he didn't. As lives went, Al's was not pristine, but none of the aforementioned transgressions applied to him.

"Let's do it, Jim. I'm ready."

"Right you are, my boy. I like your attitude," replied Jim. "I see from your records that this is your first polygraph, so I'll be as detailed as you require. If you have a question, ask it, but our golden rule is, once you're hooked up and the polygraph is turned on, the only thing you'll utter is either yes or no. Okay, let's go over some of the ground rules. First, I'm going to go over the questions and hear your answers. The polygraph is initially not turned on or, as I like to say, you're not online. Once I'm convinced you understand the questions, we'll establish a baseline for you. To do this, I'll ask you some mindless questions where you tell the truth and some mindless questions where you deliberately lie. Next, we'll go online—you and the poly become one. We'll place a sensor on a finger, on one wrist, and around you chest. You and I will then work together at establishing your baseline by going over those mindless questions again and again. Al, just look at this baseline as a target for all further questions, a target you might see at a firing range. Your bullets, that's a metaphor for your answers to my questions, just have to approach the bulls-eye. You don't need to ever hit the bull's-eye—just hit the target, and you're home free. It's when one repeatedly misses the target that eyebrows get raised, and people start to think that maybe you're lying."

"Al, listen up. You do understand when I'm talking bullets and targets, that that's a metaphor for my questions and your answers, and if your answers miss the target and we can't figure out why and you won't help me understand why, then you're out the door. And that's no metaphor, sunshine, so don't lie to me."

"Jim, how do you and I establish my baseline or, to use one of your metaphors, establish my target?"

"Al, not to worry. That's why I get paid the big bucks—I establish your baseline for us, based on your responses to those mindless questions, and let's just leave it at that. You just cooperate, cooperate, cooperate and graduate, graduate, graduate, but remember—just hit the bloody target. In other words, don't fuck with me. Understand?"

"Once your baseline is established, I'll ask you some questions of a more substantial nature—not many—about foreign contacts and a couple of other questions about counterintelligence. Just answer truthfully, and don't be surprised if I ask the same question more than once. Now, here's something you'll have to take on faith: believe me, it works. Once I turn off the poly you're free to talk at will, but I may have other questions, like what were you thinking when I asked a particular question. What this should mean to you is that I see signs of evasiveness on your part, or maybe I'm thinking you're a fucking liar. So you and I need to clarify any and all ambiguities, and you need to level with me, or I'll bust your chops—figuratively speaking, of course. So whatever you were thinking when the machine was on, spit it out, and hopefully the next time there'll be no ambiguities and we can both go home and not kick the dog—again, figuratively speaking. Now, that's pretty elementary, isn't it, Sherlock?"

"Signs of evasiveness—what does that mean?"

"Remember bullets and target. What it means is that you're missing the target by a mile, Mr. Earp."

Sarcasm again, thought Al. Was this an Agency tactic? Unnerve him, then pounce—try to catch him in a lie? His hump was out to lunch, no help whatsoever. Jim was like a laser, too focused or too simple to be even remotely intimidated by Al's hump.

"So, telling you what I was thinking will result in a better polygraph? I find that hard to believe—what if I were thinking of embarrassing moments in my life that only I know about? And what if I choose not to embarrass myself in front of you? Then what?"

Jim said angrily, "Now listen, hotshot, I've heard it all. After fifteen years you can't say anything I haven't heard again and again and again. Anyway, unless it's crucial to your ex-am-min-a-tion, no notes will be taken. I just want to get you through your poly. After all, it is your poly, not mine."

Al reflected that he had crossed some line. It seemed that, while questions by him were encouraged, difficult-to-answer questions were not, and questions whose answers might divulge crafts of Jim's trade were not to be asked and if asked would not be answered.

"Okay, let's do it, Jim."

"Wow, not so fast, Trigger. More Foxtrot Yankee India to come.

"Well, it's like this, sunshine. I only administer your poly. The big boys at adjudication review your results as well as your Bravo India and God knows what else—they have the final word. It's pretty simple, Al. You just have to ask yourself how badly do you want to be an Agency employee, and if the answer is not too badly, then don't cooperate—you still may be accepted, but probably not. I don't know how adjudication thinks, but that's not the issue. I'll do my level best to work with you and get the best possible poly up to the fat cats. Look, Al, I'll even shine your fucking shoes if that's what it takes. Remember—cooperate, with a capital *K*. If you cooperate, you'll graduate, and that's not a metaphor, sunshine. That's the truth."

"What's adjudication?" Al was becoming more nervous and was even thinking of getting up and leaving, but his curiosity won out. He bent his head lower, hoping his hump would somehow intervene on his behalf, but it didn't.

"Al." Now Jim had his head in the palms of both hands and looked utterly forlorn, like he'd explained this a thousand times—and he probably had. "I just administer the poly. I work with you. I try to get the best possible results, and then the results are passed up the chain, so to speak. They're the guys that clear or don't clear you. Once you leave this building, you and I will never meet again." He added, "Thank God."

In the back of Al's mind were the words *perspiration, respiration,* and *blood pressure.* How could talking about past transgressions, even very embarrassing ones, alter any of these three physiological indicators? Or was this just a ruse to get inside his head to ensure he fit some Agency-mandated profile? He'd never know the answer to that question—or so he thought—but cooperate he must; this was just too tantalizing to pass up. Al sat for about a minute as quiet as a church mouse.

Jim's nerves were clearly wearing thin. "Don't clam up on me, Al. You've been put in for a very high-level clearance. Once you get your 'tickets' it will probably mean more money in your back pocket. You can understand that, I'm sure. You've got to work with me, boy. Can we please get started?"

Al thought, *Yes, money, I do like money, can do so many wonderful things with money. It'd be nice to have a lot one day.*

"Oh, tickets. What are tickets?" Al could only mumble this question, knowing full well he'd suffer the verbal wrath of Jim.

After inhaling deeply, Jim explained that by tickets he meant clearances.

"Ahh, okay, Jim. Can we get started, please? I really do appreciate you taking the time to get me up to speed—after all, this is all new to me. I'm sure you understand."

"All part of the service, Junior. You remember what we talked about a short while ago? I'll go over the questions with you, and you respond either yes or no, just yes or no—no comments or questions—and only say yes or no one time, and no yep or nope, and try to refrain from clearing your throat. And when you're online, no grunts or groans or twitches. No deep inhaling either. You got it, bubba? Oh, farts, particularly no farts, please. It skews the results like a force-ten gale right out of Joseph Conrad. I know you're not hooked up yet, but try to sit perfectly still, face forward—well, in your case as forward as possible— and breathe normally, and for God's sake never hold your breath. Last week some clown passed out—thought he'd died or something, stupid shit. Okay, sunshine, you ready?"

Jim went over the questions; they were all pretty basic and had to do with friends in the wrong places, membership in any anti-American organizations, visiting embassies or countries hostile to America, or intending to somehow subvert American interests. If Al could answer any of these in the affirmative, he'd be a flaming traitor in the mind-set of the CIA, but he wasn't a traitor. Al thought, *This is going to be a cake walk.* He and Jim discussed each question in detail again and again. It took about an hour, but finally Jim was satisfied.

Jim got up and attached a blood pressure cuff to Al's upper left arm and then a flexible, coiled, black rubber strap, which measured respiration, around his chest. Al thought this might be why women poly'ed other women and men poly'ed men, but maybe not. A little pink-colored thumb cup slotted neatly over his right thumb. Jim then unceremoniously examined Al's hands, carefully focusing on the palms and all ten fingers.

"What are you looking for? They're clean. Mind you, the nails are pretty crappy. Not dirty, just not properly maintained. My mother was quite a stickler about my nails when I was a kid—used to insist they not be bitten and routinely filed them with an emery board—but it did no good, so finally she just gave up."

"Whatever. Al, enough of memory lane and your mommy. Every once in a while some smart ass tries to beat the system by dusting their hands with some kind of moisture-absorbing bullshit. They think that no moisture is better than too much moisture. Even if undetected by me, it never works, and if it is detected by me, they're starting off on the wrong foot for sure."

"Okay, Al, let's do some baseline calibration. Al, you're hooked up now, but the machine isn't on, so we can natter as much as you like. I'm going to ask you to answer some real basic shit, like your name, what day is today, and what is four divided by two. You know the answers to those questions, right?"

Al nodded. "I guess."

"You guess?" Jim sounded belligerent. "You're no Einstein. Are you Quasimodo? Al, for the one zillionth time, yes or no even when off-line."

Ahh, Al thought, *Jim is aware of my hump, after all. Don't let me down, baby—shield me from that blunderbuss.*

"Listen up, Al. Don't nod during the poly. I want you to answer the first two questions correctly and the last question incorrectly, so I will say something like: 'Is your name Al? Is today Tuesday, which it is? Is four divided by two equal to three?' So, you answer yes to all three, knowing full well you're lying to that last arithmetic question because four divided by two is two. Now, I may ask the same question more than once or even change the order, but you're a clever lad—you can figure it out. Right, and don't just answer yes to everything that comes your way. Think about the question, and don't forget when I ask you if four divided by two is three, you lie, you lie, you lie. You say yes."

Al gave a halfhearted nod.

"Al, remember no nodding. You're really starting to piss me off. What did you say your college major was? It certainly wasn't following directions."

Jim continued, "Okay, I don't think we have to practice. Just say yes to all the damn questions, but know when you're lying, because you really do know four divided by two is two, right, sunshine? You do know that? I'm pretty sure you do."

"Yes."

"Okay, listen up. I'm turning the machine on, so no chattering, just yes or no, please, and no squirming about. Find a spot on the wall or floor and focus on it. Let your mind go where it chooses to go, but listen to my questions, please."

"Okay, you're online, Al."

As soon as Jim said "online," Al sat as upright as his hump would allow, stared at a crack in the floor, and earnestly listened to Jim's three questions, which he asked several times without much of a break in between. No matter how inane the question, Al forced himself to focus intently on each question and each answer. Even so, twice he almost answered no to "Is four divided by two three?"

"Okay, machine off. Well, sunshine, you almost blew it a couple of times. Four divided by two is not three, but you were supposed to answer yes, you know. You did lie, but you almost answered no twice. Anyway, we're almost up to the best part. Oh, one more thing: there's a possibility your test will be audio recorded. I don't think that's the case today, but I never know what those clowns upstairs are up to. They're not checking you out; they're checking me out. We have some evolving ground rules here about how we question or don't question candidates, and as I don't want to lose my job, I follow those rules to the letter, and if anyone asks you, please back me up."

"Sure thing, Jim, no problem."

"Al, these counterintelligence questions I'm going to ask you are straightforward. I'm going to cut the number of questions down to three. You're only twenty-three; have never had access to classified material, so you say; have never left the country, so you say; and have a clean police record, so you say. Okay, here's the questions, and I assume you'll answer no to all three. Have you ever met with any foreign intelligence officers? Is anyone prepared to pay you or offer you favors in exchange for classified information? And finally, do you consider yourself to be a bad security risk? Okay, too easy. What do you think? I can change the wording if you like."

"You're right—too easy. Let's get going."

Al was almost in a panic because, unsolicited, into his mind came that terrible ordeal in eighth grade at the grade school prom. *Oh, my God*, he though. *I can't shake it!*

Jim hooked him back up in a jiffy. "Okay, you're online."

Three questions from Jim, three "no" answers from Al. Three questions, three answers. Three questions, three answers. This continued for most of the next fifteen minutes. No. No. No.

"Machine off. What's up, Al? Are we going to lock horns again? Is this going to take all fucking day? Adjudication's going to have a field day if this poly goes forward. Maybe 'too easy' means something different to you than me. We need to talk. What's bugging you, man? If you're not prepared to open up, we may as well call it a day. Anyone looking at these results might assume you're lying about one or all of these very important questions, so, what the fuck's up? Your bullets are not only missing the target but missing the wall the target's nailed to. Even I can see that, and I'm not even a trained adjudicator."

"Nothing—I told you the truth. I'm surprised your machine can't figure that out. I told you the truth. I'm no traitor."

"Al, settle down. Please remember: perspiration, respiration, and blood pressure. It's a fucking machine like your lawn mower, but right now it's a very unhappy machine—refuses to cut the grass. You've got to tell me what's swirling about in your brainless head. Listen, I got to make a pit stop. You want a break? I'll be back in five. Think about it."

"No, I'm fine."

Al didn't know what to do. This was all of a sudden becoming an excruciating ordeal. The thing that was eating at Al had happened when he was a kid, about eleven or twelve, at a grade school dance in the gym. The boys held hands, formed a circle, and skipped to the music clockwise while the girls skipped counterclockwise. When the music stopped, you danced with whoever was opposite you—simple and supposedly harmless. Sadly, it was anything but harmless. One of the girls, named Shirley, was a tall, skinny, very black girl in pigtails and huge dark glasses, always beautifully dressed. Once, when the music stopped, Al was facing Shirley, and he refused to dance with her. Several other boys also refused. Shirley ended up in tears; she was heartbroken.

Al felt so ashamed, and he apologized and tried to console her and apologized but to no avail. If only she had gotten angry, but she was too polite for anger. In retrospect, who was he to discriminate? After all, he had a hump. Funny, no one ever took an unfriendly attitude toward him because of his deformity, but because Shirley was black, no one would dance with her. Afterward, Al always tried very hard to be extra polite to Shirley, but she was always cool toward him. No wonder, for before the dance he'd treated her as a friend. She moved the following year, and that was that, but he still cringed when he thought of that gym and Shirley. He tried never to think about it and would never discuss it; he had behaved very badly and was quite ashamed of himself. He would sooner die than narrate that story to anyone.

After Jim closed the door behind him, he headed to reception. As soon as the receptionist saw Jim hurrying down the hall, she knew something was up and that Jim was unhappy.

Even before Jim could open his mouth, she said, "Yes, I know— cancel your afternoon appointment. The guy you're working with is driving you crazy. Yes, I've heard it before—you're going to kill him or toss him out the window or slowly strangle him with a blood pressure cuff. Yes, I know—life's a bitch and then you die."

Jim looked at the receptionist, said nothing, smiled, nodded, did an about face, and returned to find Al full of the fidgets and very, very nervous.

"Listen, Al, are you going to fill me in? What's bugging you? If you're going to clam up, you might as well leave, and I'll turn in what I have."

Al's heart was pounding. "It's like this. When I was in grade school ..." Al related his tale of woe and ended up with "and she was utterly, utterly heartbroken."

"You know, Al, I'm going to level with you. I very seldom do this. At first I thought you'd killed someone or might even be a traitor. Remember: perspiration, respiration, and blood pressure. That's all this machine can measure, and when the machine is getting mixed signals to very important questions, it becomes confused, and—guess what—so do I. I only know you're very anxious, but I don't know what you're anxious about unless you tell me. So, in future tell me. Okay, numb nuts? *Comprendez vous?*"

Anyway, it's off your chest now, so let's retake our poly."

He hooked Al up again, asked the same questions, and got the same answers.

"Okay, machine off."

"How'd I do?"

"Well, it looks a bit better. Not a hundred percent, but better—at least you're hitting the wall—but remember I am not an adjudicator. Interpreting polygraphs is more of an art than a science—and you didn't hear that from me. I'll send this forward. I can see what you're thinking, Al. You think I said if you open up, your poly will be perfect. Actually, I said 'it might improve,' and it did, slightly. Sometimes there's no improvement whatsoever. Anyway, it shows you're cooperating. Adjudication likes that. I'll be sure to note that."

"And, Jim, your recommendations will be what?"

"Al, I'm no fucking psychiatrist or any other word ending in 'ist.' I have a degree in social science and some special training—about nine months; that's it. I would never recommend or not recommend anything or anyone, and adjudication would ignore me anyway. If I recommended everyone who sat in that chair, I'd be sued nine days to Sunday, and I hardly get by now, financially speaking. Remember what I said—if they want to do a background investigation on you then your poly's probably okay. If your Bravo India comes up roses, you're in. I can almost guarantee it."

"Thanks for your help, Jim. I would—"

Jim didn't let Al finish. "Just get the hell out of here, Al. I'm going to get really hammered tonight, so help me b'jesus. Leave."

Al left with no farewell, no cordial handshake, and only a curt, professional nod from Jim and a halfhearted wave by Al. It was worse than he'd expected but interesting. *But how did Jim know I almost twice botched that simple math question? Four divided by two is two, not three. I had to force myself to lie. I'm not a natural-born liar, and I felt uncomfortable lying. My lies must have elevated perspiration, respiration, and blood pressure, and the almost botched responses must have elevated those parameters to an even greater degree, and that's what the polygraph 'told' Jim—how it 'told' Jim, I have no clue.* Then it hit him: *Perspiration, respiration, and blood pressure. The machine has no microphone, no comprehension—my verbal responses were not being heard or measured by the polygraph, so in essence an audible response is for Jim's benefit. Jim correlates what I say with what the machine is telling him. The machine tells Jim, well before I answer, what my body is 'thinking,' and my verbal responses either confirm or contradict what my body is telling Jim. So, four divided by two is three. Body says no. Mouth says yes. Therefore, we have a lie; so my verbal responses are another variable in the overall equation, and there's probably more. This is probably annoyingly simple, but it is fascinating.*

Al further reasoned that a sociopath or habitual liar might be better able to defeat the polygraph or at least mislead Jim. For now, though, that was of no concern to Al, who continued to ponder the idea of a truth zone and what Jim did to figure out if a candidate was merely being evasive, telling a full-blown lie, or telling the truth. *Very interesting*, thought Al. *I may have to look into working as a polygrapher if I'm hired into the Agency … would be kind of cool to be known as Al, the polygrapher. Could prove to be a babe-magnet.*

On the way out Al dropped off his visitor's badge and signed out. He skipped to his car, a brand new Ford Mustang convertible, V-8, British racing green, with whitewall tires and black leather bucket seats. It had been a graduation gift to himself, and he knew he deserved it. God, he loved what money could do. He fired her up and flipped on the radio. *More boring news about the election*, he thought. *Yes, I know, Ronald Reagan handily defeats Walter Mondale, a landslide, forty-seven states. Who cares? Now give me some music, baby, and none of that country and western crap.* With that he sped off, whistling a happy tune.

CHAPTER 2

I wake to the sound of waves crashing against the rocky shores of Whitby Harbour; it's six, Greenwich mean time. As usual the gulls are squawking, but their squawking never wakes me; I'm used to it by now and have been awake since half five. Occasionally I put some scraps out, and as soon as I turn my back, they dive in; they're always hungry. Life's tough this far north, and you have to get it when you can or maybe not get it at all. Winters in England are long, cold, and blustery, especially if you live on the eastern shore of the North Sea. At six, it's still pitch dark; the sun won't even think of putting in an appearance for a few more hours and will begin to set about four. At times, when not too busy, I take a few minutes and watch the sun rising, a mug of very hot coffee in my gloved hands. The sight, as the sun rises over the North Sea, all golden and bright and warm, makes me unusually pensive, almost melancholy; at these times I realize how much I love my England and my mum and dad. Some time ago I moved in with my parents after splitting up with my boyfriend, an older, unfriendly man set in his ways who'd recently found God and insisted I also find Him or suffer the wrath of both him and Him. My boyfriend was just too much, over the top. While I'm not irreligious, I am undecided at this time and reserve the right to make up my own mind, one way or another—and most likely not today. I'll straddle the fence for as long as I can. Anyway, I got pig sick of his incessant nagging and left him with no notice, not even a note. He never tried to track me down, so that was the end of him, the old bugger, and I'm thinking he felt the same about me.

After washing, I have a quick study of myself in the oval mirror over the sink in the loo. At eight stones I am, as they say, as fit as a fiddle. I've lost a few pounds since moving into the hotel. Father said it suits me; Mother, never one for disingenuous flannel, says I'm getting too skinny. Anyway, I'm thinking not bad for a lass of twenty-three, give or take. My shoulder-length, undecidedly auburn—or is it just dark brown?—hair requires a good brushing several times a day or it snarls and takes on a life of its own. In my younger years, Father would braid my hair by the fire over a cup of hot cocoa—me, not him. He was more often than not on beer. It's a nice memory. As I add makeup, I notice my eyes look a bit tired and puffy, but my makeup kit will soon take care of that. All in all, when my war paint is in place, I look pretty darn good. At times I fancy I look like Veronica Lake, but who am I kidding? Certainly not Mother; she calls a spade a spade. If I say Veronica Lake, she'll say Veronica Lake, not likely. Anyway, today should be a fine day, but first a few chores.

Four rooms have early morning wake-up calls, and I'm on duty. The kettle begins to sputter and almost whistles, but not quite. One by one I carry the tea trays upstairs, knock on the door, wait for some sort of response, and then enter and conveniently deposit the tray. No words except "Morning"—much too early for idle chitchat. After morning teas, I hoover the cocktail bar, sweep the upstairs stairs, and polish the brass in both the cocktail bar and the other, less-than-ornate local's bar. The cocktail bar is for residents of the hotel; all the locals frequent the larger, more stoic local's bar, where drinks are a few pence cheaper and, some might say, the company better. My next job is to restock both bars; Father is supposed to do this, but, as he's getting on, I usually do it—and never fail to remind him that he's a slacker and a lay about. I take a quick survey of what needs restocking; go out to the bottling shed; load up the handcart with bottled beer, lemonade, and other nonalcoholic cordials; and proceed to replace the empties. Father usually takes care of the dead soldiers by refilling the empty wooden crates and having them returned to the brewery. He also takes care of the barreled beers and spirits; he must do a pretty good job, as we have a reputation for supplying some of the best draft beer in Yorkshire—and from real wooden barrels, not kegs. Yes, the bars are Father's kingdom while the hotel and kitchen are Mother's, and those kingdoms make up the very successful Duke of Yorkshire Hotel, in which I am now a key and, yes, keen player. I help both my parents, not just Father. To Father I'm just a skivvy; to Mother a commis chef. I love cooking, not baking. To my mind baking is like taking an arithmetic test. I prefer a pinch of this or a pinch of that to a liter of this or a gram of that. As commis chef I help Mum prepare bar snack meals for the locals and delightful main courses for our residents who eat in our formal dining room, usually dressed to the nines. Some well-heeled locals also eat in the dining room, feasting on duck à l'orange, steak and kidney pie, chicken Italienne, filet steak, goujons of plaice, and other tasty dishes, accompanied always by English new potatoes and fresh veggies and very infrequently by salads. I dislike salads—very boring—and in England it's hard, though not impossible, to find fresh ingredients, especially in winter. The fare at the Duke of Yorkshire Hotel can compete with just about any hotel from Lands End to John o' Groats, and Mother deserves all the credit. She and Father took over the hotel about three years ago when he was made redundant—no golden parachute for Dad. They had little savings and signed on with a brewery to manage a pub; the pub turned out to be the Duke of Yorkshire in Whitby, Yorkshire. They both soon realized that making a go of the Duke would be a challenge requiring long hours, good people skills, and an ability to control one's temper, something Mother can never do. Father fitted right in—he'd managed one thing or another his entire life—but while Mother could cook, she just wasn't used to cooking for more than a handful, and at first more food spoiled than got sold. However, over time she did catch on, and she can now cost out a meal to the last farthing.

After restocking the bars, I finally have the opportunity to sit and have a cup of coffee. The coffee's instant, no sugar, and plenty of cream for me. I'm on breakfast duty today, which begins sharply at seven and ends sharply at nine. Mum usually does breakfasts with Bill, assistant chef, who she alternatively dislikes and hates—from her perspective he doesn't have a single redeemable characteristic whatsoever. He's bald and short, very short. He's a fair chef with a penchant for drink and regularly gets blind drunk on his day off—not tipsy but blind. A month or two ago the man nearly died. He passed out in an alley not far from the Duke, but lucky for him a passerby found him and notified the authorities, who promptly wrapped him in tinfoil and took him to the hospital not too far off, just up the hill on the other side of Esk Bridge. The lads never let Bill forget about the tinfoil; they now call him the tin man or Tiny Tin. The local lads are a tough bunch, always ready for a giggle as long as it's at someone else's expense. Anyway, as I was saying, I don't like doing breakfasts; there's little opportunity to experiment, and like most hotels in England, our breakfast usually consists of eggs any way residents like them, bacon, sausage and blood pudding, porridge, beans, toast, fried tomatoes, orange juice and at times fresh fruits, kippers, and if Bill's up to it freshly baked rolls served hot, right out of the AGA. Of course, coffee or tea is always on the menu. Most prefer coffee, some tea, and a few an eye opener that Father sees to.

After breakfasts, I prepare staff lunches. Including me and Bill, there are seven that literally run the Duke day in, day out, every day. The seven doesn't include my parents, who run the staff—and at times runs them ragged, especially Mother. The staff have nicknamed her Hitler—never to her face, of course, but she's aware of the nickname and is secretly proud of it. She'd rather be feared then taken advantage of any day. Mum's quick to anger, and three things can really set her off. Her knives and her pen are two. Everyone on staff knows not to touch or borrow her knives or her pen, which she now carries in her wicker basket that goes wherever she goes. When she wants a knife or a pen, she wants it now; she doesn't want to go hunting. Of course, the third is Father, who can get on Mother's bad side without really trying. Usually, offering what he considers to be helpful advice about her chain smoking is more than enough to put him in the doghouse, and she's constantly on his case about not pulling his weight, being bone idle, and, yes, drinking too much, especially at lunchtime. The last, especially, never fails to cause a row. Fortunately, their rows are short-lived. Mother's far too busy to waste time rowing. In fact, if the truth be known, it's not a row at all. It's very one sided: she will lash out, leaving Father with that whipped-cur look, all sunken shoulders and sorrowful eyes, as if to say *What did I do?* To console himself, Father will inevitably pour himself a couple, read the *Whitby Gazette*, published each and every Friday, and enter into idle bar talk with the locals about the overbearing role of women in British society.

The hotel's Mother's only source of income and has to succeed, year in and year out—"no doubt about that," as she would say. There really is no room for failure. Mother can't stand shirkers, stupidity, thievery, or liars. More than once I've seen staff handed their cards and told to leave, on the spot, now, pronto, and to never return. With those remarks she'd go to the till, take out their wages, and pay them off. There's no such thing as a second chance once Mother has made her mind up. She soon got a reputation, but there's always a queue looking to be hired.

Most know her to usually be fair, and as long as you pull your weight you have nothing to fear from Hitler—nothing but hard work. She expects staff to work as hard as she does, and if they don't, they're out the door and usually with no references. She can be as hard as nails, but someone has to be hard, and it certainly isn't Father, who would prefer to be merry and leave the tough calls to Mother.

Today staff lunch is steak and kidney pie. I can throw that together in a heartbeat with English peas, a rich and creamy gravy, and mashed potatoes with plenty of butter, and the pastry's hand thrown. Around ten in the morning, the staff gathers at the kitchen table. I always eat with the staff. There just isn't room enough to do otherwise, and even if there had been, I do consider myself to be staff first, daughter second. Like anything, I suppose you'd get an argument from some about that. At the table there are several discussions simultaneously in progress. We never discuss religion or politics or anything that might be in the dailies. We aren't being politically correct; it's just we're not interested in any news that's trying to make us smart or inform us of something. Our imagination and interests end where Yorkshire ends, and we usually discuss things like personal relationship, the price of a loaf of bread, and just plain gossip, nothing earthshaking. After lunch, everyone washes up their own plates and cutlery. I'm stuck with the pots and pans—so much for special treatment.

Today's Tuesday, my half day. Mum and Dad are also off, so a run to the seaside town of Scarborough is planned. I love Tuesdays: first Cash and Carry to restock the larder and then lunch at a small café just off the main thoroughfare. I usually have a cup of piping hot tea and a sandwich made from brown bread, and I usually finish off my lunch with a scone loaded with raisins—no jam, please. Sad to admit, I don't like sweets. Today will be extra special because Mum intends to purchase a brand new microwave oven. It's the latest gadget on the English market, and we just have to have one. We both love gadgets. Today's also special because the American Al will accompany us. He's a nice young man from Washington DC who periodically visits England on business—what business I don't know, and Al has little to say about that. Mother is very interested in what Al does to earn a living. I'm pretty sure she knows Al and I have something special going on and just wants to make sure he's a dependable sort of chap who can put bread on the table. She hounds him with this and then that question, but he discreetly dodges all forays with evasiveness and politeness, never getting the least bit annoyed. I have no special man in my life, but whenever Al shows up, we pair off and are inseparable. I like him very much in spite of his hump, maybe even because of it. Yes, he's a hunchback, a birth defect that's hardly ever seen these days. Most hunchbacks are terminated well before they ever see the light of day. Very sad if you ask me, but no one will ask me. Everyone's gotta do what they gotta do, but terminating an unborn because of a hump seems a bit extreme. Just look at Al: well adjusted, happy, the salt of the earth, and I'm beginning to have more than friendly feelings for him.

Al almost always has a sly, elfish grin on his face that I find frightfully attractive, and he's not autocratic or controlling by any stretch of the imagination. He's quite good-natured and easygoing, almost to the point of being a pushover, but I think not. I believe he'll only be pushed so far—then, watch out.

By eleven, we're off to Scarborough. I always drive with Mum in the passenger seat. Father and Al occupy the backseat. It takes about an hour to get to Scarborough. The route takes us past RAF Fylingdales, a joint British and American air base with no runways. As we approach the entrance to Fylingdales, an uphill climb, we're met by sight of three huge white domes that the locals call golf balls, and they do look like monster-size golf balls growing on the moors. Each golf ball is connected by an above-ground tunnel that's used to transport shift workers into and out of those domes every eight hours. What's inside those domes? I don't know—plenty of secrecy? Al probably has something to do with these golf balls, as he lives in the RAF Officers Mess. He even has a batman, all prim and proper-like, who shines his shoes on a daily basis as long as he leaves them outside his door. I really don't care what Al does; I just know I like him a lot. As we approach Scarborough forty-five minutes later, we pass by the North Sea, very close-like, waves crashing right onto the road. We have to be careful and wait for a break or we'll get swamped. This sea of ours always seems to be angry, mad about something, one gale after another. God knows why. We English are a wonderfully fair-minded people by and large; the land is lovely, the traditions memorable, and it's hard to find a better place to live. I know I'll never leave, no matter what. Lately, I've been so sentimental and am wondering if I'm falling in love with Al. I can see in his eyes and manner, and from the things he says and doesn't say, that he has strong feelings for me.

At Cash and Carry the boot is quickly loaded with supplies, and then it's off to lunch. At lunch, Al follows my lead with a cup of tea and a tongue sandwich slathered with butter and a tiny bit of spicy English mustard. It's quite tasty and new to Al, who explains that Americans by and large are not keen on organ foods and that most have never had a sandwich made from sliced cow's tongue that has been pickled and compressed for several days. Anyway, once Al gets over the notion of eating an animal's tongue, he quite enjoys it, or I think he does. Something about Al is you don't always know what's going on in his head—and I always thought Americans were so transparent. I wonder if it has something to do with his job. It's possible I'll never know what he does, but for now, I'll leave it at that. I do like the way these small cafes put their sandwiches together: brown bread, no crusts and quartered diagonally; usually just a single slice of meat, two at most; a bit of lettuce and tomato; and plenty of soft Irish butter. There's always a twisted cucumber slice for garnish, which no one ever eats. The last time we were in this particular café, Al ordered a ham and cheese sandwich, which apparently is quite common in America. He got one ham and one cheese sandwich. We all chuckled about that, but he ate both without hesitation. He's quite good-natured that way; maybe that's why I love—sorry, like—him so much.

"Well, Al," Mother says almost defiantly, "how long are you here for this time? You're here so much you may as well take up residence and save your government air fare, which I'm quite sure adds up to thousands of pounds each year."

Unabashedly Al responds, "I'd like that very much, yes, very much indeed, but can't afford it just yet. Maybe sometime down the road. There's so much about this land of yours that I love. It's totally different—just not the hustle and bustle I'm used to—and this far north the people seem content and certainly know how to have a good time."

"And is there anything else about this land of ours that you love, Al?" Mother says as she casts a gaze in my direction.

I blush. Al blushes. Father just clears his throat. No one says a word.

Mother lights up. She's thinking, so we'll be quiet till she snuffs her ciggy out. There's something about Mother and smoking; whenever I think of Mother, she's always smoking, and there's a protocol to her habit. First, she always smokes Players, never tipped. She'll shake the pack, assuming it's open, until a cigarette almost mysteriously surfaces. The cigarette will pass from the pack to her right hand and then to the center of her lips. Her lighter, usually a BIC but sometimes a more expensive lighter—probably a present—springs to life, and with a single inhalation her cigarette is alight. She'll now inhale and hold the smoke in her lungs for no less than five seconds, almost like a sommelier savoring a rich red wine. She'll then slowly exhale, straight up, always straight up—never to the left or right or straight ahead, and it's not because she's concerned about annoying a neighbor with her smoke, because she doesn't give two monkeys about annoying anyone. In her opinion, if they don't like smokers they should move or even emigrate. As she exhales, the right hand with cigarette between her thumb and index finger moves to her forehead, where it will rest until the next drag. Excess ash is deposited in a nearby ashtray, and—another habit— the cigarette never rests in the ashtray. This drill continues until the cigarette is within an inch of its life, at which time it is, almost viciously, crushed into many little pieces.

"Well, Al, I guess you have nothing to say about that, but your silence speaks volumes, and no need to further embarrass my daughter, so I'll drop the subject, at least for now."

Both Father and I roll our eyes. It appears Al, without opening his mouth, told Mother exactly what she wanted to hear. Anyway, Father likes Al. He doesn't care where Al wants to live or what he does to earn a living, especially if Al doesn't want to talk about it. If Father likes you, he likes you, and if he doesn't like you, he won't like you, and no matter what you do to get on his good side, he still won't like you. Mother, on the other hand, tends to be more analytical; she doesn't like to take things at face value. She likes to attack you from different sides, different angles, and then see how you react. That way she'll have some idea how you might react down the road. I'm pretty sure she's fond of Al, but as a son-in-law? Well, that's another story, and only time will tell, but I'm certain she only wants what's best for me. I ignored her advice about moving in with that wretched older man. Everything she said about him turned out to be true. I was very foolish and selfish, and Mother and Father were terribly hurt but eventually forgave me for being so stupid and hard-headed. One thing about me: if you tell me not to do something, I'll do my best to do it.

"Well, Mrs.—" Al starts almost timidly.

Mother interrupts, glares in his direction. "Looky here, boyo, no Mrs. this or Mrs. that! You call Father, Jim, and you know my Christian name is Nan. Use it, please! And, Al, we've got to talk. Stop hiding behind your hump or using it as a shield of sorts to fend off what you might consider intruding. No one at this table means you any ill will. In this family we accept people for what they are, not for what God gave them or didn't give them. In fact, all the attention you get in the pub, I'm starting to wish I'd been born with a hump."

"Hear, hear, Nan. Well said," chimed in Father.

Well, blow me, I think. *Mother and Father agreeing on something. This might yet prove to be a very auspicious day.*

Al has that hard-to-penetrate look on his face, almost like a sheet of plain white paper. I have no idea what he's thinking, but I'll find out later when we're alone. I hope his feelings aren't hurt. All Mother is trying to say is "lighten up, man."

Mother takes out another Players and lights up. After several deep inhalations followed by painfully slow exhalations, it appears she's about to continue prying into Al's affairs. Father takes this opportunity to try to lecture Mother about the evils of smoking.

"You know, Nan, smoking will one day ruin your health, maybe even kill you. It's a proven fact it's dangerous—you know, the lungs, cancer, the big C. I wish you wouldn't smoke so much."

If Al weren't there, Mother would wipe the floor with Father, but for my sake, I suppose, she puts on a mask of civility, responding to Father's concern with feigned, frigid politeness that I quickly see through.

"Thank you, Jim, for your concern, but I've been smoking since I was fourteen, and you know what they say about old dogs and new tricks. I enjoy smoking—it's one of the few things in life that gives me pleasure. Now, you also are a slave to habit, so just run along to the Charles Dickens and have a beer or two. Remember no more than two halves and not the strong German stuff you seem to enjoy so very, very much. I'm sure you know where the Charles Dickens is, just up the road, on the right. Now, chop, chop, off you go, and if you're lucky we'll pick you up after we look into this microwave thing in about an hour, so keep a look out for us and try not to be too friendly, mite."

Mite, not mate, I think. Whenever Mother is really ticked off with Father, it's *mite.* She would never, ever use the word *mate.* Too masculine a word and all too common, a word most of the locals use to excess, and Mother certainly thinks that, in the overall scheme of things, she's a peg or two above most locals, if not all locals.

Without even a glance at Mother, Father slinks out mumbling something about the bloody women in this family.

Father doesn't ask Al to go. He knows Al isn't much of a drinker and never a daytime drinker, and I don't want to share Al with anyone, even Father.

"Anyway, Al, how long are you here for this time? It really is quite nice having you here, and please disregard Jim's nagging and my bickering. We're really not such bad people—maybe we occasionally do stupid things, but never wicked things?"

"Sure, Nan, not a problem. I'll be at RAF Fylingdales for a fortnight, and I also have to visit Harrogate for a few days, but I'll be staying at the Fylingdales Officers' Mess my entire stay, a couple of weeks."

"Harrogate? why Harrogate? That's a big spa town an hour or so west—plenty of very ritzy hotels and such, certainly not like Whitby."

Al, caught off guard by Mother's probing, is not only speechless but motionless. Like they say, he's been frozen in his tracks. He tries to utter a sensible response, but no words are forthcoming, only an incoherent, stuttering, babble of low intensity; for some reason he just doesn't know how to answer that question.

"Oh, okay, Al, I retract the question. Relax. You should be able to think a wee bit faster on your feet, bucko. You're not a very good liar. You need to work on that. You know, have a story in your back pocket, something like 'I go to Harrogate to visit a friend from home or visit a friend of a friend' or some such rubbish."

Mother continues: "And you're still being quite canny about what you do for a living? My God, Al, you're so secretive. It must be some job." With that she looks in my direction as if to say, *Well, what do you know?*

"I've no idea what he does, Mother. He won't tell me, either."

I uncontrollably avert my eyes but am telling the truth, though I'm sure Mother believes me to be lying. She hates not knowing, being on the outside.

"Now, Al, you can take a lesson or two on lying from my daughter. If they gave out awards for lying, she'd get an Oscar, no doubt," Mother says with a half grin but also half seriously.

I think to myself, *Yes, Mother, as a child I had to learn to lie to get by you and get around Father—anyway, all white lies,* but I say nothing, for I'm sure she can easily come up with tons of tales of me lying and her catching me red-handed. Father's different. He'd cut me some slack as long as it wasn't a whopper.

I would never dare utter those unsaid thoughts aloud, even in jest. One can never take Mother lightly, and if one does and she isn't in the right frame of mind, you'll suffer the consequences, for sure.

With that we finish our lunch and as usual have to wait for Mother to finish her ciggy and coffee; she never drinks tea. She seems to relish making us wait, down to the last sip and final puff. She crushes out what's left of her cigarette, and we're off. Al pays and leaves a fifty-pence tip. Mother grumbles, saying fifty pence is far too much, twenty would have been more than enough, and she wishes certain Americans would stop throwing their money around. We then drive to the kitchen shop three streets over. The traffic is horrible, but Al's as happy as a lark, saying the traffic isn't so bad, only a nuisance. Fifteen minutes later we arrive at the kitchen shop.

A tall, austere man greets us. He's neatly dressed in a dark suit, white shirt, and bold yellow tie. Initially he has little to say, but when he hears Mother is interested in buying a micro, he warms up and even manages to put a smile on his large, oafish-looking face.

"Yes, Mrs. McKay, all the latest technology in the North of England. Those Americans have nothing on us—we only carry the best microwaves and at reasonable prices."

He knows Mother from previous visits. She doesn't like him at all and always refers to him as "that little man," even though he's at least six feet with a head the size of a football. She always says he should have been a fisherman, not a salesman. In fact, she once remarked, "That little man at the kitchen shop has eyes like a cod, but a cod's a lot smarter."

"I'll do a demo for you, Mrs. McKay, if you like."

All Mother says is, "I like."

With that, he fills a cup full of water from a nearby tap and has it boiling in seconds.

"In your hotel, you can use it to heat up all sorts, like leftovers, and it's ideal for defrosting, but you have to make sure you don't defrost to the point of cooking. Most don't actually cook with micros, but some do. They're still fairly new in the UK, but I've sold a few to Mr. Steel of the White Swan, a competitor of yours, I believe."

I wonder if this is some sort of marketing ploy. Mother not only dislikes Mr. Steel of the Mucky Duck but thinks his menu atrociously bad; most meals are not freshly made but brought in frozen. She's often said she would sooner see herself dead then eat at that pub, which is just a couple of streets over from the Duke. Anyway, if she likes the micro she'll buy it, and if she dislikes it, she won't, even if the Queen herself has dozens in her kitchen.

As it turns out, both Mother and I are over the moon about this gadget. It'll save stacks of time defrosting frozen leftovers and making sure veggies are served piping hot. Really hot is an unexplainable passion of both Mother and me—not warm or hot but very hot, on plates heated in the AGA. Of course, she doesn't act too excited in front of the little man, instead behaves as if she really doesn't like the micro and is only buying it to please me.

"Oh, one more thing, Mrs. McKay—don't ever put anything metal in your new micro, could ruin it—all sorts of sparks and smoke—and my shop will not be responsible for any damages you or your staff inflict on your micro. Understand that, please. It's all in your user's manual. Read it, and watch out for china that's ornate, may have metal bits and bobs somewhere."

While I take mental notes on how to use the micro, Mother appears on the verge of exploding. She hates it when anyone talks down to her, especially someone she believes to be far above his proper station. I know we have to get out of there, and sharpish, so I stow several questions to be researched later in the user's manual with Al at my side.

Mother writes out a check and leaves, saying nothing, not even a by your leave. Al lugs the boxed micro out of the shop and just manages to get it loaded into the car. We swing by the Charles Dickens to pick Father up. He's obviously had more than a few halves and sleeps all the way home. I'm thinking, *Father's going to get it in the neck later tonight—thank God I'll be out.* Al has invited me to the Officers' Mess that evening for a dance, a formal dance. I will meet some of his mates and the RAF station commander as well as the USAF commander. In fact, all the officers not on duty will be there. I bought a new dress with Mother's help. She said it was lovely, and if Mother says it lovely, then it's lovely. I really have to be on form tonight—don't want to let the home team down.

On the way back we swing by the trout farm at Pickering. We walk around the trout pens and throw some food pellets to the fish and watch them scramble; the water boils with activity. Mother buys a few dozen trout; I know she's dying to see how fish and her new micro cooperate. The fact that the little man told her not to cook in the micro makes her want to prove that some things, like fish, can be successfully cooked. I guess she and I are alike that way. Tell us not to do something, and, bingo, we'll do it, or at least try to. In less than thirty minutes, we're back on the road.

"Margaret, will you please drop me off at Fylingdales? I've got a lot to do to get ready for this evening—bought a new dinner jacket at Spanton's. He did a good job of contouring it for my hump—hope you'll like it. I'll get a taxi later and pick you up about seven at the Duke. Is that okay?"

"Sure, Al. I'm sure I'll like it. They do good work, and the fact that you're a visitor will make Mr. Spanton even more attentive than usual."

Twenty minutes later I draw up at the gate; the guard recognizes Al, opens the gate, and waves us through. I turn right at the fork in the road, watch my speed, and we're there. The mess is a one-story, drab-colored building probably built during World War II. It's the Officers' Mess; the Sergeants' Mess is just up the road on the right. I'd been in the Officers' Mess a few times for drinks, but tonight is a special occasion, very formal, a dance, a real dress-up affair—not quite a summer ball, but nice, really nice. I do love these kinds of things.

Al gets out, says good-bye to all, and is gone. Father doesn't stir; he's out like a light, in la-la land, not knowing that later that evening Mother will be all over him, justifiably unrelenting in her criticism.

Mother starts in again, saying, "You know, Margaret, Al really likes you. It's very obvious, even to the most casual observer, which I'm not. Do you have any plans, anything I need to know about?"

"I know he likes me, and I'm quite fond of him as well, but we'll see. Many things to think about—can't make any snap decisions. We'll see. You know I have other things, other people to consider. I can't just pick up and bobby off to America."

She perseveres, like a wolf pack on an injured elk. She knows I don't want to discuss Al but continues her probing nonetheless.

"Now listen, Margaret, please don't put your life on hold for me and Father—we'll manage. And as far as snap decisions, sometime they're the best—not always, but sometimes—and when it comes to you, I want nothing but the best. Don't overanalyze everything, dear. Follow your heart, girl. You're young, so have a good time when you can, and from what I can see there's not dozens of other would-be suitors knocking at your door. Remember you're a long time dead, so grab some happiness when you can."

I nod pensively; leave it to Mother to notice that they're not flocking to my door. Oh well, that's Mother, never one to beat around the bush, and she's right. She finally lets me off the hook, but I know two things for certain: first, I'll never leave Mum and Dad, and, second, I will never leave England, not for anyone, not even Al.

It's a lovely drive from RAF Fylingdales to Whitby, over the moors that are so barren and forlorn except in spring when snow-white lambs punctuate the landscape and in early fall when purple heather blankets huge patches of moorland. We arrive in Whitby about thirty minutes later. The Duke of Yorkshire is at the end of Church Street. Church Street is still cobbled, very narrow, shops on both sides. The Duke of Yorkshire is at the foot of Whitby Abbey. The abbey is built on a large plateau and overlooks Whitby, the North Sea, and the Duke. A hundred ninety-nine steps must be climbed to reach the abbey. Henry VIII knocked the abbey down—some religious thing I don't quite understand. Now it's just ruins, but not a ruin out of place, and the grounds are handsomely maintained. It must have been majestic before it was destroyed. The first thing any sailing vessel would see when entering Whitby Harbour would be the abbey, in all its glory and majesty, reaching skyward toward God. I suppose that was the plan all along.

Bill comes out and helps us unload; Father disappears into the bar for a sneaky one, as he calls it. Mother goes for a lie-down. Ten minutes later I find Father sipping a half, sitting on the settle next to the bar. He's reading the *Gazette*, his glasses pulled halfway down his nose; the right stem is missing. Father refuses to get it replaced, saying that these are just fine—"they'll see me out." I study him as he reads his paper. He looks haggard; all these late nights are just too much for him, and his compulsive drinking isn't helping, but late nights and drinking are part of the business. Father would like nothing better than for he and

Mother to slip home about seven, watch some telly, have a couple, and turn in no later than ten. Mother, on the other hand, thrives on late nights and the crowds and the socializing. If she had to turn in by ten, she'd kill herself or maybe kill Father. Anyway, slipping home about seven is totally out of the question. Someone has to keep an eye on the business, and when Mother and I stay till closing, sales are up 20 percent.

Yes, I'm thinking, *in a year or two, running the Duke will just be too much for the pair; they'll end up in some wretched home or worse.*

Before I can say a word, Father groans and puts down the paper. Father and I have a good relationship; we speak what's on our mind. Not so with Mother. You always have to be a bit wary with Mum. You never say what you're thinking because you don't want to cross that line and set her off. Since that line is a moving target, you never say what you're thinking for fear of unleashing the drill sergeant in her. That's why Father routinely calls her a martinet, sometimes even a bloody martinet, but always to her back.

"Margaret, I suppose I'm in the doghouse again. I did nothing wrong—just a couple of halves. You know, it's not a crime to be friendly in this country."

I shoot back, "Oh, come off it, Father. You've been drinking that strong ale again. When will you learn? You know you just can't tolerate it, especially as you eat so little. Next you'll be telling me they tied you down and poured the stuff down your gullet. Exactly how stupid do you think we are? Now, Father, how many did you really have, the truth?"

"Well, don't tell Mother, but about five—the strong German beer I like—but it wasn't my fault. People just kept buying me drinks, and I have to drink each and every one. I'm kind of a sociable chap like that, you know. What should I do when someone says 'have one on me, Jim'?"

"You can just say 'No thank you.' You're getting on, Dad—you've got to look after yourself and help Mother more. I'm trying to pick up some of the slack, but me and Mum can only do so much. You've got to start pulling your weight and stop all this bloody daytime drinking—it just makes you very tired and very lazy. Mother said the other day you're going to have to start paying for your drinks if you don't shape up, and I'm pretty sure she means it."

I get up to get ready for the dance. As I leave I hear Father pouring himself another and mumble something about the "bloody McKay women." I don't know where he picked up that expression, but it seems to be on his lips more and more; maybe we're all too hard on him. I don't know about that, but I do know he shouldn't leave all the heavy lifting and worry to Mother.

There are two bedrooms and a bathroom over the kitchen that then lead to the attic. I share one of the bedrooms with Emily, a Yorkshire lass with a broad Yorkshire accent. She and I get along well; she waitresses tables and after all diners are served helps in the washer-up room where all the cutlery, crockery, and pans are washed by hand. On Emily's day off, I grudgingly waitress while Mother and Bill prepare meals. On busy nights, we serve twenty to twenty-five meals in the dining room and up to twenty bar snacks, bringing in several hundred pounds, which is no small change. Thank goodness tonight we aren't snided. I enter the public bar in my bright blue dress that sweeps the floor as I walk. I'm thinking I should have gotten higher heels, maybe even stilettos. That way my dress wouldn't sweep the floor and not require cleaning as often, though I doubt I'll ever wear it again—certainly not to the mess. I'm agile in heels, no matter how high. I'm sure I could teach Ginger Rogers a thing or two. In my mind I think I look pretty darn good; Dad concurs as he pours me a sweet sherry, which I plan to sip till Al shows up. He's always on time—very reliable these Americans. Mother comes in to check me out.

"Very nice. Yes, Margaret, very nice indeed. I hope Al likes it. If he doesn't he's a fool, and I'll tell him so. Anyway, back to the kitchen, and if I don't see Al, you two have a grand time. I'll leave the front door unlocked."

"Thanks, Mum, we will, and no need to wait up—not sure when we'll be returning."

I have to watch the sherry; at times it gives me heartburn, and I don't need that tonight, no way. Father gets up, grumbling, to serve a couple of residents in the cocktail bar; he hates work and just wishes everyone would bugger off home so he can have a few more and go to bed.

Father leaves—most likely to check on the beer flow in the cellar—and will probably be gone for a bit. Mr. Steed comes over and sits next to me on the settle, pint in hand. The settle is informally reserved for family and close friends of the family; locals rarely sit there, not that they'd want to. Mr. Steed is a man of about eighty. Most of his lower jaw was shot off in World War I, leaving him badly scarred. He's a lovely man who lives at the old people's home just down the road across from the antique shop. It's within easy walking distance of the Duke, even on bone-chilling nights, which tonight is not.

"Hello, love. How're you doing tonight? You look smashing—if I were forty years younger, I'd give you a tumble."

Still flirting at his age, I think. *Probably a good thing.*

He drinks his pint in gulps; usually eight or nine good gulps and he's ready for another. Seems like serious beer drinkers never sip, always gulp. They say it tastes better, and that's why beer is always served at room temperature—it's too difficult to gulp ice-cold beer. I'm not sure I quite believe that tale, but I've heard it more than once.

"I'm fine, Mr. Steed, and I'm sure forty years ago you were quite the dashing young man, probably loved by all the ladies?"

A little flannel, now and again, never hurt, I'm thinking, and if anyone deserves it, this veteran does, for sure.

"Well, love, to be quite honest, I was never attracted to ladies. I liked mine a bit on the wild side, the saucier the better—more fun. After the war, I wanted all the fun—and all the beer—I could handle, but when I hit seventy-five I kind of slowed down. Trying to do what the doctor ordered—you know, cut down on the ale—but, Margaret, when I stop drinking all together I can't sleep, and when I do doze off I sometimes call out, or so they tell me, call out to me mates, those killed in the war all those years ago. I can't seem to shake them—so many young lads just smashed to pieces. Oh, the sights I've seen, Margaret."

I reach over and squeeze his trembling hand. He settles down. We chat till Al shows up, at which time Mr. Steed takes another seat nearby, but not before a nod and a wink to Al. As Mother's in the kitchen, Al gives me a brief peck on the cheek. Al knows I'm not fond of affection in public, even holding hands. As if to be more annoying, he gives me a second peck. I look in his direction, eye to eye; he sits with a sheepish grin on his impish face.

Two of the younger locals in the bar notice that I'm a bit miffed with Al and laughingly call out, "I love you, Margaret. I love you, Margaret."

I just smile and wave. No way am I getting in any kind of pissing contest with these boys. I don't want them coming up with some uncomplimentary nickname for me.

"Margaret, you do look swell, really beautiful—that dress suits you perfectly. Anyway, before we leave, I want to speak to you about a few things."

"Sure, Al, no problem, and I might add you also look very nice— rather splendid, one might even say. Black suits you. Yes, all the ladies will want a dance with you." He did look good in his dinner jacket, which did an excellent job of masking his hump. "Al, be a dear and go say hello to Mother before we leave."

He stays in the kitchen for about ten minutes.

In that interval, I'm wondering what Al can have to say that's so urgent. What if … what if he were to ask me to marry him? How should I act if he wants to marry me? It could be quite awkward. I can't leave England, ever, nonnegotiable, and I will never leave my parents, who rely on me, and I would miss them terribly, and I'd end up making Al miserable, and he's too nice a chap for that. Father seems to be getting frailer every day. There seems to be no easy solution. I'm of a mind to just keep things as they are, but Al may see things differently.

Al returns with a grin; he enjoys talking to Mother, who undoubtedly lit up a fag and blew smoke straight up, probably coming very close to setting her hair alight. She most likely continued to hound him about why was he so important that America could afford to send him to Yorkshire four or five times a year, and, of course, she would inevitably add that she always enjoys his visits. Bill and the rest of the kitchen staff would inevitably have chipped in their two cents, much to the chagrin of Mother.

"Will you have another sherry, Margaret? Sherry is so sweet—too sweet for me. I think I'll just have a gin and tonic."

I refuse. Father pours Al a light G & T, and Al offers to buy Father a drink. Of course, Father accepts.

"Anyway, Margaret, I want to speak to you about RAF protocol. This is your first formal visit to the mess, and everyone will be turned out in their best dress, and as this is an RAF do, we must put our best foot forward. Please … I'm just trying to give you a few pointers, so don't take this the wrong way. My first do was a disaster. In fact, because of my many missteps, I was afraid for a while they'd move me to the Sergeants' Mess, but I managed to weather that storm, thanks to Squadron Leader Menteith, a great mate of us Yanks. You'll meet him and his wife Jill tonight. Here are a few pointers, and remember I'm just trying to be helpful, and you may even be grateful later tonight."

"If I introduce you to someone by their Christian name, like Bill or Piggy or Dan, then you're safe to call them by their Christian name and their wives also. You see, rank drives the whole process. I'm considered to be the equivalent of an RAF flight lieutenant, which is equivalent to a USAF captain. Now, anyone who outranks me, like a squadron leader, wing commander, or group captain, must always, without fail, be addressed by their rank or 'sir.' Some may even insist, especially the younger ones, that you address them by their Christian name, but never do that. There is only one exception, and that's Squadron Leader Menteith; all the officers call him Monty. He talks a lot but has a good heart, and as I've said, for some unknown reason, he really likes Americans. Oh, beware—just about everyone we meet will outrank us, and if you're not sure, follow my lead or call them sir or ma'am."

While Al probably didn't intend to lecture me, he did, but I know he's just trying to give me a heads up, and for that, I'm appreciative. Thank goodness Mother's in the kitchen; she would not have been as understanding and would end up lecturing Al in return.

The cabbie comes into the Duke and gives Al a nod. We have to be there by eight, so we're off.

CHAPTER 3

We walk arm in arm; she looks lovely. I can see she's having difficulty with her heels on the cobbled street; she almost stumbles into an all-out fall once or twice, but I save the day. As there is no sidewalk this far up Church Street, we're forced to walk pretty much in the center of the narrow, unlit street. Fortunately, there's little traffic. The cabbie, about twenty paces in front, has already reached his cab and fired it up, lights on, heat probably blasting for the pair of us. It's cold, but not dead cold, and there's no wind, thank God.

"You better keep an eye out for Black Dog, Al. He might be lurking down one of these snickets, ready to pounce."

"What's a snicket?"

"Oh, that's Yorkshire slang for a narrow, dark alley. Around these parts snickets usually go down to the sea front; an alternative word would be shortcut. But don't worry, Al, they're perfectly safe, even at night and even if they were on the unsafe side, I'd look after you."

She giggles. I'm sure at times Margaret must think I'm a really naïve American, thinks I'll believe just about anything she says, and she's probably right.

"I'm sure you will, but Black Dog? Not sure what you mean, Margaret. Fill me in, please."

"Al, you've read Stoker's *Dracula* I'm sure. Well, Whitby Harbour is where the count returns to England. He takes the form of a black dog and terrorizes the countryside, always on the lookout for new victims, sucks the blood right out of them, you know; so in these parts, we always keep a wary eye out for Black Dog, who just might be Dracula masquerading as a—yes, come on, Al, get with the program—a black dog. Not much gets by you Americans."

She's taking the mickey out of me, teasing me in a gentle, almost childish way. I don't mind. In fact, if the truth be known, I quite enjoy it when she goes that extra mile to poke a bit of fun at me. And, unlike her mother, she too can take a little ribbing now and again.

"Margaret, do me a favor. Don't change, ever. You know, no one in my ever so brief life has treated me as a normal human being. It's the hump—no one wants to offend me or hurt my feelings, so everyone pretends it doesn't exist, and everyone intentionally filters out any humor that might be considered even remotely hurtful. That's why most of my conversations are without any humor whatsoever and usually quite uninteresting, and that's why I really do enjoy it when you take the mickey out of me. Makes me kind of feel normal, one hundred percent normal, I mean."

"I understand, Richard."

"Richard, why Richard?"

"Al, you must know, come on, King Richard the third, the king with curvature of the spine. Some even say he had a hump, not a large hump but a hump nevertheless, and a hump by any other name is still a hump. 'My horse, my horse, my kingdom for a horse.' I believe he said that and died in battle, one of our warrior kings, forever disgraced by Shakespeare."

"That's quite funny, Margaret. I appreciate that wicked, slicing kind of humor. Yes, please do call me Richard when I appear to be taking myself a bit too seriously. It'll keep me on my toes, encourage me to lighten up a bit. Do you also call that edgy, sandpaper sort of humor 'taking the mickey'?"

"Between you and me Al, I'd call that taking the piss. It's a bit more cutting than taking the mickey, so you'd better be careful what you ask from this girl, because you just might get it—and then some. But as to your request, kind sir, I'll do my best not to change."

"Yes, Al," she continues in a more sober tone, "England's an old country, much older than America, full of legends and lore, ghosts, and all sorts of mysticism and such. I love this land. You know, Al, not far from the Duke of Yorkshire, just up the road on the right, Captain Cook sailed off to explore the new world. He, himself, never returned— got eaten by cannibals in Hawaii, I believe—but his ship the *Endeavor* did return, and the lads on that ship had plenty of tales to tell, plenty of woe. Maybe one of *Endeavor*'s crew is following us down this rickety old street right now, on the lookout for booty or blood, maybe even your blood, Al." She giggles again, almost busting out into a laugh.

"Margaret, you really do have an overactive imagination. Here's the cab. Let me get in first—then you won't have to slide over. I really do understand your love for this grand old land of yours, your England."

"You're a good lad, Al. You know, I could get used to you being around on a permanent basis. Anyway, I want to have a really good time tonight. Meet everyone and dance till I drop, wear me legs down to wee stumps."

"Yes, that's good, Margaret, but you know the mess is very, very traditional—some might say almost stuffy. Need to fill you in on just a few more traditions—you know, RAF traditions."

"Not another lecture. You'd think I was brought up in the back of beyond, like I'm poor ol' ignorant Liza Doolittle and you're Rex Harrison, trying to learn me better manners-like. Okay, fire away, Rex—I'm all ears."

"Well, it's like this. Where we'll sit in the dining room has already been arranged, by rank of course. So look for your name and stand behind your chair. As you're my guest, we'll be sitting next to each other or directly across from each other. When the station commander and his wife sit, we all sit. There's nothing more embarrassing then having to jump out of your seat—tell me about it. Once we sit for dinner, we stay sat till the cheese tray's taken away. So, if you have to go to the loo, go before dinner. There are very few exceptions to this tradition—only medical emergencies. Oh, and when the decanters of port and Madeira are being passed around, they never touch the table—hand to hand, if you please. They're quite heavy to start with but by the time they reach us, they'll be manageable."

"Gorblimey, Rex, anything else? I wouldn't want to show you up, me dear. Why not tell me how to recognize a fish fork from a dessert fork so I don't end up eating my sweet with the wrong fork."

"Margaret, please. You know I quite like it when you're a bit silly. I just want everyone to like you and think I'm the luckiest man in the mess."

"In the mess? You mean England, me lad."

"The group captain will begin by toasting the queen and president, in turn. A couple of 'hear, hears' will fit in nicely, thank you very much, and one more final thing: it's a set menu. The only option you have is to eat what's on your plate or not eat at all. Not sure what the starter is—some kind of fish I believe. The main meal is roast beef and Yorkshire pudding, roast potatoes, onion sauce and peas, plenty of gravy, I should think. You may ask for a particular cut if you like. I believe you like yours blue, hardly warm in the center, so I ordered ahead for you. Desert is sherry trifle with whipped cream followed by cheese and biscuits and, of course, the port and Madeira. There will be speeches, usually brief—amen to that. The group captain's not long winded. The only other speaker is Commodore Dodson, a genuine war hero—World War Two, that is—in charge of fleets of ships sailing between America and Great Britain delivering much needed supplies. Believe he had a ship or two torpedoed out from under him, both sunk, but he managed to survive. He's now the lord mayor of Whitby—that's why he wears that huge ceremonial gong around his neck."

"You know, Al, I've met the commodore a couple of times. He comes into the Duke now and again for a couple of pints. He seems like a nice enough chap, though we never really got any further than a simple greeting or brief discussion about our horrible weather. The commodore's not much of a talker, usually sits alone, kinda like thinking about days gone by, and not necessarily the good ol' days. Father likes him, but Mother's undecided."

"How so?"

"Mother thinks he has a roving eye, a bit of a rogue—you know, zipper problems. That's a definite no-no in her book. His wife's kind of a miserable old thing. She's a lot younger than the commodore but acts as though she were ninety—very posh. Has kind of an elitist view of the world; one might even call her a snob, and her only justification for being snobbish is her husband. I believe her father was a sheep farmer whose land holdings were parsimonious. As we say in this country, she's really full of herself to a fault."

"Well, Margaret, I say God bless the commodore. He's approaching eighty-five, and if he still likes the ladies, good for him—must be something in the ale he drinks. Anyway, more power to him. His wife ought to be more cooperative, if you get my drift."

"I get your drift, Al, and by the way, Mr. Know It All, how do I address el commodore and his missus?"

"You ask the darnest questions, Margaret", as I scratch my head then my hump as if looking for a clever response to a fairly straight forward question.

"*Chérie*, I don't know—just call him sir or Commodore Dodson and Mrs. Dodson. I believe commodore is a rank, but perhaps not. He never wears a uniform and, believe me, if he were entitled to wear a uniform, he'd wear one. Anyway, at these dos he doesn't roam around much, so we'll have to seek him out and pay our respects, almost as if he's a royal holding court."

"Al, you know *cherie* means darling, not dear but darling. It's a very intimate French word denoting more than friendship and much more than just a casual relationship. Please don't use it lightly."

"It was intentional, and I mean it."

"Good, that pleases me very much. I always said you were a good lad, Al."

"Margaret, I'd like to have a chat with you after the dance. We can get a taxi and pop down to the Goathland Hotel, have a nightcap. There are a few things I want to discuss with you, important things."

"Sure, Al. Not another FYI, I hope."

"Hardly—anything but. Oh, I forget to mention, Margaret. The station commander, Group Captain Stanis, has invited you and me for drinks, in his office immediately prior to us motoring over to the mess—his car, his driver. I think he just wants to meet you. He knows me already, but not very well. I have a bit of a reputation, unfortunately a bad one but not too awfully bad."

"And why am I being singled out to meet the group captain?"

"Well, as this is your first big do, he'd like to meet you, have a bit of a chat, a chin-wag if you will. He's very British, anything but down to earth—kind of like Ronald Coleman, starched knickers—but very nice though also very standoffish, and he's not the least bit shy, just standoffish, if you know what I mean."

"I do—a baritone with all the right credentials down to a very posh English accent, a different generation than you and me. Us commoners refer to men like him as frightfully, frightfully, and don't worry—I'll take the starch out of those knickers. And what about his missus, Al?"

"She'll already be at the mess, organizing. Yes, she's a real organizer, or so I'm led to believe."

Thirty minutes later we three hop into the station commander's car on our way to the mess. In less than thirty minutes Margaret has not only wooed the station commander but earned the sobriquet "RAF Fighter Pilot." She is unusually charming and more importantly matches the group captain drink for drink—two very large gins, little or no tonic with no ice or lemon. They are both as steady as the Tower. The group captain is more relaxed than I've ever seen him, and the pair swaps stories as if they'd been mates for years. I feel a wee bit tipsy and am unable to down even half my second gin for fear of adding to my already questionable reputation.

The roast beef and Yorkshire pudding are delightful. Margaret is more than delightful; she's ravishing and makes not a single misstep. She instinctively knows what to do and what not to do. While the dance floor is small, it's adequate for the type of traditional dancing that's taking place—no rock and roll, if you please. No band or DJ either, just records of an almost bygone era, mostly songs that remind all of the war. I can see Margaret's having an especially good time dancing with the brass and some of my mates.

"You know, Al, I now see why you gave me those pointers. Everyone's so polite and proper, and everyone seems to know what to do and when. Even the junior officers seem to be on form—no one's put one toe out of place as far as I can see. I now understand why one misstep on my part would have proven to be most embarrassing—a single misstep by anyone would have been most recognizable to all, as the entire evening appears to have been choreographed down to the final cheerio."

"I know, Margaret, and I'm so pleased you're having a good time. Ah, Squadron Leader Menteith's coming our way. You met him a while ago, but he was tied up with the group captain at that time."

"I know, Al. That was only ten minutes ago. I'm not that forgetful, not yet."

"And Squadron Leader Menteith," Margaret says as Monty comes to a full stop, as if on parade playing to the crowd, heels banging together.

Monty is about sixty plus, which means he was more or less a kid when flying Wellingtons in WW II. At times when I look at a man of sixty I just can't imagine what he looked like at twenty, but I've seen a few photos of Monty at twenty, and he's the spitting image of himself with a few pounds added: round, wide-open face, slicked-down hair—or as they say in England, 'the Brill Cream boy' look—bushy eyebrows, and never without a smile. However, the most memorable thing about Monty is his temperament, which is flamboyant and, yes, charming. He's quick to laugh, always ready for an argument or a story, and rather loud even when not making a point. I really do like Monty; he befriended me the day I arrived at the mess and is always helpful, kind of like a father with a British accent.

"Monty, where's your lovely wife? Al's been telling me all about her. I'd love to meet her."

"She's chatting to WingCo Blake, talking about some such nonsense. They both enjoy hiking and camping and are now comparing notes on camping in Scotland. I needed a break. My idea of camping is in London at Whites with a G and T in one hand and a full house in the other."

"Squadron Leader Menteith," Margaret asks, "I understand you flew Wellingtons in the war?"

I can see Monty's fascinated by Margaret; he can't take his eyes off her, and I know that he knows that she knows nothing about Wellingtons, wouldn't know a Wellington from a Lancaster, and is probably too young to even remember the war, but Monty being Monty is as gracious as any royal.

"Well, Margaret, first call me Monty, please—everyone above the rank of flying officer calls me Monty—and as regards your question, well, just about everyone in this room over the age of sixty was in the war and most likely all flew in one thing or another. After all, this is the RAF. The war didn't discriminate—if you could get up in the morning and put your britches on, you were probably fit for duty, and all of the older officers in this room did their duty. I was a tail gunner; shot down two and a half Jerries—the waist gunner got the other half. Probably lucky to be alive, but that's another story. This country's so liberal today, I expect the law to show up at the mess one day and arrest me for killing Jerry."

Again Margaret puts on the charm, saying, "Monty, and I'm not being funny, some of these officers do look as though they should be retired, rest on their laurels. They did their duty. Now it's their time to kick back. Apparently, as you say, most are real British heroes. Don't they have some sort of pension they can fall back on? I see the American officers are so much younger, all forty and under."

"Well, Margaret, it's like this. These RAF blokes can all retire if they want to, but they don't. They love what they're doing, and if they want to stay on duty, they should be allowed to stay till they drop; they earned that. Now the American Air Force thinks differently. It's all about promotions, promotions, promotions. If you're not a major by thirty and a colonel by forty, you're forced out—turn in your uniform, go back home to Iowa, sit on the porch, drink beer, and watch the corn grow. It really is up or out. In some ways it may make sense, kind of like natural selection—you know, the survival of the fittest—but one can become too concerned with promotions and what it takes to get promoted. Getting promoted can becomes an end in itself, and getting promoted means filling all the squares first while properly doing your job becomes a distant second. And when your job comes in second, there may be a price to pay, and the price is that one becomes a careerist, spending more time monitoring your progression when you should be monitoring your performance, and you become very, very focused on out-performing those you're competing against, in other words making yourself look good, especially to your superiors. So, how does one consistently outperform one's contemporaries, you might ask? Well, you might do this by trying to garner all the credit for a job well done or backstabbing your colleagues or taking shortcuts. By taking shortcuts I mean getting the job done early and below budget, but shortcuts may lead to failure, and failure requires explanations to management that may lead to tall tales and deceit, which to any officer should be offensive and avoided at all costs. Anyway, Margaret, I'm rambling, but what I've just said is jolly well true. Promotions should be earned by performing well, not by becoming a careerist."

"Now, Margaret, permit me to point out a few of my mates, please? You may have been introduced to most, but you don't really know much about them. You see those two squadron leaders to your left? They both piloted Lancasters in the war, and I believe both were shot down at least once. That wing commander to your right was shot down and spent three years in a German POW camp. The group captain flew Spitfires in the Battle of Britain, a double ace. He was one of the few that Prime Minister Churchill was referring to in that famous speech of his—'Never was so much owed by so many to so few.' I heard that speech firsthand—me, part of a bomber crew—and it brought a tear or two to my eyes, even though I wasn't the 'few' he was referring to, but

Bomber Harris was quick to point out that we bomber boys did our fair share to win the war and with many more casualties."

"Anyway, now's not the time for war stories. Tell you what, you and Al come up to the mess some evening for drinks. We'll have a few and chat, and I've got a story or two that'll leave you rolling in the aisle and others that will bring tears to your eyes."

He laughs loudly, but not so loud as to be heard all over the rather small room reserved for dancing and light conversation.

"Monty," I say, "rumor has it that you'll be retiring soon. Any truth in that?"

"Well, Al, if the buggers at Strike Command have their way, I'll shortly be forced to retire and spend my senior years running a tuck shop at some local university, selling pencils and snacks, what, what. I'm only just sixty—plenty of tread still left on these tires. Seriously, I think I'll be okay for a few more years. Not many young lads are joining the RAF, not like the old days. Back then, they were queuing up to fight. Plenty didn't make it home either—very sad. Kids are a lot different today: no sense of duty, no sense of country—they just want to acquire things and have fun, fun, fun."

"Plenty of Americans never came home either," I say.

"I know that, Al. Firsthand experience. A bunch of your lads stayed with my mother during the war, near RAF Alconbury, down south. Their plane went down in the Channel, a training accident of all things. All dead. My Mother was very upset. Never quite got over it. Till the day she died she talked of those boys, and they weren't much more than boys. Knew all their names and had a special story that she liked to tell about each. The pilot was the oldest, a first lieutenant, twenty-four years old. You know, Al, if you and Margaret are ever down Cambridge way, there's a beautiful American cemetery there—pristine, well maintained, lovely, almost poetic. Each headstone's a work of art. You should take the time to take a look someday. Every Fourth of July, the locals plant American flags adjacent to each headstone—quite a sight. Us Brits just paying respect to our mates."

"We will, Monty," I say.

That's the second time Monty has linked me and Margaret. That "you and Margaret" strikes a chord. It sounded good, kind of natural-like.

"Margaret," I whisper, "getting late. Can we move on, have a drink at the Goathland? It'll still be open."

"Sure, Al."

"Whoa, where're you going, Al? Parlor football's coming up—Yanks against the RAF. I seem to remember you did quite well last time, scored two goals I believe, but we still thrashed you. Our lads are very aggressive—broken bones not unusual. That's the only way to play if you want to win—be aggressive, full speed ahead."

"Al," Margaret asks, "What's parlor football? Sounds like fun."

"You have two teams, usually junior officers with the occasional squadron leader thrown in. In the bar each side lines up—about seven or eight per side. Nobody really counts the numbers—if you want to play, you play. The object is to try and advance the football, which is usually a pillow of sorts, into the opponent's goal, which is usually defined by a couple of posts. The only snag is you're sitting on the floor, and the only way you can move is to lift yourself off the floor with your arms and with your legs propel yourself this way and that. The ball can only be shifted with your feet, like proper football. Like Monty said, it's a very aggressive game, and you have to be careful not to be kicked in the wrong place, which unfortunately frequently happens."

"Ooh, Al, I'd like to see that, but I know we have to go. Better make our farewells."

"Sorry, Monty. Have an early start tomorrow. A couple of lads to check out in a week or so—got to prepare. Also gotta get Margaret home—want to stay on the good side of her mother. I know you'll understand."

"Cheerio, Al, take care, and if I were you, I wouldn't let this one get away."

It's approaching midnight. We say our farewells to the RAF and USAF. The cab's freezing cold, and it's a different driver. The Goathland Hotel, being a country pub, disregards any and all pub closing times, even though it's the law. Farmers out haying in the summer or seeing to their stock in winter have to have a few pints before bed, and the publicans are eager to comply. The Goathland's only ten minutes away, practically all downhill from the mess. A roaring coal fire greets us; the pub is toasty warm, and we sit a few feet from the hearth, drink in hand.

"Chin, chin, Al, you do look solemn. What's on your mind?"

"Well, it's like this, Margaret, and please don't interrupt. Let me finish."

"How will I know when you finish?" She stifles a giggle, probably feeling the wine.

"Oh, you'll know, Margaret. You see, I've come to the realization that I'm hopelessly in love with you and want you to be my wife. I do understand your great love for England and the Duke and your parents, so I would never dream of asking you to leave your home, but I have a few ideas I want to run by you. Well, it's not very original, but if we marry, and I pray we will, we could pretty much carry on as we have in the past. I'll pop over here five or six times a year for a couple of weeks, and we can phone regularly. While I'm here we can rent a small flat nearby—won't be able to stay in the mess. I can retire in about fifteen years, at which time I'll take up permanent residence in Yorkshire as an Englishman—yes, an Englishman. You see, once we're wed, I can apply for UK citizenship. Oh, by the way, I have this ring—kind of customary, you know. Well, what do you say?"

"Al, for some time I've been half-expecting you to propose. Ordinarily, I would have said no for all the reasons you just enumerated, but I do love you also, and your solution to my dilemmas seem quite attractive to say the least, and I don't want to lose you, really. We're both reasonably young, and when you do retire I might even give up the Duke, and we could make up the lost time. We might even buy a small cottage on the moors and, as they say in fairy tales, live happily ever after."

"Let's have a look at that ring, Prince Charming."

With minimum scrutiny, she slips it onto her finger—perfect fit. A huge smile follows. We embrace but without too much emotion.

"The ring's lovely, Al. You got yourself a wife, boyo."

On the way back to Whitby, I surreptitiously stroke my hump. My good luck piece didn't fail me; God, I love that hump. I knew I'd done the right thing: if I hadn't suggested she remain in England, she would have most certainly declined and broke my heart. Over time this arrangement will work, and when I retire, I'll emigrate. This arrangement might even be a good thing; I'll never be around long enough to get on her nerves. I will undoubtedly miss her a great deal, but I'd rather miss her than lose her altogether. There's no way we could have continued if she had rejected me—word would get around, and

I'd be too humiliated. If this arrangement is to work, children are out, no doubt about that. I'm sure Margaret will agree. While I'm away her first obligation will be her parents, and, yes, of course, the Duke.

Several days later we're married at the local registrar's office in Whitby. We only just manage to get the license and paperwork sorted out, with a little help from the locals. It's a quiet affair—her family and close friends only; no one from the States is invited. Monty is my best man, and Tessa, a childhood friend of Margaret's, is her bridesmaid. Margaret's mother, Tessa, and Margaret wear cream-colored dresses with long, flowing skirts, cream-colored gloves, black handbags, and parasols to match. They do look smashing. Following the ceremony a reception is held at the Duke. It's a huge success, with plenty of singing and dancing and, of course, drinking. Monty makes a brilliant speech poking fun at me, telling a few funny stories about the naïve American who came to England a few years ago and is now more English than the English. How the American, while driving on the wrong side of the road, never misses sheep, dogs, buses, or telephone boxes, and it's never his fault. They just jump out in front of his car. How when he first arrived at the mess, he kept such a low profile he earned the nickname the gray ghost.

As time wears on, Margaret's father is becoming annoyed. When the old grandfather clock in the corner strikes twelve times, he anxiously asks me, "Al, don't these people have homes to go to? I'm buying, and these Americans really know how to drink—not a sipper in the bunch. And the RAF, they're no slouches either—all gulpers, even some of the wives. They'll ruin me, for sure."

"You're right, Jim. This will be costing you a bob or two, like pissing away a fortune. I do hate seeing good brass being wasted, but it's for a good cause, and, yes, I too do like money, maybe more than you, maybe more than you could ever imagine."

"No fear, Jim. Transport to the patch, where all the officers live, will be leaving in fifteen minutes."

Next morning I'm up at six, and with only four hours sleep I'm off to RAF Fylingdales. Getting married hadn't been on my agenda, and I have commitments to the Agency, so we have to postpone our honeymoon to a future, yet to be determined date, and a week or so from today my TDY's over and I'm back to the States, not to return for at least three months.

As lead international polygrapher for all government employees holding Agency clearances in Great Britain, I'm responsible for ensuring that these same employees remain good risks, have broken no Agency policies or procedures, and are safeguarding government secrets. I need to also confirm that they are not sharing classified information with agents of foreign governments or being careless in behavior or speech. I do this by administering polygraphs. I don't put my schedule together; I'm just given names and locations, and I show up. At RAF Fylingdales there are many Agency employees with clearances that need to be regularly renewed, so I visit Fylingdales and its environs several times a year.

I'm only responsible for administering polygraphs; the questions I ask are scripted well in advance and can't be altered without permission from my supervisors. I cannot be creative and inject new questions either. There's a particular protocol, and no deviations are permitted, full stop. This approach to the polygraph is fairly new—a significant change from when I was first interviewed by Jim about five years ago. The cowboy mentality, cursing, and ridiculing, are no longer permissible. Polygraphers need to stick to the game plan; they're monitored and checked up on, and any deviations from protocol will be met with remedial training and, if that fails, dismissal.

Polygraph results, along with background checks, police records, security violations, travel history, performance appraisals, and financial disclosures are used by adjudication teams to determine if individuals can continue to maintain their clearances and continue to work for the Agency and provide for their families. No clearances, no work. It's as simple as that, and that's why the Agency takes what I do seriously, very seriously indeed. They want the process done right and, more importantly, done fairly. No one wants to yank someone's clearances unless there's no alternative, so I'm painfully conscientious in the performance of my job, bending over backward to assist examinees. As long as they're being honest and cooperative with me, I'll do my best for them. If the contrary turns out to be the case, I'll cut them no slack, for who knows what secrets these examinees may know—certainly not me. I have no idea what these individuals do on a daily basis or what secrets they may know. That's not part of my job description. I just need to find out if treachery or deceit may be lurking in their hearts and if they have disclosed or are willing to disclose secrets whose unveiling could cause serious damage to my country.

The polygraph is, without a doubt, the single most important part of all inputs into adjudication. Properly administered polygraphs should provide sufficient input to adjudication for them to determine if an individual is lying, telling the truth, or just being evasive. Tests are often administered repeatedly, back to back, the polygrapher doing his best to capture results that identify lies and reveal the truth. The polygrapher doesn't decide what's true or what's not true; he just minimizes evasiveness. Adjudication makes the final determination of lying and to what degree and to what questions. Lying about associations with foreign agents is very serious; lying about associations with hookers or lying on tax returns is serious but not grounds, in themselves, for pulling a person's tickets. Off-polygraph questioning about online polygraph results is my forte; catching a person in a lie and having that person admit that he lied makes the job of adjudication much easier. Adjudicators love polygraphers who can repeatedly turn that trick, and I'm their man, and I know it. Confessions make it easy to pull tickets, to prosecute where necessary, and to subsequently minimize damage from intentional leaks and rogue employees.

In the second golf ball, second floor, I patiently wait for Jack Thompson, an Agency employee of some ten years who is responsible for compiling and sending satellite data collected by the military back to Agency Headquarters in Langley. I, as it should be, know nothing about satellite data; I only know what little I do know from the unclassified job description on Jack's annual fitness report. I have just finished going through Jack's personnel file and see no red flags. I've polygraphed Jack several times in the past, and while there was some, to be expected, evasiveness about how he lived his life, I felt he would not be evasive or have any problems with the important counterintelligence questions.

There's a knock at the door; it's Jack. He enters, literally cap in hand. I'm always amazed that so many Americans pick up English customs, even if only over here a couple of months. Jack has a flat cap in hand, something most Yorkshire men wear but most Americans do not. I'm not sure if Jack realizes that a flat cap is a working-class cap—no one in the Officers' Mess would ever be caught dead in a flat cap. I suppose the same could be said of the Sergeants' Mess, but that's another story.

We shake hands perfunctorily. Jack's hand is sweaty, a little shaky. No small talk, not even about the diabolical Yorkshire weather. This is normal and to be expected; people being polygraphed just want to get it over with—the quicker the better and as painless as possible.

"Okay, Jack, let me get you hooked up. You know the drill. I'll get you calibrated, then a few straightforward, easy-to-answer questions about your lifestyle, and then a few easy-to-answer counterintelligence questions, and you're off. The questions haven't changed from the last time. Want a quick review?"

"No, Al. Let's get this over with. I've got work to do. Number one antenna's a bit off-center—"

"Hold on, Jack, you know the rules: no shop talk. I don't need to know what you know, and I certainly don't need to know about number one antenna. Now please, Jack, let's focus on just one thing, and that's getting you successfully through this poly. Remember you're here voluntarily and can leave at any time, and I'm here to work with you and help you get through your polygraph as quickly and easily as possible."

"You say that every time, Al, but if I leave, I lose my tickets, and who'll pay my mortgage? Will you?"

"Jack, you knew the rules when you signed on. The rules haven't changed. You will be routinely polygraphed every few years, and the fact that you're stationed overseas means you'll be polygraphed more often than most, and the more you travel outside the UK, the more you'll be polygraphed. You know that, so why try to make out that this is something new?"

I'm getting that feeling again. No one likes polygraphers, but that's my job, and Jack has to live with it. He knew the rules when he first signed on ten years ago.

"Okay, Al. Let's get on with it please. Let's get this over with."

Before leaving on this current TDY, I checked in with the intelligence unit responsible for Northern England. There'd been no security issues at Fylingdales, no suspicious rogue agent, no leaks to the media, no Agency-requested investigation by MI-6. I also checked in with the local North Yorkshire police. Jack had had no run-ins with the local law. His annual appraisals were solid. Financially, he's a scrooge. Because of the lack of any suspicious information, I assume that Jack's probably been true to his country. I further assume that Jack will easily clear, as he always has.

I don't like to boast, but about four years ago as a new Agency hire, I devised this scheme of using past polygraphs to help polygraphers decide if an interviewee is lying or telling the truth today, in real time, as he's hooked up. After many sleepless nights, I came up with the "truth-corridor." As long as an individual's responses to my questions fall within his truth-corridor, as displayed on my monitor, he's telling the truth. After many tests where I correlated questions and lies as well as questions and the truth, I found that the truth-corridor works, always works, no exceptions. The only hitch is new hires with little or no history of taking polygraphs. Previous methodologies will have to suffice in these cases, but over time the truth-corridor will apply to them as well.

"Right you are, Jack. I'm already logged on, but give me a minute or two to launch the right programs and then we're off to the races. You do remember, Jack, that the first round of questions is the calibration questions."

And I almost, but didn't, say, "and the calibration questions will establish your truth-corridor."

"Of course I do, Al. I've played this game several times already and am as prepared as I'll ever be."

The calibration questions are intended to establish a baseline not only for my equipment, but for Jack. The baseline calibration questions are straightforward. White is white, white is black, one plus one is two, one plus one is three, today is Wednesday when it is actually Friday, and on and on. For each calibration question where the answer is true, such as one plus one is two, the polygraph establishes a low digital value based on consolidating pulse, respiration, and blood pressure readings (how the Consolidator software exactly works is foreign to me, as it was devised and implemented by mathematicians and computer scientists using my test results). For each question where the answer is a lie, such as one plus one is three, the polygraph establishes a high digital return. By horizontally connecting Jack's highs and horizontally connecting Jack's lows, my machine establishes and displays a truth-corridor for Jack. Today's truth-corridor is automatically and seamlessly merged by the polygraph with the five polys Jack has previously taken, establishing his target truth-corridor.

As long as Jack's responses to the follow-on counterintelligence and lifestyle questions fall within the target truth-corridor as determined and displayed as an *X* by the Consolidator, give or take 10 percent, I'll believe Jack's telling me the truth or only being mildly evasive—in other words, not a threat. When all of Jack's responses are inside the truth-corridor, he can leave. Of course, significant deviations well outside the truth-corridor will be scrutinized and discussed with a follow-on poly by me the next day. After several attempts, if all the results for an individual who has had several previously successful polys don't fall within the truth-corridor, I become very suspicious and make the necessary remarks and forward his package to Langley, where a final determination will be made. I never and can't make outright recommendations about polygraph results, but if I choose to poly an individual only one time, adjudication always extends that individual's clearances—kind of a wink, wink, nod, nod. That's how much I'm trusted and respected. If, however, an individual is poly'ed several times with poor results, well outside the truth-corridor, adjudication will take a very hard look and on a case by case basis decide to extend or not extend his clearances. I'm totally out of the picture by the time adjudication gives thumbs-up or thumbs-down.

Finger and blood pressure cups are in place, as is the chest coil; it's like Jack's being put to death rather than just being interrogated. We breeze through the calibration questions, and within fifteen minutes I have established and am displaying Jack's updated merged truth-corridor.

"Okay, Jack, power off. Now, relax. Take a deep breath if you like. Find a point on the floor and focus. Listen to the questions, and truthfully answer either yes or no—no comments or clarifications, please. These are the all-important lifestyle and counterintelligence questions you know so well."

Every time I say "and truthfully answer" I feel like I'm playing a game of sorts with the interviewee. On my monitor I can see an agitated response, which usually means a lie or evasiveness. A relaxed response usually means the truth. Responses are displayed on my equipment well before the interviewee answers verbally. An agitated response—a lie—will breach the upper limit of the truth-corridor while a relaxed response—the truth—will appear in the middle to lower-middle of the truth-corridor. The Consolidator really does all the work; it amalgamates temperature, pulse, and blood pressure into a single value and displays that value on my monitor relative to the truth-corridor. The results of the Consolidator are displayed to me well before Jack's brain even understands the question. As Jack's brain is forming a yes or no and moving that response to his lips, I already know what his response should be.

As an example, to the question "Have you ever associated with a member of a foreign intelligence service?" I can immediately see a relaxed response near the bottom half of the truth-corridor. Jack answers no, which fits the pattern, and I'm certain he's telling the truth. Of course, the question is asked several times with no embellishments. We don't use questions with double negatives, exceptions, conjunctions or any convoluted phraseology, as this would confuse the Consolidator. Now, if Jack were to answer yes to the question about associating with a member of a foreign intelligence service, which has never happened, I would switch off and immediately call for security.

The next question has to do with receiving favors for classified information. Same results: the Consolidator says no, and Jack says no. Things are going great—I should be able to wrap Jack up shortly.

The final question has to do with associating with media people on a permanent, even friendly, basis.

For this final question I see an agitated response well outside the upper limit of Jack's truth-corridor, which means Jack is probably preparing to lie. His answer is no.

I switch off.

"We got to talk, Jack. My machine doesn't like that last answer, not at all, so let's talk. What's going on in that head of yours? We're almost done. You're doing very well, so why are you having trouble with that last question?"

"Don't know, Al. Let's hook up and try again, please."

I agree, but we'll get the same results so why bother.

"Any more ideas, Jack? Hey, I've got a good idea—how about you telling me the truth? What were you thinking about when I asked you that last question? Level with me, Jack. You don't want your results going forward when they might raise eyebrows, do you?"

"Well, Al, it's like this. My wife and I have friends, a couple. We go out together every Friday. He's a reporter for the *Whitby Gazette*, but I never talk shop with him and he never asks questions, and he's a nice enough chap—English bloke, you know."

"Okay, Jack. I'm glad you got that off your chest, but I wish you'd told me the truth as soon as you walked in that door. Would have made my job a lot easier, and if you haven't been talking shop, and he's not pumping you for information, then we should be okay."

Not waiting for a reply, I hook Jack up again, hopefully for the last time.

This time the agitation level has attenuated, and Jack's results just manage to snuggle up inside the upper limit of his truth-corridor. I'm satisfied the relationship with the local reporter is harmless, and as Jack has already passed all the other counterintelligence questions, I can send him on his way.

Jack leaves. No handshake, no smile, no words—he just leaves. Jack is not a happy camper, but I don't make the rules, and he knows that.

The second and last interviewee of the day is Larry Kurtz. He might prove to be a tougher nut to crack. He's only had two previous polys on file, so establishing his truth-corridor will be difficult, though not impossible. His previous poly was indeterminate, but the Agency renewed his clearances because they had no reason not to. Now, three years later, adjudication might not be so generous.

Larry walks in, sullen and defiant. We shake hands; his are bone dry.

"Let's have a look at those hands, Larry."

I meticulously examine Larry's hands, front and back, and smell them, too.

"Really, Larry? Powder? you know it's against the rules to try to mask your perspiration and confuse my equipment. I could just end it right now—is that what you want? You know what that would mean. I'm sure you do."

"No, Al. It's just that I'm so nervous—haven't slept a wink for a week. I'll go wash my hands."

In the interim before Larry returns, I note this incident in his folder. Adjudication will not like this. Larry returns shortly. I recheck for powder or any other foreign substance. He's clean.

"Anything you want to talk about before we start, Larry?"

"No, Al. Sorry—I've never done anything like that before. This whole drill is pretty nerve-racking, as you can imagine. Sometimes wish I'd never got involved with the Agency. You know, I recently read that the United States is the only country on the planet where anyone and everyone working for the Agency, excepting the director, have to pass a polygraph—and on a regular basis."

"But that's nothing new, is it, Larry? You knew that when you came on board. So why's it such a big deal now?"

Larry smirks and morosely shakes his head but says nothing.

"Okay, Larry, let's move on. I'll ask you a series of calibration questions; then I'll review the counterintelligence and lifestyle questions. First you'll answer them off-line. I'll then hook you up, and we'll run through the examination. If I see any deception, we'll stop, turn off the equipment, and have a little chat, then continue. If you have any questions, please ask them now. Remember I'm here to help you, and also remember you're here as a volunteer—no one put a gun to your head. Any questions?"

"No questions, Al."

I hook Larry up and quickly run through the calibration questions; I'm anxious to get home, back to the Duke to see my new wife.

I rapidly move forward, establishing Larry's truth-corridor. The machine merges today's results with the previous two polys Larry has taken. A rather wobbly, wide, interviewee-friendly corridor is established, but it's still good enough for me to work with.

The fact that the corridor isn't tight should make it easier for Larry to pass. He really has an edge with so few polys under his belt, I'm thinking.

Larry's counterintelligence responses are within his truth-corridor and near enough to his previous results that I feel he's not a traitor or potential threat.

However, the results of his lifestyle questions are a total bust. The three lifestyle questions are straightforward and have to do with breaking the law, associating with individuals the Agency might disapprove of, and sexual misconduct. For all three questions Larry's answers are miles outside his truth-corridor, on average 30 percent or more. Between Larry's last poly and today, something has changed in his life. Something or someone has rocked his world—and not for the best. The fact that he's so far outside his truth-corridor tells me that he's not only being evasive and self-rationalizing, he's lying through his teeth. I do my best to get to the root cause of why he can't get by the lifestyle portion of the examination, but Larry won't open up. He doesn't offer any possible reason or excuse for his unacceptable results; he just keeps saying that he's telling me the truth and has no idea why his results are so poor. Even if Larry had decided to make up an excuse—that is, to tell me more lies—it would most likely have made his results worse. Telling a lie to justify a lie certainly won't help him, and he knows it, and that's why he, more or less, just dummies up. If Larry had decided to tell the whole truth, he would, in all probability, have incriminated himself, which would mean he'd lose his tickets and be packed off to the slammer. Larry is definitely in a lose-lose situation; he'd have been better off just not showing up and changing to a job where a polygraph is unnecessary.

I grudgingly unhook Larry for the last time. I can't do much more. I'm sure he can see by the look on my face that his results are less than stellar, well outside his truth-corridor. While he knows nothing of the truth-corridor, he knows that I know he's a flaming liar.

"Well, Larry, here's what's going to happen. I'll send your results forward, as is. Something's going on in that head of yours, and you choose not to discuss it. By taking that position you make my job most difficult, pretty much impossible, but that's your right. Your counterintelligence exam is pretty good, but your lifestyle is shaky, very shaky. I'm not sure what adjudication will do. Their options are to renew your tickets, not renew it, or bring you back home for a more in-depth exam with equipment much more elaborate than this mobile unit of mine."

"Do you think they'll pull my clearances?"

With great difficulty, I shrug my shoulders, intentionally not making eye contact.

"Larry, do you want me to level with you?"

"Yes, please."

"In my mind, Larry, you're being totally uncooperative. I will note that in my report, because if I didn't I would be derelict in my duty to the Agency. You refuse to discuss the anomalies in your poly and offer no help to me whatsoever. Why? I have a few ideas based on the questions and my experience, but I know nothing for certain because you're not helping your cause. I need explanations. I'm feeling you have some personal issues that, right now, don't affect your work, and in my opinion you're not an immediate risk to the Agency or the host country, but right now there's nothing more I can do. You're a smart man, Larry. I'm sure you can understand that."

"You may as well leave now, Larry. I'll get your package back to Langley tomorrow. Good luck."

"What do I tell my management? They'll ask for sure."

"That's up to you, Larry, but if I were a betting man, which I'm not, I reckon they'll be calling you home for a much more intensive reexamination, so you might think about clearing up any loose ends you might have on this side of the pond. But that's just a guess, Larry. I could be wrong."

I'm thinking that Larry's has some issues with the law here in the UK. Maybe illegal drugs, some sexually illegal inclination that the Agency feels is abnormal, maybe the wide-scale selling of alcohol or cigarettes bought on base to the locals, or, or, or. It could be anything; it's not my bloody concern. Any one of these transgressions—and others—could impact lifestyle results and even bleed over to the counterintelligence exam. Any one of these could prove to be disastrous to Larry personally if it surfaced and extremely disastrous to the Agency if someone tried to use that information to blackmail Larry. Who knows to what length he might go to keep his secrets secret? Anyway, rather than leveling with me, he prefers to leave it a crapshoot. Maybe adjudication will give him a break for a second time, but they'll most likely recall him and all his belongings and eventually cut him loose. He appears to be a loose cannon and is probably lucky not to be going to prison—a cold, damp English prison where the only sport he'd be able to view would be English football, rugby, and cricket—oh, yes, and horse racing.

I methodically put Larry's package together; it's already too late to have dinner with Margaret. I can't and won't give Larry either thumbs-up or a thumbs-down. Adjudication can easily figure out what I've figured out: he's a liar. Of course, Larry may be more cooperative in the States, feeling he may be somehow immune from English law, but that most certainly would not be the case. If he has committed a crime in England, he'll be deported for trial and punishment. As things now stand, I don't know what Larry's fate will be. I suppose that's his problem. I did everything he'd let me do.

In addition to my previous comment about the hand powder, I record just one handwritten note:

Refuses to cooperate.

Between Larry's polys and my rather cryptic notes, adjudication can sort things out. They're usually on the ball. After all, they've all been polygraphers at one time or another, and you don't get to be an adjudicator by being slow on the uptake.

Postscript: On my next visit to RAF Fylingdales, Larry is gone. I don't pursue the matter or ask questions, but it doesn't surprise me. Clearances are not a God-given right, and the Agency isn't in the business of handing out clearances like they're sweets. Larry was just too much of a risk.

CHAPTER 4

That was about twenty-five years ago, twenty-five years of wedded bliss—well, most of the time anyway. And in all that time Al must have crossed the Atlantic at least two hundred times, preferring the eastward, seven-hour flight to the westward, eight-and-a-half-hour flight. While the shorter flight time was important, it was getting back to Margaret that really mattered; getting back to living in England was a close second. From London's Heathrow, Al would catch the tube to Kings Cross Station and then ride the train on up to York, first class, and have a brilliant lunch that might consist of egg mayonnaise as a starter followed by an eight-ounce rump steak, medium rare; chips, and Brussels sprouts always overcooked to a soft, soggy consistency. Al always had plenty of tomato ketchup on his chips; Margaret, who often met him in London, preferred malt vinegar. If she were really hungry she'd jam a few chips between a folded slice of buttered bread, calling it a chip butty. Al also had adopted the English custom of amply applying spicy English mustard to each piece of beef he so eagerly devoured, and if he was still a bit peckish, there was always the cheese board with English cheddar, the sharper the better. Dessert usually consisted of rich, creamy, not too frozen ice cream—one scoop, always vanilla, and never chocolate sauce—to be followed by regular coffee, the blacker the better—never milk, cream, or sugar.

Al's retirement after fifteen years never came to fruition. He just never had the savings to retire to that little cottage in the English countryside, and Margaret had derived far too much satisfaction from running the Duke for him to ask her to pack it in. The work, however, was backbreaking; she was on her feet fifteen hours a day, and that combined with too many late nights and budgetary woes was turning Margaret into her mother, something she refused to acknowledge or even think about, but it was true nonetheless. The clearest sign she was becoming Nan was that about five years ago she started referring to men she wasn't overly fond of as "little men." Anyway, Al was approaching retirement, voluntarily or forced, and he was only middle aged, plus a bit, as was Margaret, plus a bit. That had been the plan all along, hadn't it: retire and enjoy the fruits of their labor? Or so Al thought. The only problem with his plan was his bank account, which was not up to retirement standards, to say the least. Al had reckoned he'd need several hundred thousands pounds in savings to lead the life he and Margaret wanted, but he had only a fraction of that. His monthly retirement check was a pittance, and it was taxed to boot. While the Duke was still solvent and generating some revenue, it had seen its heydays. If properly approached, he could see Margaret selling it off in a year or two but not walking away with a ton of cash. One thing he didn't want was to live hand to mouth, on a paltry budget just waiting for his next retirement check to show up, and this was something he didn't want Margaret to have to deal with either. He'd misled her time and again, not telling her the reality of his finances, not telling her the grim truth that they might have to hold on to the Duke indefinitely, wait till the economy turned, or, just as her parents had done, spend the rest of their lives in servitude to a business, albeit a business they both loved and enjoyed.

Both of Margaret's parents had passed some time ago. Her dad died from lung cancer. When wheeling him out of the flat for the last time, Margaret told her father to put his feet on the bar of the wheelchair. His response was, "If I knew there was a bar down there, I'd have had a drink before leaving." He died that night. A few years later her mum died from some smoking-related illness. She didn't suffer at all—just popped her clogs one morning, no fuss, no bother, the way she would have wanted it. At first it had been difficult for Margaret to adjust to being lord and master of the Duke and, as she related to Al, so difficult to find and hold onto good staff. Just running the place was more than a full time job, so Margaret had little time to experiment with new recipes or even resurrect some of her Mother's old standbys. Even so, if she ever did sell the Duke, she'd miss the locals, the socializing, and most of all the cooking and interactions with the residents. How her Mother had managed, and at her age, was something Margaret could not fathom.

It seemed to Al that Margaret was being overtaxed with too much responsibility and too little to show for that responsibility. When he'd visit, usually on business but occasionally on vacation, she found it difficult getting time off, and all the trips they planned to Ireland, Scotland, and the Continent never materialized. It was just as well—too expensive—so Al spent the bulk of his time either hiking regardless of the weather, fishing moorland becks, or just hanging about the bars serving pints as a stand-in barman or delivering bar snacks to the locals as a stand-in waiter, and if the kitchen was ever under intense pressure, he'd fill in as head washer upper. Al was always short of cash, and his credit cards were nearly always maxed out. He even started lying on his Agency financial disclosure forms by underestimating his debt. He didn't want to appear to be a spendthrift if his spending habits were ever looked at, which rarely occurred and only with sufficient justification.

"What a predicament I'm in. I need more money, more brass, more dead presidents, whatever," he grumbled to his hump, who was always a good listener but not much of a conversationalist.

The cost of living in England was half-again what it was in the States, but no way would Margaret ever consider moving to the States, so Al had to face up to that reality and deal with it. He'd gotten his UK citizenship years ago—something he kept out of his Agency personnel file. He stored his British passport in a safety deposit box. No one knew except Margaret—more deception. If any one of these deceptions were known to the Agency, he'd be in hot water, but Al was clever enough not to let this or any other of his flimflams affect his polygraph. He knew the baseline questions by heart, helped established his own legacy truth-corridor on a regular basis, and every other year breezed through his poly, which was usually administered by a less than conscientious coworker.

Many years ago the Agency had updated their approach to the administration of the poly. First, they adopted, at Al's suggestion, the truth-corridor approach for determining results—that is, was the interviewee telling the truth, lying, or being evasive. In fact, Al was on the testing team that validated the truth-corridor. He'd even got a small financial award, which he immediately spent on airline tickets, business class. The truth-corridor was Al's baby; he knew it inside and out and could manipulate results with ease. The second change was that the Agency did away with the lifestyle portion of the polygraph. It had always been controversial and considered too invasive, and it tended to keep good people from applying for work at the Agency.

Besides, if an individual did have a shaky lifestyle, it would most likely affect his responses to the all-important counterintelligence questions, so not much was gained from the lifestyle questions, which had always made the job of adjudication much more difficult. Al's truth-corridor approach was a godsend to adjudication; earning many kudos for Al. On several occasions he was taken out for drinks by adjudication and was toasted; some even toasted Al's legendary hump. He could do no wrong in their eyes and was even asked to become an adjudicator with a marginal bump in salary. He refused, knowing a promotion would cancel out any future trips to England, future trips paid for by Uncle Sam. No one knew or even suspected that Al had married a Brit, and he intended to keep that little secret under wraps. However, when he declined the promotion, he was labeled as someone who had reached his own level of incompetence and was content at that level, wanting to go no further up the promotion ladder. Al's management said they understood, but he never made GS-15. In Al's mind, turning down that promotion was the cause, the only cause.

That very same year, the year Al refused to be promoted, another disturbing scenario played out in his life, a scenario that further alienated him from Central Intelligence. Al and other polygraphers were identified as nonessential during a brief but heated government shutdown, forcing them to remain out of the office for over a fortnight. Al wasn't worried about the money, as he expected the forfeited pay would be reimbursed, and it was. What did bother him was the fact that the cover facility that he worked in had been compromised—blown by the Agency itself. Central Intelligence knew the ramifications of empty parking spaces and the conclusions that could be drawn. One day no parking spaces available after eight in the morning; the next day dozens of spaces were available all day. And, guess what, when the shutdown ended, there were no parking spaces available after eight. For weeks after the shutdown ended Al couldn't make eye contact with any non-Agency employee; if he did he invariably got a wink or a sly smile, and a couple were even bold enough to quietly say "I know you're CIA." Al found this all very disturbing. His mentors had sold his sorry ass down the Suwannee and could possibly have put him and others in harm's way, but when this scenario was explained to management by Al, management turned a blind eye to his safety. Their response was that being furloughed was required at the time, so stop your whining and get back to work. Management had the solution to Al's grievance within their grasp—to declare all personnel working in a cover facility as essential—but they chose to ignore that solution.

Al came to a life-altering decision after the shutdown, one that could send him to the slammer for the rest of his life: he decided to go rogue. It wasn't an easy decision, but then again, it wasn't a tough decision either. His lust for money finally overcame any and all loyalty to the system, and being dead-ended at GS-14, plus other real or imagined grievances, sealed the deal. He decided he needed to go rogue to acquire the financial assets required to settle in the UK and live the life he'd always imagined, like a country squire and his missus. What he needed would be hard to come by, and he was still looking. He had to find someone who had access to information that would fetch dollars. That someone also had to have a history of unethical behavior or, at a minimum, poor judgment. He'd been on the lookout for months, but no joy to date. When a candidate showed up to be polygraphed, if he or she had questionable results Al, against all protocol, would surreptitiously find out what that individual did and what information that individual had access to. He found it amazingly easy to get someone to talk about what they did at the Agency. Nearly everyone Al examined was a blabbermouth; they weren't necessarily boasting, more just wanting to let someone know just how important they were, and who better than your friendly, trustworthy polygrapher? No, getting people to talk wasn't the issue. Finding the person worth listening to? That was the issue. The name of the game was accesses, and most individuals within the Agency didn't have access to anything that could be of any value to anyone, and so far no one with the right accesses and a shaky background had shown up for a polygraph. Perhaps the next interviewee would be the one, the one that Al could somehow tap into and become a rich man.

Roger England, a good, solid name, a name not to be toyed with, maybe even a harbinger of things to come, a harbinger to my future life in England, maybe, Al thought.

Roger worked in the south of England. His polygraph results were poor, and adjudication requested he return to the States to be repolygraphed. They had specifically requested that Al conduct the poly. Al had already read Roger's annual performance appraisals as well as his job description and had also studied his most recent polygraph results. They were definitely not good. He was hiding something. Al didn't really care what Roger was hiding; he only hoped to parlay Roger's poor results into cash, plenty of cash. Did this Roger England have access to the kind of information that could net Al a first-class retirement, or would he prove, like so many others, to be of no use whatsoever?

* * *

Roger arrives early, very early. He's agitated, pensive, and more than just a bit moody. If he loses his tickets, he'll lose his job, and there isn't much need for what Roger does outside the Agency. Roger's a courier; he runs a small clock repair shop in the basement of his home in Surrey, England. He's a busy man; people come in and go out on a regular basis, even late into the night and, sometimes, very early in the morning. If you want Roger to repair your clock—no watches, please—you can bank on a wait of eight to ten weeks. It's steady income, though not enough to cover even his mortgage, much less his other expenses. Periodically, however, he gets an encrypted e-mail from the Agency, and in it is an assignment. He'll meet someone, somewhere, and will usually end up exchanging Agency cash for information, intelligence information that takes the shape of a disk, a wad of papers, even a microchip, and only recently flash drives. Roger usually has no clue what the information he receives is all about, and he doesn't care; having little curiosity is a big plus in this business. Later a second courier, broken clock in hand, replenishes Roger's stash, picks up the information, and somehow gets it back to the Agency. How that's done Roger knows not, and again he really doesn't care. That's it; that's all he does for the Agency, and he's handsomely paid, and he enjoys the travel and the opportunity to live in the UK. Like Al, Roger's vivacious wife Connie loves Roger's income, and if the money goes, Roger's pretty sure she'll walk, taking their young daughter with her. In spite of all that he loves his wife. He knew what she was like before they married; she loves, absolutely adores the finer things in life and feels she's entitled to them. If Roger can't deliver, someone else will. She's that kind of girl. She's only passing this way once and fully intends to make the most of it. Connie, for whatever reason, also loves New Orleans's style cooking but can't cook a lick and has never even been to Louisiana, so at least once a week she catches the train into London to visit Fortnum and

Mason. Several hundred pounds later she returns home carrying tinned crawfish etouffee, tinned crawfish and cauliflower soup, tinned butter-pecan roasted sweet potatoes, and even something called goat's cheddar grits—in a tin of course. Each week a different theme but always either French, Cajon, or Creole and always tinned food; just open the tin, into the micro, and, voilà, high-class New Orleans style cooking eaten in front of the telly sipping some red plonk and watching *Masterpiece Theatre*, one ridiculous soap after another, or so Roger thinks. Connie never goes to Harrods—too many tourists, and most can't speak a word of English, a very unsophisticated lot and certainly not the sort she'd want to rub elbows with. As long as she has her looks and her figure, one way or another, Connie's one woman who always gets her way—especially if the patsy is Roger.

Connie's English. She met Roger about seven years ago in a tiny village in the south of England. She's the daughter of a publican and had a younger brother, Ian, whom she absolutely adored. Ian and Roger became great mates, did just about everything together. So Roger, Ian, and Connie spent a lot of time together, and Roger had to work hard at wooing Connie while Ian was at work. Fortunately Roger's hours were fairly flexible with only a few trips now and again, and he managed to convince Connie to become his wife. His substantial wallet and huge, by English standards, home made it easy for her to say yes. On a night four years into their marriage, both Ian and Roger were blitzed, way over the limit, so drunk they were almost unable to walk, so they chose to drive. Roger was driving, on the left of course, and the country roads were less than narrow. A sheep, an evasive maneuver, and it was all over, but not until their car had flipped several times. Ian instantly died at the scene. Somehow in all the confusion Roger managed to convince the police that Ian had been driving, as he lay nearest the driver's side—neither ever wore seat belts, and both had been thrown from the car. To this day Roger has no idea what triggered the accident; he can't remember a thing though he hardly got a scratch. The family was devastated, especially Connie. She was never quite the same, becoming broody and irritable. She refused help of any sort and only recently, three years after the crash, has she got a tentative grip on life, returning to normalcy—or at least what was normal for Connie. In the process of returning to normal, she nearly drained Roger's saving to the tune of thirty thousand pounds. In only a couple of months, as if trying to make up for lost time, she spent money on new clothes, travel, new furniture, and a second car—one for her, a slightly used yellow mini MG, of course a convertible. Roger didn't mind. She was back—well, almost back—and she was happy. If the truth ever surfaced that Roger had been driving drunk the night of that fateful accident, he would not only lose his job but lose his family as well and probably end up in an English prison for several years. DWIs are taken very, very seriously, and when someone is injured or killed the sentence is stiff, almost as stiff as for axing your neighbor to death for stealing your newspapers. Roger had reconciled his lies to the authorities by believing that Ian would want it that way, and, good lad that he was, Ian probably would have. Now, however, it's time to pay the piper in the form of his periodic polygraph and in the form of Al, the polygrapher. Roger failed three examinations in the south of England, just outside of London, but he can't open up, can't tell the truth. It's a matter of two evils—damned if you do, damned if you don't. If he tells the truth, the Agency will notify the English authorities, and he'll end up without a wife, without a job, and with a new residence—one that has the word *Prison* somewhere in the address line. If he doesn't open up, he fails his poly and loses his clearances, his job, and most likely his wife, who'll hang around just long enough to make sure Roger really is a tosser and to find another wallet, perhaps an even thicker wallet. Roger's approach up to now has been to put on a blank face and lie: "I have no idea why my results are so poor, can't understand, very confusing to me also." But time is running out for him.

Roger enters the room, meets Al, and hardly notices his hump, too nervous to notice anything or even care. He hasn't shaved in days, and he knows he looks as though he could do with a good scrubbing. When he'd seen his reflection in the hotel mirror that morning, his eyes were bloodshot, deep set, and had that far away look; in a word, he looked like shit. They shake hands, all very formal. Roger knows that Al knows he's in a pickle; he can see it on Al's face.

* * *

Al hoped to capitalize on Roger's situation—if only Roger had the right accesses and would play ball; maybe even play ball without ever realizing he was playing ball. Before Roger showed up, Al made sure all recording devices in his interview room were turned off. This was not unusual and would raise no red flags; interviews were seldom recorded anyway, and when they were it was for training purposes only. Al certainly required no training.

Before proceeding with the examination, Al tried to get beyond Roger's haphazard, almost vagrant-like appearance. He saw a man of about forty with dark hair and receding hair line; a round, almost circular, face with boyish features that appeared to have recently aged; and black, horn-rimmed glasses. He was stocky but not overweight, just a couple of inches shy of six feet, and dressed in jeans and a blue denim shirt with the sleeves rolled up—all very casual, like he was trying to look cool and nonchalant.

Al tried but learned nothing from Roger's demeanor other than that he looked exhausted and slightly confused, more than just frayed around the edges. His demeanor gave no clue as to how he might react to a pitch, so Al had to be cautious and first determine just exactly how desperate Roger was. He didn't know why he even bothered trying to suss out how Roger might react based on his appearance and composure, as though the fact that he needed a shave would indicate if he was a liar or could somehow be seduced into willingly giving up classified information. Al had never been big on using body language or physical appearance as an indicator of motivation, regardless of what his superiors told him and regardless of how many studies they encouraged him to read.

"Well, Roger, you know why you're here. Your prior three examinations are very, very poor. If they're not any better on this side of the Atlantic, they'll probably yank your clearances. No clearances, no work, no money. You'll also lose your self respect, and your family will wonder what's up, and you'll have to leave jolly ol' England, and finding a new job paying your kind of salary will be most difficult, especially in this economy. Like I used to say when I lived in England, 'a bit of a sticky wicket, old boy', for you that is."

Al was laying it on heavily, painting a worse-than-worst case scenario, but all the drama was necessary, especially if he were to somehow subvert Roger, and all the drama could very well prove to be true, especially if he found Roger to be of no use. Al looked on Roger as a kind of conduit, a connection between himself and prosperity—real prosperity, not merely a dreary, parsimonious pension that, when taxed, wouldn't even pay the mortgage on a little country cottage with an acre or so of land. If Roger couldn't help him, Al would do his job and let the devil take the hindmost, certainly doing no favors for Roger just because his last name was England.

"I'm assuming, Roger, you and your family will move back to the States if things don't work out. You can't remain in the UK unless you have a British passport or you've had the foresight to have your English wife identify you as a legal alien in residence. Takes a year or two, or so I'm told. I'm sure you know that. I hope you were prudent enough to get all the necessary paperwork in place to move your family back stateside. Emigration into this country is not a cakewalk, you know, and the DC area's pretty expensive. Suggest you move out west—not California, maybe Wyoming, not too expensive, but bloody cold. A lot colder than your family is used to. Family may not enjoy that, but you have to do what you have to do—you know, to get by."

"Wyoming? I'll kill myself first. Look, Al, I'm already a nervous wreck. You don't know my situation and what's at stake. So, please lighten up, and, no, I haven't made any plans to move my family back here, and I haven't even bothered to get a British passport—never thought it would be necessary. I never thought the Agency would sell me out."

"Nobody's selling anybody out. This is your fourth try. The previous three were miserable—nothing marginal about any of them. No one wants to pull your tickets, but you leave the powers that be no choice. It looks to me as if you're just not cooperating, and I don't know if you're a traitor, a petty criminal, or Jack the Ripper. Surly you must understand. As they say, 'the ball's in your court'—it really is your move, old chap. You need to cut bait or fish, and by 'cut bait' I mean cooperate, and by 'fish' I mean resign—it's your choice. So you either cooperate or resign, and by cooperate I mean work with me. If your results are still poor and you refuse to resign, you'll almost surely be cut loose by adjudication, and that's a fact."

Again, Al was laying it on thick, intentionally trying to rattle Roger. He had no idea what was going on in the man's head, and he really didn't care as long as Roger thought another failed polygraph so horrible that he'd do anything to successfully pass this, his fourth attempt.

"You know, Al, I've been in the field for some time, plenty of ops experience. I know a few things about this and a few things about that, and I know names, and if I chose to speak to the right people I could—"

"Whoa, whoa, Roger. Stop right now if you please! I'll just pretend I didn't hear that, but what you're talking is treason. Remember you signed papers pledging your loyalty and swore an oath to safeguard and protect classified information. If you should, in moment of anger, compromise classified information, you won't have to worry about future living accommodations. Uncle Sam will incarcerate you for the rest of your wretched life in a federal penitentiary, and what will happen to your family thousands of miles to the east? Think about that before threatening disloyalty, or maybe you have already been disloyal and this is why all your results are so very poor. Anyway, let's move on, Roger. So far no real harm, *so far*, but think before you speak in future, please."

Against all protocols, Al took the first step. No turning back now. *In for a penny, in for a pound as Margaret might say.*

"Tell me in detail what you do in England, Roger. I'm curious. You seem like a nice enough chap. Hard to figure out why you can't successfully answer a couple of easy counterintelligence questions. You have successfully answered them in the past, as your records clearly show. It's all very confusing to me. You don't look like a traitor—a bit ragged round the edges, but not a traitor."

There, it was out. He'd broken protocol. Only in very special circumstance, and with Directorate approval, could a polygrapher ask that type of question. Al had no need to know "in detail" what Roger did. If Roger took the bait and had the right accesses, maybe both of them would do well from this brief encounter.

Without hesitation, likely trying to please Al and maybe, in the process, gain a few brownie points with the Agency, Roger responded.

"Of course I'm not a bloody spy! I'm a courier stationed in England. I meet people here and there, give them money, and in return get information, which I pass on to a second courier who brings it back to Headquarters, here in Northern Virginia. Not much to it, no risk. I've been doing it for years. I usually meet different people, but occasionally a familiar face turns up. So far, no problems. It's a good job. I get to travel, and I feel I'm making a contribution to the Agency's mission and helping our country win the war against our enemies."

Bravo, bravo, well said, thought Al.

"And, Roger, you have no idea what the information is all about, the information that gets exchanged for Agency cash? I mean you have no idea what the contents are. Really, old boy, I find that very difficult to believe, and if that's the case, are there ever any special circumstances where you might know the contents, in detail?"

"No, I usually don't know the exact contents of what I'm picking up, but at times I kind of know, in a general sort of way. Like, take my next assignment. I'm meeting this guy. His name's Jim. I've met him several times before in Ibiza—that's a small island, part of the Balearics in the Mediterranean, belongs to Spain—again, the same hotel, the Sunshine Hotel, not very big but fairly ritzy, right on the beach, a lovely horseshoe-shaped bar with friendly barmen. Most speak English fairly well. In the past, I came to the Sunshine for a night or two. Me and Jim meet in the bar, have a drink or two, go for a walk. Somewhere I slip him the loot, he gives me a small package, and I'm on my way back home. Very, very easy. I'm supposed to meet him again in a couple of weeks. That's assuming I still have a job. If I lose my tickets, my rendezvous with Jim will be called off, have to be rescheduled with another courier. I won't be very popular with my handlers back here. God, I'd do anything to get through this poly, just to scrape through. My next poly is years off, and a lot can happen in years."

"Look, Roger, work with me, but please remember, and I'm sure you know this already, but I must remind you. If you tell me anything of a serious nature and it involves a serious crime, I'll have to report it to the authorities today, now. That's not my rule. It's the Agency's. You do understand. I just want to make sure we're both on the same page?"

"Yes, of course I understand. I'm not a fool, you know, Al."

If you're not a fool then how did you manage to get yourself in such a predicament and, Roger, if you can't help me, you're going down, big time, Al thought as he scratched his itchy hump—a good sign, usually meaning he might be coming into some cash.

Al had to reinforce the idea that serious crime resulted in serious consequences. He didn't want Roger spilling his guts and then expecting to breeze through his poly. He had to keep his personal secrets to himself, or Al's already tenuous control over his psyche would become more precarious. Al didn't really care why Roger was blowing his polys, just that he was failing and by a large margin. Al was only interested in this Jim fellow, what he was passing over to Roger, and whether this package could somehow prove valuable to himself.

"So when did you say you're meeting Jim?"

"Two weeks from tomorrow—everything's already arranged. He's kind of a strange guy, this Jim, real Middle Eastern, tall and thin, on the top side of fifty, bald, always wears a white suit and white tie, like in the old black and whites. Jim's not his real name, or so I'm guessing, but for now I call him Jim. In fact I don't even know his real name—maybe it is Jim. It's just Jim, no last name. Also, he wears very thick horn-rimmed glasses, black—poor eyesight, I'm guessing—kind of like the pair I'm wearing right now. If you know what you're looking for, he stands out in a crowd—kind of like you, Al."

"Yes, I see what you mean, but in the right light I'm nearly invisible—just kind of blend in, hump and all."

Blank looks from Roger, as if to say, *Say what?*

"Just kidding, Roger. Please continue."

Roger made no reply to Al's humor; it might have even gone over his head, as he was now in catapult mode, just hurling bits and pieces of information in Al's direction.

Roger went on gushing information; Al couldn't get him to shut up. Wanting to think, Al called for a break and took a little walk down the hall to the restroom. He had a lot of details, but the parcel—what was in the parcel, and was it worth anything? Probably was—why would Uncle Sam buy information with no value? But if he was able to somehow get what Jim had, who would he sell it to? How could he cash in on what Jim now had? Anyway, once he secured the parcel he'd then worry about off-loading it, for a price. One step at a time. *Don't get ahead of yourself. Keep your eye on the ball.* He retraced his steps after a pit stop.

"Okay, Roger, this is all very helpful. You do seem to be a real asset to the Agency. Yes, I can see just how important you are, and it would be very unfortunate if you did lose your tickets. I can see from previous results that you're not a double agent or playing fast and furious with Agency information. What I see from your previous polys are personal issues that are most likely affecting your responses to the counterintelligence questions."

Al was now in bluff mode, trying to make Roger feel more secure, making Roger feel he was on his side.

"Do you agree, Roger?"

"Yes, of course, without a doubt. I'd never double cross my country, Al."

But I would, thought Al, *in a heartbeat*. He needed just a few more pieces of information from Roger, who was in no frame of mind to realize or even guess at what Al was plotting.

"Now, Roger, just out of curiosity, my curiosity—I'm thinking of writing a book one day, Agency Publication Review Board approved, of course. How do you pay, Jim?"

"In cash—and quite a large sum. I know that from the thickness of the package containing the bills. They're hundred-dollar bills wrapped in brown paper. Someone told me about the hundred-dollar bills sometime ago, wanted me to be extra cautious when handling the loot, as I call it. Maybe twenty thousand dollars, and that's more than we pay anyone else, especially for one pickup, and I've picked up parcels from Jim a couple of times. All in all that's a good chunk of change, and scuttlebutt has it that the intelligence in the packet we receive from Jim is worth millions. Oh, and before you ask, the money's dropped off at my house, in the south of England. A different person each time … no, that's not completely true. Sometime the same person does show up. I just never know in advance. I have a little clock repair shop. Broken clocks come in—money comes in. After the exchange, repaired clocks go out—intelligence goes out. I don't know who came up with this clock-shop thing, but we've never failed, kind of like a good old grandfather clock—as long as you keep it wound and don't move it about too much or play with the hands, it'll go off each and every hour. I never unwrap the money or check it out—not necessary. All of my operations have been successful—never a foul up, not one. My ops run like clockwork, no pun intended. I'd like to think I'm one of the reasons we're so successful."

"I'm sure you are, Roger. Look, Roger, let's just stay focused on Jim and your next visit to Ibiza—no more talk of clocks. I don't want you darting here and there and everything all running together and maybe confusing yourself and me. I know you're under a lot of pressure, so, again, let's just for the moment stay focused on Jim. Okay, so you have no idea what's in the parcel you pick up from Jim, but you believe the contents may be worth millions? Is that a fact? For a second time, you have no idea what the contents are of the package you pick up from Jim? Please, Roger, just answer that one question."

"Well, if you recall I said 'I usually don't know.' I've been to Ibiza more than once, and from what I understand from my handler that works at Langley, and who is also one of the contacts who collects the parcels from me in England, the contents are …" Roger pauses, perhaps having second thoughts, but then continues—much to Al's satisfaction.

"What I understand is that the parcels from Ibiza may contain information that has something to do with Iran trying to build a nuclear weapon and their progress toward acquiring a nuclear capability. Oh, by the way, Al, it's more of a tube than a parcel—about three inches in diameter and a foot and a half long, light gray, fairly sturdy. Looks to be almost bombproof. The info in the cylinder must be worth a pretty penny, or why would we pay Jim so much? And Ibiza's not that far from the Middle East and all the troubles they're having. Who knows? Probably classified documents of some sort. Like I said, Jim looks like an Arab or a Turk, very aloof and not very talkative, but we get on okay. Like I said, he always wears the same clothes: white suit—"

"Hold on, Roger. Please stay focused. Later you can have the floor and say whatever you like. One more question if you please, and don't ramble—just answer the question. So, as far as you know, the contents have to do with the Iranians and their initiatives in acquiring a nuclear device. Based on your description of the cylinder, I'd guess the papers might be blueprints of sorts, but that's just a guess, and it's well known to the public that Iran is years away from building and testing a nuclear weapon—or so the newspaper say. So why is the Agency paying twenty thousand big ones unless …?"

"Roger, please provide a logical ending to that question. It'll serve as a baseline for your upcoming poly. It's important you tell the truth, the complete truth, and don't even think about being evasive. So end this question: So why is the Agency paying twenty thousand big ones unless …?"

"Unless Iran is very close to developing the Bomb," mumbled Roger.

"And, Roger, how do your handlers at Langley know the information they're getting from Jim is genuine? That's the last question but one. Level with me, Roger."

"Because we've had previous drops of lesser consequences, and the information was cross-checked, vetted, and validated by us and found to be perfectly accurate and one hundred percent correct. This final drop, again according to my handler, will probably—and I stress *probably*— have sufficient intelligence to prove conclusively that Iran is on the brink of joining the club of nations who do have or shortly will have nuclear weapons."

Bingo! Al was about to burst with excitement but cleverly masked his jubilation.

I figured all along that he knew more than he was saying, trying to act as ignorant as an ass. Thank God I had the patience to tease that last piece of information from him even though he was holding onto it like an English bulldog clamped onto an intruder's leg, thought Al.

"Okay, Roger, final question—promise. When you were on this island, did you ever feel you might be in danger of someone, anyone, bashing your skull in and stealing the loot from you or the cylinder from Jim?"

"You know, Al, me and Jim have an arrangement. Probably sounds a bit queer, but it's true. He has no backup, and I have no backup. You see, I know for a fact that I have no backup, undeniably, and on my first visit to the island I tailed Jim nine ways to Sunday, and I'm certain he had no backup. We chatted about backups over a drink and agreed that backup for the sake of security was not needed—an unnecessary expense. You see, Jim wants to sell this information to us for what he considers to be a fair price, and we want to pay Jim for his information and, maybe, future information, so why would he or us upset the apple cart? It's a perfect arrangement. A win-win situation for us both, and a few thousand dollars isn't going to break the Agency, right? It's not like we plan on mugging Jim after the exchange. No way."

"So Roger you're sure this Jim fellow has no backup"?

"Well, at first I believe he requested backup from his handlers but they nixed the idea. Cost cutting I believe and like I just said it's a perfect arrangement."

"So how do you know he may have requested backup, Roger?"

"A casual remark by Jim over a margarita."

Al's brain was in overdrive. Jim might be an easy mark on Ibiza, and if Roger knew, and his handlers knew of the possibility of Iran going nuclear, then the secretary of state and even the president must know, but they were all waiting till the last piece of the puzzle showed up from Ibiza and waiting till that info was corroborated before acting. *Somewhere, right now, someone, some group, must be planning some kind of assault against Iran, an assault that will be executed if the info from Jim is validated.* War planning must be going on; a nuclear Iran would never be tolerated by the United States or the West. So if all of Al's assumptions and Roger's input proved to be true, that cylinder not only contained a treasure trove of information justifying war but a treasure trove of cash, maybe destined for Al's saving account. Never in Al's wildest imagination did he think someone like Roger would come along and possibly set Margaret and him up for life, albeit unintentionally.

First things first. He had to get rid of Roger and then figure out how to separate the man in white in Ibiza from that cylinder.

"Okay, Roger. Thanks. I'm sure you just helped yourself a great deal."

Al had decided. He was all in. All systems go. He was mentally booking flights and accommodations, arranging for spending money. On his way back from Ibiza, he'd surprise Margaret, hopefully with a little gray tube in his carry-on and a plan to exit the workforce and slip into comfortable retirement. He might even try growing roses, English roses, but that was a way off, though not so far off that he couldn't imagine a garden full of luscious, red roses, only red—no pinks or oranges and certainly no yellows. Yuck, not yellow.

Al wondered what had prompted the Agency to initially send Roger to Ibiza. Probably the same old story: money. Someone pops into an American embassy or consulate somewhere in the world with sensitive information to sell, convinces some State Department employee that the information may be useful and worth acquiring, a price is agreed to, and an exchange planned. Anyway, it didn't really matter what the man in white's motivation was, and it mattered even less why Roger just happened to show up in Ibiza. That was all history. In Al's mind what really mattered was somehow procuring this juicy bit of intel and cashing in on it. And therein lay the rub: "somehow procuring" was the key to his success or failure. Al didn't want to kill the man in white, Jim, or even seriously harm him. He'd just have to wait till he was in Ibiza, suss out the situation, and act accordingly and forcefully, never looking back.

One small problem still remained: how to get Roger cleared this time around. He was certain Roger had major emotional issues brought on by guilt and would never clear without some help; his responses to the counterintelligence questions would most certainly be well outside his truth-corridor, a corridor that Al still needed to establish. Al didn't care what the man's emotional issues were, just that his poly result were good the first time, all within his truth-corridor. If Al couldn't get Roger to pass his poly, and his tickets were pulled, a new courier with new dates to Ibiza would be in the offing, and Al would be screwed. No way then would Al be able to figure out when Jim would return to Ibiza with that cylinder. Al examined Roger's previous three polygraphs, telling Roger he needed complete silence, no interruptions.

I can't change where the Consolidator maps his responses relative to the truth-corridor; those responses get mapped in real time as I'm testing him, thought Al, *but I can rig his truth-corridor and ensure all of his responses to the counterintelligence questions fall inside his newly manufactured, bogus truth-corridor. I'll skip the merge step. No one will know.* Roger's results would satisfy adjudication, as they were interested only in results that fell outside the corridor. Given their workload, they spent little or no time on results that looked conclusive. Al manually adjusted Roger's virtual truth-corridor so all his responses, based on the previous three polygraphs, would fall inside that corridor. That was no problem. This was something Al had done dozens of times during the testing of the truth-corridor as it was being evaluated by the Agency for implementation and use by polygraphers and adjudication. No baseline calibration of the equipment or of Roger was required. Roger's truth-corridor was in place, electronically displayed in bright green on his monitor; it took Al less than ten minutes to establish the mock truth-corridor. They could go straight into the counterintelligence questions, and the results would be electronically and at the click of a mouse e-mailed to adjudication, several miles away.

"Okay, Roger, let's start. Focus on just the questions—they're the same questions you've heard at least three times. Remember: focus on the questions, nothing else."

Al hooked Roger up and proceeded to ask the questions without any rehearsal. Al could see the results were not good, but because of his tinkering with the truth-corridor, all the results ended up inside Roger's truth-corridor. This would please adjudication, and if all other inputs to adjudication were satisfactory, Roger would clear.

Al made one cryptic electronic note to adjudication before releasing the results: "Fully cooperated."

"Well, Roger, much improved. I think you can plan on taking your next trip to Ibiza. Oh, that story about me writing a book? All a sham. I couldn't write a book if my life depended on it—not enough patience.

I think what helped you was talking about your job and what you do for a living. It kind of suppressed what was previously going on in your head just long enough for you to totally focus on just my questions and filter out unwanted thoughts. It's a technique I developed some time ago, and, for you, it seems to have done the trick."

"Like I said, I see no reason for you not passing, but it's really not my call, Roger. You should know for sure in about a week or sooner. I'll put a rush on it—after all you're quite the important man."

"Oh, and, Roger, remember not to let any of the polygraphers' little secrets out, if you please. Don't discuss my techniques with anyone, especially your handlers. Anyway, Roger, the best of luck to you."

"Sure! Great, Al. No fear, and thank you very, very much."

* * *

Roger was elated. He loved this guy, hump or no hump. Now he just needed to get back home to England and Connie and the kid. He jogged to his car, so glad to be free from another interrogation, at least for several years. He just wanted to get back to his hotel room, shower, and shave. Then he'd get a good meal and a couple of brews under his belt and make plans to return home. First, though, he'd call his handler with the news that he had very probably passed his poly.

Never once did Roger even consider that discussing an active op with Al might be wrong, dangerous to say the least, and maybe even treacherous and disloyal. His tickets would not be yanked, and that was far more important than discussing Ibiza with a polygrapher. After all, polygraphers were true-blue, real American heroes, themselves polygraphed annually and routinely investigated and reinvestigated just to ensure they were always on the up and up. Roger had no doubt that Al was true-blue, a real American hero who, like himself, would die before sharing information with enemies of the republic.

* * *

Al also left after saying farewell to Roger, and he returned to his flat. It had been a long, arduous day, stressful to say the least, maybe even a bit dangerous. He too needed a brew or two. He picked up the phone, called Margaret, and told her he might be home in a couple of weeks.

No definite dates, but this might be his last crossing of the Atlantic. She was ecstatic.

After hanging up, Al mentally fenced with adjudication. Had he outwitted adjudication? He thought yes, most certainly. *No way can adjudication fathom what I've just pulled off,* he thought. *They're just not in my league. I created an electronic voodoo truth-corridor for Roger, and no one's the wiser. It really is true that information is power. I suppose I should feel very guilty, but I don't. I guess I'm really very, very wicked, a broken moral compass,* he thought as he stroked his very, very wicked hump. *But I don't give a damn. I just want the loot—I need the loot, Amen.*

And in fact adjudication thought Al a wizard. He'd done what he was supposed to—help keep Roger on board—and they were pleased to extend Roger's tickets for six more years.

CHAPTER 5

Ahmet woke to the sound of his wife rummaging through his suitcase. She made no pretense of being quiet and no pretense of allowing him more sleep than she thought he required. She had decided he needed no more than six hours, and six hours was all he'd get. He rolled onto his back and elevated himself onto his elbows. She went through every piece of clothing with a pocket. As she searched, she made indistinguishable, almost guttural sounds, and her breathing was nearly frantic, coming in dots and dashes almost like Morse code with a stutter.

"He'll have plenty of sleep when he's dead, and when he's dead, I'll have a little piece of mind," she moaned.

Ernna instinctively knew she was being watched. She figured if she made enough noise he'd eventually get up, and she couldn't wait to hear what kind of story or line or lie he'd try to fob off on her this time. Today he was going on yet another TDY, as he called them, and he'd only just returned a fortnight ago. In the past, she'd never really bothered about her husband's travels, just assumed they were part and parcel of his very secret job, so secret it was hard to imagine that all the secrecy was actually justified. Ahmet, however, had assured her it was, and so for years she dolefully accepted his explanations without unnecessary prying or unnecessary complaining.

Up until five years ago, five long years, Ernna had been reasonably content with their relationship but then that idiot brother of hers, after too much to drink at a small neighborhood get-together, said to Ahmet that one thing he really enjoyed about the job was meeting women of all sorts and all characters on a regular basis.

All her half-tipsy husband could say was, "Yep, part of the job description. Someone has to do it. God, I love my country."

Ernna overheard this quite clearly but was not annoyed or even surprised; she could only think how much she disliked her philandering brother, who had the morals of a bitch in heat. She continued to focus on what her brother was saying, and since he was half-drunk he spoke much louder than he intended.

Mamet slyly said to her husband that he'd take any opportunity to bed any women so long as she wasn't unconscious. Both her brother and Ahmet thought this unusually amusing, giggling and then laughing so hard that they had to put down their drinks to keep from spilling them.

"Mind you," said Mamet, "if she's unconscious, she can't say no." Again, hysterical giggling came from the pair of intelligence operatives.

The possibility of Ahmet being a womanizer was remote, or so Ernna thought, but what the pair next hinted at forever unsettled her, and after that Ahmet couldn't even leave the house without his wife having or nearly having a panic attack. The intimation, overheard in bits and pieces as Ernna plied them with additional glasses of vodka, was that on their last op Ahmet had almost been killed, and if it hadn't been for her brother he'd have been dead. They both also thought this unusually funny, but upon reflection a few minutes later both agreed it really was a very close call, never to happen again, or so they hoped.

She confronted her husband the next day about it, and he told her not to believe a word of what she heard the previous evening because it was all drinking-related man talk and far from reality.

"Oh, that was the vodka talking, Ernna, and you know how that brother of yours can exaggerate. And anyway, to tell you the truth I can't remember a thing I said after dinner. It's all a blur, and I've a bit of a hangover, so please give it a rest."

"What do you mean," she shouted, "give it a rest? I'm concerned, so don't tell me to 'give it a rest.' Anyway, go get yourself killed. I don't give a damn—just make sure your life insurance is up to date. I don't intend working if you get yourself killed, and please for my sake don't just get hurt and expect me to nurse you back to health or push you about in a wheelchair. If you end up in a wheelchair, I'll do us both a favor and push you into oncoming traffic. Understand?"

Ahmet just nodded and said nothing. He wasn't in the mood for a row.

Later that day Ernna called her brother and demanded the truth, wanting to know if Ahmet had had a close encounter with death.

"Ernna, my sweet, I swear on our father's grave nothing like that ever happened, and I don't even remember saying anything of the sort. I had a little too much vodka. You know keeping up with your husband is quite a task, and as I just said, I don't remember a thing."

"You know, Mamet, when we were children, I tried to throw you down the cellar steps a couple of times and failed. Oh, how I now wish I had persevered. You're such a liar. You never forget a thing when you drink. You could go to Canada and drink Canada dry and remember all the details. I know that for a fact. I'm your sister, sad to say, and I know you never forget, no matter how slammed you are. In fact on several occasions you have even boasted about your brain cells and their immunity to alcohol, and while your legs may go a bit wobbly, you brain is always on duty, or so you told me."

With that, she hung up, still wishing she had thrown that lying brother of her down the cellar steps and broken his neck. It would have been so easy, so justifiable and explainable.

Yes, Papa, he slipped and fell down the stairs. I saw the whole thing. He was always fooling around and never paying attention. And that would have been the end of her lying brother, and she wouldn't have had a single regret. She was sad that that fantasy of hers was not fulfilled.

Maybe they can't remember a thing and with a bit of luck Ahmet might even die from his hangover, but that doesn't make what that ass of a brother of mine said last night not true. Ernna just couldn't let it go.

From that day on, Ernna had dreaded with a passion Ahmet's TDYs, wondering if this one might be the final one, the TDY that left her a widow, and today he was scheduled to leave on yet another.

* * *

Ahmet, who'd given up all possibility of any more sleep, was now undressed and facing the toilet, urinating.

"For God's sake, Ahmet, close the door. We've been married so long that you don't even feel it necessary to shut the door when relieving yourself so I have to look at your backside, all puckered up and droopy? How sad. Do you think I find the sound of splashing pee attractive or your backside, with as many wrinkles as a prune, a turn-on? How pathetic, and now you don't even bother flushing the toilet? You're so different. When I first met you, you turned the volume of the TV up so any sounds you might be making were muted and didn't offend me.

Mind you, at that time I was your girlfriend, not your wife, and that makes all the difference, I suppose."

The sound of Ahmet's electric toothbrush kicked in, but that didn't frustrate Ernna's attack.

Ernna raised her voice to a bit less than a yell.

"And, my dear husband, how's your blood pressure? Even the doctor has cautioned you—it's regularly high, very high, and now he tells you no caffeine, no salt, plenty of exercise and water, and not too much booze. Is that not a fact? This is another reason I think you should pack in your job. You know when your pressure's up—that full feeling in your face, numbness around the eyes, as you explained to me. That's your body telling you to take it easy. Don't work too hard. Cut down the stress. Well, when you get that heady feeling, you could stroke out or have a heart attack you know, Ahmet. Not good, and if you die that's one thing, but don't expect me to feed you chicken soup or wipe your behind or sit up all night holding your hand because you're frightened. If you have a stroke it's on your head, and you suffer the consequences by yourself. I've been warning you for some time, and you just ignore me. So be it. Anyway, enough about your pressure, or you'll soon be accusing me of giving you high blood pressure, like I'm some kind of Typhoid Mary."

Ahmet heard every word that his wife had just said. He too was worried about his elevated blood pressure, and everything she said was true. His pressure was pretty good when at home or the office, but when on an op, a stressful op, he could feel his pressure elevating by the numbness in his face, especially immediately below both eyes. This certainly concerned Ahmet. He didn't want to have a stroke and certainly didn't want to be nursed by Ernna—assuming she'd have the job. *Maybe after this op is done, I'll file for retirement, maybe even receive a medical disability, but then again maybe not.*

"Well, Ahmet, where are you off to now? Every month or so, you go here, you go there. You never take me with you. In fact, you never even tell me where you're going. What if you turn up missing or dead—what do I tell the authorities? I'm clueless. Oh, is this my story: he works for the government, a very secret job. I, his wife, don't know where he's going or when he's coming back, or if he's coming back at all. Ahmet, you do expect an awful lot from me. I'm your wife; it's supposed to be a partnership. Can you not let your job go, just now and again, for me?"

Ahmet turned off the shower and hurriedly dried himself and began dressing. He couldn't believe it. She'd remained quiet for three whole minutes. What bliss.

He could see she was now lying on the bed on her back, eyes open, just staring. It was a flat, blank stare, focusing on nothing or perhaps focusing on infinity. She looked so very sad.

"Ernna, you knew all this before we married, and that was a long time ago. It's my job. When you were younger you used to think my job was intriguing and mysterious. Now all the mystery's gone, and you're acting like an old hag—you're becoming quite the nag, you know. If you're not careful, you'll end up like that crazy mother of yours. I don't think she's thrown away a newspaper in twenty years. And, please, in future leave my suitcase alone. I'll now have to rearrange everything again."

"Rearrange? I'll show you rearrange," she yelled as she leapt off the bed

With that, she kicked his clothes in his direction. Not a dainty, delicate kick but the kick of a footballer aiming for the goal—and the goal was Ahmet's head.

"What is this white shirt and white suit for? And look here—black glasses, and you have perfect vision. Are you going to some kind of fancy-dress party? If you wear this absurd outfit, you'll not only look ridiculous but be totally unbelievable. Everyone will laugh at you. They'll think you're some kind of senile old simpleton. Mind you, I don't know what your job is, but if looking ridiculous is a part of the job description, then voilà, you've succeeded."

"Ahmet, Ahmet, Ahmet, so different, so very different. Your work is getting to you. Can't you change jobs before you have a stroke or give me one? Why do you do all this traveling? Is there no one else at your office that can stand in for you now and again, or are you at the top of someone's shit list? Mind you, if you are, I completely understand. You do have some very irritating and annoying habits."

"No, No, No. We all travel, and I'm not at the top of anyone's list, and please stay away from my case in future and stop profaning. I will only be gone for a few days, and I shouldn't even be telling you that, but you're right and, yes, the job is very frustrating and lately very stressful, but I get paid well, and if my country asks me to serve, I serve—no questions. Anyway, Ernna, when I return we'll take a holiday, wherever you want to go—maybe a few nights in a glitzy hotel in the city or the seaside, or, yes, maybe a cruise. You think about it, and we'll book it when I return."

Ernna, apparently not placated, got tearful. Ahmet knew that the truth was, she wasn't a very happy woman, and the principal cause of her unhappiness was his job, long separations, and the frightening possibility that he might not come home one day, and for what? She had no idea what he did for a living or who he even worked for. All she knew was what he told her, and that was squat. He begged off answering most questions on the grounds of national security, and then in a rage she would lash out at him. "Yes, I know—it's secret, very hush, hush, and me your wife. Who do you think I'd tell your precious secrets to? I have no close friends at all, and your secrets are obviously more important than your wife's mental health. It's no wonder I'm cuckoo." He'd heard that refrain more than once.

"You're always planning to take me on holiday but usually don't mean what you say. When was the last time we took a trip? You're just trying to shut me up so you can leave me with a clear conscience. I know your job's very important to you, and I also know you can't talk about it, but please try and understand that I need some of you. Our government can't have all of you—just a small piece for your Ernna. You're never home before ten, and you're off very early in the morning. It's not good for us. I get so very lonely."

Ahmet knew in his heart that what she said was true, but he also knew that his next mission was critical to his career and more critical for his country. He and Ernna's brother had given birth to this current operation and sold it to their supervisors, who then sold it to their government. Shortly he'd be off to Ibiza one last time. Previous handoffs to the CIA, via that chatterbox Roger, were just tantalizing bait, though credible bait. This final handoff would seal the deal; then and only then could he relax.

"Okay, when I get back from this trip, I'll take two weeks off. We can go wherever you like. Now come, give me a hug before I head off to work. I don't want to leave you in tears or hurling hateful insults at me. We've been together a long time. Please walk me to the car."

* * *

She did. She put on a brave face but was steaming inside. She hated it when he spoke to her like a child; at times she was so angry she wished him dead—or at least severely injured. She would think about a vacation, get some travel magazines, and plan a very expensive holiday, but she knew it would never come to fruition. He'd be too busy, too tired, too this, too that. But she'd plan it anyway and raise hell when he backed out. Maybe she'd even go so far as to put down a large deposit, a nonrefundable deposit. She'd have a think about that. He was such a tightwad. He'd have to choose between taking time off or losing the deposit, on his credit card of course, not hers. She brightened up a bit; lately she'd quite enjoyed making him miserable.

She watched as he drove off. He took the first left. The first left was the way to his office, or at least she thought his office, as this was the turn he took every day when he was allegedly going to work. The airport was in a completely different direction. So he had to check in at work before going to the airport, probably to pick up tickets, as no tickets were in his case. She'd checked on that. She'd hoped to find out his destination, but no such luck. What she would have done with that bit of information she didn't know, but knowing something, anything would have been comforting. It was the not knowing that drove her to distraction.

* * *

Ahmet executed a few standard maneuvers, taking unnecessary turns, on his way to the office. He wanted to be sure he wasn't being tailed, and he wasn't. Even though it was Saturday, his friend Mamet met him with a cheery hello.

"How's my sister? Did she go off on you again, try to make you feel guilty, shed a few tears? I'm sure she did all of the above. Ernna can be a real cow. She knows that you have to travel, part of the job. I should never have introduced you two, big mistake on my part. Anyway, you'll be gone for only a few days. Later today she'll be on the phone trying to get information from me. Of course, I'll plead ignorance, which is really not the case. If she calls more than once, I won't take her calls, or if I do, I'll be curt, not say much. She'll soon get the message. Women, to me, can be very amusing and sometimes even interesting, but when they become unnecessarily assertive and boorish, they really do let their side down."

"Yes," said Ahmet, "and this chauvinistic attitude of yours is why you've been married three times and can't keep a girlfriend for more than a couple of months, and you say you dump them? I can say I find that difficult to believe, my friend. You need to treat women more like real people with real feelings and aspirations, not like some trinket to be discarded on a whim or captured on a charm bracelet like some trophy."

"Ahmet, you're an old sea dog. Do you really believe all that nonsense? Someone's been poisoning your mind. Who? Come on, fess up."

"Well, it was that course on diversity that I just completed. Makes a lot of sense if you think about it, and the instructor, a woman, was lovely and smart. Being smart is always a plus, but not too smart and never an overachiever. But, yes, I do believe what I just said, and guess what? You're on the list for the next class. It's mandatory, you know."

"We'll see about that," was all Mamet said.

Ahmet liked Mamet, his brother-in-law. Unlike himself, Mamet was very laid back and never agonized over anything. Mamet also did a lot of traveling, with too many frequent flyer miles, too many layovers, too many secrets, and too many encounters with mysterious women, and while all these encounters and the mystery of the job didn't necessarily bother Mamet, they did bother his spouse or girlfriend or both, whichever the case happened to be. Wondering women made for wandering women, and wandering women did not make for lasting relationships, but as soon as one jumped ship, another was hooked, reeled in, and put on the barbie.

"Listen, Ahmet, this is your final trip to Ibiza. After you hand off the cylinder to Roger, the ball's in the Agency's court, as the Americans like to say. Just take the money from Roger and give him the cylinder— it's loaded, sealed, and ready to go. Here it is. Don't lose it, for God's sake. A lot's at stake, my friend. We're all counting on you. Again, just give it to Roger, take the money, and come back home. You have an open ticket, very expensive, so you should have no trouble catching a flight, even if it's not a direct flight. Just get off that damn island. Make sure no one's following you, especially after you've passed that cylinder off. From what you tell me Roger is quite the talker, wants to spend quality social time with you, have tea maybe, even philosophize a bit. Forget it. As soon as you make the pass, get the hell out of there. If you can do it all in less than a day, all the better. Understand?"

Without waiting for a reply, he continued. "Ahmet, I have to stress again to you that the contents of the cylinder are irreplaceable. If they're lost, we're doomed and the mission is a complete bust. The Americans will never accept copies or last-minute substitutes, so for God's sake don't let that cylinder out of your sight."

"Please, Mamet, put more pressure on me—the agony's ecstasy. I can hardly stand it. You're such a good friend, you're worse than my wife. We hatched this plan, and if it fails both our necks are on the chopping block. Well, I better be off. Let me stuff that cylinder into my carry-on now. I suppose they'll be no problems with airport security?"

"No, it's passed security several times, once or twice with you, I believe. Anyway, there's nothing threatening or banned in it—just papers, no classification markings—and the cylinder's not made of lead, so there's been no attempt to foil security. If they insist on you opening it, then open it, and if they question you, use those cover stories that black ops told you to use. Those yokels at the airport have no idea what those blueprints represent."

"Yes, I know, Mamet. I'm not some junior sleuth. Remember I also know the contents and their importance to our nation, and please be a bit more understanding if my wife calls. Or should I say 'that cow,' as you like to call her."

"I'll do my best, but even as a child she always had to have her own way. We nicknamed her 'Moo' because of her never-ending bellowing for attention. At times we even appended adjectives like silly Moo, but more often than not the adjectives would make a holy man blush. Today I just call her 'cow'. You know, as a child she tried to throw me down the cellar stairs—and there were more than a few steps. I'd almost forgotten that. Such a selfish, odious child, but I will do my best to be understanding, for your sake."

With that, Mamet drove Ahmet to the airport. Ahmet was nervous and muted while his brother-in-law never shut up, always talking about women and his latest conquest or latest failure, and whenever there was a failure, Mamet's cryptic explanation was "probably gay."

* * *

Back in Yorkshire, Margaret was jubilant. Al was expected home in a couple of weeks, exact date unknown. Years ago, she'd finally gotten Al to tell her what he did and who he worked for. She wasn't surprised;

she knew it was something secretive and clandestine, but a polygrapher? Quite boring stuff, almost pedestrian. She'd been hoping for a "007," but Al would just have to do. They never spoke of what Al did again—no need to—and she never quarreled with Al or felt trumped by his job. She had a life at the Duke and intended to live it to the fullest and not mope about making herself and the staff edgy and irritable. When she saw Al, she enjoyed his companionship and his love, but when he was in the States or on assignment, she put her nose to the grindstone and worked at making the Duke the best hotel in North Yorkshire.

Al was approaching retirement; she could hardly wait. It would be paradise having him around all the time—or at least she hoped it would be paradise. She only hoped he didn't eventually start to get on her nerves, or worse, get underfoot. Al could help run the place till they decided what to do next, but she wanted to hang on to the Duke for at least five more years, till she was on the low side of fifty, before deciding on what to do for the rest of her life. Relocating to the States, however, was a nonstarter.

She knew his finances were not as healthy as he'd like, but they'd manage, or as Mother used to say, they'd "get by." The Duke was more of a success then she admitted to Al, and she had even stashed away fairly large sums of cash in two Swiss bank accounts. Why two? She didn't know, but two seemed better than one. Money would not be an issue when Al packed in his Agency job, and once or twice she even alluded to these bank accounts, where the account numbers were, and what the passwords were. She told him that if anything should ever happen to her, the money was his to do with as he liked. Al asked no questions; maybe it was her ego talking, but she was pretty sure he didn't like the thought of something happening to her, of her not being around.

* * *

I'm on duty tonight with the new chef, Dougal. It's Friday evening, and there are enough bookings to fill the dining room to capacity.

It's lots of fun working with Dougal. He has a great sense of humor, even when faced with one demanding situation or another. He's also a pretty fair chef and isn't afraid of long hours and hard work. I like his work ethic and attitude. I hope he stays on forever and doesn't get snapped up by some posh hotel with bags of money, like the Royal in Scarborough.

"Margaret, a challenge—two trout ready for the pan. The challenge is we eat the eyes right out of their skull, uncooked."

"Okay … you first, Doug," I laughingly reply.

With that, Dougal digs out an eye with a fork, pops it into his mouth, and swallows with a grimace; a large glass of water follows.

"Bloody awful. You're up, Mags."

I dig out both eyes with my fingers, pop them into my mouth, energetically chew them, and swallow.

"Bloody lovely, Doug. I win. You owe me a gin and tonic after last orders."

"I can't believe you just did that, you mucky pup, and it'll be a large G and T, and you can count on that."

Several hours later, last orders are in. It's approaching ten—long day. I hope the Duke's guests had a nice time, good food, good company, and good wine. I remove my pina and head for the bar, as is my custom. When Mother was alive, heading to the bar after last orders—a fag in one hand and a gin in the other—was the highlight of her day. Father would have already turned in unless Al was on this side of the pond; when that was the case, he'd make a special effort to drink sensibly so he could have a bit of a natter with Al.

Me, I always spend an hour or so in the bar socializing. It's good for business, and I do enjoy a drink or two—helps me unwind prior to closing up and bed.

Dougal will finish up in the kitchen and make sure the staff stays just long enough to properly clean up and prepare early morning teas but not too long. Staying too long may mean overtime, which can be a killer in this business. Doug will then take his setter, Daisy, out for a walk and then sneak off to bed. He seldom drinks and has probably forgotten about our bet. The bar is very busy—another goodnight. More money on its way to Switzerland. Maybe the economy is finally turning, as BBC-1 has recently reported.

I see that Bob's on duty this evening; he'd been our barman for years—very reliable, well dressed, broad Yorkshire accent. As most in the place are from Yorkshire, I consider his accent a plus.

"Now, Margaret, are you well?"

I smile. In Yorkshire many conversations begin with "Now'" and end with a question mark; what follows almost always feels like a chat between family members. I like that.

"Well, Bob, I'm as well as one can expect and better than I probably should be. Al's coming home soon, maybe for good, or so he says, but like Mother would say, 'don't believe 'em, till you see 'em coming through the front door.' I'm pretty sure she was referring to Father, who worked the oil fields in Persia in World War Two. He was always coming home and finally did, but not before quite a few false starts."

"Yes, that certainly sounds just like your mother."

He pours me a large gin and tonic.

"Oh, that one's on Dougal. He left the money a while ago, said you'd understand."

"I do, Bob. Thank you."

I take a sip. I'm not much of a gulper, though from my family history one might think I should be. I guess that bad gene passed me by, and thank the good lord for that. "Cheers, Doug."

Mother didn't like Bob very much, but not to the extent of calling him "a little man," and Bob probably didn't like Mother very much either, but they needed each other. She felt he never leveled with her, thought he just said what he thought she wanted to hear. He probably did. Bob just wanted to keep the peace; he didn't need any run-ins with Mother. She held the stronger hand, and she knew it. Mother could be such a martinet. If you had any dealing with her, you learned that quickly and watched your tongue lest you got it bitten off.

I recognize one of the new flight lieutenants from Fylingdales. He comes over and sits on the settle next to me. We chat about this and that and, of course, the dreadful English weather. So much has changed at Fylingdales. The American military is gone, but a host of American contractors remain. Thank God for those contractors. Without them there'd be no reason to send Al over, and that would make my life more difficult—more difficult but not impossible. The three golf balls were dismantled years ago and shipped back to the States. The moor was returned to its original, pristine state as promised. New technology—a stationary radar, electronically steered—appeared; the locals call it the wedge. Apparently it does what three golf balls did at four times the speed.

The flight lieutenant's pleasant, a Welshman. They call him Taffy. I hardly hear a word he says after he tells me that Squadron Leader Menteith passed away a short while ago A heart attack. Monty always joked about how his smoking would eventually do him in, and it probably did. Odd. He survived the war—Jerry couldn't kill him, but a pack a day did. Mind you, he was knocking on eighty plus a bit. No one goes on forever, and it was quick, Taffy says. So sad; he was such a nice man, outgoing, friendly, a real credit to his country and the RAF. Al will be very upset, but I won't tell him till he returns home, hopefully for good.

I excuse myself, turn in, and have a little weep. I think of me and Al's long-dead infant son—congenital heart disease. An unplanned child followed by an untimely death. Monty represented the RAF at the funeral. Most people avoid funerals if they can, especially if the deceased is a child. Squadron Leader Menteith volunteered; he was that fond of Al and just that kind of man. I'm sure the station commander appreciated Monty's gesture—kind of took him off the hook. I nod off, thinking of Al and that impish, sly grin of his.

* * *

At the airport in Ibiza, Ahmet finds the nearest restroom and in the first empty stall opens his suitcase and dons his disguise: white suit, white shirt, white tie, dark glasses. He's thin, tall, and bald, not a hair on his head. When he reappears, he's the man Roger will be looking for. He quite enjoys this taciturn character in white, even down to his white socks and white plimsolls. He will intentionally go out of his way to socialize only with Roger and be reasonably antisocial, though not rude, with anyone else trying to strike up a friendship or random conversation. He wants to remain unidentifiable; he wants to remain neutral, like camouflage. When he's gone he wants not only to be gone physically, but to have no mental pictures of himself floating about. In a word, he wants to vaporize: here one minute and gone the next.

At check-in at the Sunrise, Ahmed presents a credit card with the surname Mohamed. There's also a corresponding driver's license in the name of Mohamed if needed. It isn't. The name's bogus, but the credit card isn't and works every time, no matter how much the charge. Mohamed has unlimited credit, but Ahmet knows not to try to cheat his government. Their auditors are tenacious; a strict reconciliation of all expenses is not a possibility but a certainty. He even has to keep receipts for any purchase over twenty pesetas. Compared to his own clandestine service, the CIA is swimming in dollars, or so he's heard.

After checking in, Ahmet makes his way to his seventh floor room; he'd asked for a quiet room, and the seventh floor is the quietest. As the Sunrise is a small hotel, there's only one, antiquated lift, and he has to wait a couple of minutes before ascending. He enters a dimly lit room and switches on a light. He's planning for a little shuteye. The cylinder's in his carry-on. He double-locks the door, cranks up the AC, and then methodically and unsuccessfully searches for electronic listening devices; he trusts no one, especially colleagues of Roger. He plans on an immediate exchange and then returning home on the next available flight. He'll most likely have to go by way of London; that's the only way he can leave the island without a reservation. All other destinations will be fully booked. London-bound flights leave every six hours this time of year—peak season, but only just.

Ahmet dozes off, but then the damn phone rings, blast after blast till he's forced to answer it. It's Roger. How he always knows what room is a mystery that Ahmet chooses not to solve. He really doesn't care, but Roger is such a pain—always so very nervous and always wanting to be so very matey. Like, *Can we have dinner, a stroll, coffee, a drink?* Whatever it is, Roger's always up to it, always so cheerful in a nervous sort of way, and he usually foots the bill, paying cash, never a credit card.

"Yes, Roger. I'll be down in half an hour—need to have a shower … Yes, we can have dinner, but I'd like the exchange to take place right after we eat, so have the money with you … Oh, so you finally did get cleared? I'm happy for you, but not on an open line, Roger—might be bugged, maybe even by you Americans. I just never know who to trust these days. I'm sure you understand. Good-bye."

Roger's tradecraft is so very poor, Ahmet opines. *It's a wonder he could be cleared to drive a school bus, but that's not my concern. Maybe the Americans aren't as clever as I suppose, but still, better to err on the side of caution. I don't want any screwups, and maybe Roger's nervousness and carelessness are some kind of ruse. Maybe Roger is really James Bond on steroids and not Inspector Clouseau. Just get the cylinder to him, get the cash, leave as soon as possible, and never return to this tiny little hellhole in the Mediterranean. That's the game plan, and I'm sticking to it.*

Ahmet gets up and heads to the shower, thinking that Ernna might just be right. Perhaps he is too old for this line of work; he'd have to discuss that scenario with his brother-in-law when he gets back. Maybe even discuss it with Ernna, but probably not. She'd get too emotional and have that "I told you so" attitude. Regardless, he first had to successfully wrap up this op before permitting himself to think about the future.

* * *

Two hours prior to Ahmet's nap, Al spots him entering the foyer of the Sunshine Hotel; he perfectly fits Roger's description—all in white except for the dark glasses. While the man in white's attire is noticeable, it's anything but unique, especially on this small holiday island where tourists from around the world flock and especially this time of year when the weather's not too hot, but comfortable enough to sit around the pool and work on a tan.

I must know the floor this mystery man in white is on if I'm ever to have a chance at getting my hands on those papers, Al's thinking as he pulls a newspaper close to his face.

I mustn't be seen by the man in white, not even a peek. My hump's a dead giveaway. If Roger's ever confronted with 'a man with a hump' scenario, he'll most certainly put two and two together and come up with me, his latest polygrapher, and our talk just a few weeks ago. Not many people with humps these days—all terminated compliments of new technology.

Al's plan is straightforward, drop-dead simple. No time to be clever or cagey—just get the bloody documents and be off. The man in white has to be temporarily disabled. When that's done, he'll retrieve the documents and hopefully not be seen by anyone, not even a peripheral glimpse. No thought of killing ever occurs to Al, just a good thump to the top of the head. Not to the back of the head, the top. That should do the trick.

After a few moments at the front desk, the man in white receives a key and then immediately proceeds to the lift. His only luggage is his carry-on.

Al's adjacent to the lift, sitting in a green leather easy chair, face intently peering into today's *Financial Times*. He can see by the floor indicator above the lift that it goes straight to the seventh floor.

What a break, one floor above me. My room is opposite the lift, and if his does also, I'll have lucked out a second time. Have to be very careful not to bump into Roger or unnecessarily draw any attention to myself. That would truly be a disaster, a real game changer.

Ten minutes later, Al's in his sixth-floor room. Using the fire exit stairwell, he proceeds up to the seventh floor; fortunately the fire exits are not locked on the outside. He then finds the room immediately above his and makes a mental note of the room number. Before returning to his room he knocks on the door then slips into the stairwell. No answer. He concludes that the room is vacant. Al returns to his own room via the stairwell and then heads down to the lobby, where he calls the front desk from a hotel phone.

"Yes, room 708, sounds like running water, may be a toilet jammed up and there's a horrible smell. Better send maintenance man and pronto"

"Yes, sir, but that room is unoccupied."

"Look, I'm telling you what I heard. I heard running water and there's a strange smell. You better have someone check it out and soon."

Al nonchalantly replaces the receiver and returns to his room, where he puts on a pair of thin rubber gloves and stuffs a twelve-inch steel pipe into his trousers before going up to the seventh floor This time he waits in the stairwell where, with the door slightly ajar, he can easily view room 708 and the lift. Soon an elderly and portly maintenance man pushing a small cart full of tools exits the lift. He opens 708, turns on the lights, pulls the cart halfway into the room so as to wedge open the door, and enters the bathroom searching for a body, a water leak, anything suspicious. Finding nothing and now grumbling to himself in Spanish, he flips off all the lights and sets about disengaging the cart from the door, head down.

Like a cat onto a mouse, Al with a single blow to the skull renders the Spaniard unconscious as he's pushing the cart into the hallway. The man quietly falls. Al then carefully moves the old man and his cart back into room 708, just outside the bathroom, and shuts the door. The room's now nearly in total darkness. Using a shim from the cart, Al then discreetly wedges open the door a couple of inches and waits for the man of mystery. Having now gained access to 708 without any fuss or bother, the second part of his plan is put into motion.

Al has no idea what room the man in white is in, but the plan is to moan and call out for help when he appears, presumably as he's heading for the lift to meet Roger. When the man in white enters 708 to render assistance to the overweight Spaniard, a sharp blow by the steel pipe will put his lights out for hours. No way can Al be seen lurking in the bathroom, not even by a cat; the room is just too dark, and he was clever enough to unscrew all the light bulbs associated with the light switch by the door. After rendering the man in white unconscious, he'll then relieve him of the documents or, if necessary, go to his room and retrieve them.

And the plan goes down like clockwork. The man in white is out for the count, and he helpfully has the cylinder in his carry-on, which he'd been taking with him to dinner. Al immediately twigs onto the fact that the documents are housed inside the canister. That most likely means Roger will be in the lobby somewhere waiting for the man in white, probably the bar but maybe not.

"Well," he says, chuckling to himself and speaking over his shoulder, "my pipe's two for two, and from what I can see neither is hurting very badly, or so it appears, but I'm certainly no expert when it comes to knocking people on the head."

Well, we've had very good luck today. We have the papers, no one can place us at the scene, and both the man in white and the Spaniard will be up and around in a couple of hours, probably with headaches, but that's a small price to pay for my happiness.

Al opens the cylinder, removes the contents, and stuffs them into his inside jacket pocket. He leaves the cylinder and metal pipe behind. He examines the man in white's wallet for identification and finds driver's license and credit card with a very common name, obviously phony, but there are also business cards with an e-mail address that Al quickly commits to memory.

Al had checked out of his room several hours earlier, making sure the front desk remembered him leaving in a flurry of noisy, planned activity. Given the age and size of the hotel, he also thought, and rightly so, that his room would not be cleaned up till the following morning or much later that evening, so he would have access for several more hours—he'd claimed to have lost the key and had paid the lost key charge. Anyway, bumping into a maid was a risk Al had been prepared to take. He collects his bulky luggage, exits via a side door, and hails a cab to the airport, to Margaret, and maybe even to tons of money. An hour later, he boards a flight to London's Heathrow Airport, feeling very proud of himself.

* * *

Two hours later with a pounding headache, Ahmet slowly regains consciousness. Before doing anything else, he searches for the cylinder; he finds it, but it's empty.

I am so screwed. He needs advice, but first he anonymously calls the front desk and reports the fate of the portly maintenance man. *What to do, what to say?* He collects his things, returns to his room, and rings Mamet.

"I can't believe this," is all Mamet says at first, over and over.

"You're gonna be in deep shit when that bastard of a boss of ours finds out. Those papers are one of a kind, not replaceable, and no one will ever accept copies. I'll call Isule and see what he wants you to do. Give me your number."

Within fifteen minutes the phone in Ahmet's room rings.

"Ahmet, Isule is so very angry with you, to put it mildly. How could this happen? You're supposed to be one of our top agents. He doesn't want to speak to you. When you get back, God knows what he will do, nothing good for you or your career. You might want to think about retiring, my friend, and that's completely off the record. You knew what was riding on the Americans getting those papers. No second chance, no second set of papers. Anyway, he wants you to stay put till he and our fearless leaders figure out what to do next. Leave a message at the front desk for Roger. You know, change of plans, had to return home, meet soonest for exchange at later date, will stay in touch, usual channels. Say nothing about losing the plans. Keep everything to an absolute minimum—no local police, either. No further contact with Roger for now. Understand?"

"You know, Mamet, I spoke to Isule about me having some kind of backup. If I'd had backup this wouldn't have happened. Isule rationalized to me that I'd already had two successes so the next should also be successful. I wonder if he'll remember that conversation … probably not."

"I don't know, Ahmet, but if we can't make things right, someone will pay, and it won't be me. The only way to make things right is to recover the plans, at any cost, and then get them to Roger!"

"Ahmet, listen, do you think Roger knocked you out? No, too ridiculous—the Americans could have had the plans for a few thousand dollars. Why take that risk? It's definitely not the Americans, and from what you tell me Roger's just too nervous to go rogue. He'd give himself a stroke. Do you agree, Ahmet?"

"Yes, of course I agree. And tell Ernna I've been delayed—not waylaid but delayed. Don't cause her any unnecessary worry or grief. All in all she's not a bad girl, and she may eventually prove to be my only and best friend. Perhaps I should think of retiring, but we'll talk about that when I get home."

"Okay. Good-bye, Ahmet, and, again, don't expect a cordial homecoming. I warned you: just follow the plan and don't dally, but you probably let that numskull Roger talk you into doing something unnecessary, like a margarita at the bar where you're in plain view of all the guests, not good."

"Not so, Mamet, but you can read my initial report. I'll be sending it to headquarters tomorrow morning by e-mail. Don't worry—by and large it'll be very vague and unclassified. They have a couple of hotel workstations downstairs."

"Okay, fine, Ahmet. I look forward to reading it. Send it to me, and I'll hand-carry it to Isule."

"Okay, bye, Mamet."

Sounds like Mamet's trying to shift all the blame to me and save his own ass. What a friend—my first foul-up in twenty-plus years, and everyone wants to jump ship and give me the deep six. I followed protocol, and I followed our plan to the letter. Some outsider got wind of what was going on, knew our plans, and intervened for their own benefit. Someone broke protocol. I'm sure it's not the Americans and definitely no one on our side, but who? Regardless, I'm the fall guy. Marvelous.

* * *

As his flight's approaching Heathrow, Al can bear the suspense no longer. He has to see those papers. He deftly pulls them from his inside jacket pocket; they're just schematics and tons of verbiage, all in some foreign tongue that he doesn't recognize. He'll have to use the language translator on his smartphone but not now. He'll check into some cheap London hotel, try to make some sense out of these documents, and then come up with a plan to hopefully cash in on the papers.

He mentally muses, *How much will the Americans pay? How much will the handlers of the man in white pay?*

To my mind they're the only buyers out there, and dealing with the Agency is fraught with risk. If the word hunchback *ever comes out, the Agency will key in on me and start looking into my relationship with any and all interviewees I've recently polygraphed. No way will Roger want to finger me—too much to lose with minimum advantage to himself, and he isn't even aware that he's the catalyst that helped me to acquire the plans. In my mind maybe the man in white and his comrades will pay to get their plans back, and they'll pay through the nose if I have anything to say, for I, at least, have a rough idea of what the plans are all about. I'll ask two million, and two million's a bargain, but why would they pay much more to me than they're getting from Roger unless the man in white just wants the plans to end up in American hands, and the money Roger was intending to pass over is really irrelevant?*

Al's getting sleepy—too much excitement for one day. He nods off just minutes from touchdown.

Early the next morning Al and his smartphone are hard at work translating the plans into English, word by word, and some of the words so technical that they can't be translated. After a couple of hours, Al has figured out that the language is an Iranian dialect and that the plans are, as he'd suspected, of the Iranian nuclear weapons program. They're very detailed, with plenty of drawings. Al not only needs to figure out what the plans are all about but, more importantly, if they're genuine. If genuine, they might truly be worth millions to the right buyer or their original custodian. They do appear to be genuine, at least from their look and feel, though Al's certainly no expert at validating the authenticity of plans dealing with weapons of mass destruction. After two days in that rattrap of a hotel, living on pizza and Indian food, Al thinks he has some of the answers.

Yes, he reasons, *details of Iran's surging nuclear capabilities, detailed blueprints and dates, locations and test results. From what I can make out, Iran will have a nuclear capability in less than a month, and they already have sufficient stockpiles of high-grade fissionable material to build several weapons. Or in desperation they can easily turn highly radioactive material over to terrorists who could quite easily make mobile dirty bombs. Shortly Iran will probably shock the world with a series of detectable test explosions that they cannot deny. Yet no one will lift a finger to stop them because no one knows the vitality of their nuclear weapons program or the extent of their madness. Western intelligence has failed miserably, failed to pick up on Iran's surge into the world of A-bombs. At first everyone will want to negotiate away Iran's threat, but if anyone dares attack Iran, she'll retaliate by, at a minimum, making fissionable materials available to all takers and wreaking havoc in the Gulf. Missile attacks on Israel, using conventional weapons, are a certainty.*

Al still can't understand why the Americans have been getting this intelligence so cheaply. At first he'd thought that the money from Roger was just a face-saving gesture to move the plans over to American stewardship, but he's having second thoughts now. Maybe the man in white went rogue and didn't realize the value of the plans, just wanted money for the plans, and twenty thousand was a nice, round number. Motivation, however, isn't what Al's concerned with. He doesn't care why the plans are being moved around. All he knows is that he now has the plans, and if the man in white wants them back, the asking price is two million. He composes an e-mail briefly detailing proof that he has the plans and that if they want them back, it will cost them two million big ones and he needs an answer within twenty-four hours. If there's no answer within a day, the plans will be destroyed. At no time does he mention selling the plans to the Americans; that just might be what they want, but he isn't sure about that either.

The e-mail is sent via his smartphone. Two hours later, his smartphone pings: an e-mail. He eagerly reads it and then reads it again and again.

He literally jumps for joy, and that's not easy when carrying a ten-pound hump on one's back. *They've accepted my proposal! They want wiring instructions!* In a heartbeat he is on the phone to Margaret. He needs the number and deposit password to one of her Swiss bank accounts. He tells Margaret to expect a large deposit into that bank shortly, at which time she's to transfer all the funds to her second bank account and close out her first. She tries weaseling information out of him but to no avail. She agrees to do what he asks.

Al e-mails the account information to the man in white or his accomplice, and shortly Al receives a second e-mail. It reads:

Okay, here's the plan. We've deposited one million into the aforementioned account. For the remainder of the two million, return to Ibiza with the plans and stay at the Sunrise Hotel. Check in this coming Friday. At six PM meet a man dressed in white at the bar. He will have one million in cash. Make the exchange and then immediately return home. Agree?

Before confirming, he rings Margaret.

"Yes, one million, and I've already moved it, no problem. The Swiss are very accommodating when it comes to money."

"Okay, good. See you shortly. Bye."

Al sends one final e-mail that day. "Agreed" is all it says. By return receipt he sees that it has been successfully delivered and opened.

Al has two days to kill in London; he relocates to a B&B not far from Hyde Park. He loves London—the sites, the sounds, the food and, especially, the people.

Life's a bitch. How can I be so lucky? I'm sure you must have had something to do with it.

CHAPTER 6

Drinks are freely flowing at the Duke of Yorkshire. I'm buying. I just got word from Al that he'll be home this weekend—home for good. I'll never again have to take him to Teesside Airport to catch a flight to London's Heathrow Airport and then on to Dulles DC. The only flying he'll be doing will be with me. What a relief. I'm so happy I have Bob buy everyone a drink or two, on the house. Word has obviously gotten around: we've got twice the number of customers I would normally expect to see on a weeknight, but that doesn't bother me. "The more the merrier," as Mother used to say, though she'd have added, "but never on the house"—a thrifty Scot, my mother. Several in the pub want to reciprocate, but I refuse, even refuse one in the pump. This is my shout, and I want to make sure Bob lets everyone know the drinks are on Margaret.

Two of the younger lads have even drawn a small caricature of Al, hump and all, on the chalkboard adjacent the dart board; he's got a broad grin on his face, right hand stretched out, thumb up, as if to say, "I'll be back soon, so watch out, world. Al's on the prowl."

"Well," one of the lads says to his mate, "maybe with a man around the house, Margaret will be in better fettle, like might even smile every now and again."

They know full well I can hear. They're just taking the piss, cheeky little sods.

I pretend not hear them and turn to see Bob, a sly, crooked smile on his otherwise deadpan face. He'd heard every word, but hopefully he'll give me some cover, and he does by staring down the lads, who move to a far corner, eyes averted. Bob probably thinks I owe him one now, but I don't see it that way, and I hope he doesn't try to collect; lately he's been getting on my already fragile nerves.

I'd recently noticed, especially when he's on duty that tipping the barman is trying to catch on at the Duke as it already has in America and some parts of Europe. Bob and I discussed this at length, and I let him know point-blank not to accept tips or encourage tipping. If someone insists on leaving a tip, he's to put it into one of the local charity boxes strewn about the place. Most British pub owners frown on tipping, and most Brits don't tip the barman. Drinking is turning into an expensive pastime as it is, and if tips do the barmen some good, they definitely do us publicans no good. Tips to the barman are usually at the expense of the owner, and if the barman feels a tip may be in the offing, he might be tempted to not charge for a drink or two or to give double measures as a way of saying thank you—kind of like a wink and a nod or tit for tat. It took me a long time to get Al to stop tipping. I explained time and again that tipping barmen is not British, so he eventually stopped. Anyway, I've a funny feeling Al was tipping just to gently let me know not to tell him what to do, or in his own words, "no one tells me what to do" and by "no one" he means me. When he's in the five-pints frame of mind, and that's self explanatory, I just ignore him and cut him some slack. However, the following day he'll get an earful, especially if he showed me up in front of the locals or, worse, Bob.

Serving drinks is the barman's job, his raison d'être, but a grateful customer buying the barman a drink, having one in the pump as we say in Yorkshire, is okay by me. That one in the pump is paid for by an appreciative customer, and always drunk by the barman after hours or when trade is slow.

After a long diatribe by me not so long ago, all Bob could ask is what about barmen who don't drink? How can they have one in the pump? I thought that question too stupid to even attempt an answer, and with a look that said "you've got to be kidding me, Bob," I left to have a chat with one of the locals. Leaving the settle can be like entering no man's land. It's something Mother never did, but I do and often, especially as it gives me an opportunity to meet local spouses and local girlfriends, who very infrequently approach the settle. If Bob had ever posed a question like that to Mother, she'd have cleaned the floor with him, but Bob would never have asked Mother such a daft question. I've never known a barman who didn't drink, and I'm sure Bob knows that's the case. Bob also knows I'm not Mother, and I guess I'm not. Then again, I won't be his patsy either, and I won't let him try to get around my no-tipping policy with some ridiculous argument that there might be barmen in England who don't drink, and a small gratuity in lieu of one in the pump is only fair. Let Bob bring forth his exception if he can, and then I'll have a rethink.

Now that said and done, tipping dining room staff is not only acceptable but encouraged. A lot more work is required to serve, silver service if you please, a four-course meal than pull a pint. The tips are always fairly shared among all kitchen staff, and anyone trying to pull a fast one with funds bound for the tip box will be out on their ear in a hurry, and they all know that for sure.

Out of the corner of my eye, I see Bob pouring Timmy, a local, a rum and black.

"Now, Timmy," I say, "what's going on here, you've only just turned eighteen and onto spirits already?"

"I know, Margaret, but it's a special occasion—all the lads are just over the moon what with Al coming home. Any road, we all miss him. He brightens up the place with that queer, downcast smile of his, and his temper's as smooth as a millpond. Nay, one might never know he's married to you."

I guess I'm getting a bit of a reputation, maybe lose my temper too easily. Leave it to a lad of eighteen to unintentionally—hopefully unintentionally—put me in my place. Anyway, I ignore his last remark. I want tonight to be special and don't want to have cross words with Timmy, who, like most Yorkshire men, is not afraid to speak his mind—especially when he feels he's in the right or has had one pint too many.

"And you're right about that temper of his, Timmy; as far as you lads are concerned it doesn't exist. Any road, Timmy, please stick to beer. Legally, you're old enough to drink whatever you want and certainly old enough to drink something stronger than lager or shandies, but stay away from spirits, especially if I'm buying. Remember too much ale will put weight on you in a hurry, and too much rum may kill you or cause you to wish you were dead. From what I hear a rum hangover is murder, might even put you off drink, and I'm sure you don't want that, now do you, Timmy? Just be a sensible drinker, please. I'm just trying to give you some good advice, lad. You know that, Timmy, or at least I hope you do."

Listen to me, talking like I'm Timmy's mum or the vicar. If I continue like this, I'll be getting a halo, and I'll have to have Al periodically straighten it, as I'm not used to wearing a halo.

"Ah, maybe you're right, Margaret. Jubilee, please, Bob."

Timmy leaves to join his mates; he's pleased to be given a Jub—makes him feel like a man, and drinking in England is still one sign of manhood, good or bad. Since I own a pub, good is what I'm thinking. Up to Timmy's eighteenth birthday, lager was all he'd been served, and Bob would usually keep count. After three or four he'd be out the door unless he wanted to drink Coke or lemonade, which he usually didn't, especially if his mates were around. Anyway, after he leaves, if he's feeling like another, he'll just cross the bridge over the river Esk, take a left along the quay, and go into the White Horse, a pub so old they say Captain Cook stood many a round there. As long as you can stand and bring glass to lips, they'll serve what you can pay for, but if you fall asleep, pass out, or make yourself sick, they'll put you out into the street no matter how cold it is, and it can get bloody cold. I can remember, as a child, throwing cups of water into the air and having sheets of ice rain down on me, and that's without gale-force winds blowing in off the North Sea.

Any road, Timmy's eighteen and can now drink whatever he wants, and he knows it and so do I, but I did mean what I said about drinking and ruined lives. Up until taking over the Duke, Father was a senior director at a prestigious chemical works plant in Sheffield, but over time he succumbed to the allure of drink. At times, as I remember, Father seemed to drink continuously and apparently drank quite a lot at work. Then came the signs his supervisors couldn't ignore: too many days off, coming in late, his breath, his appearance, bad decisions, and especially his arrogant attitude toward his subordinates. After several warnings, he was told to leave and with little compensation—no golden parachute for Dad. Mother was frantic. Thank God, the Duke came up. Thank God Mother loved cooking, or they would have had to go onto the dole, but they didn't. Over time things sorted themselves out, and while Father did try to be abstemious, up to a point, he was always a relentless drinker, sad to say. For the rest of his life, he never fully understood the grief he caused Mother.

At times, when she was feeling low and we were having a quiet chat after closing, she would angrily refer to Dad as that alcoholic, and maybe she was right. I preferred to think of him as a man who enjoyed drink, like so many from his generation, and he never got nasty or belligerent. He was always kind and in good humor, though according to Mother bone idle, and he probably was. But in his mind and at his age, he just wanted to kick back and enjoy the time he had left, and drink would play a big part in his life till the day he died.

I still miss him very, very much, and in spite of what Mother said I'll always remember him as a good dad, kind and gentle, tolerant and forgiving.

At no time was any serious thought given to getting help for Dad. First, he would never have agreed. Second, word would have gotten around the village, and the shame to the family would have been unbearable, and guess what, nothing would have changed. Father was just too set in his ways, and regardless of the consequences he would not change, and even if he could change it would not have been for the better, or at least that's what I'm thinking.

There's a loud crash. To my right I can see that Wilson has fallen off his barstool; he's not hurt. A drunk seldom gets hurt when he falls—too limber. He just rolls, unless he's falling down stairs, in which case it can be quite ugly, very messy, with blood everywhere. Any road, Wilson's head missed the square, reddish tiles by at least a foot, and it'll take more than a fall to do any real damage to that farmer's body, made hard by fourteen-hour days of plowing, planting, and haying. God only knows Wilson and others like him deserve some fun. Everyone's laughing hysterically.

"Pick me up, or pass me down my drink" is all Wilson has to say. So his mates pick him up and gingerly set him on his stool. I notice his older brother stands a wee bit closer than usual, making sure he doesn't fall a second time. These boys, they're all good lads. Wilson's not embarrassed in the least, probably won't even remember falling. His brothers will see that he gets safely home, but he's on his own come sunup. Drink will make you do some foolish things—some good, some not so good—but that's another story.

"Bob, make sure no one gets too drunk—you know, really over-the-top drunk—don't want any lawsuits or bad press in the *Whitby Gazette*, and I certainly don't want anyone getting hurt. They're all locals, and all will be walking home, probably singing a tune or two. One more drink for each, then close up if you please, and don't waste that rum and black. You drink it if necessary, and make sure the younger ones stick to beer—don't want them being sick outside the Duke. The staff won't want to clean up their muck, especially if they're feeling a bit under the weather themselves."

This being sick can be catchy, like a chain reaction. If I see someone throw up after a good gag, it causes me to gag and might even make me sick. One has to be very careful about these things; even the sight of someone's muck, all yellow and full of big sticky bits can make some sick, especially me, or so I'm thinking.

"Oh, and if you're on duty tomorrow morning, Bob, hose out the gents before even going in, then give it a good mopping."

"Yes, Margaret. I got the same orders from your mother years ago."

Listen to Bob, talking like he and Mum were close friends when, at times, she gave serious thought to sacking him, and he could never quite get used to taking direction from a woman, especially a tough-minded woman like Mother.

Last orders might be easier said than done, no matter who's buying. Dougal and a friend have just finished a seltzer-water fight outside the pub. Several empty seltzer bottles lay on the bar, and the pair are soaked to the gills. They're both in high spirits, just laughing and laughing. I so enjoy seeing folk, especially young folk, having a gay time. There's so much pressure on them, what with A levels and O levels and learning computers and the like. It's no wonder so many just pack learning in and return, like their dads, to the land or the pits. Anyway, those against drink seem to resent fun, or so it appears, always pointing out the evils of drink and always forgetting that pubs are a grand old British tradition. Many a successful man has spent more time in pubs than he'd care to publicly admit, and some might even say they got a better education, or at least a better understanding of folk and what makes them tick, in a pub than the classroom. Father always said he didn't trust people who didn't drink, and I'm sure he meant it, but then Father's someone those against drink might use as their poster child. Any road, I always say everything in moderation. Oops, there's that halo of mine. I'm always trying and usually succeeding at doing what's right, but doing what's right can be kind of habit forming and a bit boring. What worries me is that when I'm on my deathbed, I'll not so much regret what I've done wrong, but what I had the opportunity to do but didn't. I think my attitude about doing the right thing was fallout from an incident that happened to me as a child.

As a little girl I always wanted to please my parents—do the right thing, make them proud—and I usually made good on that. However, one day while shopping with Mother, I pocketed a little toy ballerina without anyone noticing. It was discovered when we returned home, and horror of horrors you'd think I'd lifted the crown jewels. We rushed back to town and returned the toy with never-ending "so sorry, so sorry, so sorry." Mother was shocked and embarrassed and most likely wanted to disown me, but Father was more understanding, saying I was just a wee lass who'd made a mistake. For months after that episode I hated walking the high street, fearing I'd be recognized as that little girl who looks so sweet but is really a big-time criminal. Mother did nothing to discourage that negative attitude I had of myself, and till the day she died still cringed at the thought that her daughter, her only daughter, was, at one time, nothing better than a common shoplifter. So from that day forward I did my level best to do the right thing, or at least what I thought to be the right thing, and at the risk of repeating myself I usually succeeded, though not always.

Off to my right I hear, "Cheers, Margaret." It's Mr. Steed holding his pint high, a broad smile on his disfigured face. So much free beer. He's in heaven.

In return, I raise my glass and smile.

To my left the Ploughstot dancers are warming up for an ad hoc show. It's a bit late. Bob looks in my direction. I nod okay. Five men are dressed in brightly striped red and blue tunics, baggy trousers, and broad-brimmed dark caps, like train engineer's caps. A sixth man, the hag, is dressed in a long skirt, padded white blouse, and a bright yellow wig. The five dancers carry blunt, metal swords. Someone with a harmonica blares out a tune, and the five lads dance in an ever-diminishing circle, first clockwise and then anticlockwise, swords high, knees high, all in time with the harmonica. Sword clangs against sword. It all ends with five swords mysteriously joined, forming a star, looking quite a lot like the Star of David. The old hag rattles the old, wooden charity box. Everyone throws in a few coppers, and as they say, all had a merry ol' time.

Like I just said, last orders are easy to call but sometime fall on deaf ears, so I tell Bob not to spoil anyone's fun, at least not just yet, but

I'm no longer buying; I'm no longer pushing the boat out. I bet Dad's spinning in his grave, wanting me to stop shoveling money out the door and to remember that this is a business I'm running; the idea is not to run it into the ground but to make a profit.

"Well, Margaret," says Dougal, looking like a shaggy old dog caught in a downpour, "that dancing looks like fun. Maybe I'll look into being a Ploughstot dancer one day, but I'm truly not very coordinated and tone deaf to boot, just like my boyhood idol, Horatio Hornblower."

"You do that, Horatio. Fun never killed anyone, but no fun can make one's life a dirge. When people feel life will never change and they'll just move from one unhappy situation to another, well, that's when they start thinking about Plan B, and you know my definition of Plan B? It's suicide. So, as Mother used to say, get out there and have some fun, and find someone to have fun with, because then fun turns into something very special, something memorable and heartwarming, and I'm sure you know what I mean."

"You're talking about love, aren't you, Mags? I was in love one time—not so long ago, as a matter of fact. I was so messed up, and by messed up I mean indecisive, unnecessarily self-conscious, and always trying to please. Any road, she knew I loved her and took me for every farthing I was worth. Dated others as well, on the sly—only just recently found that out. So I guess I've learned me lesson, which is never to fall in love."

"I think you might have learned the wrong lesson, Doug. Don't give your heart to just anyone, and don't give it unconditionally and certainly not overnight. Take your time, make sure you're compatible, and if it's mutual, then lay on all sail and don't waste a minute."

My goodness, my halo's starting to slip again, and Al's not here to straighten it. One of my golden principles is never to give advice on affairs of the heart. My track record is abysmal. I better stop pontificating, or I'll get a reputation as a bad-tempered know-it-all, when in reality I think of myself as a hardworking woman with an eye to getting into a wee bit of bother every now and again.

"Anyway, Dougal, let's discuss something more cheerful than lessons learned about this or lessons learned about that. Let's discuss food—in particular, staff lunches for tomorrow. If you've time, make something special, for Al's sake, something to celebrate his homecoming and hopefully his final homecoming. I see you and Daisy shot some pigeon this afternoon. How about stewed pigeon breast au gratin in a red wine sauce with mashed potatoes and fresh country peas on the side or sprinkled on top? In other words, pigeon breast piled high onto mashed potatoes swimming in a red wine sauce then topped with grated cheddar cheese, under the grill till the cheese melts. For dessert, make a ruhm doo. We have all the dates, fresh fruit, and essence of rum you'll need. What the staff doesn't eat, we can put on the menu. What do you think? I can help if you need a hand. I haven't done a stint in the kitchen in some time. Yes, I'd quite enjoy that. What do you say?"

"Ah, Margaret, that sounds jolly good to me. I'll even freeze a portion for Al. I'll use a really sharp English cheddar and some cheap red plonk. If I get into trouble, I'll give you a shout, and I can guarantee you that I'll get into trouble. That extra micro you just bought will really come in handy, for all sorts. I can heat things up twice as fast or defrost in one and heat up in the other. The options seem unlimited. If you ever do get a third micro, we'll need a conductor to orchestrate their use, but as you know, we still do all the cooking in the AGA."

"Yes, I know, and so we shall continue using that old AGA until new owners show up and we get the heave ho. I've been approached by several tradesmen encouraging me to replace the AGA with gas, which is easier to use and always available—no coal required. It'll be difficult for me to switch to gas. That AGA was here before Mother, apparently before the Second World War. I remember my first day here. When I came into the kitchen, a huge stockpot was on top of the AGA, loaded to the gills with bits of this and pieces of that just boiling away. Mother said that fresh stock makes the best soup, and if there was one thing Mother excelled at, it was making soups; her mulligatawny was out of this world. I wish you'd known her, Doug. She was a grand lady but with an evil temper, could even be a bit vindictive, but as I've now been doing her job for quite some time, I can understand why—and I don't have Father to contend with."

I carry on about the good ol' days and Mother and Father for another thirty minutes and then turn in, hoping I hadn't bored Doug too much. I'll balance the till's receipts against the cash tomorrow morning. We only just started taking credit cards, and this made our balancing act a bit trickier; once the day's receipts are calculated I'll enter the take into my books. Like most in the business, I keep a second set of books. The money that goes to Switzerland never gets entered into the book I use for tax purposes, but I do like to keep a record of my ill-gotten gains—therefore, the second set of books. I suppose this second set of books, if discovered by the tax man, would make my life uncomfortable, but if I paid taxes on everything we took in, I'd have been out of business a long time ago, and now there's talk of a minimum wage. If that happens I may have to pack this place in or raise prices, and that'll drive the locals away, at least temporarily.

I can hear Bob closing up and then locking up downstairs. Here in the North of Yorkshire, locking up isn't really necessary. There's been no thieving in years. I can't figure out why we even have a constable, what with no crime to speak of; maybe to ensure pubs close and open on time, which our constable never does very well. If he ever comes in after hours and we're still serving, we'll buy him a pint or two, and he'll be off home as happy as Larry. Anyway, thinking about crime causes me to panic a bit.

How did Al come by all that money? He retires, and all of a sudden millions show up in my Swiss bank account. It sounds fishy to me. Maybe I should have been more forthcoming about our finances, let him know we aren't at poverty's door. But if he thought the Duke was flourishing, he might have delayed retirement, figuring he'd be in the way somehow, and that was something I just didn't want. We're not getting any younger. We need to spend more time together, and while I know Al doesn't have a roving eye, it would still be nice to have him where I can keep an eye on him. Like Mother used to say: "Men will be boys given half a chance." Mother never really liked most men, always thought of them as small, mean, and selfish. She never cut most any slack, especially Father. Anyway, Al's so pigheaded; he'll do what he plans on doing regardless of the Duke or me or the Queen of England. He's just that kind of guy. All that money, though—it's hard for me to reconcile in my mind how he could have come by it legally. Just hope he doesn't end up in one of Her Majesty's slammers. I'm getting drowsy, beginning to nod off. This weekend, probably Sunday, we should be back together. If I knew the exact day and time of his arrival, I'd pick him up at Heathrow, but I don't. Always all this mystery, and for a polygrapher, practically a desk job, or so I'm thinking. What if he's some kind of spy or double-agent or something out of the pictures? Any road, there's no sense in conjuring up "what if's." I've already got too much on my plate now. That's one thing I'll not miss, no sirree; no more mystery.

* * *

"What do you mean by 'will be delayed'? He told me he'd be back tomorrow afternoon!" Ernna was screaming at her brother, nearly at the top of her lungs, like the two of them were children again. The grin never left Mamet's face, though the situation was serious—and if he wasn't careful, the situation might become much worse. He tried to look more concerned, but his face wouldn't cooperate. He even tried to put on an expressionless face but failed there, too. The grin persisted, and this further angered Ernna, who couldn't understand why Mamet seemed so glib about the whole situation.

"So, my dear brother, you can't or won't tell me why Ahmet will be late or what happened to him or where he is? Do you take me for a fool? Where is he? Tell me the truth, and don't beat around the bush. Tell me now, or on our father's grave I'll …"

She paused just long enough to take a breath. But before she could restart, Mamet jumped in like a Spanish matador doing his best to gracefully sweep aside all her questions and all her idle threats—if they were idle.

"Sister, it's all confidential, but he is not ill, or dead, or even seriously hurt. I have spoken to him at length. He must remain in place for another couple of days to finish up what he started. If he doesn't successfully finish his job, his career may be on the line and he might be forced to retire early on half pension. Ahmet wouldn't like that or you, I think. You know you have some serious shopping habits, so be careful what you ask for. Having your darling Ahmet round the house 24-7 may not be as much fun as you think. Remember—he's my best friend, and I know all his irritating idiosyncrasies and bad habits, like the way he whistles, almost uncontrollably, all the time, and he can't even whistle. So annoying. Why can't he just hum, and the way he examines his face with that tiny blue mirror? Four or five times a day for about a minute. It's like he's counting pimples or wrinkles or nose hairs, and he has too many nose hairs to count. Sister, you should speak to him about those nose hairs—not very attractive, I'm thinking."

"Mamet, I only shop because I'm lonely, and as far that mirror thing, he does it at home also. He worries that his face is in decline, and it is—he's getting older. We're all getting older. He and I need to be friends again, even on half pay. If something bad happens to my husband, even though you're my brother, I will cut you into tiny little pieces and feed you to Mother's chickens, and after that I'll go to the press and tell them the whole story, at least what I know. Do you understand me? And as far as Ahmet being forced to retire, well, that would be a godsend as far as I'm concerned. Ahmet's too old for this game you two play, and that's one of the reasons his wrinkles are getting deeper and deeper. And his neck? Don't get me started on that, please."

"Please don't talk about going to the press, Ernna. You'll get us all into serious trouble, especially yourself, and maybe even jeopardize the security of our country. And please speak more quietly, or the police will show up and arrest you for disturbing the peace. You're causing such a ruckus. It's embarrassing, and you're making a fool of yourself as well."

"Brother, if something happens to Ahmet, I will make a serious fool of myself and you too and whoever the hell you work for. I'll be on every talk show that'll have me, TV, radio, and the Internet of course. I may even start my own blog and call it 'Ernna's Misery.' I don't give a damn about you, me, or this wretched country of ours. This country will suck the life out of you, if you let it. Right now, half pension sounds pretty good to me. We'd get by, start new careers, open a book store, maybe go back to university, teach who knows what. At least we'd be together. We'd be poor, but we'd get by, my brother. Yes, we'd get by."

"Well, I suppose if you just want to get by, but your husband doesn't just want to get by. He wants a full, fun-filled life for the both of you after he retires, not a bookstore. Of that I'm sure."

With those words from her brother, she fell to her knees sobbing, nearly hysterical. All she could say was "God, how I hate this country," again and again.

Mamet looked on, hoping she'd run out of steam, but she carried on yelling, pleading, threatening, and wanting information about her husband. Her tirade went on for another five minutes.

"Well, you say you've spoken to him. Let me speak to him so I know he's okay. In the past you've lied to me, so maybe you're lying again. Maybe you're a habitual liar who won't ever tell the truth because of your job, or maybe you just enjoy tormenting me, your sister."

"Ernna, I can't let you speak to Ahmet. I would get into very serious trouble, maybe be demoted, and I'm very sure you would upset Ahmet and prevent him from successfully finishing up our little job, which hopefully will be finished in a couple of days, one way or another."

Mamet remembered Ernna as a child, a young adult, and now, the present. *She's such a moo; she's always been a cow and always will be. I feel so sorry for Ahmet having to put up with her and all her drama—a real drama queen. Ahmet should have left her years ago. She's just not cut out to be the spouse of a government operative, can't take the separation or the not knowing, but she does like the money, and can she spend.*

Ernna, without any help from her brother, picked herself up off the floor, worked at regaining her composure, and, like a drunken sailor, staggered forward for one final face-off with her brother, who she was beginning to loath.

"You just don't understand. You're so shallow, Mamet. Water off a duck's back. Nothing bothers you. You don't brood or sulk or even get lonely. You have no real friends, just acquaintances. Nobody can hurt you; your shields are always up and locked in place. If they told you Ahmet were dead, there would be little pain and no tears. Within fifteen minutes you'd be trying to figure out who might be your next partner. My dear brother, one day you'll wake up and realize you're all alone—even that cow Ernna will have washed her hands of you. Now, my brother, take me to our mother's house, please."

"Yes, of course, but I'm not going in to see her. She's lost touch with reality since our father died many years ago, and she's getting worse. She's got tons of newspapers in every room. I can't figure her out. If Social Services come by, she threatens them with a butcher knife, so they go away, but they'll return if she becomes dangerous or the house smells too bad. Okay, let's go."

"Oh, I see you have a different car, my dear brother. Of course a Mercedes and a red one, leather seats. Ah, yes, it's a convertible too. I guess your girlfriends like the color, and it does smell new, brand new, and I bet it has all the bells and whistles and like the adverts say can go from zero to sixty in five seconds, or is it six seconds?"

"You know, Mamet, you're afraid to get involved. Our mother is not crazy but does have a few strange habits, and her hygiene is excellent. I see her at least once a week, and we have nice chats. We talk about our father, growing up, growing old, a lot of nice things, and she very much enjoys talking about Ahmet; she quite admires him, you know. Mamet, I'm sure you're a very brave man, would probably die for your country, but when it comes to your family, you're a coward. Mother would love to have a chat with you now and again but knows you're uncomfortable around her, so she doesn't push it. At least try to give her a ring now and again. Here's her house. Not such a long drive, and the yard is reasonably well maintained. I'll take a cab home, and let me know if you hear anything about Ahmet, good or bad. Don't worry, I won't fall to pieces in public and embarrass you and your cronies, and if Ahmet is dead, I won't go public, no fear. I'll be as quiet as a well-fed lamb—wouldn't want to embarrass you or our beloved country."

Mamet slowly and silently drove off. He didn't want to alert his mother to his presence. All he could think of was Ahmet, Ahmet, Saint Ahmet. *Everyone loves Ahmet, even my own mother.*

If Ahmet can't somehow recover that cylinder and make the exchange with Roger, he'll be more of a devil than a saint to our management, and there will be a price to pay. Ahmet will have to pick up the tab.

* * *

Ernna proceeds up the gravelly footpath to the front door. Without knocking, she enters her mother's house. The door's always unlocked, night and day. She smells for any distasteful or unpleasant odors; there's none.

"Mother, Mother, it's Ernna. How are you?"

Mother is seated in the living room having a cup of tea, black with plenty of sugar. She's surrounded by newspapers, all in neat, five-foot-high piles, not a paper out of place. Ernna ignores them or at least tries to; she's seen the accumulation grow month by month, year by year.

"I have some sad news, Mother, Ahmet may be in trouble or hurt or God knows what. I'm so very worried. I can do nothing. They tell me nothing, only that he will be delayed. Mamet also tells me nothing, and I'm his sister. I love Mamet, but he's no help whatsoever, and I'm sure one day I will kill my dear brother. Maybe you can have a word with him, see if you can learn anything."

Ernna's mother is approaching seventy, but eighty would have been more believable. She's lean and frail, with hands so gnarled one could easily believe she scrubbed floors for fifty years. She hardly ever leaves the house and always sits in that same old white rocker wearing that same old drab black cotton dress. Her long gray hair, while regularly washed, appears never to be combed, there's never a hair in place. Her face is sad and drooping—droopy eyes, droopy cheeks, droopy chin. It's almost as if she has no neck, just a series of cascading folds of skin from her chin to God knows where. Sadly, the droopiness is not countered by bright, sparkling blue eyes; her hoary eyes are gray, dull gray. They haven't sparkled in decades and are more concerned with what they saw then what they might see.

"Ernna, what can I learn from Mamet? He seldom talks to me on the phone, and I haven't seen him in months. What do you wish to know? What do you wish me to ask my son?"

"Everything, anything, and what does Ahmet do, and when will he return home? It would be a comfort to me if I knew just a little of what he does. Do you understand?"

"First things first, Ernna. I see you staring at the newspapers again. Do you understand about the newspapers, why I collect them? Do you want to understand? I may have told you this already. Well, I'll tell you again, but I can see by the look on your face you'll fail to listen, fail to understand. I started to collect them the day your father passed, many years ago, and will continue to collect them till the day I die, at which time they will all be hauled off to the dump. I only read the headlines on the front page, and why do I do this silly thing? And it is silly to most outsiders. Even your brother thinks I'm weird, maybe even a bit senile, but believe me I do not hear voices; no one tells your mother what to do. Anyway, every day I get the paper. I read the headlines and add it to a stack. Then I brew a nice hot cup of black tea and sit and try to think of a special, joyful time me and your Father had together that somehow might relate to the day's headlines. Like if there was a headline about unemployment, I might think of the fun times we had in our youth when we were both without jobs and living on the dole, or if the headlines concern bad weather, I might think of the time our roof caved in because of a severe storm and we just laughed, opened a bottle of red wine, and relaxed till help arrived. For another example, suppose the headlines focused on a recent crime spree by an unknown assailant. I would think of the time I was mugged, strangled, and nearly murdered. Your Father was so understanding of my fears and so very gentle and so sweet to me. This silliness of mine usually takes about fifteen minutes of quiet time, but after reflecting back in time, I feel refreshed, ready to face another long, dreary day—and they are long and lonesome and dreary when you're old and alone. Well-intentioned young people come round every now and again, try to get me into a club or maybe go out and play bingo with them. Occasionally a group of older people stop by—out for a walk, I suppose. They just want to talk, lend an unasked-for helping hand, but I think they're just hoping for that extra special bowel movement, kind of like a reward for being kind to me, but if the truth be known they're just waiting for God. They have no future, no life. Like me their past is their future; that's why they keep reflecting on what happened, not what might happen. I don't need these people, young or old, so I act crazy now and again. They usually leave me alone, but there's always that extra-special do-gooder I have to chase off my property with a butcher knife. Look, it's a rubber knife."

She pokes herself in the leg to prove it's harmless.

Ernna's heard this story before but patiently listens till the old lady finishes, sighs, temporarily closes her eyes, and slowly rocks.

"Now, Ernna, let me tell you something about your Ahmet and what he does, and not a word to anyone. I've never told you this before and will not again, and no questions because this is all I truly know. Understand?"

Ernna nods, an exasperated quarter-nod. Ernna's nod is kind of like she's rolling her eyes, but she's using her head to ridicule her mother, not her eyes. She wonders what kind of nonsense her crazy mother is going to come up with today.

"Ahmet is an intelligence officer for our beloved country. He collects information about the enemies of our country and the harm they are trying to inflict on us, and hopefully he and his colleagues can use that intelligence to fend off attacks and save lives. It's a very dangerous job, and apparently he's very good at what he does. That's just supposition on my part. Now, what he does on a daily basis, I haven't a clue. You may ask me how I know these things. Well, many years ago, your Father and me had a party; we'd just moved into this lovely house and felt like celebrating with the neighbors. You and Ahmet were invited, of course; again, your brother failed to show up, too busy dallying with agreeable females. Well, your darling husband had too much to drink, and I think you two had just had a terrible row about his job and what he does. He needed to confide in someone, so he chose me and your Father. I think we were not completely surprised; he was always so very coy about what he did. Anyway, he made us promise not to tell a soul, and up to now I have kept that promise, but times have changed and so have you, and Ahmet may be in some sort of jam, so it's good you understand that his job is not just an ordinary job, and you must appreciate the risks he takes for us all."

"Of course, Mama, but why wouldn't he tell me? After all, I am his wife, and I suppose this means my dear brother is also an intelligence officer or, in the vernacular, a spy?"

"I have no idea what your brother does or doesn't do. I think Ahmet feels you're too emotional for him to confide in you, too unpredictable. He wouldn't want you to get yourself into trouble by speaking too freely. You know he's right; of course, you are a very emotional girl. Now, my daughter, you must try to be more understanding, less smothering. Try not to love him too much, and try not to worry yourself into an early grave, but more importantly develop interests that will keep your mind occupied and not be overly preoccupied with Ahmet. Speak to him calmly about your concerns. Explain to him that you don't like the present situation and want change. He's been on the front lines for well over twenty years. Maybe he does need a change and just refuses to admit it to himself. Maybe he'd like some soft job in some embassy somewhere, but for now, be patient and see what the future brings."

Mother is over the top, so supportive of Ahmet and so very unsupportive of her own daughter. I must get going before I explode; she's as mad as a hatter. Ahmet will never retire to any cushy position anywhere. He just loves tormenting me, and I'm sure lays awake at night trying to figure out how to make me more despondent. I will die in torment, but no use taking out my frustrations on my loony, never-throw-a-newspaper-away mother. I've never heard so much crap in all my life—may God forgive me for being so disrespectful to the woman who gave me life—and even if what she says is true, he'll never change, and if he loves his job more than me, then to hell with him.

"I will, Mother. I must be going. Say a prayer for Ahmet. I have given up praying years ago. God's never home to listen, and if he hears, he chooses not to respond. Maybe God is also an intelligence officer, too preoccupied for his family."

"Don't blaspheme, my daughter. Prayers have helped me get through the drudgery of daily struggles; prayers can isolate you from the horrors of the real world and from the horrors of self-inflicted wounds. Prayers help you float from day to day with less pain and less anguish. Prayers are like armor that protects us, but we only have armor. We have no swords or spears to fend off the demons, to attack them, to retaliate and gain peace of mind and everlasting salvation. Alas, one day these demons may win out and devour us all, and one day the darkness may extinguish the light and all will be lost, but I have hope that this will never happen, and this is why I pray."

"Good-bye, Mother, and may God be with you and forgive us all for our transgressions and forgive me, an unbeliever."

The door silently closes behind Ernna. In less than a minute she has a cab on the way to pick her up. A small group of well-dressed, stern-faced neighbors is heading for her mother's front door. *Do-gooders. Why won't they just leave the old fool alone, let her die alongside her newspapers? If I were in her place, I'd use a real butcher knife to get rid of one or two of those good-for-nothing do-gooders, and to hell with the rest. Mother and her demons—if there are demons and they're looking for someone to devour, let them eat the old fools first, and let Mother be at the top of the menu.*

CHAPTER 7

As usual, the weather's cold, damp, and unpredictable. By noon, if the fog clears and the sun comes out, it might just be pleasant enough for a lunchtime stroll through Hyde Park, but one had better bundle up and wear one's Wellingtons or be sufficiently alert to dodge the leftover puddles from yesterday's downpour. London weather, even in early winter, can be miserable. Daylight hours won't exceed nine, the sun won't rise until half eight, and the bitterly cold wind can knock the unwary off their feet and send them crashing to the ground. Finally, most of the offices in the City, especially government offices, will be bloody cold in the morning and take at least an hour to warm up enough for winter apparel to be removed and stowed. Then MI-9 agents can log in, check their e-mail accounts and calendars, and either finish up unfinished business at the office or return to the streets of London to investigate rumors, question contacts, and, as time permits, do a quick check of the latest gossip with the local bobby over a cuppa.

Jason had been lucky enough to catch a cab just outside his flat in Chelsea, and the cab is now drawing up to his office just across the street from Hyde Park. His office is housed in the old Columbia Club, which in its heyday served American servicemen and women in the capacity of a hotel of sorts—no food served and no room service, just a bed, clean sheets, and a loo. Of late, it has been remodeled and several high-tech offices now occupy three floors where approximately thirty civil servants work nine-to-five shifts seven days a week. These are the offices of MI-9—not field offices, but offices that house the entire cadre of this little-known counterterrorist organization that has broad powers to investigate suspected, planned, or actual acts of terror that have occurred or might occur in London and only London. The rest of the UK is the responsibility of local police constabularies, with help, when required, from MI-5 and MI-6.

MI-9's charter, as written and subsequently blessed by Parliament, further calls for its operatives to ensure that Her Majesty's citizens residing in London come to no physical or emotional harm when being questioned by MI-5 or MI-6. And while it is never said or written, the implication is that while information is crucial in the fight against terror, civil rights must not be abandoned and roughing up Londoners, especially people of color, who are a vital resource to MI-9, will not be tolerated. The head of MI-9 regularly reminds her agents in e-mail after e-mail not to bully, intimidate, coerce, or ever lay a finger on anyone under suspicion unless verbal "persuasion" fails and physical force is absolutely necessary, and then only the minimum required force is to be used. These are the ground rules her people will work by, and what the agents of the more illustrious MI-5 and MI-6 do are of no concern of hers unless credible and verifiable proof of misconduct is forthcoming, in which case an investigation will take place. If there is sufficient evidence that agents of other intelligence organizations are not playing by Her Majesty's rules, she'll have a good chin-wag with her counterparts and get things sorted out in a hurry, her way.

Jason pays the cabbie, unlocks the front door, enters, and immediately pushes the antiquated thermostat up to a more-than-comfortable twenty-six degrees Celsius. Even though the interior of the Columbia Club has recently been renovated, the pipes or guts of the building, as everyone likes to call them, were left as they were when the building was initially constructed—thus the infrequent, though quite noticeable, clunking and clanking as hot steam surges through cold pipes. By not replacing the guts of the Columbia Club, twenty thousand pounds was saved. This meager saving was looked on as MI-9's contribution to cost cutting as well as lowering the national debt, though additional fuel consumption, due to inefficient plumbing, more than offset the onetime cost saving of twenty thousand. Jason's always first in—not that he's overly keen, but he's a poor sleeper, so rather than lie in bed thinking and playing "what if" mind games, he comes to work with the idea of being first in and first out, a cause and effect relationship that seldom plays out. As Jason is senior and Chief Pettigrew's right-hand man, he's the last to review finalized data analysis sheets and interrogation reports before they go to Ms. Pettigrew for sign-off. If any report is found to be unsatisfactory, it'll be returned to Jason by Chief Pettigrew, accompanied by a blistering handwritten critique, usually in pencil. A blistering critique means that Jason didn't properly do his job or perhaps did a rush job, so rather than do a rush job, Jason is usually third last to leave. Second last to leave is Susan, Ms. Pettigrew's girl Friday. While Susan's birth certificate clearly says her Christian name is Sue, she prefers Susan, thinking it more posh. Before heading home for the day, Susan dons her bright green Wellingtons and the rest of her winter kit and then scours all three floors of the Columbia Club looking for open safes, open blinds, unstowed classified, phones off the hook, lights left on, electric kettles not unplugged, chairs not grounded to their desk, and any other breach of security or safety. Any discrepancies noted will be righted. Susan will then discuss each discrepancy, no matter how slight, with her boss. The following morning an e-mail is prepared and sent outlining the offence and suggesting remedial actions by the offender; these e-mails are known as Susan's nasty grams. Because of Susan's good looks and effervescent personality, several of the younger lads have intentionally contrived to violate closing-up procedures so as to get a nasty gram and then try to use it as an opening gambit for some sort of rendezvous, which to date has never occurred. Ms. Pettigrew is always last out, and her last chore is to push the thermostat down to an uncomfortable twenty-one degrees prior to locking up and proceeding to her chaffered limousine, which will take her to her comfortable Mayfair flat by one route or another, but never the same route two days in succession.

A pair of highly polished wooden staircases to the left and right of the front door make their way to the second and third levels of the Columbia Club; there are no lifts. All floors on all three levels are of solid oak, highly polished and highly buffed, so highly buffed that the glare from the summer noonday sun, as it passes from one overhead window to another, may impair one's vision for a second or two if stared at too long. The second and third floors contain one office after another, like rooms in a hotel, a rather low-class hotel; each room has four identical desks, and each desk is equipped with a workstation, a secure phone, an insecure phone, and several drawers where personal property and unclassified hard copy can be stored. Classified hard copy is stored in the vault—second floor, west wing. The vault also contains a bank of servers; anything virtual is stored on these servers, and generally speaking all virtual information is shareable. In addition to these local servers designed primarily for MI-9 use, there is a second bank of servers that MI-9 accesses at MI-5 off-site facilities. The servers at MI-5 are primarily used for interagency secure e-mail, sundry Oracle databases that MI-9 plugs into, and various calendars for meeting coordination.

If one moves to the exterior of the Columbia Club, one sees a featureless building not more than thirty feet from Bayswater Road, nondescript in every sense of the word—one three-story gray building among many three-story gray buildings—and this was the reason the run-down Columbia Club was chosen to be the home of MI-9. It is unabashedly plain, not invisible but easy to look at and not see and easy to forget. After all, keeping a low profile is what being a secure facility is all about.

As senior agent, Jason's office is on the ground level, straight ahead, first office on the left. Jason likes this arrangement but for one thing: first office to the right is the office of Chief Pettigrew. The crack of her heels on the wood floor announces her pending arrival seconds before her rather pointed, ample bosom arrives, followed milliseconds later by the rest of her. Ms. Pettigrew is a matronly spinster, fiftyish, five foot two, eleven stone, with short, graying hair and off-white eyeglasses that hang on her rather pointed nose and small ears; a lanyard keeps her from ever misplacing her much-needed glasses. Her large, round eyes are royal blue with ample eyelashes and more than sufficient eyebrows. With the exception of lipstick, almost imperceptible, she wears no makeup, not even nail varnish. She always dresses in trouser suits, a knit blouse, high heels, and a cardigan. Each day it is a different color cardigan: Monday is sail white, Tuesday is emerald green; Wednesday is electric blue; Thursday is ebony; and Friday, her favorite day of the week, is bright red. She adores red.

Chief Pettigrew feels the cold more than most, perhaps due to her age or perhaps due to a mild case of pernicious anemia, and if it's one thing she doesn't like, it's being cold—hence the cardigans and the extra office heater surreptitiously planted by Susan under her rather large, sumptuous, mahogany desk. Together, the cardigan and hidden heater work at keeping the chief toasty warm. On the jacket of her suit, adjacent to the first top button, right side, is a cameo, a cameo she always wears regardless. Most wonder if there is some significance to the cameo— maybe a personal loss or lost love or just a family heirloom—but no one dare ask out of respect or, better yet, out of fear, fear of a chief who's not shy about exercising her authority on a whim or calculated with premeditated malice. Some might even say she can be vindictive, but she, in return, might say, "If you mess with me, watch out."

The one thing that sets Ms. Pettigrew apart from her contemporaries is her intellect—plenty of gray matter and brainpower harnessed and focused on safeguarding the nation of Wellington and Churchill. Back in the day she was an undercover operative stationed in Berlin and was among the first few to predict the downfall of the Berlin Wall and the subsequent implosion of the Soviet Union. At that time she worked for MI-5. Years later, because of her continued successes in the field, she was handpicked by the prime minister to organize and run MI-9. As chief of MI-9 she is responsible for the safety and security of the City, London, and there she'll remain till retirement, which is always just round the corner; which corner is still unclear and anybody's guess, especially hers.

Jason shares his office with Aubrey, a rotund six and a half–footer with a penchant for expensive clothing, especially suits and especially deluxe shoes, of which he probably has dozens of pairs, all leather uppers and leather lowers. If Aubrey ever sees the words 'man-made' in lieu of leather on a pair of shoes, anywhere, they are immediately rejected without ever a second look. Aubrey's face is round and full, with jet-black hair so long he's constantly combing it, to the great agitation of Jason, who believes combing one's hair in public is rude and ill-mannered, kind of like chewing gum or endlessly sniffing one's nose instead of blowing it. Small, piggy-like eyes are dwarfed by a rather large nose that sits atop a fairly large mouth with lips that might be considered nonexistent. Aubrey's mustache is so thin that, in the right light or wrong light as the case may be, one might assume he has no moustache at all. Aubrey's face is a cacophony of contrasts: small eyes, big face; large nose, scissor-like lips; large mouth, thin moustache. These relationships perfectly describes Aubrey, a man who stands for nothing, or to put it another way, stands for everything: Labor today, Tory tomorrow; devout today, atheist tomorrow; harmony today, discord tomorrow; and on and on. Aubrey just wants to zip through life with minimum effort and minimum grief, to go with the flow, and hopefully, in the process, keep everybody happy and off his back. The one thing Aubrey will not compromise on is going out of his way to impress lovely, young women—ladies or not, eligible or not, clever or not. The only prerequisite is that they must be lovely.

To describe Aubrey without describing his hands would be like describing Superman and failing to mention the fact that he can fly. Aubrey has large hands, hands so large that the word *huge* might be most appropriate; his hands are the hands of an eight footer, the hands of a giant, hands so powerful that one can crack open something as small as a walnut or split open something as large as a melon. At infrequent times Aubrey's hands take on a life of their own, and if annoyed and they subsequently close around someone's throat, the slightest pressure will snap necks like dried kindling. To date no necks have been snapped, but several have been intimidated.

Aubrey can never find gloves in all of London that properly fit, so to fend off the cold he wears black woolen mittens that his mum knits. There are never, ever any office jokes about his black mittens or his mum, and while mittens do make driving a bit more challenging, they more than make up for that minor inconvenience by keeping Aubrey's hands comfortably warm, for if the truth be known, the hands that can break mechanisms designed to improve one's grip can't bear the cold. Chilly hands result in clumsy, tingly fingers that can't insert coins into parking meters and white knuckles that must be soaked in tepid water to restore circulation. Finally, Aubrey never wears jewelry of any kind. Watches, rings, necklaces, nothing made of metal or plastic ever comes within spitting distance of his body. His wife moans about him not wearing his wedding ring. His explanation to her is that a man in his position doing what he does can never wear jewelry for fear that jewelry can be traced back to the owner and might be the cause of him being injured or worse. Jewelry, he explains in all sincerity to his gullible wife, "is like fingerprints. Fingerprints don't change, and a man's jewelry doesn't change either." He usually ends his little lecture to his wife by asking her if she wants him hurt over a wedding band, and how does a woman answer a question like that?

On occasions, usually after a couple of drinks at his local, Aubrey laughingly pokes fun at his wife's naïveté for believing his lame explanation for not wearing his wedding ring, but when the barman asks him why he dislikes wearing all jewelry, Aubrey feigns hearing loss and hastily changes the subject, for not wearing any jewelry is his excuse for not wearing his wedding ring. Aubrey can't be bothered explaining the obvious to the oblivious, as too much explaining mangles the story.

Jason knows that Aubrey's explanation to his wife is a load of codswallop. Aubrey doesn't wear jewelry because he fancies himself a ladies' man and wants to appear to be single and available. Jason also knows Aubrey, no matter how hard he might try, couldn't score in a brothel. He'd be too busy preening and boasting about his unparalleled shoe collection and his latest acquisitions from Bond Street. Most working girls and potential "dates," as Aubrey might describe them, would figure that he's just window-shopping, not wanting to be separated from his brass, and they'd leave looking for others who are prepared to have fun, drink, and most importantly spend. To Aubrey's credit he's persistent, keeps trying, especially at the office, which he describes as his hunting grounds but to no one but himself.

Jason sussed Aubrey out from day one. *When it comes to women, he's a real tosser, and that will never change unless Aubrey has a complete makeover, an epiphany, and learns to relate to women as individuals with minds of their own, stops trying to impress by being disingenuous, and stops trying to use his employment credentials as some kind of magic skeleton key to the hearts and loins of every attractive female he meets, on the job or no.*

Jason outranks Aubrey by minutes—yes, minutes. They both went through the same training, graduated on the same day, and were MI-9's first two agents, but Jason's surname comes alphabetically in front of Aubrey's, so Jason is most senior and team lead. This really riles Aubrey, since his academics and overall fitness are far superior. Being team lead has its perks: a desk near the window and nearby radiator, and, most importantly, whenever there's a meeting or briefing with the chief, Jason gets the nod while Aubrey sulks in the office, usually occupying Jason's chair with a view of a footpath and one nondescript bed-and-breakfast after another.

However, all things considered, the pair gets along rather well, and if it weren't for Aubrey's habit of avoiding nouns and overusing pronouns, Jason might even have considered him to be a mate. Aubrey frequently, but not always, starts a sentence with a pronoun or, if he wants to be very, very annoying, an indefinite article like *an* or *some*. He'll continues substituting pronouns in place of nouns at such an alarming rate that within ten seconds Jason's lost or mostly lost, has no clue what Aubrey's talking about or where he's going or how long it'll take him to get where he's going, wherever that might be. His written reports, while usually accurate and to the point, are phrased the same as his speech patterns, and when Jason finally figures out what Aubrey means, he'll proceed to edit Aubrey's written words with a sprinkling of nouns, proper and otherwise. Fortunately, Aubrey doesn't mind minor tweaks to his verbiage, which, aside from murdering nouns, is analytically insightful—a very big plus when intelligence data needs to be sliced and diced for meaning and sliced and diced again, down to the molecular level, for extrapolation and decision making.

Today Aubrey's running a bit late—too much claret the night before. His wife had organized a dinner party for some friends she wanted to impress, and how better to impress them than to parade Aubrey out in his finest attire, and, of course, she'd drop a casual word or two about her husband being in the employ of one of those famous MI organizations. She left it at MI because MI-9 would not do—too small and much too obscure. Aubrey's wife had hoped that this dinner party would be the ticket for her and her pompous husband to be added to the guest lists of those in attendance. To Aubrey's relief her little charade worked and he could relax and not be told he hadn't tried hard enough or why couldn't he be a bit more outgoing, a bit friendlier, a bit chattier—to which Aubrey could have had no response, as he really didn't care to be added to anyone's social calendar. If it weren't for his hounding, social-climbing wife, he'd have been at his local hours ago on, at a minimum, his fourth gin and tonic instead of amusing the neighbors.

Anyway, after they've gone, I can relax and enjoy some of that, but she abhors sport, any sort, and she won't stop nattering. So if I'm to enjoy it, she'll have to turn in as soon as the door closes behind them.

Both visiting couples, when saying good night, assured his wife that they would soon be invited for drinks and canapés.

She beamed while Aubrey thought, *Goody, goody.*

The front door gently closed, and they were alone.

"Before you turn in, please get me a top-up. It's exquisite."

"Yes, the claret is rather delightful—kind of on the dry side, usually from Bordeaux, in the south of France. Cost thirty pounds a bottle not including VAT."

Aubrey rolled his eyes, thinking, *She definitely looked that up. She knows squat about it and couldn't find that place with one of them and a map, and I'm surprised she didn't tell me it's red. She's always trying to impress, even me. Why can't she just relax and enjoy?*

"Sure thing, dear. It's on its way, but I want to watch a bit of telly with you—you know, kind of snuggle up. It's been a lovely evening, and I believe we were quite popular. I'll clear the mess up tomorrow when you're at work catching bad guys."

"Some other time, dear. Not now. Actually, I have a bit of work to wrap up. You know it's official, and I can't even think about removing it from there till you leave. You understand, I'm sure, so be a pet and just run along."

He'd almost said bugger off rather than run along, but that would have bordered on being cruel, and while Aubrey wasn't normally mean-spirited, last evening he'd felt a bit churlish, a feeling he'd attributed to too much claret and too many people getting up close and personal and wanting to be his friend.

As she headed upstairs he can hear her chuntering, "I'll put a flea in that Jason's ear when I see him; I will do that indeed. He demands too much from my Aubrey."

Actually, Aubrey's briefcase was nearly empty, just a few crosswords and a how-to book on building birdhouses. Aubrey would never bring official papers or official magnetic media home—or for that matter build a birdhouse—even if he wanted to, not in a thousand years, but his wife was at him to do just that, and this how-to manual was his cover, as if to say, "See? I've been reading up on it, so give me some time, please. I'll need to buy one, not too powerful, a jig saw, and I don't have the brass just yet, so just be a bit patient. It's months till spring, and we won't ever see any unless that tom of theirs gets run over—he kills them just for fun as soon as they touch down."

With that Aubrey grabbed the remote, found BBC-2, figured out what the score was, and fell asleep.

It's half nine when Aubrey finally arrives at the Columbia Club, also by cab, as there are no parking within walking distance and only one pay and park for thirty quid a day, which equates to about six hundred a month, which equates to a minor spend up on Bond Street, where ties go for fifty guineas and shoes can go for a month's parking. As he opens the front door, he's hit by a rush of cold air. Aubrey, like Jason can't stand being cold or even a bit chilly; it causes him to add layers then he overheats, perspires, and become so tired that he has to head for the loo for a snooze in the farthest stall—up to thirty minutes of pretending. He immediately pushes the thermostat up, something he will later deny to Jason as well as Ms. Pettigrew. As he enters his office he's greeted, as he's always greeted, by those two most annoying words.

"Hello, mate. Running a bit late today, are you? How'd your do go last night?"

"Oh, hello. How are you? I see she's not in yet, so I'll have a quick read if it's okay with you, and as regards your question, it was more than a disaster—it was boring, down to the last slurp and last swallow. Everyone else had a wonderful time, and now we're on another one. When will it stop? Pretty soon we'll be booked solid for weeks on end, and all I want to do is visit my local or watch it and occasionally drink too much and fall asleep on whatever, but she loves those kinds of things. She's such a people person. It gives me the heaves, to be quite honest. I just don't like most of them, if the truth be known."

"Sure, knock yourself out. Have a quick read of whatever you like."

He's at it again, thought Jason. *As soon as he walks through that door, he starts talking gibberish, one pronoun after another. What's bloody awful? What 'she' is not in, and he'll read what? And why ask my permission? It's going to be a slow day, so he can walk in front of a red, double-decker bus for all I care. I'll not give him the benefit of asking for clarification. I'm pretty damn sure he does this just to get on my nerves, but maybe not. Just can't figure him out.*

Jason swings his chair one-eighty and gazes out the window, almost forlornly. *My life's slowly ebbing away. Just one big case, and maybe I can transfer back to MI-5 or even MI-6, get some recognition, maybe even a promotion. God only knows I can use the extra money. Now I seem to be doomed to spend my final days with this aging lothario and his misguided use of the English language. Perhaps if I were a better sleeper I'd be a bit more tolerant, but he's got to be the most annoying chap in the City.*

But Aubrey doesn't do anything to intentionally annoy anyone; his mind just works that way. Like a chess player he's always two or three conversations into the future, anticipating the give and take of a normal conversation. Pronouns substitute for nouns as a way of minimizing repetition, as a way of helping him multiplex several successive sentences into meaningful—well, almost meaningful—sentences, and if that means only he knew what he's talking about, then so be it. When he was a child, every effort was made to encourage him to use nouns and to speak in complete and meaningful sentences, but all efforts failed. His friends and family, when confused as to what he intended to say, would gently ask for clarification, which he eagerly provided, mostly always avoiding proper nouns and much of the time avoiding common nouns. He rather enjoyed this added attention, something he seldom got as a precocious, overweight child. At school he was bullied by most, but around puberty he and his hands grew to such a size that Aubrey terrorized just about anyone he wanted to. He never lived to regret the hidings he regularly handed out to those sloths that had for years humiliated him, boxed his ears, and sent him on meaningless errands like fetching a pocketful of smoke and bringing it back without losing an atom. Talk about a lose-lose situation; his pockets were always empty, and if he refused the errand, he'd usually be tormented for the remainder of the day.

Aubrey is a senior intelligence analyst, grade 15. Aubrey excels at what he does, and what he does justifies his fifty thousand a year. He's got a keen, analytical mind almost as methodical as the chief's but not quite. It might be a stretch to say his investigative skills are unparalleled or Sherlockian, but the skills he picked up as a Manchester copper are certainly formidable, earning him the nickname Bulldog, a nickname Jason is aware of but never uses. In fact, no one except his wife uses it, much to the annoyance of Aubrey. His wife, on the other hand, will use it when she's trying to be coy or romantic, and it's at these times that Aubrey, under any pretense, dashes off to his local, which fortunately is within walking distance, because "bulldog nights," as he calls them to his mates, require five or six large gins at a minimum.

While on the streets of London tracking suspects or knitting elusive clues into evidence, Aubrey has a way of ingratiating himself to the public. He can be most charming and appears to really care, and maybe he really does. Therefore, most people like him, trust him, and readily share information with him; those intimidating hands of his, continuously in motion and aboveboard as if ready to pounce, are a plus. The scarcity of nouns seems to catch suspects off guard, making them less wary and more apt to intentionally or unintentionally cooperate. Misconstrued questions can and often do result in unexpected responses that not even Aubrey could have anticipated.

While Aubrey doesn't dislike Jason, he can't figure out what makes the old boy tick. Or is it that Jason is just too complex to categorize or figure out? To Aubrey, Jason's like a zombie; he infrequently smiles, is never overly animated or friendly, and is always profound and serious. But Aubrey knows he's good at his job, has a good rep. *There he sits, like he's one of them, gazing out, just waiting for recess so he can run out and pull pigtails. He's so insufferable—probably needs a bit of a giggle or a bit of something, something that'll loosen him up a bit. It's like he's just going through the motions, very sad indeed.*

Jason's short, very thin, balding, an untidy dresser with high cheekbones and a dimple right in the center of his chin. His Asian-like eyes seem to be looking over one's shoulder rather than straight at whoever he addresses, and he has big ears—not large but big. He's at least fifty, maybe more, and weighs in at exactly nine stone seven, a weight that hasn't changed in twenty years.

Aubrey's mumbling to himself as he logs in. "If only mine had begun with an *A* or *B* or *C*, I'd be team lead right now—not fair. I'm a lot younger, a lot brighter, and definitely better-looking than him. I will go places; he will vegetate until he either retires or dies, probably at his desk or gazing out. He's definitely not a self-starter or a go-getter. Like that Ol' Man River, he just keeps rolling along, heading out to God knows where."

Online, Aubrey continues scanning placement ads for intelligence-officer positions in London but finds nothing new, only the same old rubbish jobs he's passed up before: jobs at MI-5 or MI-6, jobs that no one else wants because they're desk jobs or jobs requiring excessive travel, especially to places where hotels are scarce and sleeping under the stars is common, even in subzero weather.

Anyway, thinking of a promotion here is a dead loss. In this one building is everyone, and most of these will be here forever, and I'm already fairly senior, so the only logical move for me is over there, back to where he came from, but I'm not even sure either of them will give me a good recommendation, especially that little bugger five feet away. Why is he always staring out, like he's waiting for something or someone?

The crack of heel against oak alerts the pair that Pettigrew's on the prowl. Jason quickly swings his chair about and begins to read the first available folder that presents itself; he hasn't even logged on yet, and it's after ten. Aubrey points his browser to the top of his history file and clicks; he'd mentally prepared himself for a cross-examination by the chief, or Her Majesty, as they like to call her.

She enters, smiling, though not a happy smile; it's a false facade that masks what she's really thinking, a Mona Lisa–type smile that's unfathomable even to professionals trained to decipher the obscure. As she enters, Aubrey vacates his chair, yielding it to his chief. She sits—no "thank you"—quite dignified, back erect, legs crossed at the ankles, hands folded in her lap. The chief is never ingratiating, pleasant, or cheerful. Being popular was an odd notion to the chief when so many tough decisions had to be made immediately after the London rail and bus bombings a few years ago. To date, there have been no more bombings, but if more should occur, her head would be on the block, and she knows it. Being popular is as important to her as being able to shear a sheep or change the oil in her motorcar. There's silence for at least a minute, which gives Aubrey time to size up his chief and her time to size up two of her most senior operatives.

Aubrey's eyes immediately shift to Her Majesty's shoes. The heels are of moderate height, and the rest of the shoe is a dull red, gilded in gold at the edges, with the toes cut away. Two toes cheekily peek out from each shoe.

Those are the most beautiful things, very expensive indeed. She's clueless when it comes to things like that. She's such a plebe. If only I'd been a bit more discriminating when we first met. My idea at that time was free sex for the rest of my life. I was such a buffoon. Nothing's free; one always pays one way or another, and usually through it. Talk about repenting at your leisure, but she's not such a bad egg. It's just that I was made for better things, and I'm sure she'd be happy married to any social climber on the planet who could put one over her head and pander to her endless idiosyncrasies like her unnatural fear of riding in one or her unexplainable fear of little ones. She can't bear being around them—always thinks they might fall and somehow break—and that's why from day one they were never an option.

I'll bet a single pair of her shoes cost more than his entire wardrobe—if you could call what he wears a wardrobe. It's more like a knickknack shelf, and why is it me, always me, leaning up against the bloody wall? It's always just assumed the most junior rises and gives up his chair when she comes in. What nonsense. Hope she doesn't adjust the arm rests again—takes me forever to get them properly reset.

Aubrey manages to internalize his whining. If he had his way, all would rise in his presence, even the Queen. Anyway, Aubrey is very conscious of his rank in MI-9 and knows when to rise and when to remain seated, and so does everyone else except Ms. Pettigrew—who never rises for anyone, much less lean against a wall—and when someone junior to Aubrey comes in, he or she leans against the wall or carries in a chair from down the hall. Chairs are never dragged, pulled, pushed, or rolled. They are carried; no one wants to mark, mar, or scuff the wooden floors.

Ms. Pettigrew turns to Jason as senior and with a smirk on her face quietly asks, "Well, boys, how's it going? Not rushed off your feet—I'm sure you're not, or are you?"

She knows things are slow and actually likes slow days, for slow days are usually peaceful days, but wants to see what kind of hokum they'll come up with today. If only they would just tell the truth; she figures Jason has been looking out the window, daydreaming, and Aubrey's been searching for that one dream job that will catapult him into a position he feels he dearly deserves, but the chief knows Aubrey's going nowhere; he's too valuable to pass on to those cretins at MI-5 or MI-6.

"Well, it's like this. I've been reviewing a few unsolved crime cases here in the City, cases that may end up being our responsibility some day. I got an in with the local chief inspector—routinely feeds me the latest intel and gossip over a drink or two."

"Of course, Jason, you know we're not crime fighters per se, but as lead if you feel this is appropriate, then proceed and good hunting. Oh, please be careful what you feed back to ..." She pauses; she'd almost said "him" but a chief inspector could be a "her"—not likely but still could be. "Yes, back to your friend, the chief inspector."

Jason nods and smiles ineffectually while Aubrey knows there's no way he can top that story. *Why does that prat always come out on top in these interviews with her?*

"And you, Aubrey, anything new?"

"Well, I've been online this morning studying up, you know."

"No, I don't know. I'm personally going no further in MI-9—as far as I can go already. No more examinations for this little duck. Next, I'd like to retire to a small seaside town and watch the tide roll in and roll out. I especially like high tide this time of year, watching visitors getting soaked by an unexpected large roller. But that's another story, and I won't bore you pair by asking for any details of what you say you've been doing. I see you, Jason, haven't even logged on, and it's just past ten o'clock, and I see you, Aubrey, are logged on, but I believe that's the online edition of *MI Today* you're looking at, and look at the pitch of those letters—must be a thirteen or even a fourteen. Are you having problems with your vision? Maybe you should get an eye examination. Anyway, I have some real work for you two. I've just got a signal in from our allies, the gallant Swiss. It seems a lady publican from Yorkshire recently had deposited into her Swiss bank account tens of thousands of pounds; the depositor cannot be identified. Now why would anyone deposit such a large sum of money into her account, and only a single transaction, yesterday? Any ideas, Jason, or perhaps we should get your friend the chief inspector to give us a hand?"

"No, not off the top of my head, but I thought it was against the law for that kind of information to be shared with anyone, even us."

"Only up to the first hundred thousand, Jason, and you should know that, but to add a little spice to the overall equation, this publican is married to an American-turned-Brit who recently retired from the CIA. Now do you have any ideas or theories, Aubrey? And, please, let's rule out the pools."

Aubrey, never at a loss for words but always fearful of saying the wrong thing or the right thing at the wrong time, jumps right in.

"Well, depending on what his position was there, maybe he got wind of something that he turned around and sold for a king's ransom. It may be worth us looking into that. You have anything else?"

"Yes, actually I do, from a source of mine at the American embassy, just up the road. She's an administrative assistant with access to Langley's personnel records. Our publican's husband, Al—no surname now necessary—recently retired as a senior polygrapher and currently resides in the UK. So I did a bit more checking and found out that he'd taken out British citizenship years ago, so if you should happen to meet him, he'll be treated with the utmost courtesy and respect and not like some cowboy. Please remember that. I then had some junior check his whereabouts after he retired—you know, travel records, police, hospitals, credit cards, cell phones, et cetera. And what do you think? He's recently traveled to the Spanish island of Ibiza, and shortly thereafter—bingo—tons of money shows up in his wife's Swiss bank account, and guess what? He's got another trip planned to Ibiza this coming Friday, and surprise, you two will be on the same flight, tailing him to see what's going on and who he hooks up with. The Spanish authorities will know nothing of our little operation—your true-name passports should get you onto the island safely, and if anyone asks, you're on holiday."

Jason and Aubrey smile in each other's direction, pleased at this unexpected turn of events—a real thriller, maybe. At least they can temporarily escape this dreary, inhospitable English winter and do some real work.

"Okay, boys, Susan's making all the arrangements. You know, tickets, charge cards, cash, hotel reservations, et cetera. She'll be in shortly, so make nice, Jason, and you, Aubrey, keep your eyes in your head. Don't stare. She's very pretty, as I'm sure you know. Some time ago I tried sending her back from whence she came, but no one would have her. I dread to think what that might mean. I'll send her over now."

The sound of the chief's heels against the rock-hard wooden floor ebb, followed by nothing but stillness till Susan just materializes, as if beamed in. With nary a greeting, she launches into the particulars of their upcoming travel.

"Okay, here's the scoop."

"Wow, hold on. Not so fast, you. I think I'll call you that from now on; it's far better. Yours is quite a common name. Now, that's unique, really. Okay?"

"Susan," Jason says, interceding, "what my colleague is trying to say is that he thinks Scoop might be a better name for you, though I personally think Susan to be superior to Scoop in every respect. After all, you're not a cub reporter out to get a scoop."

"Yes, sir, please call me Susan. Susan's my Christian name, and while I've been here for almost a year, I'm still on probation, but if I do well, I'll be made permanent, and I don't think Ms. Pettigrew would want her personal secretary called Scoop. Yes, I'm pretty sure of that."

"Please don't call us sir—makes us sound old, and there's only one of them in this room," responded Aubrey with a sly smile on his face.

Jason lets that jab go, thinking, *She's very pretty, not too young but young enough to still have a girlish figure and a lovely smile. Probably thinks I'm old. Well, I am, and at times I feel twice my age.*

Susan's demurely dressed, wearing flats that she changes into upon arrival each day. The flats are not quite sandals but not as formal as required by the MI-9 dress code. Jason had previously noticed this minor transgression and thought about having a friendly chat with her but over time ruled that out. If the chief didn't mind, why should he? Now Aubrey certainly wouldn't have missed that opportunity of chatting up Susan if he'd noticed, which apparently he did not. The rest of Susan's attire is ordinary, almost bland, almost surely from Marks and Spencer's rather than some boutique in Mayfair where only people like Aubrey can afford to shop.

Yes, she is lovely, thinks Jason, *about five seven, nine stone, great figure, and a face that can break hearts in the blink of an eye, and she's single.* But the one thing that strikes Jason most is her shoulder-length brown hair that frames her very attractive face, giving her an almost angelic look, a look of complete innocence and trust. When she smiles, the only thing missing is a picture frame.

Aubrey has also mentally sized Susan up again, finding her more than just attractive. *Have to try and score with her, be more forthright, but not today. Too many other things going on. Maybe when I return. I see she's still not wearing one. Anyway, focus. Not now. Don't let her be a distraction—time enough later on.*

Susan glances at one and then the other, wanting to make sure it's okay to carry on and not wanting to appear to take charge, but the chief did say to give them their itineraries, no chitchat and straight back to her office. That's her plan, and that's what she does. Within fifteen minutes she's out the door thinking Aubrey a flirt and Jason moody, almost unfriendly, opinions she'd previously formed.

"Okay, Aubrey, we leave the day after tomorrow, early flight, Heathrow. Our man will be on the same flight."

"There's a brief résumé in my packet but no photo. He's in his early fifties, white, and—hold on, he's a hunchback. So even the pair of us should be able to find and follow a hunchback. Not many of those huffing about these days. We'll discuss our plans tomorrow, but I'm thinking I tail him off the plane, and then you tail me to make sure I'm not being followed. We're all in the same hotel, but we must never lose sight of him or not know where he's at, and we'll see what develops. What do you think?"

"You're the boss, boss. She really is lovely. Anyway, I think I'll leave early. I've got some to burn up, and not much going on. See ya."

Jason knows Aubrey; he knows he'd pop across the hall and try to score a few brownie points with Susan, but the chief will soon get wind of his intentions and give him the heave ho. Jason spins his chair and looks out the back window. He blankly stares, thinking of nothing, just staring, unblinking, a single tear rolling down his left cheek.

The office is as peaceful as a tomb. Nothing stirs, even the invasive humming of the electronics morphs into silence. And there she is, Clara, his wife, walking toward him, smiling, not too far off, waving. Jason knows if he moves a millimeter she'll be gone. He must extend this moment for as long as possible and then relive these seconds over and over when he desperately fights to sleep the good sleep and desperately fights to replace the lifeless Clara with this vibrant, smiling young woman. Clara died on a bus in the City returning to their flat after work; she died at the hands of terrorist thugs out to make a point. What point? Jason still can't answer that question. At the morgue he insisted on seeing her one final time. The mortician had discouraged him, but he'd been adamant. All but her face was shrouded. The lower left side of her face was missing, as was part of her skull, and all her lovely long hair gone, burnt off by the blast. He dreaded to think what the rest of her looked like. After five minutes of utter silence, they'd led Jason away, but her face would haunt not soothe him for an eternity. They said she died instantaneously, but Jason doubted that; he'd heard that tale before, and the tale was that the victim died with no pain, no suffering and death had occurred immediately.

Maybe, maybe not, thought Jason. But not every lifeless victim dies with little pain and little suffering, and he prayed to any god who would listen, and his prayer was that Clara had not suffered from either fear or pain.

Clara's death happened before Aubrey and MI-9. He had been an information technology officer at MI-5, with no fieldwork experience, but when he heard about the formation of MI-9 in the wake of the blasts that shook a nation, he enlisted and trained to be a field agent. His motives were pure and honorable, almost noble, but nothing could bring Clara back. Anyway, the last few years had been quiet, no big cases to solve, and he'd begun to sour on MI-9 and longed for MI-5, where the chance for promotion was good and the work more steady. He needed something to take his mind off Clara but knew he would never forget her and really didn't wish to. Maybe this Ibiza thing would do the trick.

The phone rings. She's gone.

CHAPTER 8

The prime minister, a man of about fifty-five, stocky, tall, with dark-rimmed trifocals and no hair to speak of, deliberately hung up the secure phone. He mused for a moment and tugged at his wing like right ear lobe with his left hand, as was his wont when excited. He buzzed his confidential secretary. Two quick buzzes meant "I need to see you now." As he waited, he straightened and centered his Windsor-knotted dark blue tie, adjusted his posture to better conform to his crimson-colored leather-clad chair, and put on his most serious of serious, statesmanlike face—all this for his personal secretary.

He's such a stickler for details. This may prove to be a very auspicious moment, and he unofficially archives everything, may write a book one day. I definitely don't want to be characterized as disheveled or, worse, slovenly.

"Well, McDonald, you'll never guess who just rang."

McDonald, a very senior civil servant and personal secretary to several PMs, both Labour and Tory, wasn't about to guess, so he just shrugged his rather feminine-like shoulders and put on a blank face with eyebrows raised. As he raised his eyebrows, his trendy, narrow-rimmed glasses with the light blue stems slid down his nose and would have impacted the floor if it weren't for a large, hairless mole immediately above the right nostril. Without any humor whatsoever he quickly reset them.

Looking at McDonald was like looking at a mature David Niven, the film star: soft, dark, wavy hair; a slightly less than full moustache; thin face; and slight build. Not tall but then not short, and, unlike David Niven, McDonald doesn't have that posh English public school accent. In fact McDonald has no accent whatsoever. Over time he'd worked very hard at shedding his accent, an accent he believed would get him labeled as working class. McDonald is Scottish by birth. He'd left the Highlands as a youngster to seek his fortune in the City, and there he remained, never to return. He even managed, under the guise of national security, to weasel out of going to his mother's funeral. He consoled himself by sending twelve dozen white roses, her favorite, at a cost of two hundred–plus pounds. To this day he grimaced when thinking of that two hundred, wishing it could have been put to better use.

It isn't that McDonald disliked the highlands of Scotland; he just felt that he'd outgrown anything North of Peterborough and considered himself a sophisticate. As a sophist he firmly believed that the civil service, like the crown, provided continuity for the people, and while governments came and governments went, the civil service would always be in place and, like a helmsman of old, steer Britain through good times and bad and McDonald would rather think of himself as a helmsman than a yob from the far north.

Politicians, he postulated, were a necessary evil. Voters incorrectly thought that, by picking the politicians who made the choices that ran the country, they, the voters, were in charge and their votes really did matter. McDonald thought this a scandalous exaggeration of the truth. No matter who got elected by the voting public, it would still be the civil service who set long-range policy that ran the country. The day-to-day implementation of this long-range policy would be managed at the local level by civil servants in tandem with their political counterparts. *It's all a matter of inertia*, McDonald theorized, recalling Newton's third law of motion. *Once policy is set and the ball begins to roll, it'll roll unabated till acted upon by a stronger force, and if that were to happen, the hand behind that stronger force will be the civil service.*

"The president of the United States, that's who just called. I just hung up, no more than thirty seconds ago. We've only met once, but he seems a very likable chap—very chatty and all."

"And what did he want, Prime Minister? He'll be calling you because he wants something, a favor, probably information. If he wanted something more concrete like money, he'd be calling China or India or even, God forbid, Brazil. You know these are the up and coming superpowers, sir. They're the ones with all the clout and all the dough. Us Europeans, and I use that word *European* with many reservations, as well as the Yanks, can't balance our checkbooks and can't get our collective houses financially in order, so the president definitely wants information. Am I not right, sir?"

McDonald knew that the PM didn't like the isles, his isles, lumped in with France, Germany, Italy, and the rest. He didn't like Britain being labeled as the western coast of Europe. These isles and their citizens were British. McDonald had been on the short end of that lecture more than once: "That's why God made the Channel to separate us from them. They're Europeans, and we're British, and never forget that, McDonald, please."

If McDonald had been more Scottish and less British, he might have said: "And that's why the Romans built Hadrian's Wall—to separate the Scots from the English," but he didn't. He didn't think much of an independent Scotland and all the headaches and heartaches it would bring to both sides of the border, though more grief to the north, he feared.

"Yes, McDonald, you're right of course, as usual. He wants to know if we have any new information about Iran's nuclear facilities. Have the Iranians had any significant breakthroughs? In a nutshell the president wants to know if Iran might be on the brink of testing a nuclear weapon. Up to now the intelligence communities in America have collectively said no, but one of their agents was supposed to deliver data to Langley, via Ibiza, to the contrary. Apparently, this data transfer was to occur in Ibiza a few days ago, but the transfer failed somehow, and this smoking gun, as the president calls this new evidence, just vanished into thin air. In fact the president has ordered a second US Navy carrier group into the Med, now passing Gibraltar off the starboard bow I believe, and they'll be within striking distance shortly. I'm thinking if the Iranians are playing with fire and about to test a nuclear weapon, both the United States and Israel will thump them and thump them hard. Of that you can be sure. And further, if the Yanks go in, us Europeans, as you like to call us, will most likely not be far behind."

"Sir, speaking from years of experience, it's quite out of the ordinary for the president to call you directly. There are channels, you know. This smoking gun thing must be of the utmost importance. So, sir, do you want me to call in the heads of Five and Six and Nine for a good ol' chin-wag?"

Recently McDonald had started dropping the "MI" off MI-5, MI-6, and MI-9. MI-this or MI-that was far too tedious and unnecessarily redundant. In fact, McDonald was thinking of just "Five-Six-Nine," but that would have to wait—had to give the assiduous politicos time to assimilate Five and Six and Nine; he didn't want to overtax their imagination.

"Oh, yes, I suppose they should all pop over some time later today or early tomorrow, but why MI-9? So small, and Pettigrew's such a dragon. No one intimidates her. She's got too much on Woolsey and Gardener. They won't stand up to her, and me? Well, I'm just a politician who could be out the door come the next general election. And you, McDonald, you're just an overpaid civil servant serving politicians. You know MI-5's Woolsey is now politicking for MI-9 to be integrated into MI-5. Save a bob or two, and while MI-9 has met the challenge, London has been safe. It's had no sparkling, well-publicized success stories preventing this tragedy or that debacle. Woolsey won't broach the subject of the integration of MI-9 into MI-5 in Pettigrew's presence, no way. Pettigrew would pitch a fit. In Pettigrew's mind no attacks against London means MI-9 is not only successful but spectacularly successful, and she may bloody well be right."

"Yes, McDonald get the three of them over here about tea time—no details as to why I want to speak to them either. Also, please invite the queen's representative to Parliament, as well as a few senior members of Parliament, back benchers as well, if you please. Don't want to be accused of a cover-up or trying to gain political clout by coveting classified information. This government needs no scandals. We've only just returned to power after a long absence."

"Yes, sir. Consider it done."

"Oh, and one more thing McDonald. Clear my calendar through tomorrow evening, and have any experts we have on Iran and their weapons programs report to me at one o'clock today. Send a limo if necessary to collect them. Just a couple will do—don't want a full house. I want to make sure I'm on form and don't end up talking a load of codswallop. Anyway, I really do need a primer on Iran's nuclear weapons programs and their quest for the Bomb."

McDonald nodded and returned to his own rather sumptuous office, an office in McDonald's mind far superior to the PM's: better views, no painted walls, just exquisite multicolored wallpaper, an immense mahogany desk, satin white crown molding, and a sixty-inch big-screen telly, high definition, where he watched all the latest sport. He first called the heads of Five and Six and Nine and insisted they appear at number ten at half-four that day, no excuses permitted. He explained that the PM had pressing business that required their presence, and, no, per the PM's directions no advance agenda would be forthcoming, and again, no, the names of the other attendees, if any, would not be shared. Please be prompt, and if transport was needed, it'd be dispatched. McDonald then had an underling contact the MPs who would attend, as well as the Queen's representative to Parliament. He rationalized, and rightly so, *Why be senior if you have to do everything yourself?*

All three intelligence chiefs refused the offer of transport. They each had their own driver and limo, Bentleys of course, that picked them up in the morning and took them home at night. They even had security if asked for, but they never did.

One o'clock came, and one-fifteen went. The PM was doing a slow burn and was about to explode when McDonald buzzed and reported that Mr. James Whitehouse had arrived and was prepared to answer questions on Iran's nuclear programs. McDonald had previously briefed the PM on Whitehouse's bona fides, which were very impressive and included speaking several Iranian dialects, significant time living in Tehran, writing two well-respected books on Iran that sold poorly, and teaching advanced political science courses at London University. In addition, Whitehouse had been cleared by both MI-5 and MI-6 with special compartmentalized access to the latest intelligence on Iran's military and nuclear weapons programs. He also had carte-blanche access to review signals from the British embassy in Tehran so long as those signals included "gypsy" in the address line. Gypsy was code for any signal that even remotely touched on Iran's nuclear weapons systems.

Introductions were made. No handshakes, just courteous nods and a "good afternoon, sir." McDonald left thinking the PM would have to be a bit more affable and stick out his hand now and again or he might be labeled as cold and aloof, which he probably was, being an Eton boy and an Oxford University-Kings College graduate, number three in a class of one hundred and three.

"Well, sir, I must say this is an honor. How can I be of service to you?"

The PM just stared, almost glared, thinking, *This is my bloody expert? He's not much more than a lad and can't even keep his hands out of his pockets. Can't be thirty-five if he's a day and yet he's so accomplished, briefing his PM like he's tutoring an undergrad at Oxford. I hope McDonald knows what he's doing.* The PM had to force himself to smile—or was it a grin, or maybe even a smirk? To ask Whitehouse his age would have been rude, but that very question was sizzling in his mouth like an egg sunny side up in a frying pan, just waiting to burst. The PM regained his composure by grinding his back teeth. Anyway, for now, he had no other options; Whitehouse was, at least for now, his only expert. He needed pertinent information in a hurry. In ninety minutes he'd be meeting with the chiefs of 5 and 6 and 9.

"Okay, Jim—may I call you Jim?"

Whitehouse shyly nodded and seemed unable to force back a boyish grin that he unsuccessfully tried to mask by slightly bowing his head and partially covering his mouth with his right hand.

"Well then, Jim, Jim it is. You see, it's like this, old boy. I've an important meeting later today and need a quick and accurate assessment of Iran's nuclear weapons programs. First let me stress I'm a politician not a scientist, and I'm certainly no expert on Iran or nuclear physics or weapons proliferation; as an undergrad I abhorred science. I'm more of a freethinker. I need your latest take on Iran's progress toward acquiring a nuclear weapon, and it must be, insofar as possible, based on fact, not speculation or supposition or guesswork or extrapolation. I need to know if Iran has the capability to test a nuclear weapon today and if no, when? I also need to know a little about their ability to deliver a nuclear weapon on target and their willingness to take such a step knowing full well that their nation would be obliterated. Yes, that's a good start, and keep it general if you please. Please, avoid things like the square root of pi to the second power. I'm sure you understand, Jim. I majored in Elizabethan literature at Oxford."

He ended by gently tugging at his right ear and then thought, *What am I nervous about? He's the one who should be nervous.*

"Sir, please remember by and large that Iran is pretty much a closed society, and when it comes to any of Iran's weapons programs, she is impenetrable. That goes double for their nuclear weapons programs, which are scattered all over Iran, a fairly large country about the size of Alaska but less snow. Please remember that this is just my assessment based on the latest intel, but unfortunately and contrary to your guidance my assessment is based on the extrapolation of existing intel, both archival and current. First, to figure out where they'll be in the future, I must speculate on where they are now, and while speculation is better than a wild-ass-guess with the edges trimmed, it's anything but precise. That said, I don't believe Iran has the ability to test a nuclear weapon today, but I do believe they will have sufficient fissionable material to build one very soon—maybe twenty-four months, maybe a bit more. But this is just speculation, not guesswork, but speculation based on the scientific analysis of available intel from several sources, both overt and covert. As far as a delivery system is concerned, missiles or rockets are a long time off, even years, but lorries or planes could be used to put a nuclear weapon into play. Sir, you did ask me to keep it general. If you log into my classified website, the scientific data that backs up my assessments may be viewed, but it's a little more complicated than the square root of pi to the second power. I can give you passwords if you like."

"No, that won't be necessary for now. Please proceed."

"Now, in my estimation, dirty bombs probably already exist and may even be in production, and they could pose an imminent threat, especially to countries in the region. They could use ships or planes or even buses for transport and remotely detonate them in congested areas, causing panic and fear but doing little physical damage. Deaths would be rare, but deaths would most certainly occur and would most likely be from heart attacks or traffic accidents, not radiation poisoning. But a dirty bomb would certainly cause a panic if it went off in Trafalgar Square or Times Square—what a mess, a real psychological blow to one's adversary."

"Sir, one important point you should always keep in mind: Iran will categorically deny anything and everything I or MI-5 tells you. They'll call what I tell you allegations and demand undeniable proof, of which I have little to none. But what I do have is speculation based on some facts and the prior behavior of Iran's rulers. I believe I told you this already, and I believe what I'm telling you now to be factual."

"Now, as regards your question as to the will of the Iranian leadership to suffer the consequences for acquiring or even trying to acquire nuclear weapons? Some leaders are prepared, others not. No one really knows what their end game is, but the odds are against Iran acquiring a nuclear capability to only generate electricity. They're trying to make a point; they want the Bomb. They want the Bomb because the Israelis have the Bomb, and they also want the Bomb because the West doesn't want them to have it. Persia was once a great civilization, and some of today's leaders in Tehran would like to resurrect that persona, no matter what the monetary cost or risk. You know, a resurgent Iran ready to slay David, who slew Goliath. The older male Iranians in power are a proud bunch longing for recognition and respect, but if they play their cards too close to their chest, their fate may be self-destruction."

"Very well said. Now tell me about inspections and sanctions."

"Well, sir, in my opinion the West will never be allowed to inspect and verify what they want to inspect and verify. Iran is hiding something, so she'll never give us a free pass to inspect those most critical locations, locations where fissionable materials are being manufactured, stored, and tested. Significant and meaningful inspections of all facilities seem to be a nonstarter, dead on arrival as the Americans like to say. Iran won't budge on this no matter how much they try to give us the impression that all things are negotiable. Again, in my humble opinion, sir, Iran will not let us inspect because she's trying to acquire nuclear weapons and most certainly does have something to hide. Iran is lying, but it's a cat and mouse game with us being the cat, and the longer they forestall us, the more time they'll have to fulfill their sordid ambitions."

"Now sanctions may be a different story. They're working—plenty of people suffering—but it's a slow process that may never be totally successful. Who knows how much pain Iran is prepared to suffer, and it's not the politicians or Ayatollahs who are suffering, not by a long shot. The blitz didn't work, and I doubt sanctions alone will force Iran to give up her nuclear ambitions. Unless we want war, sanctions are our best way to inflict pain, but it's certainly not a long-term solution. The only long-term solution is to destroy their nuclear facilities or for Iran to allow inspections and prove to the world that her nuclear ambitions are limited to producing nuclear power for peaceful purposes only, and that'll never happen because Iran's lying to the world, in my humble opinion. She wants nuclear weapons and is secretly working very hard to get them; again my opinion, and there's always the possibility that I'm wrong, but I doubt it. What we need is actionable proof, one way or the other."

"Well, sir, that's it. Mr. McDonald said to keep it brief and high level, and I only had an hour's notice and little or no preparation time. I'm putting a Powerpoint briefing together that captures in more detail what I've just said. But, sir, doesn't all this beg the question: how many Western leaders, especially in Washington, want war with Iran? Some do, others do not, but John Q. American has had it with Iraq, Afghanistan, and the Arab Spring. They do not want another war— full stop. They see these wars as accomplishing little except draining their country's coffers and sending American youth to early graves or rehabilitation centers. Many see every war since Korea as accomplishing very little. Americans want the focus to be on America first: reduce the deficit and unemployment, get the economy going, and overhaul their retirement and healthcare systems. If there is to be a war with Iran, the Americans want proof, undeniable, undisputable proof, something along the lines of a Pearl Harbor, a unifying factor—you know, an event that will cause all good Americans to rally round the flag and send their young men and women off to war singing, like World War One, marching up Fifth Avenue singing 'The Yanks Are Coming.'

"Sir, you look a little disappointed."

"Yes, what you said about undeniable proof is key, but that proof may be hard to come by, but I'm sure that conundrum is actively being worked on, even as we speak."

"Anyway, thank you, Whitehouse. So if I may paraphrase what you've already paraphrased for me, you believe Iran wants to acquire the Bomb and is diligently working to acquire the Bomb but probably doesn't presently have the Bomb, but probably could get the Bomb soon but not too soon. You also believe that Iran probably has deployable dirty bombs. You believe meaningful inspections and verifications will probably never be permitted, and while sanctions are hurting them, they're probably insufficient to cause Iran's leadership to rethink their long-term nuclear strategies. And finally you believe the American administration will probably only wage war against Tehran if there is sufficient proof that Iran is making significant progress toward acquiring the Bomb, and to date no one has defined what 'significant progress' is, but I assume testing a nuclear device would be considered sufficient proof, probably. Is that right, Whitehouse?"

"Yes, sir."

"I'm surprised, Mr. Whitehouse, you didn't say, 'Probably, sir.'"

"Sir, you did say that that conundrum, sufficient proof, is being worked on. May I ask by whom?"

"Yes, you may, and you have …"

The PM thanked Whitehouse and buzzed McDonald, the back door opened and closed with hardly a sound, and then all was silent.

Well, that was a bloody waste, the PM thought. *Nothing new, only a lot of probablies. What Whitehouse said has been in the dailies on and off for the last year or two. The only important point is that Whitehouse firmly believes that the Iranians are liars and that they are in the process of building a nuclear bomb. The only thing lacking is proof that Iran is a liar, and that's what the West needs, some form of credible, undeniable intel that Tehran is actively working at building the Bomb. Apparently, per the US president, that proof may have been in Ibiza a few days ago. If the West ever gets its hands on verifiable proof, proof that Iran is covertly trying to get the Bomb, it will have no qualms whatsoever about eliminating those nuclear facilities, and Iran knows that. But there's no real proof and therefore insufficient justification for an attack. The West was wrong in Iraq; there were no weapons of mass destruction. Its suspicions about Iran might also be wrong, but if that's the case, why is Iran acting so coy, on the one hand appearing to be helpful and cozying up to the West and on the other appearing to be playing for additional time?*

The PM's right ear lobe was raw from tugging—too many variables and not enough answers.

He buzzed for McDonald, who quickly appeared with a question or two of his own.

"Sir, how do you propose to respond to the president? We don't want to appear to be dragging our feet; this Ibiza, smoking-gun scenario must be terribly important for them to come to us for intel on Iran's status vis-à-vis weapons of mass destruction. If there's concrete evidence that Iran's playing fast and loose with the truth, it may be just what's needed for the United States and its allies to systematically dismantle Iran's nuclear weapons facilities, and 'systematically dismantle' is a euphemism for destroy. Sir, I really do believe we must provide the States with our assessment of Iran's ability to field a nuclear weapon and soon—the sooner the better."

"Of course you're right, McDonald, but let's talk to our intelligence chiefs first and see what they have to offer. He only just called this morning. If our intel chiefs only know as much as Whitehouse, we'll just have to tell the president 'nothing new,' and we'll follow up with a signal detailing what we do know for a fact and what we think might be happening. I'm very hesitant to include anything Whitehouse thinks may be happening—even he's not completely certain of his own opinions."

"Of course, sir, you're right, and we'll know in a couple of hours what Pettigrew, Woolsey, and Gardener know and what they're thinking."

"McDonald, one question if you please. You know Whitehouse with all his talent and connections doesn't know much more than you or me and just about every cub reporter in the City. While he's a boffin, he can't manufacture proof that Iran's a liar and is building nuclear weapons. We can't give the Americans what they need to justify an attack if we don't have proof. Am I right or not?"

"Right, sir. I would have thought that was quite obvious. We're not in the business of manufacturing proof, but I don't believe that's the case anyway. Some American hawks, and they're in the majority right now, have been wanting to take out Iran's capability to go nuclear for some time, and to them this might prove to be the ideal time, but they have to retrieve what was apparently lost in Ibiza first. What I believe is that the Americans are trying to get answers and are going to all their friends with questions, just hoping something meaningful turns up. Unless I miss my guess, they'll do what it takes to figure out what happened to that smoking gun of theirs."

* * *

While Whitehouse was meeting with the PM, across town Jason was seated in Pettigrew's reception; Susan had rung for him a few minutes earlier telling him Ms. Pettigrew wanted to speak to him and could he please come to her office at once. Jason crossed the hall, but the MI-9s chief was on an overseas call, so while he waited he chatted to Susan.

"Well, Susan, you've been here close to a year. How do you like it? Most folks are good enough, and your boss, once you get to know her and her rather inconsistent habits, is more than just okay. I've been working for her for years, and I'm still in one piece—had my butt chewed out a few times, but who hasn't? Now, how's my mate Aubrey been treating you?"

"He's such a dear. Offered to take me out for drinks this Friday, after work, and said he'd help me make permanent staff. He said he and the chief are tight and he'd put in a good word. For a big man, he's as sweet as sweet can be, and him no wife or even a girlfriend—or so he says, but I'm sure he's lying. And the way he talks, almost in riddles. I have a hard time following him but eventually do understand what he's getting at. It's quite comical if you ask me—makes him more endearing and more interesting."

"Susan, you do know Ms. Pettigrew has rules about MI-9 employees dating each other. It's called fraternization, and it's definitely a no-no. You and Aubrey going out for a drink might be considered a date, and that's just not permitted, especially if you're looking to make MI-9 a career. A group of MI-9 agents out for a special occasion may be okay, but she frowns on that also. Intelligence operatives and their support are supposed to keep a low profile—you know, make no waves, remain inconspicuous, just kind of blend in. If a group of us are out on the town and one of us is made, then all of us are made. And she really frowns on the misuse of alcohol and its consequences. Like me old mum used to say, 'there's a baby in every gin bottle,' and, Susan, you'd be wise to not believe everything Aubrey has to say. For every rule the chief has there's a good reason for that rule. You know, if you listen to Aubrey and do what he says, you'll never be made permanent and—"

There was the buzzer calling for Jason. He rose, smiled at Susan, and headed for Pettigrew's office, which was tucked away at the east end of the Columbia Club. He knocked once, opened the door, entered, and sat where he always sat: in the plush, light green Victorian easy chair a few feet from Pettigrew. It seemed to Jason that the green chain was closer to her desk than usual. Maybe the cleaning people, but maybe the chief was very slowly getting hard of hearing. He would watch out for that.

Without a smile or any greeting of any sort, Ms. Pettigrew straightened her back and went eyeball to eyeball with Jason.

"Well, Jason, I've three things I want to speak to you about. I'll take them in ascending order of importance, from bottom to top if you please."

It was her want to always enumerate to Jason what she intended to speak to him about up front. Fortunately for Jason, three was the maximum to date.

"Aubrey's been hitting on my secretary. Aubrey knows my rules. Susan may not know the nuances of all my rules, but she will before she goes home this evening. He works for you; please have a word and nip this in the bud. I want Susan to do well, but if she believes every line someone tries out on her, I'll have to cut her loose, and I'm just the person who can do it. Anyway, does Aubrey have issues of some sort that I don't know about? Why is he continuously on the prowl? You need to remind your partner that he has a wife who, if she had a mind to, could make problems for him, and problems for Aubrey are problems for MI-9, and problems for MI-9 are problems for me. And, guess what? I do not like problems that affect how we do business. There are thousands of pubs in London with thousands of dolly birds out for a fling, so why doesn't Aubrey try his luck with one or two of these fun-loving dolls? And finally, again, please ask him to not use his association with MI-9 to try to impress. Will you do that for me, please, Jason, or shall I talk to Aubrey myself and maybe even enter a few adverse remarks in his personnel file?"

"No, I will. Aubrey's a good agent and academically smart—ran circles about me. We trained together; he still feels he should be my boss, but he does as I tell him, and I'm certain we'll get this sorted out and it won't happen again."

"I hope you're right, Jason. She's young, and he's slick—a bad combination under the best of circumstances, and considering we're responsible for the security of the City, well, you know, Jason. I don't have to draw you a picture. I've seen it before. People try to hide things, see each other on the sly, but it never works out; it all eventually comes out, and hearts get broken and careers busted and security compromised. Remember, Jason, there's two things I just won't tolerate, and that's a security compromise and bad press. If necessary I'll send you pair to the wall if either happens."

Not a smile on the chief's face, not even a smirk or shake of the head. She continued unabated.

"Okay, number two. How are you doing, Jason? And don't look at me as if to say, 'What are you talking about?' This is not the first time I've asked. Sometimes, Jason, you look so sad, just staring out that window, vacant, not a friend in the world. Have you ever thought of therapy? You've got to move on, Jason, but it will be terribly difficult. Have you not tried to meet other women? You and I started MI-9; you were the first I brought on board, even before your training. Back then you were very motivated. I later found out why. MI-5 didn't want to part with you, but I soon convinced that troll Woolsey that I needed you, and eventually she acquiesced."

She stopped, hoping Jason would say something, for she really liked him and hated seeing him so miserable and unresponsive to life. But as his immediate supervisor she could only do so much. She didn't want to be overly intrusive, just helpful.

"You're right, Chief. I thank you for being concerned, but no matter how hard I try, I can't get my Clara out of my mind—her mangled body, so tragic. Her death was without purpose. I mean, she wouldn't hurt a fly, but she just happened to be in the wrong place. Bloody bad luck. But I'm working on it. If I only slept better. I won't go on meds. I've seen what they did to me mum. She became addicted to sleeping pills, and they slowly ate her brain away—all cognition and self-awareness gone, as one boffin told me. I think I'm on the mend but who knows; I certainly hope so, but I still miss her very much."

"I'm sure you do. You know, Jason, my mother had a saying—'if you can't get over the death of someone, then you might as well jump into the grave with them,' or something like that—but what she was saying is that life is for the living."

Jason said nothing; he didn't know what to say. She didn't understand that he and Clara were soul mates, very close, not easily separated, even in death.

"Something a little more philosophical, Jason. Have you ever heard that old standby 'If you stare long enough into the abyss, the abyss will stare back at you'?"

"Yes, Nietzsche, I believe, but please don't ask me what it means. I haven't a clue."

"You know, the last time we spoke you said you occasionally see your Clara, like a dream, like a misty soft, dream is the way you described her. You said she's smiling and waving to you as she walks toward you. I'm not sure if it's a dream or not—may even be real for all I know. We humans aren't as clever as we'd like to think. Anyway, the next time you see her, please do me a favor. Try to hold the image as long as possible—study her every gesture, every move, especially her face, her mouth. Maybe she's trying to tell you something. Will you do that for me please?"

"I will."

"Now for number three. I've had the PM's personal secretary on the phone—you know, that odious civil servant McDonald and his supercilious, jumped-up ways. In just over an hour I've an appointment with the PM. Agenda unknown. Attendees unknown, but I do know it's at Number 10 in their large conference room, so they'll be guests aplenty. I know you still have contacts at MI-5. Any rumors? I always like to be prepared. Maybe he plans on dumping me, which would make those hypocrites Woolsey and Gardener very, very happy, or maybe they plan on reintegrating MI-9 back into MI-5, in which case my resignation will be on the table, pronto. I could never work for Woolsey; we go back too far, and she can be so two-faced, such a bitch, excuse my French."

"Well, Ms. Pettigrew, I got some gin from several sources. You're right, some in MI-5 want MI-9 back in the fold so to speak. Some don't like such a small outfit pretty much having the same clout as MI-5 and MI-6, regardless of our responsibilities. The fact that Woolsey and Gardener don't like you is no secret. They'd like to see you taken down a notch or two, but from what I've heard, there's no definite plans to either replace you or to have MI-9 subsumed by MI-5, so I'm guessing this meeting has got to be for something else—something no one, not you, Gardener, or Woolsey is even aware of. I'm betting they'll be others present, so be careful what you say. The PM's new, and he'll want to cover his butt by having allies in the room or at least impartial observers who will most likely have nothing to say but will be taking copious notes, for sure."

"Okay, thanks, Jason, and remember what I said about your wife—watch her every movement, every gesture. Jason, on the way out have Susan ring for my car; I'll be out in ten. Just need to get bundled up and turn off the electrics."

"Will do."

* * *

McDonald loved his job. For anything that needed to be done, there was an underling. While he was watching sport, underlings were busy greeting the limos, preparing afternoon tea, collecting and closeting brollies and winter weather gear, and on and on. It was grand being the apex predator. Life was good, but after all he'd earned it. After all those years of service, he now deserved all the perquisites that he had. He was at the top of his game. The best advice he'd ever had as a youth was that he should manage his own career: don't just take or seek out any assignment; take an assignment that'll help in moving up the ranks and making connections with the right people, the power brokers, the ones who'll decide who gets promoted. Now, he was personal assistant to the prime minister and not just this PM but future PMs; the job was his for the rest of his service. It was like he had achieved tenure, and his job was cushy. If very infrequently things didn't pan out and there was some kind of kafuffle, one could always point fingers at an underling or even the PM himself. McDonald just had to keep his personal life in order; as there was no Mrs. McDonald that was quite easy. In his spare time he enjoyed sport of any sort; he was an avid reader; and he enjoyed fine food, cooking, and of course music. He didn't drink, not a drop, and occasionally enjoyed the company of women but as friends only. He firmly believed a man and a woman could just be friends, and it worked for him. Finally, he had no skeletons in his closet, and he intended to keep it that way till the lid of his coffin was nailed shut. Because of his ordered and sedentary life he was very judgmental but kept his personal views to himself, though he was sure his judgments and opinions showed up in his manner and attitude toward others. Even his handshake, he'd heard through the grapevine, was condescending.

He'd have to put in an appearance this afternoon, make sure the PM had everything he needed for his upcoming conference with the MI ladies. As the PM hadn't buzzed, he assumed he had what he needed, but he'd better check, so he sauntered down the hall, knocked, waited for the PM to respond—which he did—and entered with a smile.

"Well, sir, may I be of any assistance? I think we're fairly well organized. The afternoon tea is on the way, just tea—no coffee and no soft drinks—and there'll be plenty of munchies. You know, biscuits of all sorts, cakes and dainty salads, ham and cheese sandwiches as well. That should do the trick, though probably most won't eat at all, especially the older ones, petrified they might get food stuck in their front teeth, especially lettuce. Lettuce has a way of not letting go."

"You might be right about teeth and food, especially sandwiches. I'm continually checking for unwanted residue myself. Such a bore. Will you be there, McDonald?"

"Oh my goodness, no. Just not heard of. You'd be surprised how many look down their noses at members of the Service—you'd think we were downstairs help or something. You'll probably know just about everyone in attendance, and if you don't know them, that's their problem, not yours. After all, you are the PM. The meeting is basically yours and our three prima donnas', if I may be so bold. The rest are there to observe, but if I know politicians some will have to have a word or two or three, so, sir, if I may suggest, don't let the politicos hijack your meeting and try to reset your agenda. It's your dance card, so you set the priorities and hold steadfast. It'll be a short meeting I'm sure, unless one of our three divas has some information of interest to you, which I doubt."

"Yes, probably so, and I thank you for your advice. Well, I'll be trotting on. Most should be having tea by now. I abhor tea, and if I'm ever in a situation where I feel I must drink it, I take it weak, very weak indeed, and I abhor tea bags as well—prefer loose tea and tea balls."

The large conference room, or more formally the Churchill Room, was opposite the PM's office, about fifty paces straight down the corridor. The PM walked past a rogues' gallery of former prime ministers, some well known, some obscure. One day his picture would be added to that gallery, but he hoped not too soon, for you had to first die, and then a likeness of you would be painted by some unimportant artist, and with much fanfare and little substance your mug would be hung adjacent to your predecessor, assuming he or she too had passed. If the predecessor hadn't, a space large enough to accommodate his or her likeness would be left.

Between the pictures of Harold Wilson and Ted Heath, the PM called in for a pit stop; the lavatory was always attended by some elderly chap, prepared to watch your 'stuff' as you went about your business. The attendant also handed out towels, not paper, and when not otherwise engaged sat on an elevated leather chair tucked away in the far corner of a room as big as two moderately sized flats. The attendant was immaculately dressed and in his heyday was probably quite the lad, dashing, and a bit of a knave. Other than seeing to the needs of those who frequented his domain, the attendant had only one other ground rule, and that was never to speak unless spoken to, and the PM intended not to speak at all, as the attendants all had a reputation for being nosy, unnecessarily chatty busybodies seeking to "help," as they would put it, those in power by offering advice. They were also known to spread rumor and to unabashedly seek assistance with personal matters. As was the custom, on the way out the PM left no more than ten pence in a small wicker basket on the sink adjacent to the hole in the countertop where used towels got deposited.

The PM entered the conference room, a bulging manila folder under his left arm. McDonald had given him the folder, said it made him look more PM-ish. All rose. With a stiff "Good afternoon" he motioned for all to sit and then sat himself, placing the manila folder well out of the way—didn't want to inadvertently knock it on the floor and show himself up. The table was round, about twenty feet in diameter, so there was no head, but the seat closest the door was left vacant for the PM. Most were sipping tea and crunching biscuits. Most were also surreptitiously sizing up the PM, who had a reputation for being quietly efficient, a backroom kind of guy who could, figuratively speaking, twist arms with the best of them. There were no servers; what you wanted you got off the trolley yourself. The PM preferred no tea or snacks. He acknowledged those in attendance by name. The PM made a mental note to thank McDonald; he saw his firm but subtle hand, for no young bucks spoiling for confrontation were present. McDonald had ensured only those who knew the PM were invited; less awkward, as this was the first time most of the attendees were seeing the PM, as PM. He noticed immediately that Pettigrew and the Woolsey–Gardener pair was separated by the diameter of the table, not a good sign. The PM wanted cooperation; too much was at stake, maybe even a war.

He remembered what McDonald had recently stated. *Yes, after all, I'm the PM. It's my meeting and my meeting to steer. I only hope that the dragon and the trolls, as McDonald calls them, will work together and not bicker as is their wont.*

The PM began He didn't stand; that set the tone for follow-on speakers. He enjoyed speaking in public, one reason he'd been the MP from Worcestershire for twenty years.

"Before we get started, this meeting will be at the Secret level—what goes on in this room will only be passed on to those with the necessary clearances and necessary need to know. If you feel compelled to take notes, please make sure you properly annotate them and secure your notes before departing."

"Well, I'm sure you're all wondering why we're here. This meeting is basically for Ms. Woolsey, Ms. Gardener, and Ms. Pettigrew, so straight to the point. America's president was on the line to me this AM, London time, which makes it the middle of the night in DC. According to his intelligence services, the Iranians may be on the verge of acquiring a nuclear weapon in the not too distant future. A nuclear-armed Iran would bring all sorts of unpleasantness to the region. If this were to be true, I'm pretty certain that would mean war. At a minimum both the US and Israel would attempt to eliminate Iran's potential for manufacturing the Bomb. If Iran is attacked, the Gulf might be closed by Iran's navy, and even if it remains open, oil tankers from the West would most likely be targeted. On land Iranian armies would most certainly attack Israel, and allies of Iran like Syria and Hezbollah might get involved. To put it mildly, it would be a mess. Let me fill you in on what I know. Then Woolsey, Gardener, and Pettigrew can respond in turn, without interruption or unnecessary questioning. What comes out of this meeting will be the basis for my response to the American president, who has asked for our assistance in clarifying Iran's position vis-à-vis nuclear weapons. Up to now, the mantra of America has been that Iran can't possibly develop the Bomb for at least two years, time enough for sanctions to really bite. As you all know, sanctions are working, but no one on either side of the Atlantic believes sanctions alone will dissuade Tehran from trying to go nuclear. Apparently, and this is right from the president's mouth, American agents were in place to receive concrete proof that Iran will be capable of developing the Bomb much sooner than previously thought, maybe even in a couple of months. If this were to be true, war in the Gulf would be inevitable. Anyway, to continue, this proof or smoking gun as the President calls it was somehow hijacked—yes, that's a good phrase. By whom? No one knows. It just vanished, as they say, 'into thin air.' The Americans strongly feel that the hijacked information is legitimate; knowing it came from a reliable source in Iran who had access and who only wanted enough money to safely leave the country. In a nutshell, on the island of Ibiza, the damning information was to be exchanged for cash, but the guardian of the information was knocked unconscious and the info removed—to where, nobody knows. Now, my question to MI-5, MI-6, and MI-9 is can they shed any light on this strange set of circumstances, and do we have any new data that might rebut or confirm the missing smoking-gun theory? In other words, do we have any information that might prove that Iran will be going nuclear sooner rather than later?"

"You, Woolsey, MI-5. You're most senior. You first, please."

Ms. Woolsey, fiftyish, nine stone, was anything but matronly. She was always dressed in either a skirt or dress, very trendy, and for her age might even have been considered a looker—from the neck down. Her face was coarse and her skin slightly mottled—too much sun in her youth that not even makeup, in excess, could hide. Her hair was of medium length, and the style was that of young women of the late seventies, teased out every which way, almost haphazardly, with a slight fringe in front that brazenly attacked her bushy eyebrows. Her hair was colored, jet black. Jet black next to her rather pale skin just didn't cut it—too much contrast. Her facial features were nondescript.

Woolsey slowly rose, as if for effect, as if she had anticipated that very question and was full of confidence. She proceeded to speak, slowly at first, as if collecting her thoughts—and she was. She did know a great deal about Iran and its relentless pursuit of the Bomb, but she knew absolutely nothing about the "Ibiza connection" as she now mentally labeled it.

"Thank you, Mr. Prime Minister. Let me first congratulate you and your party—quite a close race, I believe, but when it's all said and done, you're the PM, and good luck. Now, to answer your question, MI-5 has analyzed and reanalyzed Iran's intentions as regards nuclear weapons and firmly believes Iran is trying to get the Bomb as soon as possible, but we have no irrefutable proof other than the fact that Iran flat-out refuses to let the West verify, through inspections, her claim that she wants to go nuclear for peaceful purposes only. Now, dirty bombs probably already exist and may even be in production, and they could pose an imminent threat, especially to countries in the immediate region. If Iran were attacked today, MI-5 feels dirty bombs would be the weapon of choice ..."

At that moment the PM made the connection between Whitehouse and Woolsey; Whitehouse must have briefed Woolsey and probably Gardener upon leaving Number 10 that very afternoon, a briefing similar to the one he himself had just received. The PM knew Woolsey had no new information and certainly didn't know what happened to the President's smoking gun or where it was. He let Woolsey continue, and continue she did, for another thirty minutes, even going into minutia from Iran's past. She touched on Alexander the Great, the Trojans, the American hostage crisis, and the failure of Jimmy Carter to be reelected. She finally got off the bully pulpit by acknowledging that she knew nothing about the Ibiza connection but would look into it on her return to her offices. In fact, as she was speaking an aid of hers was out the door and back to MI-5, mentally composing a signal to Mediterranean Division, soliciting information about events on Ibiza that might somehow be related to Iran's quest for weapons of mass destruction.

As Woolsey droned on, Pettigrew absentmindedly went over a litany of reasons why she loathed both Woolsey and Gardener. They had all trained together, and all three entered duty the same year. At that time they were good friends with one difference: Woolsey and Gardener were ambitious, very ambitious, and they intended to do what was needed to move up. They became master careerists, knowing who could help and what positions would inch them closer to the top. If they had to step on someone to get ahead, then so be it. They cultivated relationships with men who could help and then discarded them as future opportunities came to light. They'd been wildly successful, both becoming chiefs of Britain's premier intelligence services, MI-5 and MI-6. Both would probably be on the honors list next January, and both might even become peers of the realm someday, maybe even baronets, but Pettigrew knew names, people they had duped, used, and wounded in their climb to the top. Pettigrew had also had relationships with men, but these relationships were based on love or at a minimum honesty and affection, not "what can you do for me?", and she could count on one hand the number of relationships. She was absolutely certain both Woolsey and Gardener would have to take off both shoes to count theirs—and they'd still come up short.

Woolsey was winding down. She finally finished.

Well, thought the PM, *that was forty minutes of bullshit. I would have thought someone in her position might have had a little more insight into what I need to know, but she jut echoed what her expert already told me. Where's 007 when I need him?*

Pettigrew felt like spitting but remained outwardly calm, icily emotionless; she was good at hiding her true feelings; she'd had plenty of practice. *Thank God, no questions,* was all she could think.

"Now, MI-6, what do you have to say?"

While Woolsey and Gardener were like two peas in a pod when it came to their careers, they were like chalk and cheese when it came to their appearance. Unlike Woolsey, Gardener was on the plump side She was tallish and always nicely turned out, but her attire usually consisted of clothes she'd purchased years ago. She never threw anything away, even if it was a bit thread-worn or a bit discolored from being cleaned one time too many. Her plump figure was matched by a plump face, with extended jowls that eclipsed and might one day engulf her cheeks. A plump nose, plump eyes, and plump ears rounded out her rotund, Mount Rushmore–like face. In fact if one word could describe her visage to perfection, that word would be *roly-poly*. Yes, she was on the heavy side, of that there could be no doubt, but to describe her as very fat might be a bit too cruel and hurtful; so perhaps it would be best to just describe her as tall, overweight, and with a penchant for clothes that her dead mother wouldn't be caught dead in.

Gardener didn't seem to rise to her feet but seemed to be standing in the twinkle of an eye. One second she was comfortably sitting, and then in a flash she was up and delivering her take on Iran vis-à-vis the Bomb. For her size she was very agile and very mobile, but to the PM's disappointment she merely dittoed what Woolsey had just said. However, it took her fifteen minutes to say what equated to "I know nothing of what recently transpired in Ibiza and less than Woolsey when it comes to Iran's nuclear ambitions."

Before sitting she looked from person to person, apparently hoping for a question, but there were none. In fact many were a bit embarrassed for both Woolsey and Gardener, at their lack of information about such a sensitive topic, and most thought Pettigrew would also come up short.

"Well, Ms. Pettigrew, will you also ditto what MI-5 and MI-6 have said?"

Pettigrew rose and began slowly pacing round the room till she stopped right behind MI-5 and MI-6; she was fearless.

"No, I think not, sir. I'll make this brief and to the point. A few days ago my office got wind of a huge transfer of cash, from somewhere yet to be determined, to the Swiss bank account of a Yorkshire publican, too large a sum to be overlooked by MI-9. On investigating, we found this publican's husband was an American who'd acquired British citizenship, and upon further investigation my people determined that this individual was about to retire or had retired already from Central

Intelligence—yes, the CIA. We further determined that this individual was in Ibiza at the time the transfer of this 'smoking gun' was to occur. We're still in the process of connecting the dots, but it seems quite sensible to me at least to assume that he was somehow involved with our 'smoking gun,' and we know that this individual will return to Ibiza shortly—this week, as a matter of fact. We have an op in place to tail him and hopefully recover the lost documents and return them. Return to whom? I hope no one will accuse me of putting the cart before the horse, as we've yet to recover the documents. Perhaps they should be returned to their original owners, perhaps to the Americans, or perhaps we keep them, at least for a while. This is all to be determined, but if and when we do recover these documents, a determination will then be made based upon their content and the wishes of our government."

As a final act of bravado, she took three paces forward and placed both hands on the back of Woolsey's chair.

"Bravo, Ms. Pettigrew! Well done," the PM roared.

"Hear, hear," said all but Woolsey and Gardener, who both felt that they had somehow failed, had been luckless, and had even been upstaged, while that shrew Pettigrew had just filled an inside straight. Both Woolsey and Gardener loved poker, but neither was very good or very lucky while Pettigrew, who actually preferred bridge, was both very good and very lucky; her advanced degree in statistical mathematics might have helped.

"Sir," Gardener interjected, "mightn't this op be too big for MI-9? Perhaps we could run it from here on out. We've far more resources, and I thought MI-9 dealt only with London and its environs and was barred by law from participating in clandestine operations beyond the borders of the United Kingdom, sir?"

Gardener didn't want to appear to be too anxious to assume control of Pettigrew's op, but she did, and she did appear unnecessarily willing to climb right over Pettigrew to please the PM. With that one question to her PM, Gardener lost status and maybe even a peerage.

"Well, Pettigrew, what do you say to that?"

"Mr. Prime Minister, that CIA employee is presently in London and shortly will board a flight to Ibiza, so I believe that gives MI-9 the lead, and we need no help from MI-5 or MI-6, and that's why I kept the details vague. If the prime minister wants a private brief that can be arranged, but I would urgently like to return to my office to fill my people in on these new developments. Sir, may I be excused now?"

"Of course, Ms. Pettigrew, and wishing you and your people jolly good luck, and you, Gardener, listen up: no interference, no participation from either MI-5 or MI-6, and if I even get an inkling that my instructions have been disregarded, heads will roll."

In her most flamboyant manner, Pettigrew collected her handbag and left. The room was dead quiet till the door slammed behind Pettigrew, who was steaming, wishing she could somehow coax Jason to murder both Woolsey and Gardener, but that emotion soon passed.

With the meeting adjourned, the PM returned to his office. He then asked McDonald to come into his office. He picked up the red phone and had a call put through to the president. He preferred speakerphone, as McDonald was present; all recording devices were off.

"Mr. President, yes, likewise. Glad to chat with you again … Yes, weather's bloody awful, which is normal for this time of year … Oh, so it's in the seventies in DC? How very, very nice for you. Anyway, shortly by signal I'll be sending you what MI-5 and MI-6 have on Iran's nuclear ambitions via our embassy in Washington, but one piece of encouraging news."

He proceeded to relate to the US president what Pettigrew had just related to him.

"Yes, no guarantees of course, but we may be able to retrieve that lost packet of yours, and maybe even this week, but again, no guarantees."

"Mr. Prime Minister," the President rejoined. "we would like the packet back as soon as possible, if possible. If and when you retrieve it, encrypt it and, via the Internet, send it to your embassy here in Washington. Then drop the hard copies off at our embassy in London, and our military will airlift it back to Andrew AFB via RAF Alconbury. Of course the contents are extremely important, but more to the point we need to know about the validity of the data. You have boots on the ground; please do what's necessary to determine if the data is valid. I don't want to be making decisions based on invalid information, something we hawks have done in the past, much to our embarrassment. Many here, especially the more liberal, find it difficult to believe that Iran is now or shortly will be capable of testing the Bomb. We now have two carrier groups in the Med; we've pulled the group that was in the Gulf back into the Med—more room to maneuver in case of a confrontation. Our allies in the region have just raised their defense condition and put their air units on alert, so your input is vital to what decisions finally get made here in Washington, and there isn't much time. We can't keep the press at bay forever, and we certainly can't remain prepared to attack Iran's nuclear facilities indefinitely. We either attack or stand down, a decision I have to make and quickly and that decision will be a no-brainer if Iran is close to testing a nuclear weapon. When will your operation occur?"

"This weekend we should know one way or the other, and I'll pass on to Ms. Pettigrew, our lead in Ibiza, that validating the information is just as important as acquiring the information."

"Good. Thank you. If you need any help from any of our clandestine services, please let me know. We have worked together well in the past, and your people know our people—first-name basis, I believe."

The PM looked to McDonald, who, with head down, slowly shook his head side to side.

"No, that won't be necessary for now, but thanks for the offer, Mr. President."

"Okay, thanks and good-bye."

"Cheerio."

CHAPTER 9

Not far from the Columbia Club, on the other side of Hyde Park, Al is ensconced in a small bed-and-breakfast. His room is on the third floor, a small, dingy garret with the loo, running water, and pay phone, with a calling radius of less than thirty miles, at the end of the hall. There was no en suite rooms and no lift. All this luxury cost Al fifty quid a night. He has to be out of his room from ten to half four so the owner can tidy up and do whatever owners of B and B's do. Dinner, if you choose to eat in, is served sharply at five, and there is no menu and no seconds—you eat what's provided or you eat out or you go hungry. Dinner always consists of one meat dish, two veggies, and potatoes, usually mashed but sometimes roasted, followed by a sweet and instant coffee, only regular. Wine is extra, always red and dispensed from a five-liter box resting on the sideboard. The owner keeps close tabs on who drinks what; there's no such thing as the honor system in this place. Al has eaten in twice. Most everything is overcooked; the veggies are like mush and the mashed potatoes watery and the sweet, usually a frozen Sarah Lee crumble or pie, is overcooked by about ten minutes in the same oven as the joint is cooked in, giving the sweet a robust, hearty flavor. The meat, well done of course, is a cheap cut of beef sliced on the bias and, as it turns out, quite tasty. There's plenty of horseradish sauce and tomato ketchup but no gravy. If you go out after dinner, you're expected to be back by ten. The front door is locked at ten, on the dot, no exceptions. If you return after ten, a ten-pound service charge is added to your bill; the ten pounds goes to the chap who has to get out of bed and let you in, usually the owner or his teenage son. The owner and his family live downstairs—not exactly a basement, as few homes in England have basements, but a kind of subterranean level where the windows overlook the garden, almost at eye level. A short set of stairs on the side of the house leads down to a second entrance that is seldom used unless the owner's out on a piss-up and trying to sneak by the missus on his way to bed, which usually doesn't work as the missus is a light sleeper. The next morning the owner gets a good telling-off for waking the missus but not much more. There is no outside staff to help; the family does everything and, considering what they have to do, does it quite well. These are the kind of digs that are just that—digs or lodgings. Al hates lodgings but thought it safer to stay at a run-down B and B rather than a posh Mayfair hotel where computers might somehow track him down. His room consists of a narrow twin bed; an antiquated dresser with a large, cracked mirror; a carpet fit for the dump; and a small, door-less closet suitable for the belongings of a traveling salesman down on his luck. On top of the dresser stands a plain white porcelain bowl and pitcher to be used for washing and shaving. It took Al a day or two to figure out how to use these nineteenth-century accoutrements. Down the hall you fill the pitcher with water and then empty the water into the bowl. You wash using a flannel and then empty the remnants into a bucket near the door. After a refill you shave and repeat the previous steps, finally emptying the bucket into the loo. If you want a shower—there isn't a bath to be found on the premises—you have to queue up on the first floor, and the water is always cold, ice cold, even in summer, and the water never flies out of the shower, just sort of trickles out so one has to stand directly under the showerhead to get wet, and it takes forever to get all of the shampoo out of your hair. To cap things off, the door to Al's room doesn't lock. Yes, there is a lock, but the key's been lost or pinched years ago. The room also has some strange, pervasive odor that Al couldn't initially pinpoint, it reminded him of his recently deceased granny, who'd hung on for ninety-five-plus years; yes, the odor was the smell of age, and that one-room, third-floor cell was just that: aged and unresponsive to the demands of the day.

Al is up by seven; breakfast is not on the menu, ever, so Al bundles up and heads for the Spotted Goose, a pub just up the road. It's pitch dark, and there's no overhead street lights, so he has to be careful not to stumble; a sprain right now could prove to be disastrous to his less than thought-out plans. From previous visits to the City, Al knows that not many eateries serve breakfast, so it's a stroke of luck that he stumbled onto the Goose, which serves an excellent full English breakfast, including English bacon, sausage links, black pudding patties, baked beans, fried mushrooms, toast, jam, and a brace of free-range eggs, sunny side up just the way Al likes them or cooked any other way one likes eggs, except boiled. Years ago the owner realized that a boiled egg can never be cooked just right; customers complain that the yoke is either too runny or not runny enough. So while eggs can be fried, scrambled, poached, or even cooked in the micro, they will never be boiled, so there's no need for egg cups. Al's fried eggs are not flipped—too risky—but the cook gently washes hot oil over the eggs as they fry, slowly cooking the yolks to a leaky, golden perfection; the whites of the eggs take care of themselves. A piping cup of freshly percolated black coffee seals the deal; for an extra three quid the coffee will go Irish.

As Al eats he reads the *Times*. As he reads he thinks about his game plan for the next few days, though it's not much of a game plan, more like a Hail Mary pass. Tomorrow it'll be wheels up at noon. Hopefully in Ibiza he'll return the canister with its secrets and receive the additional million, in cash, in large bills as he requested. The cash will then be packed in his case and checked through; paper cash shouldn't set off any alarms, as cases in the UK and Ibiza are scanned for explosives and sniffed for drugs, but cash money is seldom, if ever, an end in itself. Putting cash between his shirts and shorts is just too risky, so there's no other viable alternative to using his checked luggage; he'd just have to risk being found out. If he is found out he has no plausible explanation planned, none whatsoever. His plan seems so simple, maybe even a bit naïve, as if planned by the Marx brothers. Could it really be that easy? Presumably the man in white will be in Ibiza, and Al wonders if he might bear a grudge for that knock on the head; no doubt he does. No additional e-mails have been forthcoming, so Al assumes they'll meet in the bar in the early evening as arranged, make the exchange, and then have a drink or two for old times' sake, even though they've never been formally introduced. Al makes a mental note to pick up the tab—wouldn't want the man in white to think him a cheapskate with him having millions. If Al thinks about it too much, he worries that something might go awry, so he tries not to think about it and hopes several strong, gin-laced drinks will see him through this night. *Maybe*, he thinks in one of his weaker moments, *I should just ditch the canister, head north, and be happy with the million I already have.* But Al doesn't look at the second million as icing on the cake; he looks at it as a necessity if he is to lead a life of leisure, excess and camaraderie, and develop gout well before fifty-five.

He feels he'll be reasonably safe in Ibiza if he stays in public places at all times, but that might be difficult. He'll do his best to be a barfly, avoid his room, and only use the loo when absolutely necessary and use the bar's loo, which, if he recalls correctly, has one stall and an impressive lock not easily jimmied.

But what if my luck does run out? What if I'm killed? After all, two million is a lot of money. Must be plenty of people pretty sore at me, especially the Americans, especially Roger, but I'm sure he hasn't tied me to his failed op, not yet. But to be killed, ugh, how sleazy, how lower class, how very, very embarrassing. What will the locals at the Duke think? What will they say? Hopefully my death will be attributed to some kind of random violence, something outside my control. Like they say on the news, wrong place, wrong time, and Margaret, she'd be devastated, but she's like her Mother, strong. She'll get over me, but not too quickly I hope.

After the exchange Al's plan is to hightail it back to the airport and catch the next flight back to the UK and then on up to Yorkshire. He hopes things will work out to his advantage, but two things continue to niggle at him. He wants to know more about the contents of the canister and is beginning to be concerned that someone might try to separate him forcibly from his prize. So today he'll address both issues, and by tonight he should be able to sleep better or at least rest more comfortably. He'll need a lot of luck for everything to come off as hoped. He'd had luck before; now he hopes Lady Luck won't forsake him, leave him in a lurch either dead, horribly maimed, or trying to explain to the authorities how a million happened to end up in his case. With that he turns his head and gently strokes his hump. "You won't let me down, will you?"

Al speaks two languages—English and American—and can understand Yorkshire at times. That's where his linguistic skills end, abruptly. From his amateurish analysis of the canister's contents, using his smartphone as interpreter, he'd figured out that the documents are written in Farsi so are most likely Iranian. The plans looked like test plans that document Iran's nuclear achievements, and if Al's translations is even half-accurate, the Iranians are close, yes, very close, to testing a nuclear device, but Al wants to be sure. In this information age, knowing secrets about Iran's weapons programs is power and money, and knowing secrets about Iran's nuclear weapons program, with bona fides thrown in, is a mega multiplier, and that's why, to Al's thinking anyway, the original owners of the documents are prepared to shell out millions for their return, but … *Why are the original owners of the plans paying me millions but according to Roger are prepared to sell them for only twenty thousand to the CIA?*

To that question Al has no convenient answer, but getting the plans into American hands must be very important to the man in white. For now, though, getting that extra million is singularly uppermost in Al's mind; after the exchange, the plans can go to the devil for all he cares.

Al had, at first, thought about copying the documents and maybe even selling the copies. He'd found the thought of selling the originals as well as copies not only intriguing but stimulating and exhilarating, kind of like soaring through the air under your own steam. Realistically, however, copies could be forged or altered and would be of no value to anyone, so he'd eventually abandoned the idea. Besides, the more transactions Al exposed himself to, the greater the risk. His best and only plan was to maintain tight control of the originals, and to do this, he had to act wisely, be smart, but most of all be cunning.

Using his smartphone, Al Googles translation services in London, keyword *Farsi*. There were dozens of hits—after all, this is London. Al selects a Mr. Abdulla Abdulla with an address on the other side of the Thames, near Borough Market. He composes an e-mail detailing what he needs: basically several short documents verbally translated, with nothing in writing. Off the top of his head Al spins, weaves, and concocts an unbelievable story of where the documents came from and why he needs them translated.

> *The contents of my documents are fictional and are to be included as an addendum to a book I'm writing; a colleague of mine wrote the addendum on my behalf, but I want to reconfirm that the documents say what I intended them to say; accuracy is very important, as this is my first novel.*

The story has as many holes as a sieve, but he figures he can plug the holes later, assuming Mr. Abdulla is interested in the job. He's intentionally left things sketchy and more than a bit vague. *If Abdulla refuses, no harm done, and if he accepts*, he reasons, *I can provide additional details on the spot, as needed. What Abdulla thinks of my story is irrelevant. I just need a solid translation and interpretation of my documents.*

Al ends the e-mail by suggesting a time and place for them to meet and asks what his fee would be. After clicking the Send button, Al walks around the park to kill time. It's cold but not unusually cold, and fortunately he has on his long gray, woolen overcoat accompanied by a bright yellow scarf nonchalantly tied round his neck. No hat—Al never wears a hat, for they keep falling off. He does look a sight, hump and all, rambling first this way and then that as if in a trance, walking in his sleep, or maybe even a bit tipsy, but Al is neither, just in deep cogitation wondering where he might be a week from today: maybe dead and, as his mother-in-law used to say, a long time dead. Twice he almost bumps into others out for a walk, and twice narrowly escapes a telling-off for daydreaming and not paying attention to where he's going, but on both occasions the offended parties, noticing his deformity, just smile and politely nod, figuring this poor chap might be incapable of properly seeing in what direction he's heading.

As he walks, he remembers that he's intentionally left his documents in his room for safekeeping. He'd made no effort at hiding them, for anything hidden has potential value if found, even accidentally, so he left them in the canister in his case in the door-less closet. He'll have to return to collect them later or be up for a ten-pound penalty. "Whatever," he mutters. "But still, ten pounds is ten pounds, and ten pounds will buy four pints of Cameron's best bitter at the Duke, and I could sure go for a pint right about now." One hour later the ping of his cell lets him know that Mr. Abdulla Abdulla has received his e-mail and responded. Al reads Abdulla's response with delight.

> *Yes, today is fine. Yes, afternoon tea for two at the Ritz at two PM. My fee is two hundred pounds plus cab fare, and you're springing for the afternoon tea. Okay?*

Al responds in the affirmative and ends with the following:

> *And for identification purposes, I'm the one with the hump. Dress appropriately, as this is the Ritz after all. One lump or two?*

Al laughs at his own dry sense of humor and returns to the B and B, where he's given a hard time by the proprietor for trying to enter his room as it is being tidied up, but a twenty-quid note silences him and his whining, sharpish. *Money solves so many problems and truly enriches one's life.* That little gem clings to the tip of Al's tongue. It won't let go, and he can't spit it out no matter how hard he tries. He finally gets its message: he must have that additional million come hell or high water. He collects the canister and a few essential bits and pieces, puts on his best set of clothes, has the owner ring for a cab, and cheerfully checks out. He doesn't want to raise any alarms by pitching a fit over the shockingly poor food, the antiquated furnishings, or the lack of hot water.

He arrives at the Ritz shortly before two; the place is mobbed. Fortunately he'd made reservations several days ago, hoping to enjoy an afternoon of palatial spoiling and overindulging in just about anything the Ritz offers, including several glasses of light, chilled champagne at ten pounds a pop. At the time of making the reservation, he'd figured he'd be on his own, but now, criminal that he is, plans are changing and changing in a hurry. So far, though, Al has been on top of each and every change. He is dutifully escorted to his table by a trim waiter in tails who under different circumstances might have been thought to be a royal, a man without peers, but alas the waiter is just that, a waiter, overworked and underpaid, even at the Ritz.

"Oh, waiter, when Mr. Abdulla shows up, show him to my table, please. We'll have afternoon tea for two, and if it's not a problem, you can start serving immediately. I'm famished, and everything looks so yummy."

"Certainly, sir, but I thought you were alone; your booking shows afternoon tea for only one."

"No, I did book for two, I swear to God, on my mother's grave. Must be a mistake on your end. Why, with all these people clamoring for attention, it's no wonder reservations get turned inside out. Anyway, not to worry—I'll take care of you when we're finished. Also, please, once you deliver the tea don't disturb us. Business transactions—you understand I'm sure. When Mr. Abdulla leaves, please bring me the check, and we'll settle up."

"Very well, sir. Consider it done." As the waiter snakes his way back to his station, he thinks, *So lower class. Why treat yourself to this lovely afternoon tea and spoil it all with business? Couldn't business wait for an hour or two? He'd be better off having tea in a mug in a pub and watch football and eat salad sandwiches followed by a Mars bar. Lower class, lower class, lower class, and he's such a bloody liar. Foreigners do get on my teat end.*

Shortly the tea trolley steams up, shimmering silver fore and aft; it's the real deal—solid sterling silver, not plated copper. On it is the teapot filled with boiling water and six extra-large tea bags oozing flavor and color, one tea bag per cup—very strong tea. A solid white tea cozy is nearby if required. There's also a pot of steaming hot water to replenish the contents of the teapot or to dilute the tea in one's tea cup—have to be careful not to get a lapful of hot water. The tea condiments are centered on a table about four feet across, rather large considering it's to be a table for one. Tea condiment included sugar, only white of course—never brown in the afternoon. There's full milk for those who prefer to ruin their tea. What there isn't, is lemon, skim or low-fat milk, or honey, but if one asks, one's waiter will cheerfully produce what one requires, though that cheerful smile will usually mask an impolite thought or two along the lines of *Aren't they common? Aren't they vulgar?* Waiters at the Ritz know how things ought to be done, and they can be caustic and sarcastic when things are not done properly, but never to the paying customer. The teaspoons, along with an army of cutlery, lay meticulously placed in front of two armed chairs. A second service had been whisked into place well before Al could even think *and Bob's your uncle.* After giving the tea five minutes to brew, Al elects to pour his own, neat, into solid white teacups. A bit embarrassed by his own curiosity, Al flips the saucer over. "Yes," he said to himself, "Wedgewood. God, I love this country". Next comes a two-tiered silver cake stand meticulously stacked with sandwiches, very delicate, handsome sandwiches, almost too good-looking to eat, enough for a tribe. They've been quartered and the crusts faultlessly removed, almost as if a Harley Street surgeon had done the job with a scalpel. There are salmon, roast beef, and pate sandwiches, all very thin and delicate, and the bread slices are color-coordinated: a brown slice, then a white slice, and then another brown. Immediately after the two-tiered cake stand is set in place a three-tiered one is nestled up against it—very grandiose and impressive, especially to out-of-towners. The top tier has melba toast and two types of caviars, both black, in silver pots, with a miniature silver spoon in each little pot beckoning. The second tier holds various cheeses, from ultra-sharp English cheddar to several sorts of foreign sticky, smelly cheeses that go well with the caviar on toast; and the bottom tier is loaded with confectionaries of all sorts and all flavors. The petits four, covered with icing sugar of different colors, look particularly appetizing. While Al is tempted to dive in, he impatiently waits for Mr. Abdulla to put in an appearance. He smells his tea. *Yorkshire Gold, no doubt.* He slowly sips his tea, remembering to keep his pinky tucked in as Margaret had instructed him, and he luxuriates in his surroundings: soft music, gay flowers of indeterminate origin everywhere; tables with pure white, *Ritz*-embroidered linens that almost touch the floor; silver running riot; beautiful light green furnishings punctuating the huge room; and the people, all beautiful people, all dressed to the nines, not a pair of jeans or open-necked shirt in sight. Al is in heaven. He only wishes Margaret were here to enjoy the splendor and the food. *She does love food, but as she says so often—maybe too often—has no time for sweets, but*, thinks Al, *she'd certainly try a sandwich or two and at least one petit four for dear ol' Al.*

Mr. Abdulla Abdulla finally shows up, ten minutes late with no explanation. In a flash he's towering over Al, unintentionally interrupting Al's tranquil thoughts of heaven on earth and almost causing him to lose his less than secure grip on his teacup. *Why didn't that bloody waiter give me a head's up? Probably still stewing about the booking mix-up, like one additional person makes much difference in a room the size of Wimbledon and hundreds milling about, or appearing to mill about. Maybe there is some order, but I doubt it, even if this is the Ritz.*

"Oh, the hump is real. I thought you were joking—you know, pulling my leg as they say in the States, and so few have humps these days. Wonder why? It's not so unattractive—at least yours isn't. Might one day be kind of trendy, like braces and bow ties were not so long ago. I bet you do stand out in a crowd—can't lose you, dare say."

Al can see that Mr. Abdulla is taken aback by his hump, embarrassed and then some, like meeting a woman one hasn't seen in months, seeing a huge protruding belly, and realizing she's pregnant. People don't know which way to look or what to say, especially men. His hump, like a bulging belly, affects people differently: some try not to even acknowledge it and just stare past it, while others acknowledge it by staring directly at it but continue talking as if his hump doesn't exist.

Still others, like Abdulla, acknowledge his hump, even allude to it in conversation but then become very self-conscious, as though they've been caught taking a peek down the front of a woman's low-cut dress, and talk complete nonsense for a minute or two. The fact that Abdulla is taken aback pleases Al; it gives him a slight edge if an edge is needed. Al slowly rises, annoyingly slowly to Abdulla's thinking.

Abdulla is a big man in every sense of the word, and his swarthy face is serious, with not a smile to be seen in either his eyes or mouth. Al figures Abdulla is not only serious but very serious to the point of being cold and impersonal and most likely arrogant from birth. Mr. Abdulla weighs in at about fifteen stone; he's six foot two, maybe more. He's clean-shaven, with jet-black hair that partially covers his ears. His hairstyle and sideburns are far too long for his age, which appears to be about fifty, and far too long for the times. His face is more oval than round, as are his puffy brown eyes. The rest is pretty standard stuff for a man his age: a nose that sniffs too much and a throat that's just beginning to sag. Al immediately notices that Abdulla has one most annoying habit: sucking air through his top two front teeth as if trying to clean them from the inside; this is accomplished by pressing the tip of his tongue against the back of the teeth and sucking. Over the next hour or two that high-pitched sound will prove to be more and more annoying. Finally, Abdulla's suit ill fits him; it's too baggy, and the creaseless trousers sweep the floor as he walks. It's a light brown suit, not tan but one or two shades lighter than chocolate, but Al has bigger fish to fry; the color of his suit is unimportant. *Must focus on getting the documents translated; that's the name of the game.*

Al doesn't introduce himself by name, just offers a businesslike handshake—a couple of perfunctory pumps, and that's that. Abdulla gets the message: no unnecessary questions if you please, and let's get to work.

"Mr. Abdulla, please have some tea. Then examine my colleague's papers. Let me know if we can do business. If, yes, the two hundred pounds plus twenty quid for cab fare will be handed over. Remember, as I explained in my e-mail, these documents are to be included as an addendum in a soon-to-be-published fictional novel written by yours truly, so I must be sure that when I reference these documents I use the proper verbiage. Understand?"

Pouring tea and collecting a handful of sandwiches, Abdulla responds. "Yes, I completely understand. As well as speaking Farsi, I do also speak English and speak it very well—maybe as well as you—and I should have no trouble with the translations. You're an American, I see, staying at the Ritz, I suppose?"

Al wasn't sure if Abdulla was being clever about speaking English so very well, trying to tell him in a semi-nice way that he wasn't just some yokel from the wrong side of the river.

"No, I'm Canadian, from British Columbia, and, yes, I'm staying at the Ritz. Now, no more personal questions, please."

Al's just being cautious; he doesn't want to admit to anything, having only just met Abdulla. For all he knows, Abdulla Abdulla might be a copper. Now he's having second thoughts about admitting to being Canadian and staying at the Ritz. Maybe he should have just dummied up, but he doesn't want to frighten Abdulla off by being too secretive or too aloof. He needs the translator's cooperation, at least for the next hour or two.

"Now, down to business, Mr. Abdulla."

"Please, sir, my name is pronounced Ab-dool-la, not Ab-dull-la. Pronounce it as if there is a couple of *O*s in it. Don't know why I'm so sensitive about how one pronounces my name, but I am."

"Certainly, Ab-dool-la. I'll be sure to remember that. Now, can we proceed?"

From the inside pocket of his dark, rather spiffy suit jacket, Al withdraws six neatly folded papers, each measuring fourteen inches by eighteen inches when unfolded. The paper itself is almost transparent and light blue; figures and writings of some sort are on the first five pages. The sixth page looks to be some sort of spreadsheet, though it contains no figures, just column headings across the top, labeled row entries down the left, and a date inside each cell. Al passes page one to Abdulla, who sets his teacup down and turns the page clockwise till the page number is at the top right.

"I see, Abdulla, that you know the correct orientation—page numbers top right. That's good. I'm even a bit impressed. It took me many hours to figure that out. Trial and error, you know, but then again I don't speak Farsi."

"Even if you did speak Farsi you might still have problems. Everyday Farsi numbers pages at the bottom, like English, but these are technical drawings, and top right is the convention, as is the light blue paper; it's some sort of government standard. Don't ask me how I know this, but I do; I guess I'm quite a clever chap. Your friend, the one who drew up these papers, must also be quite clever to know the ins and outs of Iranian technical documents."

Al isn't even going to try to answer that question, if it had been a question. This time he does dummy up, as if he hadn't even heard what Abdulla just said.

Abdulla examines page one for about five minutes. After returning it to Al, he is given the second, and so on. The sixth and last is examined more rigorously, in excess of twenty minutes, and then returned.

In that time Al has drunk three cups of tea; taken a few sips of champagne; and eaten several sandwiches, caviar, toast, cheese, biscuits, and mountains of petits four.

"Well." Al cranes his neck to the vertical and successfully makes eye contact with Abdulla after the translator returns page six to him.

"I should have charged you more than two hundred, but a deal's a deal. I assume you just want a synopsis of what the addendum to your book is all about, no real details. For real detail, I'd have to keep the documents overnight and charge you an additional five hundred pounds."

Again, Abdulla makes that high-pitched hissing sound, as if he's beginning to doubt all or part of Al's story and the more he doubted the more he suspected that Al's not only lying to him but using him for something he hadn't signed up for.

"A synopsis will do just fine," Al says as he hands over the two hundred twenty pounds in a large, sealed manila envelope while trying very hard not to appear annoyed.

"No need to count it—it's all there," Al says as he picks up a petit four with yellow icing sugar. He wolfs it down, whole. Delicious.

Abdulla resumes speaking. "The last page is key; it references the previous five. But why would your colleague write a fictional account of the development of a fictional nuclear weapon in Farsi, when you don't even speak Farsi, and now you need a translator at two hundred pounds?"

Al has anticipated this question.

"My colleague is also my friend; he lives in Paris but was born in Iran and lived there for many years before immigrating to France. He speaks not a word of English. He's a university instructor specializing in nuclear physics with a very creative mind. I basically told him what I needed through his wife, who speaks both fluent English and fluent French. I'm not a scientist by any stretch of the imagination. I write fiction and needed some help with some technical details that my friend provided many months ago, and before you ask, I don't speak French at all, and it's not your business how or why I befriended a man who I might have trouble conversing with. Now, no more questions, or I'll be charging you, and, yes, I do eventually plan on having the plans translated into English but didn't want to unnecessarily incur that expense until I was sure of their content."

Thank God, thinks Al, *he didn't ask me why my friend didn't write the plans in French, which would be easier to get translated. I should have developed a better storyline, but I didn't. But, as I'm paying Abdulla, he just needs to do my bidding, and that's that.*

"Okay, got the picture, as you Ca-na-di-ans say." He'd pronounced *Canadian* a syllable at a time, as if reminding Al his name is Ab-dool-la and to get it right.

Al wonders why Abdulla is almost taunting him, perhaps even openly questioning his honesty. It's a mystery to Al. Perhaps Abdulla is again making the point of their equality. Maybe yes, maybe no. Al doesn't know or care to know. He isn't here to befriend Abdulla, just to get a loose interpretation of the documents that he stole from the man in white in Ibiza

"Well," Abdulla continues, "I also am not a scientist, but I can make out what your friend has put together. As I previously said, the final page references the first five. The first five are major components for the creation of a nuclear weapon, according to the copious annotations and notes at the bottom of the page, and that's why page numbers are top right. My goodness, your friend really does have an active imagination, but it's all very high-level, something suitable for a novel, a spy novel I'm guessing. Each component is then broken down into subcomponents; in all there are thirty-six subcomponents that are enumerated in table form on the sixth page—numbered, as one would expect, one through thirty-six. When all thirty-six subcomponents are completed and tested, one has the Bomb and, voilà, success. Oh, voilà is the French equivalent to 'and Bob's your uncle,' as you Ca-na-di-ans might say, or is that an English expression?"

Again, more satire. Al's beginning to think there might be more to Abdulla than mere translator, but no, the man is too easy to read, too simple and pedestrian. No way is he an agent from any country or even law enforcement. He's smart but not clever.

"And Mr. Abdulla, the sixth page is critical to my novel. I assume there are dates of completion for our thirty-six subcomponents? Would you please paraphrase those dates to me?"

Abdulla is handed page six again. He intently studies it for a second time and then restudies it for a third.

"Yes, my friend. Again, please understand that these subcomponents are all very high-level, and I certainly have no understanding of how they're intended to fit together to create one big boom. In reality, each subcomponent would be made up of hundreds of individual workflows, each with their own timeline, but for your fictional account of the development of a nuclear weapon, thirty-six components will do. No other details are necessary. In fact, additional details might confuse the average reader. I should think your scholarly friend kept things simple so as not to overwhelm your protagonist, most likely a nontechnical politician or businessman. Am I not right?"

"Bravo, Ab-dool-la. My lead character is a foreign correspondent with 'connections in high places' as they say. He spends many months surfing the Internet learning about the Bomb; he then creates these documents with the help of a few trusted cronies and tries to sell these plans to anyone dumb enough to fork out good brass. Quite insightful of you, Abdulla, but, please, let's keep this quiet till my book is released, which won't be for several more months. Now, let's get back to page six, please. What completion dates did my friend in Paris ascribe to each of the thirty-six components?"

"That's easy. They're all finished—yes, tested and completed, and have been for several months. I noticed that straight off the bat as they say in your Ca-na-di-an movies, or is it films or, perhaps, the pictures?"

Again that hissing, like a cobra attacking a courageous mongoose. Al begins to wonder who's the mongoose and who's the snake, but it doesn't matter. The time for this interview to end is soon, very soon.

"Excellent, Abdulla, that's exactly what I wanted to hear. My publisher will be most pleased. My book is on track, and when it's completed I'll send you an autographed copy. Now let's finish this lovely tea, and you can be on your way, two hundred plus pounds richer than when you came in."

Al motions to the nearest waiter and requests more strawberry jam. In what seems like a flash, a lovely sterling silver pot loaded to the gunnels with strawberry jam is returned, and returned upon a silver salver to boot.

"Ta, thank you, waiter," Al says as he scoops out some jam with the tiny silver spoon provided. He liberally applies the captured jam onto the biscuit he's eating, doing his best not to drip jam onto his dark black suit. The one drop that does manage to escape Al's gaping jaws falls harmlessly onto his serviette.

Abdulla glares at Al. There's more hissing, almost nonstop.

"Oh, my Ca-na-di-an friend who is really not Ca-na-di-an. One observation from this dark-skinned foreigner who lives on the wrong side of the river, if you please. I suspected right from the start that you were not Ca-na-di-an, but now I am certain of it. You referred to 'good brass,' an English expression, and 'Ta, thank you' is Yorkshire, of that I'm positive. I believe you're English, and for the record I very much dislike the English and your attitudes about Iran and our great Ayatollah, and I hope your book bombs, and I doubt very much you can even afford to stay at the Ritz."

Bingo, thinks Al. *He went for it like a trout to a worm.*

The hissing stops. Abdulla had sprung his trap, probably thinking he's ensnared an Englishman, caught Al in several lies, and showed him for what he really is—a liar, an English liar—but Al is marching to a different drummer.

Al had figured Abdulla might be up to something and needed to find out if his excess curiosity and uncalled-for sarcasm had anything to do with Ibiza. He'd needed to get Abdulla to show his true colors. It was obvious that Abdulla hadn't believed Al was Canadian, so Al provided him with the necessary "proof" to confirm his suspicions. Al's deliberate use of the phrases "good brass" and "Ta, thank you" was intended to give Abdulla the opportunity to vent his frustrations or to continue the game. If Abdulla had wanted to continue the game, Al might have been snookered and might have had to leave with Abdulla's motives still a mystery. Fortunately, Abdulla took the bait and exposed his real and only motive. Abdulla's only reason for trying to outfox the fox is to lecture Al on the evils of being British. That sets Al's mind to rest; at least Abdulla isn't a threat to himself or his quest for the additional million.

"You're right, Sherlock, or should I say Ab-dull-la? Got me dead to rights. I am English and proud of it Now bugger off before I put the boot in, and please don't make a fuss. After all, this is the Ritz, and after all I'm British, and you're God knows what you are, and if you're so unhappy here, why not piss off back to where you came from?"

With that Abdulla leaves, though not before grabbing a handful of sandwiches and stuffing them into his brown jacket pocket. As he exits he looks in Al's direction and mouths, "Bloody English."

This makes Al feel even better. Abdulla is certainly no threat to Ibiza; he's more a threat to himself, immigrating to a country he dislikes and making no effort to fit in. *Probably be going on the dole in the not too distant future. What a fool, and as arrogant as they come.*

Al settles the account; a 20 percent tip seems adequate and brings the bill to an even two hundred pounds. *Worth every farthing.* He then checks into the Ritz, just to spite Abdulla, and mentally ticks off the "staying at the Ritz" entry on his bucket list, a list compiled only yesterday. If he does succeed in getting that extra million, he'll have to assemble a new bucket list.

Again, Al's room is on the third floor, but this time it's not lodgings but a suite of two good-sized rooms and an en suite bathroom. The sitting room has it all: lush pastel velvet furnishings of the softest fabrics; stand-alone brass pole lamps with beautiful multicolored shades that match the furnishings; a big-screen TV with Netflix; and in the corner a bar made of mahogany that one can walk behind and serve one's guests or, even better, one's self. There are even a couple of bar stools. Al can hardly believe his luck: a bar stocked with bottles of good-quality spirits, bottled British beer, and wine to suit all tastes. Not a miniature in sight. There's also an ice maker, and if one feels a bit peckish, room service is just a phone call away.

Ah, the good life. I can hardly stand it. What did I do to deserve all this? Mother would be so proud. The annual migration, each and every Fourth of July like clockwork, to Beacon, New York, for the family picnic was the highlight of her summer, and here am I staying at the Ritz, shelling out five hundred quid a night, just for a place to place my head but with so much luxury it's hard to believe. I think I'll have a large gin and tonic right now, just one, a sneaky one as Margaret's dad used to say.

The dimly lit bedroom is accessed from the sitting room via a portal three door widths wide and as high as a standard door. The bedroom furnishings match the sitting room in color and style. The king-size bed is so high a stool is required, but the pièce de résistance is the bathroom, which is truly palatial. It has a chandelier dead center, but the bath is most amazing in that within easy reaching distance of the bather are five light green pull chords that go up through the ceiling, bound for unknown destinations. Each chord is neatly labeled: *waiter* if one requires a drink while bathing, *laundry* for additional warmed towels as needed, *butler* to help one dry and get dressed, *maid* to help the ladies in and out of the bath, and *madam* to scrub one's back or whatever else needed scrubbing, or so Al imagines. These chords had been disabled years ago but left in place as a testament to the days when the rich not only rented rooms but rented entire floors so their staff would be close by to do whatever needed doing and respond to the pull of a chord.

"The Ritz, the Ritz, the Ritz," Al almost sings as he puts one foot on the stool and falls into bed, careful not to spill a drop—and he doesn't. "I love the Ritz."

As he lies in his bed he goes over what he thought he knew yesterday and knows for certain today. *Thanks to Abdulla, I now know that Iran has developed the Bomb, and well ahead of any timetable the West thought possible.* Actually, Al doesn't really care if Iran has the Bomb or not. He'll still exchange the documents for the million in Ibiza tomorrow, but those little pieces of information Abdulla provided him might come in handy and might add more brass to his already large cache. Now, his second dilemma has to be addressed, and this dilemma will be much easier to address than the first, to wit, *how do I keep someone from forcibly separating me from my documents before I'm ready to exchange them and receive my million?*

That's easy; I'll overnight express the documents to the Sunrise in Ibiza, care of myself, and then collect them when I arrive. This he does, and they are posted within the hour. Except for addressing the envelope, Al doesn't have to move a muscle. The concierge has a young lad collect the envelope with the documents inside, take it down to the local GPO, and post it; the canister is discarded. No tip required—after all, this is the Ritz. *God*, thinks Al, *Life is good; I do so love money.*

181

CHAPTER 10

The clock is approaching twelve; the weather has taken a turn for the worse, much colder; the sun is at its apex and will shortly begin its rapid descent westward. One can expect, this time of year, limited undiluted daylight and only a spattering of direct sunlight. A dry, frigid breeze blows across the park and through the poorly sealed windows and warped doors of the old, mostly wooden, Columbia Club. Even though the furnace has been roaring since enabled early this morning, Jason cranks the thermostat up a few more degrees but to no avail; only time and the advent of more unbroken sunlight for longer periods of time will warm the interior enough for winter gear to be removed upon arrival. By two in the afternoon twenty-four degrees Celsius is a possibility, and then its downhill from there. By two in the morning the temperature of the interior will chase the temperature of the exterior, and the only thing that will be missing from inside the Columbia Club is the weather.

"You know, you can set it to a hundred, but it'll not warm up till it's good and ready. It's been running steady for hours, and it's only just habitable; it's not too bad if it's not blowing, but with that wide-open park just across there, it seems to blow all the time, nonstop. 'Have to dress warm or suffer the consequences; this is England you know.' That's what she always said, and she was dead right. I should have worn my long what-cha-ma-call-ems. Anyway, as long as it doesn't freeze up or explode, we should be able to get something done today. Thank Him above that we're really not so busy, or she'd be at us to get back to our icy rooms and get some done. I don't know how she does it. Just sits there all day long as happy as him; the cold doesn't seem to affect her, but going to the loo for the ladies must be a real challenge what with all their gear requiring rearranging."

"Aubrey, let's forget the weather. Tell me one more time what Pettigrew said. It's not like her being so cagey and evasive. Normally she'd just have Susan fill us in. Must be something very important, something the PM said or plans on doing. I wonder if it has anything to do with us going to sunny Spain tomorrow. Hope she's not thinking about canceling our op."

"She said for us to stay put till she shows up in about forty-five minutes—well, thirty-five now. She has some important information for us that she won't discuss on the phone because of its sensitive nature. She's worried about them and their maybe eavesdropping on her conversations. I tried a few gentle interrogation techniques on her, but she soon twigged onto it. Just hung up—very rude if you ask me. Why is it them that's in power think they can be rude, downright rude, like her just hanging up? Like a steamroller—squash all opposition, squash all the little people, like me. My goodness, if I acted like that toward her, I'd be looking for another job, of that I'm sure."

"By 'them,' Aubrey, I assume you mean reporters?"

"No, by them I meant the chief."

"No, the first them."

"Of course I did. I didn't mean the flipping dragon ladies. I would have thought that was very obvious. They usually prey on the royals, politicians, and maybe one of them now and again, but I wouldn't put it past them to try and pick up a bit of scandal on some high-ranking public servant, especially one of the MI ladies. They've no conscience whatsoever. Just get the bloody story and a few incriminating or embarrassing photos and maybe even a few direct quotes. Where they come from is irrelevant. The more salacious the better, just to sell a few more and get a few more hits on their bloody websites or their blogs. It's no wonder we're discouraged from having them as friends or even acquaintances."

"Again, by them you mean reporters and such."

"Yes, them reporters, that's what I do mean. You know what they call ten thousand of them chained together at the bottom?"

"Yes, not enough. Aubrey, you use that same line for solicitors, politicians, movie stars, union leaders, and anyone you're lampooning or just take an idle dislike to. Fortunately your dislike is temporary, or half the population of this country would be holding their breath under water."

"Aubrey, I'm checking my e-mails again. Nothing's out of the ordinary. I even have a mate at MI-5 that I chat to now and again who says nothing's special going on, though he tells me some folks in Mediterranean Division are putting in some overtime. Plenty of pizza this evening—you can count on that. It must be something that she picked up at Number 10; that's why she's being so coy. My God, it just took me a minute or more just to open one e-mail, and that's no exaggeration, and no attachments either. Network's dreadfully slow again; it's no wonder we never meet our deadlines. At times I can drink a cup of tea waiting for the results of a straightforward search or simple save—very discouraging. All the network people at MI-5 can say is 'inefficient queries,' and from what little I know, they might be right, but why is the code inefficient today that was efficient yesterday? I'm no programmer, and thank the lord for that. I once had a mate, a computer programmer by trade, showed me what he did. Worked all day staring at a screen, all he looked at all day was numbers and symbols and words you can't find in *Collins English Dictionary*. All day he was rearranging one line of code or writing new code as he called it. Well, one day he just up and killed himself with a rope tied to an overhead pipe. It's no wonder—all that thinking, all the time, just warped his brain. Oh, oh, Aubrey, just in, and you're going to love this from one of the muckety-mucks at MI-5 security. We have to reset our passwords again; apparently now it's every sixty days and, guess what, our strong passwords have to be very strong, like nine characters, mixed uppers and lowers with a couple of numbers and special characters thrown in for luck, and no words—at least no English words. Oh, and listen up, the password czar says we're not to write our passwords down anywhere. Not in your desk or wallet or handbag or on your wrist—nowhere, full stop. And if you'd like a longer password, it can be up to thirty characters but no repetitions please. Who in the name of God can remember thirty characters? This is borderline insanity, or maybe that border has been crossed or even double-crossed? What they do suggest we mortals do is put our new password into a classified e-mail and then send that e-mail to ourselves, encrypted of course. That way if you forget your password, you can open that e-mail for a bit of a memory refresh. They even suggest a subject line, and that's 'My Password'—how clever. Those clowns are so bloody pathetic and not the least bit helpful if you ask me, and we haven't had an intentional breach of national security in years. Mind you, there was that chap back in the eighties. Some say he was a mole passing secrets to the Poles. Then, abracadabra, he just vanishes. Some say he was smuggled out by the KGB; others say he ended up in the Thames wearing cement shoes. Anyway, I don't know. Well before my time."

"But don't you need your password to log into our mail server?"

"Bingo. You got it, Aubrey; stowing your password in an e-mail just doesn't make sense, at least not to me, but, as you know, I'm not all that bright. I know passwords are important; some of the information we deal with is very sensitive, even classified, so we need to protect it, but all the MI's have good physical security, and here at MI-9 each room is alarmed. Everyone working in this building has been vetted time and time again. No one can always remember a very strong password; that's why people write their passwords down somewhere. They don't want to embarrass themselves by admitting that they forgot it; and it's so much of a hassle to reset it and generate a new one; and when you do forget your password and request a reset an e-mail is automatically sent to the network mastermind, which results in a black mark against your account, and after so many black marks you get called in for mandatory password remedial training, and guess what, the whole process is automated, never touched by human hands or seen by human eyes. They call that a smart system. I bet even Pettigrew writes her password down, probably in that old Rolodex of hers. And changing it every sixty days is definitely not smart. Just when you get it memorized, you have to change it or get locked out of all your accounts, and then the real hassle begins. What genius came up with sixty days? Maybe we should change it every day just to be on the safe side, and as slow as the network is, changing your password could take some time, which is okay when we're slow, but we're very seldom that slow."

"One day I can see it, Aubrey—smart loos. You have to enter a user ID and password to use the loo. If you forget your password, you really are in deep shit, literally. The government wants to know how well your plumbing's working or not working, as the case may be—all in the name of moving everyone into regularity. The chancellor of loos figures a regular nation is a happy nation, and a happy nation is a more productive nation, and the more production, the more taxes."

"Well, Aubrey, can't blame Pettigrew. She's not the genius that gave birth to password madness. Everything about MI-9 is slaved off MI-5, with the exception of our people, who take orders from Pettigrew. Some of our specialty software and databases also belongs to us, but if MI-5 wants to see our data, they probably could arrange that and we'd be none the wiser. Think about it. All our servers, workstations, and standard, off-the-shelf software belongs to MI-5. MI-5 even owns the furniture and pays the rent on this relic. Pettigrew has no real budget of her own; we're just too small. MI-5 also pays our salaries and benefits, and I'm sure all required password-change edicts are annoying to her also, so you can bet your bottom dollar someone at MI-5 is responsible for this sixty-days thing. I know for a fact that MI-5 and MI-6 are still on one hundred twenty days, so someone has it in for us or maybe has it in for the boss. You know, I used to work with a chap who was about to retire. Told me he never had problems remembering passwords. Said he always took a pencil and marked the keys of his keyboard with the first three or four characters of his password; once he figured out the first three, the rest just naturally fell into place. Of course, periodically he'd have to refresh the pencil marks. He also had to make sure he avoided too many vowels; the more vowels, the more often the pencil marks have to be refreshed. If security ever came poking about, he merely rubbed the marks off the keys with his thumb. Never had any trouble whatsoever, and in all the time he worked for MI-5 never had a password reset and surely never had any bother about someone trying to hijack his password."

"And do you do that?"

"Me? No, of course not, Aubrey. That would be against protocol, and you know me—never break protocol. That would be a security violation, wouldn't it? I don't want security on my tail, so I try to do what they ask and am usually able to. Well, not to worry. Things will somehow sort themselves out. We Brits are pretty clever when it comes to circumventing officious, well-intentioned, but senseless rules."

"Anyway, speaking of senseless ones, I think I'll go have a few words with her, across the hall, help her put together a very strong one. In fact, it'll be so strong she'll need my help remembering it, and I'll be so helpful and so sweet, she'll bend over backward to show her appreciation, or that's what I'm hoping for anyway. I might even ask her if she'd like to go out for a couple later. You know, after."

Half-listening, Jason marches on. "Yes, times are changing, Aubrey, and not necessarily for the best. PINs and strong passwords as well as networks, browsers, social media, response times, and of course bits and bytes are what it's all about today. Yes, computers are the name of the game, and the pair of us better get on board, because if we don't get on board, we'll end up working for some boffin straight out of Cambridge or Oxford who's clueless about what we do on a daily basis but does know his bits and bytes. Oh, so you're going over to see Susan."

"Listen up, mate, we need to have a talk, and put your serious face on, please. For God's sake, Aubrey, pay attention and don't look so bloody bored. This is important. Pettigrew's been keeping an eye on you and Susan, and she doesn't like what she's seeing. You know she's dead set against fraternization, and she believes you two are very close to crossing that line. If you ignore my advice as a friend, then you do so at your own peril, and Susan will most likely be sent to MI-5 or discharged for underperforming and insubordination, so keep your associations with her to a minimum, and keep your conversations to work-related topics only, and please keep your hands off her back, arms, legs, and any other part of her anatomy you find attractive, especially in the work environment, and please don't associate with her off duty, either. Aubrey, I can't give you a direct order—this is not the RAF—but please heed my warning. If you truly like Susan, give her a wide berth. I know Pettigrew a lot better than you. If she thinks you're just blowing her off, there'll be hell to pay, with a due date of just around the corner."

"By God, old boy, you're sounding more and more like a stuffy old one or, better yet, an old fuddy-duddy. You'd think you were her dad or something, and as far as she's concerned, word has it that back in the day she had a fling or two or three, but now that she's gaffer it's everything by the book—her book—and no exceptions allowed. Anyway, I just want to give her a few pointers on how to choose a good strong one that she can readily remember and not have to write down. No harm in that, is there now, I ask you? I don't think so. I think you two are getting your knickers in a twist over nothing. I'm just being sociable and helpful. One would think MI-9 would encourage things like that."

Jason just shakes his head, turns, and says nothing while Aubrey, almost stealthily, heads in Susan's direction. Jason pulls up his chair to within a few inches of the radiator and intently stares out the window, hoping that Clara might put in an appearance. He wants to take Pettigrew's advice and see if Clara was trying to tell him something, but for the time being she refuses to materialize. He knows he's most likely hallucinating when he does see Clara, but maybe hallucinating is a good thing. *The thought of her being gone, completely gone, in the blink of an eye might just be too much for me, and Plan B might become a viable alternative to living a life with little sleep and no hope for the future. Anyway, there are too many distractions today, and Clara never liked distractions; she wasn't much for multitasking.* He thoughtfully smiles to himself. *She couldn't knit a black scarf and watch telly at the same time, and talking and reading a map, with me at the wheel? Well, that was a recipe for an argument, for sure.*

Look at me. I'm starting to get maudlin. Soon I'll be in tears, and Aubrey will be consoling me on my loss though my loss was years ago, but no one can possibly understand how I feel or how I felt about Clara, especially Aubrey, whose wife is more of a nuisance than a comfort and a joy. Anyway, better get my mind off Clara. I know I'll never get over her. Perhaps we should have had children, but I just didn't want to share her. Life's becoming more and more tiresome and uninteresting, but for the time being I must stay focused on this upcoming op to Ibiza.

What kind of bombshell is Pettigrew coming back with anyway, or maybe there's no bombshell whatsoever and just my overactive imagination? Guess I'll know shortly.

Jason can hear Susan giggling across the hall as if there's no tomorrow; he wonders if Pettigrew has spoken to her about fraternization and its consequences. If Susan can't see through Aubrey's humbug then she'll have to pay the price, and paying the price is a bitter pill for anyone, especially one so young and so very pretty.

The front door opens; at this time of day it can only be Pettigrew. Aubrey's back in a flash, almost on tiptoe. They can hear the crack of her hard heels on hard wood floor. Rather than going to her own office, she turns left and comes into Jason's. Aubrey immediately vacates his chair, allowing his chief the opportunity to sit, which she does of course—again without a thank you, smile, or nod.

"Blimey, Jason, it is cold in here. Why not turn the heat up? I hope my office isn't this cold. You should get a little space heater, tuck it under your desk, at least keep your feet warm. Of course, now that I think of it, that's against MI-5 regulations, so on second thought better not. If you do, keep it a secret, between you and the space heater, and don't let me twig onto it or I'll have to order it removed, immediately if not sooner, as we used to say back in the day."

Pettigrew knows that there've been several recent e-mails explicitly and succinctly banning space heaters of any sort from any and all MI-5 controlled facilities, but based on her seniority and dislike of Woolsey she chooses to ignore them.

Jason smiles and nods, eager to hear what Pettigrew has to say about her recent meeting with the PM; he doesn't want to waste time discussing the virtues of space heaters, and if Aubrey weren't present she'd drone on about Woolsey and what a bloody tosser she is and how she can't manage a sweetie shop much less MI-5. Pettigrew never swears, says that it shows a bad command of the English language, but when either Gardener or Woolsey is the subject of a conversation her language quickly degenerates, becoming salty and blue rather than prim and proper as one would expect from the chief of MI-9.

Ignoring Aubrey, as if he weren't even in the room, she proceeds to fill Jason in on what had recently gone down at Downing Street.

"Well, Jason, it's like this. I hardly know where to start. From the news media you know that Iran is allegedly trying to get the Bomb, and there have been unsubstantiated rumors that they are very close. Tomorrow, you're tailing our hunchback to Ibiza, no disrespect meant, and there is most likely some connection between Iran's military ambitions and this man. One of America's agents was unable to receive documents that conclusively prove that Iran is about to acquire the Bomb, and the man you're tailing may be the reason why. That conclusion, my conclusion, is based on one thing: follow the money. Your missions are severalfold. First, protect the hunchback from any harm whatsoever, and I mean that—he is British, after all. You'll be on Spanish soil, so be careful what you do and what you say, and try not to get yourself arrested—be discreet. If necessary, and only if it's truly necessary, coordinate with Spanish law enforcement, but that's only to be done in an emergency. I don't want your cover blown; you're too valuable to me. Once your cover is blown, you won't be able to work any country in the Euro-zone. Next try and secure any documentation our hunchback friend may be carrying that addresses the issue of the Bomb vis-à-vis Iran. Finally, and this is paramount, you are to try and determine the validity of any bomb-related documents that fall into your hands, and that's right from the mouth of the PM. I just finished talking to him on my cell. Yes, I like that expression: 'fall into your hands.' How you are to accomplish this—that is to say, verify the validity of any documentation that falls into your hands? Well, I don't know, but improvise, improvise, improvise. I can't exaggerate the importance of what you're doing. If Iran gets the Bomb, they'll be yet another Middle East war, bigger than the others, and no one wants another war, especially if it's not necessary. Oh, by the by, make sure you have phone numbers. Susan, or perhaps I should call her Scoop, will supply you with all the necessary numbers, and don't forget your mobiles. Take the disposable ones, and before coming home smash them and trash them. No fingerprints of course."

Aubrey cringes but says nothing. What can he say? He knows that "scoop" comment was a direct slam at himself.

Jason tries to make eye contact with Aubrey as if to say to him that yes, she really means business, but Aubrey's eyes never leaves the floor. In fact, if the truth be known, Aubrey is following the antics of a small black beetle out for a stroll, as if on holiday. Aubrey is sure that the beetle doesn't realize how close it might be to dying, being inadvertently crushed by anyone in the room. Death can be like that—never see it coming till it's too late, and then, bingo, you're dead. Aubrey figures if the beetle makes it safely across the room, he'll return from Ibiza safely.

"Oh, one more thing, Jason: no bodies if at all possible. No bodies whatsoever. No Spanish bodies, no American bodies, and most certainly no English bodies—and, yes, that's right from the PM also. Bodies mean publicity, and we want no publicity. This operation must remain clandestine, and, remember you're forever sworn to secrecy. When it comes to your little visit to Ibiza, no matter how things turn out, you dummy up and never use this little episode to try and impress, even tangentially. Get my drift, Aubrey?"

Aubrey again cringes and says nothing, eyes no longer on the floor but tightly shut as if to say "for God's sake please give me a break."

"Ms. Pettigrew, I need some clarifications on a couple of points. So we're to somehow relieve the hunchback of this documentation and somehow determine if the documents are genuine or not, and we're to do all this without annoying Spain, and also do it all in a quiet, peaceful sort of way, and as the PM says, no bodies? Sounds rather daunting to me."

"Jason, let me remind you that this is why you and Aubrey are a part of my team. Doing daunting things is part of the job description, and I expect nothing less than daunting from you pair—you know, for God and country and all that tommyrot. I expect what you're really asking is can you and your mate here use force, lethal force or otherwise, if required. You know I can't authorize lethal force, especially against a British subject. Now, those individuals our hunchback is going to meet may prove to be a different kettle of fish. Remember—improvise, improvise, improvise. I should think you'll do everything in your power to finesse this op. Make sure no one gets killed, including yourselves. If someone gets banged up, slightly bruised, I should think we could manage to sweep that under the carpet, especially if you manage to acquire the docs and come up with some kind of proof as to their validity. Jason, a lot of careers and a lot of lives are riding on this op. Many of our people have been discouraging the planned use of military force against the Iranians for various reasons—many do believe the Iranians are not lying, and then there are pacifists in Parliament who don't want war, full stop, even if Iran does get the Bomb. Appeasement hasn't worked in the past. Why do they think it'll work now? However, if the Iranians make us look like fools and are in the process of acquiring the big one, some kind of attack by the West and Israel will be required, and heads will roll. Sex scandals have brought down governments in the past; only God knows how this scenario—Iran getting the Bomb—would affect the PM and his party, even though political and military choices were made long before the present PM came to power. If we did blow it and did wait too long, and Iran will soon get the Bomb, the only good fallout will be that the dragons at MI-5 and MI-6 will most certainly get the chop. How I'd love to see that—putting those two old witches out to pasture. Somewhere in the Shetlands I should hope. Fortunately, I'm small fry, and at worse I'd just be asked to tender my resignation and go quietly off into the sunset, or so I'm thinking. And if that were to occur, you, Jason, might end up as Chief MI-9, assuming there is an MI-9."

"No, thank you, Chief. One or two more questions if you please, ma'am. How did the man with the hump come by these documents? Has anyone up or down the chain provided us with this piece of intelligence?"

"It's really irrelevant to us, Jason. We just need to get the documents, but I do believe the PM said that someone commandeered them in Ibiza whilst they were on their way to American intelligence. That's all speculation, but I rather suspect that explanation to be true. Think about what we know for certain: an American agent in Ibiza was prepared to receive documents, our hunchback is on the island, the exchange fails, our hunchback's wife end up with a cool million in her Swiss bank account. Any more questions?"

"So why's he going back a second time? He's already made a bundle. Makes no sense to return to the crime scene, now does it?"

"Again, Jason, irrelevant. Maybe more blackmail, a change of heart. Who knows, but we're assuming he's got control of the documents, and we want the documents, and we're prepared to do what it takes to get the documents. Understand? Any final questions?"

"Firearms. They could be checked through with the pilot's approval and a letter of authorization from you."

"Jason, absolutely not, and why would you need firearms? You have Aubrey, and I'm sure after the verbal jabs I've just given him, he's ready to take on all comers. And please remember—no bodies; though a few banged up ones, well, that's okay."

To avoid further questions Pettigrew gets up, returns to her office, and inadvertently squashes Aubrey's new best friend. All Aubrey can think is, *Not good. We may be coming home in boxes, and she'll be pretty upset, but she'll be on everyone's guest list, and that'll cheer her up.*

To Pettigrew's way of thinking she's been walking a fine line between fantasy and reality, and she doesn't want to continue dancing around any more of Jason's rather pointed questions. Actually, she was somewhat disappointed in Jason asking so many questions. She'd been given her marching orders by the PM, and she'd asked no questions. She'd passed them down the chain, and now it's up to Jason and Aubrey to deliver one way or another, and deliver they must; failure isn't an option. She has no idea how Jason can meet the objectives of this operation, but Jason the clever one and Aubrey the muscle might just be able to pull it off.

Susan hears the bang, bang of her boss's footsteps as they approach; they grow louder and louder. She immediately sits up straight and with a quick, abrupt toss of her head shakes her hair out of her face and begins formatting a résumé she's edited several times already. She knows that she's under scrutiny because of her rather close association with Aubrey, who she likes a great deal. Yes, she knows fraternization will not be tolerated, but they're just friends, or so she'd thought. The last time he'd sat next to her he gave her thigh a gentle squeeze, which had confused her to no end. *After all, he's a married man even if he does say otherwise, and I thought we were only friends, and now he may want to be more than just friends, which might be okay with me, as I enjoy his company, but then again perhaps he was just being matey—very baffling, to say the least. Getting mixed up with Aubrey might prove to be a bad idea—too much baggage. Now Jason, I like him a lot also, but he's so uptight. He seldom smiles—not shy I'm thinking, but always preoccupied, off on cloud nine. He needs to lighten up and have some fun.* She continues thinking of Aubrey and Jason, but her thoughts are soon interrupted by Ms. Pettigrew, who is not a happy camper.

"Susan, bring me the latest classified intelligence folder on Iran if you please and a cup of coffee in my office, now, and be quick about it. And make sure it's hot, very hot—micro it if necessary."

Pettigrew reads the folder and then goes online for additional updates. *So many classified links, so many passwords—thank God for my Rolodex. Yes, things are definitely heating up in the Gulf. Iran's calling up reserves, and all her air bases and air defense units are on high alert. Iran is planning to block the Gulf to western oil tankers in the event of an attack and also planning to counterattack Israel and Western interests in the region.* Pettigrew sighs; it's been a long day, and tomorrow might even be longer. She rings for her car, puts on her overcoat, turns the space heater off, and heads for the front door; it's one of the few times she's left before Susan, who will soon follow her chief out the front door.

"Susan, lock up the classified on my desk. Tomorrow you and I are going to have to talk. I'll leave it at that for now, but sooner rather than later you'll have to decide if you want to be a part of my team or just a part of the steno pool at MI-5. Anyway, good night, and have a pleasant evening, and don't forget to turn the thermostat down, way down."

Susan knows exactly what her boss is talking about; it's Aubrey, and what her boss is saying is choose: choose between a solid career at MI-9 or getting tangled up with a very nice but very married Aubrey. Susan is flummoxed; she doesn't know what to do. After all, a job is just that, a job, and she knows she can land another and land one quickly, but she's grown rather fond of MI-9, even quite fond of the chief and Jason, sad old Jason who rarely smiles and never laughs, ever so stoic and reliable, and to many young women ever so boring, plus he's getting on. Many of her friends look for men who are a bit edgy and unpredictable, not necessarily over the top but exciting and hot. She's played that card, in spades, and for every danger-man it seems there'd been a danger-disaster, some of titanic proportions requiring months of quarantined emotions before giving the next danger-man an opportunity to please her or break her heart. The one thing all these danger-men had in common was their ability to lie, even when lying was unnecessary; and while they'd lied often, they'd been anything but consummate liars. When they'd lied, she'd known, and over time their lies trumped any feelings of affection she might have for them, and she'd soon moved on, heartbroken but none the wiser. Actually, if the truth be known, she likes Jason a great deal. It was kind of a nice change, liking someone reliable, someone you could always count on, but poor old Jason is still wed to a dead woman and just can't let her rest in peace and give himself a little happiness or even give himself the opportunity to be happy. Yes, she'd miss them all, but to choose between Aubrey and a job would be difficult.

Anyway, she'll discuss her dilemma with Aubrey tonight; they have a date at her local at eight. He's arranged for a taxi to pick her up at her flat; they'll meet, almost as if it were accidental, so mysterious and so staged, and she half-hopes Aubrey will show up with a stick-on moustache. She enjoys the mystery; it's fun. However, she has to be realistic and is now more or less leaning toward ending future trysts with Aubrey before trysts become liaisons. After all, just for a change, she'll have to be practical and think of her future, and Aubrey's evil, affectionless wife could prove to be a handful, and this is why Ms. Pettigrew wants her to choose. The chief doesn't want to see MI-9 in the tabloids or have to listen to Aubrey's wife screaming down the telephone.

Yes, she thinks, *I'll definitely set things right with Aubrey. I'll give him his marching orders this evening; it's business and business only—and no funny business from here on out.*

Again Pettigrew, a second time, says, even louder, "Susan, good night, and have a pleasant evening."

Startled, Susan submissively responds. "Yes, ma'am. Look forward to our little chat tomorrow, and have a nice evening yourself, what's left to it."

She's chosen and feels better about having chosen. *Tomorrow I'll tell Ms. Pettigrew that I'll be more professional as far as Aubrey is concerned, and tonight I'll follow through with Aubrey. He can be so charming, so convincing, but I'll stick to my guns, hopefully.*

She can hear Jason and Aubrey chatting in the next room but can't discern what they're actually saying and makes no attempt to understand what they're talking about. Locking up Ms. Pettigrew's classified is first and foremost on her mind, and she doesn't want to forget that. She's already in hot water; leaving classified out all night would put her into boiling water, and she'd end up sending one of her nasty grams to herself, something that has never happened so far.

* * *

"You know, Jason, this is rather a sticky wicket. No matter how things turn out we could be hung out to dry, especially if things go south once we arrive there."

Jason can't help noticing that the tone and texture of Aubrey's dialog has changed. As the pressure gets ratcheted up, his abuse of pronouns becomes less offensive and less obvious.

"So let me see if I understand what she just told us," continues Aubrey. "I'll encapsulate it if I may. Get the documents, determine their validity, no bodies, no weapons, and improvise, improvise, improvise. Well, I'm damn sure everyone involved will be packing, especially the Yanks, and if anyone ends up dead, it'll be one or both of us. Am I right?"

"Well, let's hope you're not right about us coming home in caskets, but I don't think Pettigrew would hang us out to dry no matter how things turn out. Then again, she only has so much power, and if it's perceived MI-9 screwed up and the PM is looking for someone's head, it could well be hers. Our illustrious chiefs at MI-5 and MI-6 would be more than happy to serve said head up to the country and the dailies. Regardless, she'd fall on her sword before tossing us to the tabloids, of that I'm sure."

"Okay, Aubrey, let's go over what we know and more importantly what we don't know, in as much detail as we possibly can. Now, we're not exactly sure why our hunchback is going back to Ibiza, but on his first visit he returned to find that his wife's Swiss bank account balance had many extra zeros. I'm also thinking he's not going back just to return the documents in good faith—that would just be too noble—and he's certainly not going back to return his ill-gotten gains. I'm thinking the hunchback must have the documents, and we should work under that premise from here on out; nothing else makes any sense. Why would he even consider going back if he didn't have the docs? So he's returning the docs to someone, but why and who? He must be getting something in return, like more money … the first payout could have been a partial payment. Yes, Aubrey, that makes sense. If that's the case, us getting the documents should be quite straightforward, a doddle. Remember Pettigrew did say a few bumps and bruises are okay. There are two big questions in my mind. First, how do we corroborate the contents of the documents? Do we simply call Pettigrew and say we've got the documents and they look legit, that is to say, they're all in one piece? Hardly. She's looking for proof of some sort. Well, from what we've been told, if we confirm the legitimacy of the docs, that's the same as saying Iran will shortly have the Bomb, and that will give the Americans and Israelis the reason they need to hammer the Iranians, but guess what? You and I are anything but experts in document validation, so what criteria are we to use to say the docs are or are not genuine? That's why Pettigrew got tired of my questions—she didn't have answers. So, in place of answers, we've got to improvise, which is another word for 'wing it,' and I suppose that's what we'll have to do when and if we recover the documents, 'wing it.' The second big question is, I wonder if our hunchback friend realizes that his life may be slowly ebbing away, like sand in an hourglass. One misstep on his part could mean that he gets whacked and we temporarily lose sight of the documents. But however things turn out for our hunchbacked Brit, I'm pretty sure you and I will eventually end up with the documents, one way or another."

"One more thing, Aubrey: we're running out of time. You've read the files. Things are going to start happening this weekend, one way or another. Either the Americans will stand down, or the Israelis and Americans will thump Iran. That's it, plain and simple. There's no way we'll have time to return to England with the documents and have MI-5 and MI-6 determine their validity, and I shouldn't think Woolsey or Gardener would want to make that call anyway. They're too careerist, and they know if they make a blown call that results in yet another war, their careers and any peerage they were expecting will be toast. Pettigrew didn't even suggest returning with the docs to Britain as an option because it's either fish or cut bait; the go-no-no decision will have to be made in the next seventy-two hours, and hopefully you and I will have meaningful, insightful input to the attack-stand-down decision. Don't ask me how, please—we'll improvise, improvise, improvise."

"Well, old boy, you're in charge, so here's the plan as I understand it. I show up at around ten thirty, carry-on baggage only. You at the front, me in the rear. We ignore each other. When he deplanes, we tail him and do our best not to lose him—just a joke, old boy. Anyway, you closely follow him in one cab, and I'm a few cabs behind. Do you know how to say 'follow that cab' in Espanola? May not even be necessary. We'll probably be picked up by the hotel shuttle, which will make things easier for us. Anyway, got to run. See you tomorrow, and, remember just ignore me, like she usually does. From her perspective, I wasn't even in this room this evening. Like I just said, she just ignored me. She didn't even ask me if I had any ideas or thoughts about this op."

"Not to worry, Aubrey. She appreciates you well enough; she just questions your motives when it comes to the ladies, especially Susan. So you're off. I'm not going to ask where you're off to, but I'm hoping it's not with you know who, and I'm very serious about that, dead serious."

"No, no, mate, definitely not. To my local for a few pints with me mates—kind of unwind, you understand I'm sure. Oh dear, you're not thinking I'm stepping out with her, are you? No, no, no, not after your warnings and her sarcasm. Cheerio. See you on the morrow."

Jason knows Aubrey is lying. He certainly doesn't have mates at his local; he has associates, colleagues, or even friends, but never mates. Mates implies flat caps, and Aubrey would see himself dead before associating with men in flat caps or women in jeans. He's too much of a snob for mates, flat caps, and jeans, and Aubrey hardly ever drinks pints, just spirits and occasionally white wine, chardonnay, 12 percent. To confirm his suspicions, he steps across the hall. Susan's gone. Hopefully she'd made her security rounds. He peeks into Pettigrew's office—nothing classified on her desk. He's the last out.

* * *

Jason tosses and turns; finally he can stand it no longer. At five he gets up and meticulously makes the bed, square corners and all. He then goes about making himself a cuppa decaf while he watches the news, which is focused on breaking news in the Middle East.

Cab fare reimbursement to Heathrow has to be submitted in a travel voucher to Susan so both Jason and Aubrey, in separate cabs, get receipts from their cabbies and carefully stuff them into their wallets. After all, twenty pounds is twenty pounds. Both separately check in and proceed through security and then on to the gate, B74. Each, as planned, is solo, something Jason can easily do today, as he feels Aubrey had played him the fool by going out with Susan the night before. They're partners; there'd been no need to lie. There's just too much at stake, and Aubrey, knowing the criticality of this op, had continued to flirt and flit in spite of—or was it because of?—the barrage of warnings coming in his direction.

At the gate both look for the man with the hump. Aubrey is wearing a light-colored suit and bright red tie while Jason is wearing dress slacks, a dark blue denim shirt, no belt, and a lightweight, dull red overcoat. They both spot Al about the same time; it would be difficult to miss him, as he sits immediately adjacent to the Jetway reading the *Times*; no way is he going to miss this flight. As their cabin zones are called, each boards. As fate would have it, Jason sits immediately behind Al while Aubrey is in an aisle seat in the rear of the plane, an MD-88, with only a slight glimpse of Jason, but following that red overcoat will be easy, dead easy.

Jason wonders what the hunchback's name might be, but more importantly he wonders if he has the documents on his person or in his carry-on, a little gray gym bag with zippers in front, back, and both sides. On his mobile, Jason has just received word from another, more junior MI-9 operative that the hunchback had checked in one large case that the operative had personally searched. He'd found no documents of any kind, and the case was made of such thin leather-like material that he doubted that the docs could be stowed in a secret compartment crafted out of the case itself. Jason's brain is racing. *Where can the documents be? On his person? On an accomplice? In Ibiza already? Time will tell, so not to worry now.* After the plane's outside door is closed, Jason relaxes. He plans to enjoy the flight with a wary eye on the hunchback, checking his every movement to ensure no second-party player injects himself onto the field of play.

Aubrey hates flying, and he especially hates sitting in the rear of the plane. Every bump is magnified, and he wonders why airlines stopped using the word *turbulence* and started using the phrases *rough weather* or *rough air*. That for some reason annoys Aubrey more than the turbulence itself. The usual bumps in the vertical when passing through clouds are expected and accepted, but the side-to-side yawing in bad weather really unnerves Aubrey. What's most unnerving is when the plane slows to what seems like a crawl on final approach. Aubrey sits there thinking that the plane will stall and free-fall to the earth, requiring perhaps minutes to die. To settle his mind and heart rate, Aubrey relives last night's date with Susan. At first, she'd been more than a bit cordial, even a little bit romantic and cuddly-like, but after a few gins, enough to give her sufficient Dutch courage, she let him have it with both barrels.

"Just friends, please, and we're to be very professional at the office. I have to think of my future, you know. I'm not getting any younger, and the chief tells me if I don't shape up, I'm out the door."

To say Aubrey had been crushed, dumbstruck, or devastated would be an exaggeration, but he'd certainly been shaken up a bit and at first wondered why she'd dumped him, but he couldn't blame the girl with all that pressure from Pettigrew and the old man. They'd parted on friendly terms and a cordial handshake, and he even helped her into a cab, though he'd refused to pay the cabbie in advance. He stood in the freezing weather waiting for the next cab, which arrive twenty minutes later. By God he hated those two words *just friends*, and he'd heard them so often but never quite got used to them. *Anyway*, he thinks to cheer himself up, *plenty of other fish in the sea. Next.*

Al continues to thumb his way through the daily he'd just bought at the newsstand near the gate; at three quid, he plans to read every word. In big headlines there's speculation that America, in partnership with Israel, is going to attack Iran's nuclear enrichment facilities and very, very soon. There's fear, even panic, in some circles that Iran has acquired and is prepared to use nuclear weapons. A decision has been made in Israel that sanctions have failed and time is running out. It appears their American allies have agreed, for they've positioned two naval forces in the Med, well within striking distance of any potential target. Planning and coordination had previously been worked out under the guise of training exercises. Iran knows that this was no bluff; an attack is likely imminent, so she, in turn, is preparing for substantial conflict and substantial follow-on initiatives knowing full well she'll lose round one but over time might inflict considerable damage to Israel and material damage to American regional interests.

Iran, hoping for international support and sympathy, has reiterated and restated the same old mantra that her quest for nuclear capabilities is for peaceful purposes only and that she has no intention of building a weapon based on nuclear energy. No one in Israel is listening, and it appears no one at Langley is listening either, but analysts suspect nothing could be further from the truth. Langley is still, a page one article suggests, searching for answers and has to have them soon, or the president, in spite of vehement protests by Israel, will cancel the attack on Iran. To Al the commotion about Iran, America, and Israel is all good news, news that most likely means no one is looking for him or his documents and the extra million is coming home to papa.

Al's quite prepared to give the documents back to their original owner, the man in white, and what the man in white does with them is irrelevant to Al. As long as he gets his second million, the man in white can do with them as he pleases, even return them to Roger or whoever. Al just wants the loot, and thanks to Abdulla Abdulla only he and the original owners know their true contents, or so he thinks.

Al relaxes and quietly hums "Off we go into the wild blue yonder," never even thinking that he might be followed or be in danger. The docs are already at the hotel in Ibiza, only he knows that, and he's quite prepared to return them—for a million of course. So in his mind there's no reason why anyone would want to harm dear ol' Al.

The MD-88 roars down the runway. At around one hundred sixty miles an hour, she gently lifts off, heading south to Ibiza.

CHAPTER 11

Ahmet paced the length of the bedroom—ten paces, turn, ten paces back—his hands never leaving his pockets, where one hand fumbled with some loose coins while the other fingered a small gold pocket watch, sans fob chain. A small piece of white cotton string attached the key to the watch, though Ahmet never wound it. The watch was from his father's estate, and he carried it with him on all operations, always in his right pocket. He liked to think it brought him luck, and perhaps it did. Every op he'd been on but one had been successful, and he'd always returned safely without as much as a scratch. Ernna, as was her wont lately, mocked him, telling him he was a fool for believing in such nonsense and superstition, but no matter what she said or how loudly she said it, he wouldn't part with his good-luck piece. While the watch had more or less failed him on his last trip to this god-forsaken spec of manure in the Mediterranean, he had returned home alive, and there was still the opportunity for him to recover his documents and transfer them to Roger or anyone else representing American Central Intelligence. He stopped pacing, sat on the edge of the bed, and placed the watch on a small night table adjacent the queen-size bed, between the hotel phone and alarm clock. The ticking of the clock was loud, incessant, and regular, very distracting if you went out of your way to listen. In a few hours, one way or another, he'd either have the documents or not—so much pressure, ceaseless and uncaring.

Even though the Sunrise Hotel was advertised as semi luxurious, Ahmet's room was Spartan, designed to be quickly cleaned and made ready for the next occupant. The parquet floor only needed a quick mopping, while the bed could be changed in less than five minutes by an experienced housemaid, and they were all experienced, all being mothers who'd successfully reared several bambinos. In addition to the bed, there was a standalone vertical lamp with a white, blotchy plastic shade, a mildew-stained white wicker chair, and a refrigerator that hummed every time the compressor kicked in. Between the refrigerator and the air conditioning Ahmet could imagine a sonata of elegant proportions, as each had its own unique rhythm, and each kicked in at irregular intervals. A set of French doors led to an outside veranda of sorts. Two cheap, tacky, black wrought-iron chairs, pitted by salt air, nearly filled the five-by-eight-foot balcony that overlooked the Med. A low, four-foot-high railing offered the sea gazer some protection from the parking lot far below, but if one were a bit tipsy one would be well advised to remain indoors. The bathroom was of standard hotel issue, white porcelain in all directions, white towels, white tiled floor, and of course the tub—no shower; all were clean enough to be an operating theater. On the counter stood, like a row of regimental soldiers, five little brown plastic containers containing Ahmet's blood pressure medications, as well as a single container of pills for gout and a single white container of Lipitor. While his blood pressure was presently under control, stress, salt, booze, caffeine, insufficient sleep, and weight gain could easily override the positive effects of the pills, or so his doctor told him. Yes, his doctor—of no particular association with the Agency—cost Ahmet a pretty penny. The bill from a Service-connected doctor would have been "no charge," but if his handlers or his management ever found out about his blood pressure issues, he'd be sidelined for sure, and Ahmet chose not to deal with the reality of the situation; he chose to ignore that reality and not only endanger himself but his operations, present and future. Ahmet thought he was clever enough to manage the moment. If he felt that tingling pressure in the upper half of his face, and his lips as well, he'd pop a pill or two, lie down, and think pleasant thoughts: the sea; a brightly burning fire on a chilly evening; a beautiful woman, not Ernna—oh my God, never Ernna. This regimen checked and then lowered his blood pressure, always and, up to now, within fifteen minutes, and he'd be back on the job no worse for wear. His doctor had also told him to purchase a mobile blood pressure cuff and learn to monitor his own blood pressure and keep a record so he, the doctor, could properly manage the effects of Ahmet's medications. Ahmet chose to ignore this piece of advice also. However, even Ahmet was smart enough to know that very high blood pressure, if left unchecked could result in a paralyzing stroke or even death, and his physician had also told him, on more than one occasion, to go to an emergency room if that tingling pressure in the upper half of his face persisted.

Ahmet suffered through several episodes of blood pressure on steroids, where the upper half of his face would go tingly and numb, making him feel a bit confused and out of touch with reality. He mentally referred to this condition of unbridled high blood pressure as "the Mask," but over time he did learn to manage the Mask. He cut out table salt, except on eggs, and caffeine, and with superhuman effort he limited his wine intake to two glasses a day, usually in the evening, which also had the secondary effect of eliminating the mild gout in his knees that he occasionally experienced. He dropped a few pounds, exercised irregularly, tried to get eight hours of sleep a day, which was impossible, and made an extra-special effort to always take his meds on time. The only thing he couldn't manage was his wife and her incessant unhappiness, but all things considered he managed the Mask well.

Ahmet was in an unusually pensive mood as he sat motionless on the edge of the bed, feet resting comfortably on the floor. His first consideration was not the op but Ernna. She was having a difficult time coping, caving in to every pressure life put in her way. When he'd first met her she was a pillar of strength and self-confidence, but over the years, what with prolonged separations; long, lonely hours and the not knowing she became more and more morose and then more and more frantic and irrational, never completely reasonable and never in control. If only he could have told her where he was going and for how long, perhaps that might have helped, but he couldn't; he wouldn't jeopardize the operation—no way. Whenever she saw his case next to the door, she knew he'd be leaving shortly. He could only tell her that he'd be leaving soon, not to worry, keep busy, and he'd see her when he saw her. In the beginning he didn't think this much of an inconvenience. In fact, to be perfectly honest, he thought it rather nice that someone could miss him so much, but over the years all the uncertainty had adverse physical and psychological effects on Ernna, effects that Ahmet could never have conjured up even in his wildest imagination. Ernna ate irregularly and subsequently lost weight; she graduated from over-the-counter sleeping pills to prescription medications to help her sleep, but she always looked tired and wretched and was always fractious. She drank too much when he was gone, and this irresponsible drinking was beginning to affect her memory. She became distant, self-absorbed, and reclusive and when Ahmet did return, she pretended that she didn't miss him at all and was looking forward to him leaving again, sooner rather than later. She had no close friends and continuously argued with her brother and mother, calling them the most hateful names she could think of at the time, and even when she calmed down, she never apologized but remained aloof and defiant. She was always absolutely miserable, deep in despair, and deeper into self-pity. Ahmet feared self-destruction might one day be an option for her, and it would be his fault for neglecting her, for placing his career over her best interests. Their marriage vows specifically pointed out that they were to be responsible for each other, especially if one were sick. Ernna was sick, very sick, an emotional train wreck. She needed his full-time attention, but giving up fieldwork for a desk job or retirement was unthinkable. A desk job not only meant less pay but limited opportunities for advancement. The Service wanted go-getters, people who were prepared to sacrifice, people who were prepared to see their family inconvenienced or even, in rare instances, emotionally sacrificed for some greater good. Also, desk jobs were boring: going to meetings, sitting around all day planning ops for others, or just killing time waiting for five o'clock and then fighting the more than abundant traffic to get home. Sending and receiving e-mails of little or no consequences might be his destiny one day but not today; he just wasn't ready to pack it all in. Ernna had known he traveled a lot when they first met, and at that time traveling didn't prove to be an issue or even a mild inconvenience. Why didn't she speak up then? There could have been some resolution. They'd agreed on no children because of his job, and that never proved to be an obstacle to their happiness; why wasn't this traveling thing resolved sooner instead of escalating into an issue of monumental proportions? It was like a double whammy: high blood pressure and Ernna, that perfect combination of catastrophes designed to sideline Ahmet, force him into early retirement, or kill him outright.

No matter how much Ahmet rationalized, justified, or tried to ignore the realities of his present life, deep down he knew change was inevitable—for his wife's sake, for Ernna's sake—but would and could he follow through? After this op, something had to be done and would be done, or so he hoped; he hoped he'd have the courage to move one way or the other and get off dead center. As much as he'd hate it, he'd have to move on, either retire or give up fieldwork; medical requirements of course would be the reason. Admitting to his superiors that his wife had serious emotional issues would end his career, and pronto; he'd be forced to hand in his papers and live a life of tedium on a disastrously curtailed budget, something he did not wish to do but for Ernna and his own health, he'd give up fieldwork as soon as he returned home from Ibiza. With so much on his mind, Ahmet had broken one of the golden rules of the Service: he taken his eye off the ball. His current op was now a distant third in his list of priorities, well behind his wife and the Mask.

His mobile rang, the sound of a dog barking. Ahmet retrieved it from the outside pocket of his sports coat. It was Mamet. While the tone of his voice was steady, Ahmet could detect a note of trepidation, yes, anxiety, which made him anxious and fearful, fearful of what Mamet might have to say about his sister. Had Ernna finally lost it altogether or, worse, opted for plan B, suicide?

This will not be a phone call that ends well, on a positive note, he thought. *As long as Ernna's okay, I can deal with anything. I can cope, but if Ernna's in trouble then I'm in trouble, and the mission can go to the devil.*

"Ahmet, listen. This is important. Isule's on his way to Ibiza. His plane arrives at fourteen hundred local, your time, today. Keep an eye out for him and make arrangements with Isule to collect the case containing the additional million. When you secure the documents, hand over the million, no questions asked, as agreed to. Please don't get clever or heroic; just hand the money over, get the documents to Roger, and return ASAP."

"Why is that gorilla coming? I thought you were coming. He hates traveling and can be so difficult at times. He knows he's my supervisor and won't let me forget it. He'll try to intervene wherever possible and just get in my way. He just wants to make a name for himself, but if things don't turn out well, he'll wash his hands of the whole situation and crucify us, you and me."

"Well, Ahmet, to be quite frank, Isule doesn't trust or even like either you or me. He thinks if he wants the job done right, he'll have to do it himself. You know, for such a little man, a little fat man, he has a rather high regard for himself, and he has never attended university or even a college, and if I'm not mistaken his fieldwork is practically nil, and that's why he keeps his curriculum vitae under close wraps—it's nothing to brag about."

"In my opinion, Mamet, he's undereducated and anything but an overachiever, but he's sly and crafty. The only reason he's our superior is because he's dodged sensitive missions where failure was an option and managed to worm his way into the hearts and minds of the politicos who run the Service. In a word he's a sycophant, a player, and I've always disliked players of any ilk. As you know he can be charming, constantly fingering the tips of his antiquated, waxed moustache or rubbing his overstuffed pot belly after a meal, like, some kind of gorilla that's just eaten a boatload of bananas. But he smiles a lot, always has a funny story at his fingertips, and is not shy about ingratiating himself to the right people, especially the ladies, who seem unnaturally susceptible to his disingenuous compliments and wily ways."

Mamet caustically responded, "You may be right, but keep an eye out for him, and don't go out of your way to antagonize him or frustrate his plans. He's really hopped up mad about this second million—thinks you blew it. He'll bring the million in his carry-on in cash, but don't be surprised if he doesn't try to somehow procure the documents and keep the money, and I believe Isule may have contacts on the island, so be extra vigilant, for God's sake. The way he's been carrying on, one might think the million is coming out of his pocket, or maybe he's hoping for some kind of finder's fee. He'll do some kind of grandstanding, and if he's able to procure the documents without forfeiting the cash, at least in his mind he'll be some kind of savior or even a hero—you know, something like 'He saved the day for the good guys, God bless Isule.'"

"Nonsense, Mamet. He's such a wart, so full of himself. You know, my brother-in-law, that 'hero business' is not only ridiculous but crap, and it's only a million after all. It's certainly not a king's ransom by any stretch of the imagination, and our budget is surely not that tight. He could end up by getting in the way. I have no idea who I'm meeting, but they know me. They or he or she will initially come forward, so they'll have the upper hand, and there may even be more than one. I'll confirm the docs are the originals and not copies and then hand over the money, no questions asked. If they smell a rat they might bolt. I don't think that's something Isule's superiors want, do you? First and foremost we want to move the documents over to the Americans, a.k.a. Roger, as quietly as possible—no fuss and no involvement by Spanish authorities and no publicity. For God's sake, we don't want our mugs plastered all over the front pages of every newspaper on the planet. When it's all said and done, our superiors want a silent transition of the docs over the Americans; this is what we want. After all, this entire scheme, success or failure, was hatched by us, by you and me. We're two of the few who truly appreciates the ins and outs of what's going on. I think, if I remember correctly, it would be appropriate to say 'it's a plan of Byzantine proportions.' Yes, that sounds impressive, and it's true, and if that gorilla blows it, it'll be his head as well as ours. Is that your take?"

"Probably so, Ahmet, but Isule sees this as an opportunity to further ingratiate himself to our current rulers, make a name for himself. I had a few drinks with him last night. You know Isule—he always drinks a bit too much and talks too much, and I'm sure he's planning some sort of ruse, so please be careful, and if anyone gets hurt, let it be Isule. You may have more to fear from Isule then the man who knocked you on the head. Isule may just end up getting you killed, and if those trigger-happy Americans in the form of Roger and any of his sidekicks are in Ibiza, and we believe they are, there may be some gun play, as they say in those American Westerns I love so much, so don't let anyone get the drop on you, partner, and don't get tangled up in your own spurs. So, my friend, there's plenty of unknowns out there. Be wary of the Americans, be wary of the Spaniards, be wary of the man with the blackjack, but most of all be wary of Isule. You know what they say."

"Yes, I know. Keep your enemies close and your friends even closer. That's so lame, so overused but so true, Mamet. I'll keep it in mind. Not to worry—I've got my lucky pocket watch with me."

"Anyway, Mamet, you're right about Roger. He's here. I've seen him a couple of times, like a little lost puppy looking for a pat on the back or just someone to talk to. You really do love American Westerns, Mamet, but you've forgotten one more player and maybe the most important. Perhaps the man with the blackjack will also have friends on the island, friends that Isule may have overlooked, making him more vulnerable than he believes. My first priority is the op. If Isule gets into trouble, he's on his own, and that's a promise."

Mamet, half jokingly, "If it were me in place of Isule, would I be on my own?"

Without hesitation, Ahmet shot back, "No, the op could go to blazes, and the only reason I say that is because I would have to tell your sister of your death, and that might just be the one thing to push her over the edge, and she means too much to me to risk such a disaster, such a maelstrom, and her going over the edge would be a lot more than a storm in a teacup. Yes, outwardly at times she does loathe you, Mamet, but deep down she loves you very much. After all, you are blood of her blood, and as the old saw goes 'blood is thicker than water.'"

"Ahmet, Ahmet, you've always had a way with words, but I appreciate what you just said. I think. Oh, and don't forget, if you do happen to get the documents—or should I say when you get the documents—get them to the Americans ASAP. Then be gone. Come home to my crazy sister; she needs you very much. I spoke to her a while ago, and she sounded so cheery and happy, but, as you know, it's all just a front, a cover for her real emotions, and she didn't even try pumping me for information about you, which is not her nature, so I'm thinking she's up to something, hatching some sort of plot, trying to figure out how to make me miserable with her uncommon, unreserved happiness. Well, go figure."

"Yes, Mamet, go figure. If you speak to her again, tell her that I miss her and love her and will be home as soon as I possibly can. Au revoir, my dear friend."

"Yes, au revoir—as long as it's au revoir and not adieu, so, please be careful, Ahmet."

"I will try, but as you know in this line of work anything can happen and usually does. Good-bye for now."

With that they both hung up. Ahmet powered off his cell. He intended to take no more calls; for the next few hours he had to focus on the op. He stretched out on the bed, waiting for the appointed hour, which was still some time off.

What tradecraft, Ahmet thought. *Perhaps it's for the best that I'm packing it in—me, discussing operational matters on a mobile. Very poor tradecraft indeed, something I learned not to do in Spying 101, back in the day, but it doesn't matter. Who do I have to fear? The one who thumped me is an amateur, of that I'm sure, and the Americans for all intent and purposes are on my team; they just want the documents with no hassle. The only wild card, as far as I know, is Isule, and he's probably more dangerous than any unknowns that I'm aware of.*

Ahmet tried focusing on how he saw the upcoming meet going down, or how he'd like it to go down, and figuring out different viable alternatives if things went sour, but how could he concentrate, how could he focus with this horrible, never-ending distraction consuming him with uncertainty and agitation? If only he didn't love his wife, just didn't care what happened to her, one way or another. It would make things so much easier, but he couldn't be that cold, that heartless. He truly loved his wife. It was his career or Ernna. There was no other choice; there was no third way. He just wanted this op to be over. He didn't care how it ended; he just wanted to go home.

As was his habit Ahmet overanalyzed his current predicament vis-à-vis Ernna. Either retire or remain with the Service as a desk officer—he'd already decided to give up fieldwork upon returning—but to leave the Service, to retire? The word *retire* seemed so final, as if the next step was the grave, and it probably was, but Ahmet had decided, in spite of himself, in spite of wanting to indefinitely defer any decision at all. Yes, he would retire for the sake of Ernna. Yes, the die was cast. Upon returning home he intended to hand in his resignation and retire, but not retire from life. He'd develop other interests, such as a hobby or, yes, hobbies, and maybe even occasionally work out at the local gymnasium with his brother-in-law. Anyway, in spite of his other interests, between looking after Ernna and avoiding the Mask his life would border on meaningless, a life without a cause or purpose. But what had to be done, had to be done, and Ahmet was never slow to action once he'd crafted a final solution to a vexing problem, or so he thought. He even looked forward to boarding a plane back home after this op, his final op, was over, regardless of the outcome. His benefits were not fully vested, but at 40 percent of his current salary, they'd get by. A small house or apartment in the country with a little land to grow vegetables, and maybe a few chickens, didn't sound too awful but awful enough. They wouldn't be able to afford much more than seeing a film now and again and eating out at some cheap Indian restaurant where most of the food was brought in frozen; even the vegetables and fruits would be two or three days old. Traveling was out of the question. Most days would be spent at home doing not much of anything, just going through the motions, taking lots of naps to kill time, to kill what was left of the rest of his life, but at least he could keep an eye on Ernna. Presently, neither had any extracurricular interests or close friends to speak of, so every evening would be dedicated to watching TV and having a few glasses of cheap red plonk. But they could change and would change and would develop meaningful interests, things they could do together—maybe even take up ballroom dancing, though Ahmet had to admit that he had two left feet and was tone deaf. Regardless, "end-stage life'," as Ahmet liked to refer to a life with no purpose, was in the cards, and the only thing he could look forward to with any degree of certainty was the grave, but it would be better for Ernna. He owed her that, but as for himself, he'd be miserable but persevere and try to put a cheery face on an ever-so-dismal, and most likely worsening, situation. He just wasn't ready to hang it up, sit around all day, and get lazy and then fat and then more lazy. But, as his long-dead father used to say, "Life's a bitch, and then you die"—and he was right; he did die.

Ahmet wondered what the man with his plans and the million might be up to. What was in his future? He'd certainly have enough money to enjoy his golden years and enjoy them in style, perhaps living in the South of France, going on Rhine River cruises, and maybe even taking cooking classes in Naples. All were possible for him. In fact, with sufficient funds anything, anywhere, anytime were all possibilities. *But*, thought Ahmet, *what's in my future? Cheap red wine, and that'll have to rationed, and the only Italian food I'll be eating is pizza from the corner deli—probably have to buy it by the slice.* Some people got all the breaks. Again he tried focusing on the upcoming second exchange but couldn't—too many distractions, all named Ernna. Anyway, in a few hours it would all be over, one way or the other, and he'd be on his way back home, but for now he'd have to be extra cautious; he didn't want to get a second knock on the head or worse and end up going home in a box.

While Ahmet did not intend to sleep, he did doze off and immediately dreamt, or was it something other than a dream, maybe an omen? But it did feel like a dream, most abstract and most symbolic, but what did the symbology represent, if anything? In the dream he and Ernna were seated in the backseat of a car, very tired. He slept on her breasts. They drew up to a plain, multistory, poorly lit building with many open windows. The second-story windows glowed invitingly. A ladder of dramatic length materialized, straight up to the top floor. Ernna was first up, as agile as a monkey. When she arrived at the second floor, she easily entered the window, was almost sucked in. Ahmet clumsily climbed, rung by rung; even though this was just a dream, Ahmet feared falling, feared death. When opposite the open window he tried entering, but for every attempt there was a corresponding failure. First the window shifted: left then right, up then down. After many failures Ahmet got a leg into the window, only a leg. The window then shrank, so Ahmet retreated. The window then commenced to grow and shrink unpredictably. Ernna beckoned. When the window was at its largest, Ahmet propelled himself into Ernna's waiting arms. He had made it. They embraced; she was smiling, beaming, like she used to beam when they first met. She was happy, exquisitely happy, with no frown lines, no anxiety, just contentment. He rolled over and awoke; Ernna's smile abated, but her frown was always in the back of his mind.

He pondered the dream, if it were a dream—maybe he'd not been asleep at all. *What did it all mean: a window with a mission, a window with a personality, and Ernna smiling and confident. What rubbish. That Ernna died years ago.*

Ahmet tried not to think of anything, especially windows, his wife, or what might happen or not happen later that afternoon. He didn't want to upset himself, didn't need an unexpected visit from the Mask, which reminded him, *It's time for my medications; yes, this time of day it's blood pressure medications as well as that famous cholesterol-busting medication.* Fortunately, other than occasionally feeling a bit loopy and drowsy, all these meds had no adverse physical effects on him, and for that he was grateful.

On his way to the bathroom, he looked out the window. From his view of the pool area, Ahmet could see Roger wandering, wandering nowhere in particular, just wandering from one end of the pool to the other. He was wearing a straw boater, knee-length swimming trunks of an indescribable color, a flashy bright red shirt, and green flip-flops. In his right hand he was carrying what appeared to be a large book. Of course, he also wore a pair of Ran Ban Aviator sunglasses; he probably thought they made him look trendy, cool. Looking cool was important to Roger. Ahmet wondered if this was Roger's idea of blending in. Anyway, it must have worked; he was alone. He couldn't make a friend no matter how hard he tried, probably couldn't even buy a friend. Roger stopped, stared seaward, and with a great deal of hesitation began chatting to a rather long, slightly overweight woman of about fifty who was lying on her back on a navy blue deck chair wearing a bright pink bikini that was far too small for a woman of her size—flesh bulged every which way but loose, thank God. Her longish body was matched by a longish face with features that were either long in the horizontal or long in the vertical; nothing was short about the lady in the pink bikini except perhaps her temper. Roger would talk, she'd answer, and on and on till she got fed up and gave him the glare that meant move on and stop blocking the sun if you please. Roger moved on, awkwardly, till he reached the far end of the pool, where he made two quick turns and returned, desperately looking for someone, anyone to chat to, but all eyes were averted. Ahmet wondered if Roger's behavior, that of a hapless loser, was some kind of cover and beneath that unlucky but planned persona beat the heart of a lion or at least the heart of a lion cub full of confidence and verve. *Impossible. No one could develop a cover like that and have it be so convincing. What you see is what Roger is all about, and that's indecisive, introverted, and most likely very unlucky,* or so Ahmet thought.

Yes, Roger's back, for sure, mused Ahmet. *It looks like Mamet was successful.* A couple of days ago Ahmet had helped his brother-in-law prep for a visit to the American consulate in town. Mamet had planned to meet with his American contacts and inform them that a follow-on drop would occur in Ibiza Friday evening at the hotel bar, same package, and if they still wanted the documents to make sure someone was there to receive them and to bring the promised cash.

Mamet had been warmly welcomed into the consulate, his bona fides having previously been vetted. He was offered tea—hot tea, not iced tea. While sipping this less than satisfactory tea, Mamet updated the Americans on what would soon take place in Ibiza. As he was about to depart, he received the usual two thousand; no questions were asked, which surprised and pleased Mamet, who was sure he'd be asked to explain why the previous exchange failed. But he wasn't asked to explain anything, so all his preparation for that anticipated question went for naught. Apparently the Americans wanted the documents at any cost, and they weren't interested in why the previous exchange had failed, as they already knew of the failure compliments of Roger's handlers. The Americans were only interested in the probability of success this time around. Mamet assured them that failure was not possible, even offering to return the two thousand if they doubted his integrity or motives. As expected the Americans declined. Mamet was then silently and coldly ushered out a side door and into a crowded shopping plaza, where he stopped off at the nearest bar for a shot. *Yes,* thought Mamet. *No one likes a snitch. Whatever. But for me what's really important is a good bottle of whiskey and a fine woman or women. That's what life, or at least my life, is all about.* The shot was downed in a heartbeat, followed by a chaser of miniature Kit Kats offered by the barman. *Now back to the office to mess with Isule's plants, but on the way back I must watch my back, make sure I'm not being tailed. Ah, life is good.*

Ahmet missed his brother-in-law. Mamet was everything he wasn't. Women described him as a bad boy, something apparently many, if not most, women, at least those under forty, liked. He was cocky, bold, lighthearted, extremely confident with the opposite sex, and presently single, though he'd been engaged at least twice this year. Yes, single, something Ahmet longed for now and again, but not always. No, not always; when it was all said and done, Ahmet did love his wife and feared for her safety, but as in all long-term relationships he did, at times, pray, maybe even mentally plan, for her demise. For this he was ashamed and full of guilt, though only temporarily.

Anyway, Ahmet, back to business, you slug. Stop daydreaming. Mamet assured me that he wasn't followed on his journey back to the office from the American consulate, ever, so the possibility of a rogue agent from the consulate knocking me senseless and walking off with the canister borders on ludicrous, if not impossible, but all the pieces of the puzzle just don't fit. We want to transfer the docs to the Americans but in a circuitous manner, not directly—too suspicious. That's why Mamet just didn't pass the plans over to the Americans: too many red flags, too many questions with questionable answers. That has always been the plan and still is; the documents must end up in American hands but not directly, or their validity would most certainly be disputed. However, thought Ahmet, '*There's a wild card out there, and I've no idea where that knave is or who that knave is working for, and he's the one that knocked me senseless, and he's the one who'll most likely be returning the canister to me this evening. And with a bit of luck I'll get a chance to even the score. No, no can do; no trouble. Just make the exchange and be off; getting even is out of the question, as tempting as it is.*

When Isule had heard that his team would be given another opportunity to supply the Americans with the documents, he'd been less than overjoyed, at least outwardly. He just said "Thank you very much" in as curt a manner as possible, dismissed Mamet, and continued watering his precious African violets. He especially loved African violets, and whenever he was away on business Mamet was left to care for them.

Mamet disliked Isule with a passion, so the plants suffered. They were therefore only watered on the day of Isule's return, no matter how long he was gone; perhaps that explained why the violets never bloomed, which caused Isule a great deal of grief and frequent visits to the local garden shop, where he was told not to fertilize, to copiously water, and not to unnecessarily shift the plants but let them stay in place, and blooms would be forthcoming. As he watered, Isule reflected on replacing Ahmet with an agent he considered more reliable. Lately, Isule had noticed Ahmet, well, not being Ahmet; he was preoccupied, almost sullen, and defensive to the point of paranoia, but Ahmet knew Ibiza, knew the players, and he and his brother-in-law had cooked up the entire scheme—with significant coaching from himself, of course. Something was eating at Ahmet, maybe his alcoholic wife but probably not. His medical records gave no clues, but in his heart Isule could see that Ahmet was on the brink, but of what? He had no idea, but after this op he'd order Ahmet to have a complete physical and psychological evaluation by Service physicians and go from there. If it was proven that Ahmet was no longer fit for duty, he, Isule, would be more than happy to give him that final push. When it came to putting old nags like Ahmet out to pasture, Isule excelled. He had no qualms about ridding the Service of people who had seen better days, and no desk job would be proffered. Ahmet would not be allowed to hang about answering the phones so his pension payout could accumulate. His separation would be voluntary, of course, but if Ahmet fought retirement his personnel file would be loaded with as much negative material as he could dig up, and Ahmet would be separated for cause. Anyway, one way or another, he'd be out the door, and good riddance. Isule disliked Ahmet, thought him supercilious and condescending. He also disliked Ahmet's brother-in-law, thinking him immature and unreliable, but what really bothered Isule was that he knew Mamet wasn't properly looking after his plants. He was sure Mamet was either fertilizing them to the point where the foliage was excessively healthy but blooms nonexistent or withholding water. Given time, he'd eventually figure out what Mamet was up to, but as far as Ahmet, there would be a little farewell party, a handshake or two, but no golden handshake, and he'd be gone, to be replaced by someone younger and less expensive to the taxpayer.

Ahmet had to keep his eyes on the ball, not let Ernna distract him, but he couldn't. He hadn't slept well, and he still had several hours till the meet that evening, so he decided to take a nap, but he was too restless, couldn't settle. He called room service and had a large whiskey sent up, neat. *Perhaps*, he speculated, *this will be what retirement is all about—bad habits, like drinking before the sun sets, a definite no-no that a younger Ahmet would have frowned on.* In a couple of gulps the glass was empty, but there was still no relief, no shuteye.

Within forty-five minutes Ahmet was up and heading to the bathroom for a quick freshen-up. He went into the bathroom as Ahmet but came out as the man in white, dark glasses and all. He couldn't settle and decided he had to speak to Roger. He walked briskly to the pool area, taking long strides as if on a mission—and he was. He whistled through his front teeth, wanting to appear jaunty and self-assured, confident of his ability to weather any storm. He had to banish Ernna from his mind, at least for the time being. He had to be Ahmet the invincible, not Ahmet the vulnerable.

Roger saw Ahmet approaching, smiled, and stuck out his right hand as if it were a magnet drawing Ahmet ever closer.

"Jim, how are you? I'm so very glad to see you."

They shook hands. Roger was absolutely delighted to see the man in white and showed it; he couldn't hide his pleasure and made no effort to hide it.

"Glad to see you, too, Roger, and, Roger, Jim's not my true name. It's Ahmet. We'll most likely never meet again, so please call me Ahmet."

"Well, Ahmet, I figured Jim wasn't your real name right from the start; it's so American or British, and you don't look American or British, more Middle Eastern—that's my guess—maybe Turkish. Am I right?"

"Yes, you're right, Roger, spot on—quite perceptive on your part. Now, down to business—plenty of time later for small talk. Roger, do you have the money? Without the money there can be no exchange. Anyway, I'm sure you know that, so I'd bet my last cent that you do have the money, in cash as agreed to, large bills. And I don't think you'd leave it in your room, so the cash must be stashed in that book you're carrying about, and I didn't think you even fancied reading, especially a book of that thickness."

"Very good, Ahmet. You're right. How very, very clever you also are."

"No, Roger, not clever but observant. I've met you on this tiny island several times, and I've never seen you read anything, not even a newspaper or for that matter not even a menu, and all of a sudden, out

215

of the blue, you show up carrying *War and Peace* or some such tome, and that book looks thick enough to hold the required sum—in hundred dollar bills, of course. Now, Roger, let's sit, please; we've got to have a good down-to-earth talk. Here, near the pool, away from others and in the shade if you don't mind. Skin cancer, melanoma—I'm sure you understand. It runs in the family, but I won't bore you with the details."

"Sure, Ahmet, we can sit anywhere you like. What's bothering you? You seem edgy. You want a drink or something? This is not like you. You're always so composed and self-confident, but now, as I've just said, you seem tense and nervous."

"Roger, stop waffling. I'm a bit confused. I'm trying to gain a little insight into who could have made me last week, who whacked me on my head and took the documents. How did they know what I was carrying? You and I are on the same team, so where's the leak? You want the documents, and we want to give them to you—perhaps *sell* is a better word, but sell for a pittance—so I'm convinced your team didn't thump me, and I'm dead certain my team didn't thump me, so who the hell else is there? How did someone find out about our plans, and who is that someone, and are they acting independently or on behalf of another government agency?"

"Oh, so that's what happened to the documents and you don't have them with you? Do you?"

"No, but please answer my question."

"Well, think about it, Ahmet. Who did you originally get the plans from? Maybe they had a change of heart, wanted them back."

"No, Roger, that doesn't make sense. There's no reason they'd want the plans back, though the plans are unique and one of a kind and, let's say, very interesting. They didn't even know I was coming to Ibiza—of that I'm sure."

"Well, Ahmet, maybe it was just a random act of violence—you know, you were in the wrong place at the wrong time. You know, a coincidence."

"Roger, I don't believe in coincidences; everything happens for a reason. A third party somehow found out about our meet and scuttled our plans, and now the documents are up for grabs, but hopefully I have the inside track. I'd certainly feel a whole lot better if I had some idea how someone knew what I was carrying and how they also knew when and where the exchange was to take place; it's really worrisome. Maybe

I'm being set up again—who knows? No, Roger, it wasn't a coincidence. Of that I'm sure. This was premeditated and well planned, but whoever planned it was lucky, very lucky, and an amateur I'm thinking, but I could be wrong. At the risk of repeating myself, how did they know I had the plans? Roger, you don't think someone at Langley's trying to pull a fast one, trying to cash in on our op?"

Roger, head downcast as if studying his naval, just slowly shook his head. "No, Langley's clean. I'm clueless myself. No idea who swiped the plans or, for that matter, why. Probably swiped for money, the root of all evil or perhaps the root of all happiness."

Roger's responses were unquestionably sincere and most honest, at least in his own mind. Not in a thousand years would Roger have thought that he was the source of the leak. To figure out that he was the one who had unintentionally set Ahmet up would have required a great deal of thinking outside the box, and Roger was too much of an in-line thinker. He always went from A to B, then from B to C, and on and on until his goal was achieved. To go from A directly to his goal, no matter what the goal, was neurologically impossible for Roger. He just wasn't genetically wired to think that way, to take great leaps from premise to conclusion.

Ahmet could only believe Roger's every word. Roger, so innocent and so unassuming, so naïve. How his planning had been found out might and probably would remain an unsolved mystery forever, but that didn't stop Ahmet from analyzing and dissecting last week's events over and over, events that left him partially, though temporarily, concussed and less than a stellar agent in Isule's mind.

"Listen, Roger, I've got to go. Nice chatting to you. Why not take a seat in the bar this evening, kind of watch my back. This deal has got to go down successfully—winner take all, and we better be the winners or there'll be hell to pay when we get back home. Oh, and one more thing: if you have a weapon, please do not bring it with you tonight. Just leave it in your room. If we can't pull this off without someone being shot, then we deserve to fail, and using a gun to intimidate is totally out of the question, at least here on Spanish soil. Understand?"

"Sure thing, Ahmet. See you later, in the bar, when the sun's well into the Med."

"Yes, sure thing, Roger, when the sun's well into the Med. When I get the plans, I'll immediately pass them over to you; and you, well you do what you have to do, but be careful."

With that Ahmet departed. Between his wife and this op and the Mask, he was certain his brain would soon explode, sending blood gushing out his ear holes and him to either the morgue or into a wheelchair, paralyzed from the neck down. His step was now less jaunty, more thoughtful and deliberate, as though this step or the next might be his last. Ahmet didn't like that feeling, not at all.

Roger returned to the pool, repositioned a deck chair so it faced directly into the setting sun, and sat. He then lowered his Aviators till they sat neatly on his nose. With not a care in the world he watched as the sun slowly settled into the sea. He had passed his poly, his wife seemed content, and during his off time he tinkered with his clocks, something he enjoyed doing. Clocks never disrespected him and never asked to borrow his credit card. Yes, life was good, and if Ahmet failed to retrieve the documents, then so be it. Let Ahmet worry about that, and if there was a tab to be picked up when all was said and done, let Ahmet pick it up.

When the sun had half-disappeared over the horizon, Roger got up and headed to the bar, though not before stopping by his room to pick up his weapon, a small .38 Special that neatly tucked into a shoulder holster under his left armpit, under his bright red, loose-fitting shirt. Roger felt there might be danger, and therefore he wanted to be prepared, regardless of what Ahmet had said; after all, he didn't work for Ahmet. Moving firearms within the European Union was always a problem but not impossible, and because of what had happened to Ahmet last week, Roger thought he might require a weapon. The weapon had therefore been pouched in from the American embassy in Madrid to a small American-friendly consulate in Ibiza; it would be returned when the op was complete. Roger seldom asked for a weapon, but today was special; he didn't intend getting whacked on the head, not by anyone. After ensuring his weapon was loaded and the safety set, he headed to the bar, feeling nine feet tall.

Chapter 12

A perfect landing: Aubrey could hardly feel the thump of the rear tires on tarmac; a second or two later the nose gear also gently glided onto the runway. Flaps flew out and up to the perpendicular; with gentle braking the leviathan slowed to a crawl. The flight time had been just under two hours, with no rough air. Aubrey gave a sigh of relief; they'd made it to Ibiza safely, all in one piece. He was always fearful of some tragedy or drama when he flew, but between browsing a magazine or two, eating a few air-hostess–provided nuts, and having a stiff whiskey, which he'd nursed for some thirty-plus minutes, time had seemed to fly by, no pun intended. As they taxied to the gate, one cell phone after another sprang to life, and chatter, in English and Spanish, seemed to engulf him from all sides. Aubrey could hardly believe what he was hearing.

"Yes, dear, just landed. Weather looks lovely, bright and sunny; quite warm, I should imagine. How's the weather back home?"

How's the weather back home? You pillock, you only just left two hour ago. How do you think the weather is back home? Bloody cold and getting colder, thought Aubrey.

"Yes, we made it safely. Give the kids a hug for me … Yes, back home in a fortnight … Okay, love, cheerio."

Another cloth-cap, mused Aubrey. *Only just got here and planning for the return. Why bother?*

On and on, one ridiculous conversation after another. Everyone was checking in with someone, all conveying the uninteresting details of their rather sad, wretched lives. In fact Aubrey was sure that some people at the rear of the plane were calling people up front, arranging or rearranging last-minute details of their holiday or talking just to hear the sound of their voice as they queued up, pulled their carry-on from the overhead, and waited impatiently for the Jetway to be put in place so they could then pop out one at a time, like fish fry being ejected from their mother. Aubrey would put a gun to his head before leading the life of a cell phone junkie: yakking, texting, e-mailing, social networking, twittering, and on and on. Mankind had become so pathetic, so lame. Most couldn't stand to be on their own for less than a micro-fart; everyone was part of some social team, some network or another. To be an individual with few or no virtual ties was tantamount to being an outcast, and no matter how one framed it, to the virtual world you were just that, an outcast, intentionally excluded from the cornucopia of enticements that the Smart Age offered, in all its virtual elegance, to all its virtual clientele.

The music in the background was vibrant and full of life, probably zumba or salsa, and most appropriate for a planeload of tourists wanting to have a happy holiday on an island with a reputation for sex, drugs, and booze. Of course, it would all be captured on their ridiculous, expensive smartphones and e-mailed or texted to their friends back home, who would applaud and rave just to make the traveler feel the holiday was worth all the expense.

Aubrey had to force himself to put aside his dislike for anyone reaching out and "touching" someone and to focus instead on his partner. He kept a sharp eye on Jason, who was tailing Al. Al was like a man on assignment, very focused; he grabbed his carry-on, the soft gray gym bag, from under the seat in front and then queued up, patiently exiting the plane with a cheerful smile for the pilot and air hostesses. Passport control and customs were practically nonexistent, taking less than twenty minutes to process and clear a plane-load. No one wanted to keep the British from spending. There was only one concourse, and it led to a line of vans and buses all heading to various hotels scattered over the island. Once he'd retrieved his mittens from the magazine receptacle, Aubrey followed Jason, who followed Al onto a van heading for the Sunrise. Four or five others also climbed aboard. Al chatted to everyone; whether from nerves or just plain friendliness he was irrepressible, almost to the point of being jovial.

Jason wondered if the man with the hump had the documents on himself or in his carry-on; he'd make no move till he could figure out what the man with the hump was up to. Locating and then seizing the documents might not prove to be too difficult, but figuring out if they were original and had not been tampered with might be another story. The van roared to life and then slowly pulled away and picked up speed as it left the confines of the airport. In about thirty minutes the Sunrise Hotel came into view. It was perched on a grassy green knoll overlooking private beaches polluted with deck chairs. The Mediterranean Sea seemed endless; hard to believe it wasn't an ocean. The van slowed, turned into an unmarked service road, and stopped just outside registration. All exited, some tipped the driver, and all collected their luggage and queued up to register. Unlike some nationalities, the British are rather good at queuing—better than a stampede and certainly more efficient. Upon exiting the van, Al donned a large dark fedora that he snugly pulled over his head. There was no way he could hide his hump, but it appeared he tried. When it was Al's turn to register, he presented a credit card and was informed of something by the woman behind the desk. Jason couldn't quite hear what she said, but the man with the hump smiled and gently, almost surreptitiously, nodded. After registering, Al headed for the bar, which was about thirty paces away. From the rear Aubrey also noticed this verbal exchange, but he couldn't figure out what was going on at the front of the queue. In about ten minutes Aubrey was registered; his room was on the fifth floor. He also proceeded to the bar for a whiskey or two before dinner, but Jason would keep him on a short lead. Two would be his limit; then he'd have to go onto wine or God forbid, beer, but to go on anything non-alcoholic was totally out of the question. He bellied up to the bar next to Jason and ordered a whiskey, neat and definitely no ice, please. Jason was sipping a half lager and lime, and the man with the hump, sitting on the other side of the horseshoe-shaped bar, was on pints. Aubrey downed his first in a couple of gulps and asked for a second. Al had nearly finished his second pint; he also was a gulper.

"You notice that he's tucked himself into the darkest part. Gets little light, and he'd be easy to miss if you didn't know he was over there. I'm thinking they keep the lighting low to keep it down or maybe aid those out for an illicit rendezvous."

"Yes, Aubrey, leave it to you. You've cracked it, mate, an illicit rendezvous. I'm sure that's what it's all about. Anyway, our man with the hump wants to keep a low profile for sure. That's an about-face from when he was in the van; now he's all business. With that dark hat on he's difficult to identify, and I'm sure that's his game, but the hump's a dead giveaway. But if you weren't looking for a man with a hump—and who is these days?—you could quite easily not see him tucked away as he is."

"You see that, the way he gulps? I bet he's had one or two in his day, and so skinny. I admire those that can drink a half dozen in a single sitting, and they don't get a beer belly, and they never go legless. Most get fat and lazy and have trouble making it to the loo and end up with wet ones."

"Yes, you're probably right. Wet ones. I'm pretty sure I don't want to attempt to decipher that. Anyway, listen, Aubrey. I was wondering if you should be sitting more over there, next to the till, a few stools away from our friend with the hump. Anyone coming into the bar or paying a tab will be coming from that direction, and once inside, their back will be to you and you can make sure nothing untoward happens."

Jason didn't nod or point, but Aubrey knew exactly where he should reposition himself. He figured if he played his cards right, he might luck out and have a third, compliments of her of course.

Aubrey downed drink number two and then rose and went to the loo. When he returned, he occupied the seat Jason had indicated. This seat gave him the clearest view of the passageway into and out of the bar, and he still had a clear view of Jason, who was sitting more or less directly across from him. Anyone entering or leaving would have to pass Aubrey, and there was nothing small about Aubrey; if he wanted to stop somebody, he'd stop them and hold them with his hands, the hands of a titan. Aubrey was strong, very strong, and the more whiskey he drank, the meaner he'd got. Aubrey was about to order another whiskey but could feel the glare of Jason looking at and through him from the other side of the bar. He changed his mind; he wasn't in the mood to set himself up for a lecture sometime down the road. Now, Susan, she was definitely worth a lecture or two, even one from Pettigrew.

The barman paced and frequently checked his watch; he was bored. For a small hotel, the bar was rather large, almost too large considering the number of drinkers presently in it, but perhaps the bar had seen better days, or perhaps it was just too early. Many continentals wouldn't even think of entering the bar till after dinner, maybe for a nightcap or just to stretch and reconnoiter, and it was far too early for dinner.

While the barman was less than busy, it took Aubrey several minutes to catch his eye. "White wine, please, and none of your local stuff either.

Anything not local will most likely do, and please make sure it's not chilled—room temperature will do quite well, thank you."

While Aubrey wasn't much of a beer drinker, he could probably match Al pint for pint, or so he thought as he watched Al gulp several mouthfuls of ale before coming up for air.

A fourth man entered the bar, a man in a bright red shirt. It was Roger England, still hoping to receive the documents from Ahmet. He looked around. Ahmet was not present, only three others, none of whom he recognized. He walked round the bar, sat two stools from Jason, and ordered an American beer, which he drank from the bottle.

Jason watched as Roger drank, sip after sip, thinking, *How can anyone drink ice-cold beer from a tin or bottle? It just doesn't make sense.* Jason liked real ale from a barrel, a wooden barrel, not a keg but a barrel, and he couldn't understand the American infatuation with drinking everything cold, ice-cold, but it was a fact of life, though not his life.

Jason wondered who the man in the red shirt might be. Would he eventually be receiving the documents; was he an ally of the man with the hump, some kind of backup; or was he just a tourist on holiday to the trendy island of Ibiza? Jason had no clue but continued watching and wondering and sipping. At the rate he was presently sipping, it would take him an hour to finish one lager, and a half lager at that.

After ordering another beer, Roger stepped out to hit the head. Immediately after Roger left, the man with the hump walked over to the front desk and picked up a parcel; Jason almost gave Aubrey the high sign but fortunately did not, as the man with the hump returned to his stool and continued washing back beer at a pretty good clip. He was now on his fourth pint in less than thirty minutes.

Al had immediately recognized Roger but could only hope he wouldn't be recognized or even noticed, tucked away as he was; the swap had to take place today, and soon. Al had to tough it out and trust in the hump and the luck of the hump. If Roger saw him and recognized him, he might start to connect the dots, and there might be a confrontation—a confrontation that could end in disaster and cause him to somehow lose that second million. But upon reflection Al figured that even if Roger did see him and did recognize him, he wouldn't do a thing, for doing something might result in him having to retake his poly with a not-so-friendly polygrapher, and Roger would rather die than have to retake another polygraph.

"Don't let me down now, baby; I need all the good fortune you can give me," Al softly whispered, almost like a prayer, as he gently stroked his hump with his left hand while his right hand was busy hoisting his pint to his gaping mouth.

Roger returned. The sun was setting; the bar became murkier, like a London fog had just blown in. Al felt more relaxed—the darker the better.

The bar was quiet. There were no TVs with the sports channels blaring, no gay background music, just a Spanish barman who spoke English and spoke it quite well. Four quiet customers; no one spoke to anyone. No one even made idle chatter with the barman. Each of the four was in a world of his own. Jason thought of Clara and her tragic, untimely death; Aubrey of Susan and that delicious smile and full bosom. All Al could think of was money and what he could do with it for Margaret and himself. The man in the red shirt, usually very loquacious, decided to play it low key and just observe. He knew something would be going down very soon and would hopefully have good news to report back to the Agency. He also wondered about a woman, his wife. What was she getting up to in his absence? He didn't want to know. Almost incidentally, he wondered where Ahmet was and when he would put in an appearance. In Roger's mind the plan was quite simple. The documents moved from whoever had them now, maybe someone in this very bar, to Ahmet and then from Ahmet to himself. What could be more simple? Of course there was a matter of cash changing hands, but the cash wasn't his, so no problem. But just in case there was some trouble, his weapon was near at hand, and to prove that, he tucked his right hand under his left shoulder, feeling cold steel—very reassuring.

***

At the top of the hour, the phone rang. It was Ahmet's wake-up call. He'd finally nodded off and fallen into a deep sleep; now he was groggy and in a very bad mood. After a face wash with cold water and a flannel, he headed for the bar for what he hoped would be his last visit to this bar, this hotel, and this island. As the elevator doors closed, Ahmet realized he'd left behind his lucky pocket watch. He decided not to return to get it; he was already late, and Ernna was probably right—superstition, a silly superstition.

"Yes, just a silly superstition," he muttered to himself. As he exited the elevator, Ahmet was followed by yet another man, a short man with a moustache and protruding belly, well dressed in a dark evening suit, dark shirt, and no tie. His slicked-down graying hair was parted in the middle.

Al immediately recognized the man in white when he entered the bar and motioned to him to come over and sit next to him. Ahmet obliged. Ahmet couldn't at first believe that the man who'd knocked him cold was a humpback, a man taller than most but because of his hump had limited visual acumen. Ahmet thought it might truly be time to retire, for while Ahmet was not a big man, he had been trained to fight with fists. If he'd not been surprised he would have surly bested Al in a one-on-one competition, but as the saying goes, therein lay the rub. He had been taken by surprise and from behind; he'd let his guard down, was being a good Samaritan, and that could have cost him his life.

"Come sit. My name's Al. What's yours?"

"They call me Ahmet."

"Look, old boy, sorry about the knock on the head last week. I just had to get those documents, and this was the most painless way that I could think of, short of … well, short of killing you. Let me buy you a drink, let bygones be bygones. Okay, mate?"

"I don't think I'm your mate, but I'll have a half—the local beer will do."

"Look, I have the documents. What about the money—do you have the money?"

Ahmet was about to shake his head, for he had no idea where Isule was with the money, when suddenly there was a scuffle near the till. There, to Ahmet's horror, Isule was being wrestled to the ground and was now in a choke hold by a huge set of hands, hands that appeared prepared to wring the living life out of Isule. A revolver lay a few feet away.

To Al's surprise, a second man from the other side of the bar came round and told the hands to let loose, but if Isule continued struggling, the hands were to choke the living shit out of him. Isule relaxed. Jason recovered the weapon and gave it to Aubrey, who stuffed it into his belt and then covered it with his jacket.

Ahmet just sat shaking his downcast head in utter dismay. He didn't know what to do. Isule was surely acting on his own, probably trying to make a name for himself. Al was speechless but wondered where the money was. Isule was shaking like a leaf. The bar was dead quiet, so Jason took a few liberties that he mightn't otherwise have taken.

"Look, you, what's your name?" Jason spoke very quietly as he glared at the man about to be strangled by the hands.

"Listen, Aubrey, slowly start squeezing until he quietly tells me his name and why he was about to shoot or at least threaten our man with the hump, or maybe his target was that tall man in white."

Aubrey did as directed. Shortly Isule, without speaking a word, begged for mercy. Aubrey loosened his grip, slowly.

"I'm Isule, an Iranian. I'm here with my associate Ahmet, there, drinking beer, dressed in white. We are partners. Actually he works for me, and I intended to hurt no one but just quietly threaten that man with the hump. He has some papers that belong to us, and he's blackmailing my country, of that I'm sure, or why else would he be chatting up Ahmet? I intended to get our documents back and get them back without paying the blackmail to that rascal. Once I'd recovered the documents I planned to peacefully leave the island with our money."

Oh, I see; it's all starting to make sense now, thought Jason.

Ahmet couldn't believe what he'd just heard. He knew Isule was a novice when it came to espionage and associated tradecraft, but how could Isule be intimidated so readily and offer up the truth with little or no resistance? Isule was a paper pusher who enjoyed highlighting missteps by his subordinates while seeking the cover and safety a desk offered. As far as Ahmet knew Isule had never even been on an op, so why now when so much was at stake?

Ahmet could only wonder at how the tables had now been turned. He had no leverage whatsoever. All his cards were now being dealt face up. His cover was blown; the mission was in ruins, and unless he was gravely mistaken, the two men with the English accents were anything but tourists. They were most likely officers in one of the MI's. It was all supposed to be so simple: trade the money for the documents and then pass the documents to Roger, sitting on the opposite side of the bar. How did the English become involved, what was their game, and where was the money? Probably that fool Isule left it in his room, under the mattress.

"Aubrey, if Mr. Isule, struggles break his neck. I want everything to be peace, perfect peace. No need to get the locals involved in what is strictly a private affair."

The barman stood, mouth agape but totally enjoying watching all these foreigners carry on, as if on a picnic, no shouting, all very civilized but very, very serious indeed. He intended to do nothing, just enjoy the show. If a Spaniard or Italian had been involved, the place would have been filled with police by now; even when not excited the Spanish could be quite noisy and emotional but not quite as noisy as the Italians—with hands waving every which way and slapping foreheads, mama mia, what a commotion would ensue.

Jason walked over to Al, who remained in the shadows with his hat on a forty-five degree angle, pulled over his face, shielding himself from Roger, who was not more than thirty paces off.

"Okay, about those documents, Al. Look, I can have my friend break your neck as well, but he'll do it nice and quiet-like—don't want to draw a crowd, and if you were to holler out or scream, he'd rip your tongue out. How'd you like those apples?"

"I don't like apples, and I've grown very fond of my neck, as it holds my head in place, and how do you know my name?" Al asked as he quickly passed the documents to Jason.

Jason continued. "Never mind that—unimportant. Look, I think I see what's going on. You're here to sell these documents to your friend, the man in white, Ahmet. How you got them I don't care, but more importantly I need help in determining if these are truly legitimate and not forgeries or somehow altered, and I think you may be able to help, and we need to figure it out sharpish."

"Why should I help you?" Al asked, looking rather dismayed and even a bit surprised at his own reckless courage in asking such a bold question of a man whose mate could put the big hurt on him in a hurry.

"I believe Mr. Isule may have some cash in his room; if you help me get at the truth, it's yours, all of it, and no questions asked."

"Well, I'll do what I can to help as long as the cash ends up in my hands, but will I be arrested when I return home to England?"

"In my mind you've broken no British laws, Al. I'm sure you've broken laws in other countries, but not in England, so you're probably in the clear, but you don't sound English. You sound American with a slight Yorkshire accent; plenty of fine pubs in Yorkshire."

Jason knew full well Al's pedigree from Pettigrew, but impressions of that magnitude would ensure Al's full cooperation. It was almost like saying, *I know where you hang your hat at night and where your family lives, and if you step out of line your body will be tossed off Whitby Pier.*

"Okay, you'll have my cooperation, promise, as long as the cash ends up in my hands when it's all said and done."

Jason now turned to Ahmet, who was listening, observing, and still mentally blown away by the fact that he'd been bested by a borderline cripple. "And you, Mr. Ahmet, what about you? Will you help me out?"

"Why should I cooperate with you? This man," he said, nodding toward Al, "assaulted me and stole papers from the Iranian government, then sold them back, and now he wants more money. These documents rightfully belong to the Iranian people. That fool Isule over there has placed me in danger and foiled my op, so why should I cooperate with you? I cannot be bought. Isule can go to the devil for all I care. As far as I can see, you have no leverage over me unless you intend to threaten me with death, and if carried out that may prove to be a blessing to me but a thorn in the side of your government. After all, there are witnesses."

Jason motioned to Aubrey with his right hand. "Bring Isule over here."

Aubrey did as directed, standing less than a meter from Ahmet.

"Aubrey, what floor is your room on?"

"Fifth floor, boss."

"Aubrey, take Mr. Isule up to your room, please. If you do not hear from me in one hour, throw his sorry ass out the window. I mean it, Aubrey, just do it. Sixty minutes from when you pair enter your room, if you do not get a phone call, teach him to fly, English-style. Oh, and on your way up check his room for the money, the money I promised Al."

Aubrey nodded. Isule's face turned white with fear. On their way out of the bar Aubrey had a whisper or two in Isule's ear, telling him not to make a sound or he'd break his bloody neck right there in the bloody lobby, and he meant it.

Ahmet marveled at the cool callousness of Jason and didn't doubt for a moment that the English would kill Isule if he, Ahmet, didn't cooperate. But he didn't like Isule, and his real mission was to get the documents to the Americans, not the British. For the time being, though, he'd play this Englishman's game.

"Yes, I'll cooperate. I'll need no restraining, but remember I'm no fan of Isule's, and if he flies, he flies. I really don't give a damn what happens to that overweight roach."

"Good, let's hope you do, because in less than an hour, my mate will be chucking your bloody friend off the balcony, and as they say, it's not the fall but the sudden stop that hurts, and if I remember correctly it's all concrete—no swimming pool near enough to break the fall. After all, this is not Hollywood."

"Please," uttered Ahmet, "stop calling him my friend. I detest the man."

"Okay, whatever, let's sit, have a chat, and maybe figure out if we can stop a war. First, let's have a drink. Compliments of the queen, of course."

Roger, at the other end of the bar, couldn't quite figure out what was happening—a scuffle followed by anxious whispers and the departure of two, all taking place in less than fifteen minutes. Apparently some kind of meeting was now in progress; the bar was too poorly lit for Roger to recognize anyone, even Ahmet. Everything was peaceful; the barman set about his duties, bringing a lager to Jason and pints to both Ahmet and Al. After a few minutes Jason asked Al to move to a nearby corner table and quietly finish his beer—no interruptions, please. If he wanted another just give a nod to the barman.

"Okay, Ahmet, first tell me how you got these documents and from whom. Documents that I assume document Iran's ability to build a nuclear device and documents, I assume, I couldn't read even if I had time to read them, and in your opinion are they truly representative of what's happening in your country vis-à-vis the Bomb, and finally why are you being a traitor to your country, Iran?"

Almost mumbling, Ahmet replied to Jason's questions, "I'm a member of a small Iranian society determined to keep nuclear weapons out of Iran. Having nuclear weapons will make us a target for the West and Israel. Several of my associates work on the Iranian nuclear weapons program; in fact, one is the nephew of our President, our leader with five syllables for a name. Anyway, his nephew stole these documents, which prove beyond a shadow of a doubt that Iran is very close to going nuclear. We want to turn these documents over to the United States so they can destroy the Iranian nuclear weapons facilities before it's too late. A few hundred hardworking Iranians will die, but if we develop and deploy a viable nuclear weapons arsenal, hundreds of thousands will die someday, and Iran will no longer be Iran."

"Ahmet, are you familiar with the contents? How do you know they're legitimate? Maybe they're forgeries."

"Why not ask your own experts? I'm sure they can verify their authenticity. With all the high-tech equipment possessed by the West and agents here, there, and everywhere, I'm sure you would have no problem verifying whether or not they are legitimate. And by the way, what is your name, and who do you represent? By your accent, I'm sure you're English."

"Okay, Ahmet, I'll answer your questions in turn and truthfully, but from here on out please let me do the asking. We just don't have time to hand-carry them back to England; we're running out of time, and decisions have to be made quickly. The United States has two fleets positioned in the eastern Mediterranean with orders to either attack Iran or stand down. A go-no-no decision is required by the president in less than twenty-four hours, so what we, or should I say I, determine here and now will most likely be the lynchpin, the overriding evidence, for whether your country gets attacked or not, and I'm guessing your position is that the documents are genuine and do show a nuclear weapon in the not too distant future, and your friends would prefer Iran gets hammered sooner rather than later, right? Finally, my name is Jason, and I represent Her Majesty's government."

"Thank you, Jason. That is my position, albeit stated rather crudely, but true nevertheless."

"Now," continued Ahmet, "this is what I know, and this too is categorically and unequivocally true, so help me God. I received the documents immediately, and I do mean immediately, after they were stolen from Iranian Headquarters for Nuclear Development, the IHND, in Tehran. There was no chance of anyone altering anything. The president's nephew told me the documents prove, in writing, that Iran is very, very close to developing nuclear weapons. There is a schedule among the documents you now have showing in detail that within a few months Iran will have the capability to disperse nuclear weapons in vehicles or aircraft throughout the Middle East and eventually will have a missiles capability, maybe within three years."

"And how did this nephew of your president come up with this bright idea of stealing these very secret plans then passing them onto you?"

"He's a friend of a friend who encouraged him to take the plans and pass them over to me. It's all very simple, actually. Once I got the plans I was to pass them to the Americans as proof of my country's real intent, but you know what they say about the best laid plans of mice and men. That man over there, Al, somehow got wind of what I was planning, blindsided me, stole the plans, and is now in the process of becoming a multimillionaire. Life can be so unfair. I still can't believe a borderline cripple was clever enough to put me off guard and steal the documents."

"Never mind, Ahmet. Happens to the best of us."

"And, Ahmet, how did you arrange to try to get the documents to the right people in America, and by the right people I mean the CIA? Disregard that question—the answer's obvious. There's embassies in Tehran friendly to America and her allies, and a word here or there about what you have would result in some kind of arranged exchange, an exchange that went sour, right here in Ibiza. And Isule, your boss, how does he figure into all this? You know, he made you look very foolish, very amateurish. I assume he's quite the rookie, probably a pencil pusher."

"He is with me, unfortunately, and believes in our cause, but he's a fool with a temper, a hot temper. He realizes our funding is strained. A million or two is significant to us, but we are prepared to pay to get the documents back so we can pass them on to the Americans. I really don't know much more. I have never seen the documents myself—they were always in a canister. But our president's nephew is an honorable man and unconditionally champions our cause and unconditionally vouches for their accuracy, so you really have no choice. You have to believe me—you have no proof to the contrary. If you doubt me and the attack is called off, then the West shall reap a whirlwind sometime down the road, of that you can be sure."

"And one last question. You and Isule, what do you do to earn a living? I mean when you're not stealing. Maybe you're just a common thief fabricating stories, fabricating plans for political gain?"

Ahmet had anticipated this question, and there could no pausing and reflecting. By his attire, education, and manner he was not a common laborer. He had to be a professional of some sort.

"We're attorneys. We practice law in Tehran. Would you like an address or the name of our firm or a phone number?"

"No, Ahmet, that won't be necessary, as I'm sure you probably do have the right people in the right place to confirm your story or maybe confirm your lies."

And Jason was right: the right people were in the right place to confirm Ahmet's story. As it happened, Ahmet had been a lawyer, but that was in another life, years ago.

Jason now had Ahmet and Al change places.

"Well, Al, can you shed any light on the documents now in my possession? Have you seen the documents, examined them in any real detail?"

"Yes, I believe the documents are genuine, and I have seen them, and they were examined by an expert. He, too, believes them to be the real deal with no alterations."

"And who is this expert, and what are his credentials?"

"Yesterday, in London, I located an individual off the Internet who examined them in detail. I paid him two hundred pounds. We had tea at the Ritz. He speaks excellent Farsi, which is the language of the documents, and he was able to come up with a rather unclear picture of the Iranian nuclear weapons program, but among those documents is a test schedule with dates, and he firmly believes testing a nuclear capability will be upon us very soon, in a month or two. In his mind they're genuine."

"So while you've looked at the documents, you really have little or no idea what the contents are, and more importantly you have absolutely no idea if the documents are fraudulent or the real deal? You say he speaks excellent Farsi. How do you know his Farsi is excellent if you don't speak Farsi at all?"

"Yes, you're right of course. Well, since his translations seemed reasonable and he spoke with an air of certainty, I just assumed what he said was true. But you're right. Maybe he was just giving me some value for my two hundred pounds, but based on what he said, I still believe the documents are genuine and do forecast an unenviable, sad future for the Iranian people if an attack is deferred. After all, many if not most Iranians want nothing to do with their country's leaders."

Jason now asked Ahmet to return; he wanted each to hear what the other had said. Jason continued.

"Well, Al, it's like this. Here's my take. While having afternoon tea at the Ritz, a total stranger convinces you that these documents are genuine, but you have no real proof as to their authenticity. If I pass your take on the documents back to my superiors and they pass it on to our American ally, Iran will be attacked with the loss of much life and the destruction of significant amounts of Iranian property. You see, Al, we're working against the clock. American forces are now in place and have been for some time and will probably be in play very soon—either attack or stand down. American intelligence somehow got wind of these documents and their contents, but they want proof that the plans are legitimate; they don't want to start a war based on faulty intel, not a second time. Their game plan, in large part, is based on these documents. Right-wing America is forecasting a resurgent Persia, a nuclear Iran, an Iran with a nuclear capability pointed directly at the Israelis, and the Americans are not very happy about that. Many prefer action now rather than later."

"And you, Ahmet, you're still sticking to your story that an insider with access to Iran's top secret nuclear weapons program smuggled these documents out and turned them over to you and you intended to turn them over to the United States? And you swear you've never seen the documents and the only thing you know about the documents is what this insider told you, and he's a traitor, and who knows who else he's betraying?"

"Yes, Jason, and my friend the insider, the traitor as you call him, has no reason to lie. After all, his motives are pure and honorable, and if there were to be an attack, he might be killed, as he works at one of the nuclear facilities that would probably be targeted."

"I'd be surprised if your friend's not dead already. Surely someone must realize that the documents are missing if they are as important as you say."

"I don't know. My friend is quite clever, with relatives in very important political positions. No one will eagerly point a finger at him—if they were proven wrong they would most certainly be punished, maybe even shot."

"And this traitor's name, Ahmet?"

"I don't think that question's reasonable. Do you expect me to give up the name of a friend? Would you?"

"Probably not. Well, we're getting nowhere, and I've got twenty-four hours to wrap this up. Okay, here's my gut. Al, I think you're telling me the truth, but I think your conclusions may be wrong or misguided. It's a tremendous leap of faith on your part to wholeheartedly embrace, over afternoon tea, what your man at the Ritz told you. And you, Ahmet, well, I believe you to be a liar, but I can't prove it. I think you know more than you're telling me, but I just can't figure out how to crack you in a few hours. Even if my friend tosses your colleague out the window, you would most likely remain steadfast in this unbelievable fantasy you've conjured up or, perhaps, scripted well in advance for a situation like this one. Or perhaps you really are telling me the truth. I can't call my boss and tell her what you two have said. She'd only tell me to get answers, pertinent answers that our leaders can use to make necessary, difficult decisions. Maybe I should have my man upstairs just beat the truth out of you, Ahmet, and you'd be next, Al."

"Probably a good idea, but it probably wouldn't work, and then you'd have to kill me. You see, Jason, I too love my country and am prepared to die for it. Americans don't have a lease on loving one's country, and the best thing for my country in the long run is having our nuclear facilities destroyed."

"You may be right Ahmet, and what good is a tortured confession? And as far as dying for your country, I'm not buying into that bullshit. My attitude is that if someone has to die for their country, let it be the other guy," responded Jason almost mirthfully.

Al had been dead quiet up to now. Suddenly, without warning, he blurted out four simple but prophetic words: "Perhaps I can help."

"What do you mean? How can you help?" Jason said sarcastically.

"Well Sir, after all *I Am A Polygrapher*. I can prove if Ahmet is a liar or not a liar; just get me a machine."

Al said this with such pride, such verve, that one might think the heavens above should open so all the archangels could band together and sing, in one stentorian chorus after another, "Hal-le-lu-jah," all for the benefit of Al the polygrapher.

"With the right machine, I can get the truth out of anyone as long as they're cooperating and do not have to be restrained. I've worked for the Agency as a polygrapher for in excess of twenty years. I'd like to think I'm a legend in my own time. I know what questions need to be asked and have received many citations for a job well done—even received a financial award right from the hands of the director himself, though it was a pittance if the truth be known. I deserved more, much more."

"Twenty years? That's a long time trying to pry the truth out of the mouths of people just wanting to work for their country: get a job, keep a job. You must have heard that line before. Thank God we have no such nonsense in England."

"Oh, please, Jason, not you, too. I assume every individual being polygraphed by me is a liar—big lies, small lies, white lies, black lies. Lies, lies, lies—everyone has something to lie about, and it was my job to get at the truth. Yes, they're pretty much forced to cooperate if they want to remain employed, and that makes us polygraphers very unpopular, kind of like we're tainted, contagious somehow, so we stick to ourselves or become lone wolves, like me, but as long as they're not a threat to the country, they pass, eventually."

"So you were unpopular. Why didn't you transfer to another career field? Why put up with unpopularity for twenty-plus years?"

"Well, Jason, it's like this. I liked the job. It was challenging, and I was good at it, very good. You know, Jason, I'm quite a clever lad, believe it or not. Anyway, if you do decide to let me interrogate Mr. Ahmet, I have one or two conditions. If Ahmet is telling the truth and I can vouch for his honesty, I get the money. If I am able to get the truth out of Ahmet, assuming he is indeed a liar, then the money defaults to me also, and I will be permitted to live the rest of my days in Yorkshire, sipping ale, with no hassle from the authorities, either on this side of the Atlantic or the other."

"Okay Al, agreed," replied Jason almost without thinking, knowing he was on safe ground making such a promise.

"Oh, and one more thing, Jason. That man in the red shirt on the other side of the bar, have him removed, please, but no harm. Just ask him to move along for the time being—no questions, please."

"Done." Within thirty seconds, Roger was gone.

"Well," said Al, "how did you manage that, so easily and quickly?"

"It's like this, Al. I told him if he didn't bugger off pronto I'd have my friend upstairs squash his balls as if they were a pair of grapes. He soon got the hint and left, but not before I relieved him of this .38. You Americans—guns, guns, guns."

"I'm not American, and I believe I've told you this before, so please remember, thank you very much."

Jason knew that this was a sore point with Al but continued rubbing it in, much to Al's chagrin and his own delight. Jason now carried on in dead earnest with Ahmet.

"Well, Ahmet, what do you think—want to give it a whirl? If Al can confirm you're not a liar, he gets the loot and you get the documents to do with as you choose, which is to probably pass them over to the Americans, in the form of the man, I assume, in the red shirt that was until quite recently sitting at the other side of the bar."

"And if he proves me a liar, which will not happen, then what?"

"If he proves you a liar, then the documents are false and the attack will be called off, but Al still gets the loot."

Wow, thought Al, *I love these odds. I do love money.*

"Sure, why not," said Ahmet. "I'll cooperate completely and be completely honest. You have my word. Now, while you round up a machine, can we take a break? It's awfully hot in here, and that beer has given me the sweats. I need to clean up."

Ahmet needed a break. With all this cross-examination and tension, the Mask was beginning to put in an appearance. He had to return to his room, double up on his meds, lie down, and think pleasant thoughts. If pleasant thoughts didn't work, he could be in trouble; he didn't want to see the inside of Ibiza's emergency room or the inside of a casket.

"Okay, break time. We've got a plan, and all in less than an hour." Jason picked up his cell and rang Aubrey then put some distance between himself and the table where Al and Ahmet sat.

"Okay, Aubrey, no need to teach our friend to fly. We're no closer to the truth, but all parties are cooperating, or at least say they'll cooperate. Take Isule down to the local lockup. Tell them who you are and who you work for and ask them to hold Mr. Isule for twenty-four hours and then let him go. If Isule gives you any static, tell him you'll have him arrested on a weapons charge. That should shut him up for a day, and while you're down there, round up a polygraph machine or get some insight on how we can borrow one in a hurry with no questions. And well done, Aubrey. Your actions will be reflected in my report to the home office and Pettigrew. Highest marks, Bulldog. Yes, highest marks."

"Oh, and one more thing, Aubrey, on your way out please stop by the bar. I have some documents I want you to fax to Pettigrew; they're plans for building the Bomb—yes, the Bomb and please return them to me on your return. Just give Susan a call and have her inform Pettigrew that a fax is on the way and what the contents of the plans are. Be vague but not too vague. Pettigrew will know what to do next, and also pass on that we should probably know if the plans are genuine in three or four hours and that when we do, we'll let her know pronto-like. Oh, and don't waste time chatting up Susan. Finally, I don't want Ahmet to know that his mate is out of harm's way, so secure him in the room, come down for the docs, then collect him on your way out to the cab. It's already out front waiting for you."

Shortly Aubrey showed up, looking very, very pleased with himself.

Jason passed the documents over to Aubrey and whispered a few words into Aubrey's ear. "Aubrey, a couple of final questions. Do you have the money, and would you have tossed Mr. Isule off the fifth floor balcony?"

"Yes, the money is in your room, and yes."

"Right answers, Bulldog. Thanks, and take care."

"Well," Al chimed in as Jason approached, "I'm sure you asked him about the money. What did he say? I mean, does he have the money?"

"Yes, I now have the money, so you can relax, Al.

"Okay, here's the plan," said Jason. "For the time being, the money and documents stay with their current owners, which are me and my mate. We take a break, get cleaned up, reconvene down here in a couple of hours, about 7:00 p.m. And, please, don't anyone think of doing a jackrabbit on me. My mate can be very persistent, and he does like rabbit stew. Oh, and phones are off-limits. In fact, leave your cells with me, and as for the house phones, stay away from them also. In fact, I'll have them disabled from the front desk just to be on the safe side. By six, Aubrey will have rounded up a polygraph machine. No fear—he'll return with a polygraph even if the PM himself has to make a call or two. It may not be the Cadillac of polygraphs, as you Americans say," he said, eyeing Al mischievously, "but it'll have to do."

"I'm English!"

CHAPTER 13

As Ahmet entered his room he immediately saw that the there was a message, a telephone voice mail on the room phone. Even though the room phone was now switched off, he could still listen. Unfortunately, it was bad news, very bad news. It was from Mamet. Ernna was in hospital, the psychological ward. She'd done the unthinkable: overdosed on sleeping pills. She was in a coma but expected to live; he was to call home as soon as possible and make arrangements to return sooner rather than later. His wife's situation was critical but stable. Suddenly, without warning, the Mask sprang to life, unconditionally exerting its full force, causing Ahmet to reel from dizziness and further causing him to feel sick, very sick: nausea, sweaty palms, sweaty forehead. With some difficulty he regained his equilibrium. On his way to the toilet, he vomited uncontrollably in fits and gasps. Fortunately the sink was at the ready. Seconds later, he popped several pills specifically compounded to control runaway high blood pressure. He lay down, but the distractions were endless and fierce, and no matter how hard he tried, he couldn't get Ernna out of his mind; he couldn't even make a poor attempt at relaxing.

What is she going through? What have I done to her? It's all my fault. I should have known; there were dozens of warning signs, and I chose to ignore them all, all for the sake of a career but in reality just a job, a job no better or worse than a common ditch digger. In my simple little mind I convinced myself that I was some kind of savior, a savior on a mission to save the motherland, but from what? Who knows? Who cares? What a fool I've been. No wonder so many new recruits quit after a year or two; they see the reality of their situation: long hours, separations, poor pay, stress, stress, stress, so they wise up and pack it in before being seduced by the propaganda that their mentors routinely peddle. And that propaganda is the mission, the op, so very important yet so very secret, so secret in fact that one cannot speak about it once your badge is retired, and one must always remember: the mission first, family second. That's it; I'm through. When I get home, it's the end of the line for me. I'm out, and I'm sure that fool Isule will be the first to second that motion. I'll do my best to beat Al and his polygraph, but if I fail, I fail, but at least the game will be over, once and for all.

Ahmet did his best to clear his head and to try not to dwell on Ernna, but that wasn't possible; the memory of her sad, weary face permeated his very existence, like a haunting that refused to dissipate with the twilight. Ernna's ghostlike features swirled overhead weeping, sighing, always out of focus. First clockwise and then anticlockwise, faster and then slower, changing colors, though the colors were always bright pastels. In spite of himself, the Mask began to relent, slowly loosening its grip till Ahmet felt almost normal; the haunting slowly vaporized into oblivion. *I have no choice. I must either return this evening or tomorrow morning, but if I leave now Jason will think I'm lying about the documents, and the attack on Iran's nuclear facilities will most likely be called off, and months of planning will have gone for naught. Isule will revel in my failure, and failure, by any name, for any reason, will be my failure, alone. It's like they say: "Success has many fathers but failure only one," and I will be the father of one of the biggest intelligence failures in my country's history. Now, of all times, Ernna, what's going on in that crazy, mixed-up head of yours, and why now? I really need to focus on beating this poly—distractions will be the ruination of me and my op and what's left of my miserable career. All things considered, I'd like to go out on a high note. I'd like my final op to be a grand success, but if I blow this poly and Al discovers that I am a liar and that the docs are contrived, then no air strikes, and that bastard Isule will use my failure as an excuse to justify his own acts of unadulterated stupidity. If Al somehow trumps my training, I will have failed—not Isule, but me. Isule may even convince our management that his was an act of bravado, courage, and cunning and his plan would have most likely succeeded if only the agents of England had not been present. And who could have foreseen that? Certainly not me or Mamet. Anyway, how did England and her merry men from some MI service or another even know that plans detailing Iran's nuclear capabilities were on this godforsaken little shit island? Better yet, how did that hunchback Al know? All very confusing and almost unexplainable, and if Isule puts the right spin on it, he might even convince some that there might be a mole in the*

Service—a mole named Ahmet or maybe Mamet. Who knows? Anything's possible when nothing is sacred and lies are blessed and know no boundaries.

The Mask had now completely subsided. Ahmet smiled to himself, feeling he had once again cheated death, once again defied the odds. *I can't blow this poly; I must convince Al that I'm telling the truth, and then I'll presumably get the plans back, pass them to Roger, and be off this tiny, insignificant wart of an island, but it's Jason that has to be convinced that I'm telling the truth. The plans will only be used in retrospect to justify the go-no-no decision to be made in the next few hours. That decision will primarily be driven by what Jason reports back to his handlers in the UK, of that there can be no doubt, and what Jason reports back will, in large part, be determined by how my upcoming poly turns out and what Al subsequently passes on to Jason. And that bugger Al, he gets the million regardless and will be free to enjoy the rewards of his ill-gotten gains, and he doesn't give a damn about anything, just the money. He doesn't care if the whole of Iran, not just its nuclear arsenal, is pummeled back to the Stone Age and has to use firewood for heat. The English can be such pompous bastards, cold as a witch's teat and hard as the hardest steel. The long and the short of it is that even though I have been lying, I'll have to outsmart, outfox, Al at his own game, but I've been trained, time and time again, tested and retested in how to beat the polygraph, no matter how expert and clever the polygrapher. I'm not even exactly sure how clever that hunchback really is. Regardless, I'm certain I can outsmart Al; he has nothing to lose. He gets the million one way or the other and probably doesn't really care if I'm lying or not. Regardless, I must relax, rely on my training. Pulse, blood pressure, respiration—that's the name of the game. The polygraph has no eyes, no ears; it's just metal, electronics, plastics, and what limited brainpower it has is all virtual. It's all up to Al to put the pieces together and determine if I'm a liar or not, and it's not rocket science. Polygraphy is an art, and the machine is just a tool like a hammer or saw, but in the right hands the job usually gets done but not always. I need to make Al the exception rather than the rule. I need to beat the tool, beat Al at his own game. I must control my breathing, control my heart rate. Remember—don't get rattled, stay calm, stay focused. Find a point in the room, focus on that point, put yourself into a semitrance. Keep the brain fully engaged by mentally naming all the countries in Europe while simultaneously counting from one to a hundred. Overload the brain as soon as the machine is turned on—anything to keep pulse, blood pressure, and respiration steady. However, I need to be alert, be aware of what's going on around me. Use my training, training, training, training. Keep a little peephole open to the outside world. Our instructors emphatically told us to rely on our training, not intuition, not instinct, and certainly not the gut or hunches. Listen to the questions from that little peephole; especially listen to the questions he'll ask up front as he calibrates the machine or, better yet, as he calibrates me. No need to lie when answering any of the calibration questions. In fact, lying when answering any calibration question would be stupid. They're all straightforward, so no need to lie, but even for the calibration questions, remember your training. Put the conscious portion of the brain to sleep; let the peephole rule. That might prove to be difficult, as Ernna will never take a backseat to anything, anybody, but I'll have to try conquering her and putting her back into the bottle, at least temporarily. Al will go over all the questions germane to Iran and its nuclear facilities prior to switching on. Answers will only be yes or no, only yes or no—no explanations permitted. Detailed analysis, if required, about any of the questions will have to be sorted out prior to the polygraph being switched on. More often than not, the answers to most questions will be no, and there will probably be an audience, a.k.a. Jason, albeit a very quiet and very attentive audience, and this also will tend to elevate my stress levels, but I must ignore Jason. Al will initially only have a handful of questions that will focus on the plans: "Did I have a chance to examine the plans?", "Have they been altered by me or anyone else?", and maybe a question or two about how I got the plans. Remember "No, I have never seen the plans,"; "No, I have not altered them," "No, they have not been altered by anyone else." No, no, no, but yes, they are authentic, and of that there can be no doubt. It looks like I'm holding all the aces as long as I can convince that numskull Al that I'm telling the truth and Iran is about to go nuclear. If Al says that I'm telling the truth that info will be passed up channel, and those damned nuclear facilities will be bombed into subatomic particles. So what if Langley gets the original plans retrospectively, if they get them at all. It'll already be too late: the go-no-no decision will be made in the next eight hours—can't keep two fleets on station in the Eastern Mediterranean indefinitely. Being the hawk that he is, the president will most certainly decide to bomb if he believes the plans to be genuine and Iran is within months of acquiring the Bomb. I just need to outwit Al, and then Iran takes a hit, a real shellacking, but only its nuclear facilities, nothing else. I can then go back home with a clear conscience, knowing that I've done well. I've got to have a clear head to outwit Al—no distractions—but that's nearly impossible, what with*

Ernna perhaps dying, or maybe even dead already, and the possibility that the Mask may make one last grand entrance and send me to an early grave, and, yes, if the truth be known, an early grave that I most likely deserve, what with all the lies and treachery I've committed for, I'm thinking, a less than grateful nation.

How romantic, thought Ahmet, *both Ernna and me passing within hours of each other. Some might think that very poetic. What bull, total nonsense. No one is going to die, especially me, and I don't even have a bucket list.*

Ahmet was in turmoil; he needed his cell, had to get the latest on his wife. Down the hall was Jason's room; after a knock and an explanation, Ahmet returned with cell in hand.

Hard to figure these Brits—one minute their ready to toss Isule out the window, and the next Jason hands over my phone on my word and says I can keep it as long as I need it and, in the process, wishes my wife well. Go figure.

With that Ahmet picked up his lucky watch and dropped it into his pocket, figuring he could use all the luck he could get, no matter where it came from. He then rang Mamet.

"Mamet, what's up? How's Ernna? Is she conscious?"

Ahmet listened nonstop for the next three minutes and said nothing.

"Good, yes, she's conscious, stable, and will be released in a few days. Thank God. Please don't let them release her until I get home, and you're probably right about the antidepressants and therapy. She'll probably stop taking the pills in a fortnight, probably start slinging them down the toilet, but truthfully, Mamet, I really do think these mind-altering drugs are dangerous and will do nothing to cure one very mixed-up lady, but I'm not a doctor, and really it's her decision. It'll take time, but when I'm with her full-time, she'll improve, and as far as therapy, within a month her therapist will be ready to cut her loose or be in therapy himself. Ernna can be quite a handful as you know, and the situation is dire. I haven't heard you refer to your sister as 'that cow,' so I'm thinking you're also worried."

Again Ahmet listened but this time for only about thirty seconds.

"Thanks, Mamet. Keep me posted. I won't forget this. Anyway, that idiot Isule really blindsided me, blew my cover; he made me look like a fool, an amateur. I'm still hoping to sort things out, but that may prove to be too dicey, even for me. Can't go into any details; gave my word—no shop talk. I'll explain when I get home, but I'd like to discuss Ernna a little bit more if you have a few more minutes."

"What happened, Mamet? What triggered this episode? Even for Ernna this is well over the top."

"Don't know, Ahmet. She's been hitting the vodka pretty hard lately. She just can't seem to cope when you're away. It's an accumulation of fears, and fears lead to anxieties that build and build till suicide becomes viable, a plausible Plan B. I mean, it's not your fault, but as you've just said, she's over the top, and I truly feel for her. The booze doesn't help matters—makes her more delusional and very forgetful. God only knows what's going on in that mixed-up head of hers, but I don't believe she's trying to make a statement about your job or you. I really don't. She's just very, very confused and can't understand why you would choose your job over her."

"Yes, I can understand that, and how are you and your mother doing? This must be especially stressful for your mother, and at her age—she's almost eighty, I believe. Is that not so?"

"Yes, as well as can be expected, but she's a tough old bird. She'll get by. Of course, we're both very upset, but it must be doubly worrying for you, being so far off, and now your op's in trouble. Shall I come out and lend a hand?"

"No, it'll be over one way or another later this evening, but thanks for asking. But, please, no questions about the op. Listen, my friend. I want you to do me a favor. Have my retirement papers ready for my signature when I return, please, and tell Ernna of my plans. That might cheer her up a bit and soothe her frayed nerves. Anyway, I should be back tomorrow sometime—midafternoon, I'm hoping. I'll catch a cab, and don't worry about me. If we succeed, we succeed, but if we fail, I fail."

"Ahmet, are you sure? Your pension won't be worth very much, and my sister has expensive tastes. And after you've been with her 24-7 for six or seven months, you'll most likely start to get on her nerves, and she'll be wishing you had a job to go to. You know, Ahmet, you can be a little controlling at times, even annoying, and I'm sure sometime down the road you'll wish you hadn't packed your job in."

"You may be right, but nonetheless, yes, I'm quite sure I want to retire, and if it becomes necessary I'll get some kind of job—maybe a night watchman or some kind of job where my background and clearances may prove to be a plus. Your sister has been playing second fiddle too long. It's time she got all the attention she needs and deserves. Anyway, must go. I'm on stage shortly, the center of attention at least for a few hours. Hope I don't blow it."

"Whatever that means. You're a good man, Ahmet. Take care, and may God be with you."

"Good-bye, Mamet."

Ahmet turned off his cell and lay on the bed, trying to relax prior to going downstairs and facing the hunchback. He wondered what Al was up to.

Probably relaxing, figuring out ways to spend his million. This whole scenario is a win-win for him regardless of how things turn out for me.

Being grilled by Al seemed much more than just a challenge; it seemed more like scaling a snow-covered mountain in his bare feet. Ahmet now had strong reservations about besting Al. All confidence in his training and his abilities had vaporized. He felt on his own, alone, and vulnerable; he missed Ernna. One or two slipups on his part would doom the op, but Ahmet was now well beyond really caring about the op. He had bigger fish to fry. He dozed till six and then donned his white outfit and headed down to the bar after jamming a few pills into his jacket pocket.

As he entered the bar, he could see that it had been closed off by management at the request of Spanish authorities. *So this is where this little charade will take place.* He could see that Jason and the man with the huge hands were chatting, both sipping water. As Ahmet entered, they nodded affably enough. There, in place, adjacent to the till, was the polygraph, presumably set up by local officials who had already departed. Al was nowhere to be seen but would most likely be arriving soon, making a grand entrance, hump and all.

Jason was speaking to the man with the huge hands nonchalantly, not lowering his voice, almost as if Ahmet were not standing within hearing distance.

"Bulldog, you did a splendid job all round, and Pettigrew will be informed. I shouldn't be surprised if some kind of promotion or bonus comes your way—you deserve it, really. Now, as previously discussed, take Isule down to the local lockup."

"Just as long as I don't get promoted over you."

"What do you mean, old man?"

"Well, for a long time, as both you and she know, I figured I should be team lead. I thought I was smarter and cleverer, but as it turns out you're the clever one, very clever, and I truly believe things would have turned out very different if I'd been running this op—and by different I mean not as good. I'm proud to have served under you."

"Okay, mate, enough back slapping. Now off you go—no need to see how this all plays out. I'll fill you in tomorrow morning. Don't forget—wheels up at ten, so I'll see you in the hotel lobby at eight, and take this half bottle of whiskey with you. I just bought it—you deserve it."

"Cheers mate," responded Aubrey.

Jason came very close to advising Aubrey not to call Susan, but he knew if the man wanted to call, he'd call. What the hell—Aubrey could face up to reality tomorrow, for he was sure Pettigrew would shortly put a flea in Susan's ear and maybe even Aubrey's, and that would be the end of that little affair, if it was an affair. Deep down Jason had to admit to himself he liked Susan a lot, but the self-imposed specter of Clara wouldn't permit it, and he was still too much in love with Clara's memory to move on.

With that, Aubrey departed, leaving Jason alone with Ahmet, both men silently waiting for Al. Ahmet quietly studied the polygraph, a model he'd never seen before. It looked antiquated, yes, very old indeed, but that was Al's problem, not his. In a few minutes the bell from the lift sounded. Al emerged with a wide smile; he'd cleaned himself up, had a shave, and looked remarkably professional. Yes, Al had gone that extra mile, knowing full well that he might be the keystone to war or peace, so he dressed and carried himself appropriately, standing as erect as he possibly could, hands stretched out as if greeting royalty, as if to say "here I am," eyes alert, hair slicked down and combed straight back, and leather shoes shined to a patent-leather sheen. He wore a dark suit, a white shirt, and a subdued light blue tie with light red hash marks. He was a credit to his training, a credit to his profession. After all, he was a polygrapher—probably the only one on the island.

Jason couldn't take his eyes off the hump. He tried but couldn't. It was hopeless, so he caved and just stared, but at least he had enough sense to keep his mouth closed. *Must be like being permanently pregnant*, Jason thought, but Al would have never agreed; over the years he'd grown very fond of his hump, thought of giving it a name but changed his mind—a bit too creepy. Even if it were possible to have it surgically removed with no consequences whatsoever, he would have most certainly refused. His hump was more than a physical attachment; it was an emotional appendage, a confidant, an arbiter, and, yes, a friend to converse with now and again.

Al eyed Ahmet, the man in white, who was sitting, back erect, legs crossed, sipping—or was he gulping?—a beer from a pint glass. He appeared full of bravado and arrogance, like he'd not a care in the world. Of Ahmet's woes, Al was clueless.

Arrogant SOB, thought Al. *Face like a hateful bull, ready to rip the matador to pieces, and I'm that matador. Just hope I haven't overestimated my own capabilities and underestimated Ahmet's. He looks so bloody confident, full of pomp, certainty. I've got to maintain my edge. Can't understand why he's so cocksure when I'd stake a king's ransom that he's a liar—though I wouldn't stake a farthing of my own money. I could use a few allies, someone to bounce a few ideas off of, someone to help me decide on an approach to best break the bull. Maybe he is a liar but feels he can overpower the polygraph and me—big mistake.*

Unbeknownst to Al, he, the matador, did have allies in his struggle against the bull. First there was Ernna, the banderillero, fleet of foot, ready to stick long, colorful, barbed banderoles into the neck of the bull and always just managing to avoid the deadly horns as his head swished to the left and then right, hoping to gore his tormentor. Another ally was the Mask, a picador mounted on a horse padded to the gunwales with thick armor made not of steel but woven, mattress-like fabrics designed to absorb the eight-inch horns of the bull, though the sheer momentum of the bull would occasionally dismount the picador, causing him to run for safety, nimbly leaping walls. The picador would jab the bull between the shoulders with a lance as close to the banderoles as possible. Both the lance and banderoles were designed to weary the neck muscles, forcing the bull to lower his head more and more, making it easier for the matador to slay the bull in the prescribed manner: a single sword thrust between the shoulder blades directly into the heart. Anything less would result in boos from the crowd, boos from Jason. Yes, Al had allies, but of them he knew nothing.

"Hello, hello, hello," said Al. "How you chaps doing? Okay, Ahmet, give me a few minutes to examine this contraption. I see it's already been set up by the locals, probably calibrated as well. All the markings are in

Spanish, but I can work around that. This, my friend, is the MX-101T. The 'T' stands for trainer; it's used to train wannabes. About fifteen years old, but by today's standards it's a dinosaur—very little brainpower in the form of advanced electronics or sophisticated computing power, and it has no memory to speak of. It can't remember a thing, like having a severe case of Alzheimer's at age fifteen. A better comparison is the automobile before the automatic transmission—very manual, very mechanical, clunk, clunk. Compared to my cell, the 101T is a dunce, but in the right hands, my hands, she'll purr like a pussy cat."

Jason watched as Al switched the MX-101T on. Just like in the movies, a dozen or so what looked to be pens or cartridges sprang to life, oscillating up and then down, the ink marking the paper in regular patterns. At the moment all the pens were in sync, as the 101T was in test mode. Al then shut the machine down and tore off the used paper. He then checked to ensure sufficient ink and paper remained for him to complete his examination of Ahmet, which should take less than an hour.

"Well, Ahmet, we're in luck. I cut my teeth on the MX-101T. I know this puppy inside and out, and if you tell me the truth, I'll help you convince Jason you're not a liar, and if I understand correctly, he'll give you the documents and you can do with them as you please. But if you're telling me porky pies, I'll figure that out, and if that were to be the case, I think Jason will make a few phone calls to his handlers, and you go home empty-handed."

Ahmet said nothing. He was preoccupied, and what Al was saying was of no consequence to him whatsoever. He just couldn't get the sight of Ernna out of his head. Perhaps she was shackled to her bed, heavily sedated, and he, Ahmet, was the cause of all her grief. He just wanted this whole sham over and over in a hurry. There was no way he could not outwit Al—no way.

"Ahmet, please sit in the examinee's chair, right here, a few feet from the polygraph, and, Jason, if you don't mind, step back and sit next to the till. And please be quiet—no interruptions from here on out. Don't worry, you'll be able to hear every word."

Jason obeyed, motioned Al to come closer, and then whispered a few words into his ear.

Ahmet failed to even notice what had just transpired and most likely wouldn't have cared even if he had noticed a few whispered, unintelligible words.

"Ahmet," said Al upon returning, "I know what you're thinking. First, you're probably thinking you can outfox me, and you're probably right, but you can't outfox the pair of us, and by this I mean me and the 101. That's impossible. You're also thinking I win no matter how things turn out, and by this I mean I get the money whether you're proven to be a liar or not, and you're right. The money does, in all scenarios, come to me, but that doesn't mean I'll not prove you to be a liar or not a liar. The consequences are high, astronomically high—war or peace. If you're a liar and the plans are proven to be unreliable, then the US Navy goes home, none the worse for wear, but if you're telling us the truth and the plans are reliable and unaltered, then it's bombs away."

Ahmet yawned, crossed his legs several times, rubbed his hands together vigorously, and frowned the frown of the bored, as though ready for a nap.

"Ahmet, please try to focus. You did agree to cooperate, but right now you seem miles away. Now, can I assume that you have never taken a poly—never, never, never—and you have never had any training in quote unquote beating the polygraph. Is that true?"

"Yes, of course. Can we just get this over with, please? And to reiterate, I have never taken a poly and have had no special training in passing or beating a polygraph, but if I did, Al, I'm sure I could not only beat the polygraph but make you look simpleminded and witless."

If Al had a nickel for every time he'd heard "can we just get this over with?" he wouldn't even be on this island, but he didn't have carloads of nickels, so down to business. By Ahmet's demeanor and bravado, Al thought him to be a liar, but now he had to prove it or better yet get Ahmet to admit that the plans had been altered and were unreliable. The best way to prove Ahmet was a liar was to catch him in a lie or, better yet, several lies.

Al walked over to hook Ahmet up. Ahmet, almost without thinking, turned both palms up and then back down so they rested on his knees. Al briskly hooked Ahmet up and then bluntly asked, "Why did you do that?"

"Do what?"

"Turn your palms up, as if presenting them to me for some kind of examination or inspection. It looks like you know it's standard operating procedure for any polygrapher to inspect an examinee's hands to ensure you haven't rubbed them with some ointment or something that will somehow skew your test results. Guess what? It is standard procedure for me to examine the palms of all examinees. How did you know to turn your palms up for examination, Ahmet, if you have never been polygraphed? Tell me that. Please, Ahmet, tell me, if you can without lying—and, remember, you did say you'd cooperate, so cooperate and don't be evasive."

"I don't know what you're talking about. Just a coincidence, I suppose, and again I reiterate that this is my first polygraph. Now, can we move on? I'd like to get this over with sooner rather than later."

"You know, Ahmet, I'm starting not to like you. Don't try to make a fool out of me. I've been at this game too long, so no more lies, please. For the time being we'll just assume it was a coincidence, but no more coincidences. One coincidence, yes. Two coincidences, never."

"Okay, let's move on. Any more lies, and I'll just have to assume you're a habitual liar and not cooperating, and I'll further assume that the plans have most likely been tampered with or are a complete fabrication. If that's the case, I'll tell Jason you're bluffing, Iran's nuclear weapons accomplishments are just a figment of your imagination, everyone goes home happy, and no one ends up with a Tomahawk missile in their back yard, okay?"

Ahmet said nothing but resolved to really try and make Al look the fool; he just had to focus, go into a trance, overload his brain, and rely on his training, which, to date, had never failed him—at least never failed him in training. But this was the real deal, and Al wasn't shooting blanks. It seemed to Ahmet that Al really wanted to get at the truth; the mantle of being a polygrapher must weigh heavily on him, and the money, at least temporarily, had become a distant second to the truth.

"Ahmet, I need to establish a truth baseline for you, so please answer these questions truthfully. I'm sure this is all new to you, but just listen to the questions and answer yes or no. Okay, power on."

As soon as power was switched on, Al could see that Ahmet's blood pressure was astronomical. If he were examining Ahmet for the Agency, Ahmet would have been immediately disconnected and sent home or to the emergency room. The Agency didn't want anyone dying or stroking out while under their control, but as Al was not working for the Agency, he chose to ignore Ahmet's blood pressure readings and focus on perspiration and respiration only, as the BP readings were off the chart and totally unreliable.

Al then proceeded to go through three baseline calibration questions that had to do with the day of the week, a simple addition problem, and a third asking Ahmet to determine if one integer was between two others; sometimes the answer would be yes, sometimes no.

The baseline calibration questions went along these lines for five minutes or so:

"Is today Thursday? Is today Monday? Is four plus three equal to seven? Is four plus three equal to eight? Does the number seven lie between five and nine? Does the number seven lie between eight and ten?"

After switching off, Al asked Ahmet to lie when answering the next series of questions.

"Ok, power on."

"Does the number seven lie between eight and eleven?"

Ahmet replied, "Yes."

"Does seven plus three equal twelve?"

Again Ahmet said yes, they continued in the same vein for three or four more minutes.

"Well done, Ahmet. I have an excellent baseline on you. Shortly I'll go over the rest of the questions with you. I'll ask you questions concerning Iran's bomb-building capabilities, and I do mean the Bomb. Okay, let's take a break. Take five, but not much more than five minutes, please. Get up, walk around, hit the head if necessary. Try to relax, Ahmet—your BP is pretty high. Elevate your legs if you like, and if you're on any meds, it's okay to take what's been prescribed."

Ahmet was unhooked.

Al sat, pondering Ahmet's results to the calibration questions—the results that were lies and the results that were the truth. There was no way he could establish a truth-corridor, as this was the only polygraph he had administered to Ahmet. Besides, the 101T just didn't have the necessary memory or necessary applications software to establish a meaningful corridor.

Even though Al could not establish a truth-corridor, he could use the perspiration and respiration results, as reflected in the inky, sinusoidal readings to the baseline calibration questions, to help him determine when and if Ahmet lied to the upcoming questions about Iran's nuclear weapons capabilities. By eyeballing the highs and lows to the baseline calibration questions, Al figured he could determine if Ahmet were lying or telling the truth to the final round of questions. It was kind of like being forced to use an abacus in the wake of power being lost to an electronic computing device, but Al had no other choice; time was short, and Jason needed answers in the here and now, not tomorrow.

"Okay, Ahmet, before we start I want to go over a few more things with you. What Jason really wants to know is, are those plans that presumably show Iran going nuclear genuine, or have they been altered by you or a colleague of yours? It looks like the Americans are firmly convinced of their authenticity. That's why there are two carrier groups in the Med. We all know this just by watching CNN, which I did just a short while ago. There's enough American firepower in the Med right now to devastate known Iranian facilities, facilities that are most likely developing weapons of mass destruction. Also, Israeli jets are on Israeli runways armed to the teeth, so this is a very serious situation. But if I find that you're lying, Ahmet, those ships will turn around, and Israel will push back."

"Can we please get this over with? You're starting to bore me with this constant repetition. The plans are genuine. How many times must I say the plans are genuine?"

"Yes, so you say, but before I hook you up, there's one more point I'd like to clarify. Tell me, Ahmet, are you Muslim?"

"Most Iranians are Muslim, so, yes, I'm Muslim, but why do you ask? Do you dislike Muslims, maybe? Can we continue?"

"And are you a devout Muslim—I mean live your life by the teaching of the Koran?"

"Yes, of course I live by the Koran, but what has that to do with my polygraph and the truth? In fact, it's none of your business."

"I understand devout Muslims are forbidden to partake of alcohol, yet I just saw you drinking the light of my life, beer. You see, I would rather forfeit my religion than give up beer, but you, on the other hand, seem to enjoy beer, which is contradictory to your religious beliefs. Or am I, simple heathen that I am, missing something?"

"Yes, I am Muslim, and, yes, I do occasionally drink alcohol. I didn't say I was a good Muslim, only that I am Muslim by birth."

"So you are not a devout Muslim as you just said, and you see, Ahmet, this highlights the fact that you have now lied to me a second time. I know for a fact that most Muslims do not drink, full stop. So maybe you're not a Muslim at all, or not a very good Muslim as you say, or just a plain bad Muslim, but your credibility has again been called into question, and very soon I won't believe a single word you say."

Al was now playing Ahmet's game: a lie for a lie. He had no idea if most Muslims did or did not drink, full stop, but Ahmet not being Muslim offered interesting possibilities. Al was in his element, happy beyond words—happy using words to his own advantage. The stakes were high, and no one was looking over his shoulder, so he could afford to be cavalier and reckless in his examination of Ahmet.

"Okay, before we get to the heart and soul of why we're here, let's review what you've previously said. First, you received the plans from the nephew of the Iranian president who had access and is sympathetic to your cause, and the plans were passed to you with little or no delay. So there is no way the plans could have been altered by either this nephew or yourself, as you or your colleagues just didn't have the know-how to change the plans and any changes made by you would be obvious. All this passing of plans took place in Iran, I assume. Is that right?"

"Yes, in Iran of course—where else?"

Yes, where else, and based on what Abdulla Abdulla told me in London, I also believe the plans to be authentic, but have they been tinkered with, edited in some very subtle way? That's the question the world would like answered, and answered quickly.

"Anyway, I almost forgot. One more point. I believe when we first met you said you and Isule were solicitors by profession, and at first I believed you. Well, an hour ago, Jason's mate asked Isule what his profession was, and, well, dear, dear, dear. He said he was a businessman buying shirts from the Chinese and marketing them in Iran, and he was even so gracious as to provide us with his Iranian office address and telephone number in Tehran for us to check if we wished. Guess what? Jason did check, and while the address is legitimate, the phone number is a bit quirky. You see, the international dialing code your friend—or should I say your associate?—gave us is not even in Iran, but maybe Isule just has a poor memory or had a hard time focusing, thinking he might be learning to shortly fly, English-style. What do you think?"

That simpleton Isule! Ahmet's brain was close to erupting. *Why didn't he just refuse to cooperate? Why start making things up, things that can be readily verified?* Isule had hung him out to dry again; this was the last straw. Between Isule's bad tradecraft, Ernna's suicide attempt, and the Mask, he was near to being over the top. He was near to breaking. He just wanted to go home to be with his wife or die of humiliation right here and now, but for the sake of the op he had to persevere.

Ahmet said nothing to Al's question, too steamed to even think straight. He just sat, looking forlorn, gently rubbing his forehead with the tips of his fingers.

"Ahmet, that was lie number three, and I suppose whether you're a businessman or solicitor is really irrelevant, isn't it? Anyway, you've got a lot to contend with, I'm thinking. I don't think you're having such a good day, but please be patient. One or two more points, and I think this nightmare of yours will be over. I believe you said you have not seen the plans. Yes, I'm sure this is what you said, so I'd like you to now examine the plans you say you've never seen."

Al passed the plans to Ahmet, who immediately and properly oriented all six pages with the page numbers at the top right.

"Wow, my friend. How did you know to orientate all the pages with the page numbers top right? I'm under the impression that only technical people, people with engineering and science degrees, know that page numbers are top right on documents of a technical nature, and you tell me you're a solicitor or perhaps a businessman, and neither is very technical. You're admittedly not an engineer. Everyday Farsi calls for page numbers on the bottom, centered. How did you know to orientate all six pages with page numbers top right? I think I know why, Ahmet. Because you've seen these documents before and most likely altered them or had them altered. But now I need to understand why they were altered, and then we can all go home. The first night I'm home I plan to drink myself stupid, and that's a promise, and again I must remind you that if you fail to cooperate, Jason will brand you a liar."

"No, not true," said Ahmet. "I just know that these sorts of light blue documents have the page number at the top right. I don't know how I know, but I just know."

Now Ahmet's greatest fear came to fruition: the Mask put in an appearance, slowly at first but becoming progressively worse as Ahmet sat and thought and sat and thought. *When will this crucifixion be over? I can bear it no longer. I must go to my room, relax, take more meds, and hopefully put this monster back into its cage before it kills me.*

Ahmet was totally confused, becoming more and more agitated, more and more willing to be bested by this hunchback, this polygrapher.

"Ahmet, I want to hook you up and ask you one, simple question. I'm totally convinced you're lying about these documents. I'm sure you have altered them, but how and, more importantly, why? I need to know that. Then we'll call it a day, and you can return to your room and home tomorrow. That one, simple question is this: 'Have you ever even been to Iran, in person, in the flesh?' That's the question I mean to ask you."

Ahmet's face dropped, hung low so his chin rested on chest. He let out a sigh and then another. The Mask reigned supreme. Al reigned supreme, in all the glory of a polygrapher who'd met and bested an archrival. Ahmet's face told the tale. He was a liar indeed—no question about that.

"I can see by the look on your face that the answer is 'No, no, you have never set foot in Iran.' Do you know what country that international dialing code is for, the one Isule willingly passed to Aubrey? I'll tell you, it's Tel Aviv, in Israel, and I'm one hundred percent certain that you and Isule Are Really MOSSAD, ISRAELI INTELLIGENCE! Am I not right?"

"Yes." Ahmet was broken, and if Al had switched on, he would have seen that Ahmet's blood pressure was off the charts. Ahmet could stroke out if not unhooked and unhooked now, but that was no concern of Al's. He was victorious, a credit to his profession, and he might have prevented a horrible conflict. He turned, winked at his hump, and headed for the bar. He needed a stiff one, large, undiluted.

Ahmet unhooked himself as Jason stepped out of the shadows wanting to make sure he understood what had just happened.

"So, Ahmet, you're an Israeli agent undercover as an Iranian agent feeding altered Iranian documents to the CIA. Documents that you somehow got from an Iranian traitor. How did you receive these plans in the first place?"

Ahmet was now fully cooperating, having been bested by Al. Logic and cunning had triumphed over training and deceit. But for the Mask and Ernna, Ahmet may have fared better, but he'd been dealt a bad hand in this, his swan song, and only looked forward to turning in his papers and leading the life of a man with no purpose, no ambition, and a pittance to get by on.

"How did I receive the documents? By mail, all of them, from an Israeli agent working as a requirements engineer in Tehran. He had access to planning documents that, milestone by milestone, mapped out Iran's plans to acquire the Bomb. I never ever even left Tel Aviv. I then passed the documents on to Roger, who sent them back to the CIA. At first the documents were genuine and easily verifiable but of no real consequences—no top secret information, just official correspondence. Roger built up a trusting relationship with me and with his superiors. I would tell him what the next drop would contain, and the next drop contained what I said. However, for this last drop I told Roger this drop would contain detailed plans clearly showing that Iran is close to building a nuclear weapon. He told his handlers, who told the US State Department, who informed the Israeli government of Iran's advances in building the Bomb. Israel demanded a preemptive strike against Iran by the West, but the US wanted to review the stolen documents first. Our current Israeli government has wanted to bomb these nuclear facilities for years, but they needed American involvement. That's all the American government really wanted—irrefutable proof before acting against Iran— and this final set of plans would provide that proof. But Al intervened, stealing the plans from me and preventing this irrefutable proof from getting into the hands of the CIA and eventually to the president, who, faced with undeniable proof of Iran's nuclear ambitions, would have ordered Iran's nuclear facilities destroyed. It's all very simple actually."

"So Mossad was acting without the approval or knowledge of the current Israeli government? Mossad, on its own, determined that these Iranian nuclear facilities should be destroyed and using falsified documents intended to manipulate the powers that be in Tel Aviv as well as the United States into bombing Iran's nuclear facilities. Is that the case, or did your government know the plans had been altered?"

Without waiting for a response, Jason continued. "So, Ahmet, the plans were altered by you, by Mossad?"

"Only the last set of plans—the ones you have in your pocket."

"I repeat did your government know anything about this op, especially altering the plans to dupe American intelligence and the current American administration?"

"That's well above my pay grade, Jason. Isule asked me and my colleagues to plan the op, but as far as who knew what, we'll probably never know, and as the strike will now most likely be called off, I suppose we're none the worse for wear—or that's how I see it, anyway."

"Yes, makes sense to me, but why didn't you just pass the altered plans over to the CIA, very straightforward, very simple? You know from Mossad to the CIA with love?" asked Jason.

"Yes, too straightforward, too simple. You know what they say about accepting gifts from friends: be careful, be wary. The CIA knows that some in Israel want Iran's nuclear weapons facilities destroyed. They would have been super cautious about accepting and acting on such a gift from Mossad; they would have analyzed the documents in great detail and most likely discovered that they had been tampered with and tampered with by Mossad. Relations between the US and Israel would have taken a huge hit. We needed a more circuitous, less friendly, route."

"And how were the plans tampered with, Ahmet?"

"Yes, good question. The completion dates were altered by Mossad. We had to prove to the United States that Iran posed an imminent threat to the region. We had to alter the dates, as Iran will not be capable of building a nuclear weapon for some time—maybe five years—and this is what the unaltered documents showed. But Mossad wants Iran's capability to produce a nuclear device destroyed now, once and for all, and so do the our politicians and the vast majority of Israelis, as well as many in power in the United States."

"I'm still confused, Ahmet," said Jason. "So who authorized your op?"

"I'm not really sure, but I believe our previous government asked for a plan that would eventually lead to the destruction of Iran's nuclear capabilities. My colleagues and I put this plan together when we received documents from one of our agents that showed that Iran would someday, years from now, be capable of building the Bomb. Anyway, to make a long story short, when we had a change of government the plan went dormant, but not for long. Then, out of the blue, the plan is reactivated, and like they say, the rest is history. I'm pretty sure it was Mossad's leadership that reactivated the plans behind the backs of our politicos, but that's just a guess. I'm thinking I'm probably right, but I could be wrong, who knows. An Iran with a nuclear offensive capability would probably spell the end of Israel and most likely Iran also."

"So, Ahmet, if Al hadn't stolen the plans detailing Iran's nuclear weapons strategy, Roger would have delivered the plans to Central Intelligence. Is that right?"

"Yes, as proof of Iran's lies and proof that Iran's nuclear weapons programs is alive and well and on track to go live very soon, and the altered plans would have proven just that to the United States. Then, if all went well, America, in conjunction with Israel, would have attacked Iran and attacked with a clear conscience, thinking they were meting out justice to a rogue country intent on destabilizing the whole of the Middle East and maybe even the world."

Jason had one final question, a question that would summarize, unequivocally, Israel's involvement in altering the plans provided to Mossad by Israeli agents working inside Iran.

"So, as you've said, Ahmet, Mossad did alter the plans, made some date changes that are probably difficult to detect. However, plans are, as we speak, in place for Iran to build the big one but not for several years into the future?"

"Yes, we changed the completion dates, and I'm repeating myself: all the actual completion dates are years into the future, and Iran is years away from building the Bomb. These documents you now have in your possession are planning documents. Over time, completion dates could slide one way or another, but Iran will not have the Bomb for years. It is intending to get the Bomb, but who knows when? After all, these are just planning documents, and things do change. Now, can I go lie down, think pleasant thoughts, and prepare to catch my flight home tomorrow?"

"Yes, of course you can, but I'm sorry, I'll have to keep these plans."

"Whatever," responded Ahmet as he left, tossing his lucky pocket watch into a rubbish bin.

"Well, Al, you did it. You may have just prevented a nasty incident and saved quite a few lives. I'm going up to my room right now and ring my director, who will pass what just transpired to the PM, who will pass it on to the president, then down the chain to the US Navy. So it looks like no strike against Iran, and we can sleep the sleep of the good, knowing we did a good day's work."

"Excuse me, sir. Haven't we forgotten something?" Al asked slyly.

"What? Oh, the money. Follow me. I'll get it for you."

In his room, Al was delighted: a million smackers, not dollars but sterling—about a million and a half Yankee bucks. He turned his head, and if it were physically possible he would have kissed his hump, but a wink would have to do. *Tomorrow back to Whitby*, he thought. *Back to Margaret and a life of swilling pint after pint, talking nonsense, and exchanging tall tales with the locals. God, I love it'.*

Jason was also in a happy mood. Al had gotten Ahmet to crack. In retrospect it all seemed so obvious, so simple, that Jason was surprised that it had almost succeeded. The Israelis wanted Iran's nuclear facilities eliminated. Its reluctant ally the Americans needed proof of Iran's nuclear ambitions, so Mossad altered Iranian planning documents to show a nuclear capability sooner rather than later. The plan was for Roger to receive the altered plans from Ahmet, but Al had intervened. How Al knew of the hand off was and probably would remain a mystery.

Jason had just gotten off his secure line with Pettigrew, informing her that while the plans were legitimate, some dates were bogus and Iran would not have a nuclear capability for years, and, yes, he had the altered originals and would turn them over to her tomorrow, along with a detailed report.

Her final words to Jason were, "Oh, and, yes, I got the fax from Aubrey. Every boffin in both MI-5 and MI-6 is examining them. It'll be interesting to see what kind of explanation the Israelis come up with, I mean about Mossad's role in the whole operation. Let them sort their own house out, I say. I'll brief the PM on what you've just told me straight away, and he can figure out who needs to know what. Good work, Jason. See you tomorrow."

After that call, Jason returned to the now open bar, ready for a real pint or two. Aubrey was nowhere to be seen; he'd probably drunk that half bottle of whiskey and was now sound asleep. After analyzing and reanalyzing what had transpired that day, he figured that if the dates were bogus, as they were, the US Navy would stand down, Israeli aircraft would come off alert, and things would start getting back to normal. He also figured he and Aubrey and Al had saved thousands of lives, at least for the time being. With those pleasant thoughts in mind, he finished off his second pint and headed toward the lift, hoping for a fairly good night, a night not interrupted by the mangled body of his dear Clara.

***

The phone rang at five; it was Pettigrew. She seemed to be very agitated, in a very bad mood.

"Listen, Jason. Bad news. The Americans and Israelis have attacked; right now they're bombing the hell out of any and all facilities that may be related to the Iranian nuclear weapons program. We were not consulted but were only told of the attacks shortly before they began, and before you ask, yes, the PM did chat to the president, and the president did know that the plans were bogus but decided to attack regardless. You two try to catch an earlier flight, and one more thing, and please don't give me any aggro. The PM would like you to turn those plans over to that American agent on Ibiza and to do it now before leaving. No one asked me what I thought. I can see it right now in my mind's eye at the United Nations—the plans held high, copied and passed around to justify the attack, even though our side knows they're bogus or at least partially bogus."

"Will the Americans inform the UN that the dates were altered and Iran wasn't expected to have a nuclear capability for years, or will they let the altered completion dates stand as legitimate?"

"I don't know, Jason. That's not our business; that's politics. The Israelis won't tell, that's for sure. The Iranians won't say much other than that the plans are forgeries, and they're partially right, but Iran did have plans in place to go nuclear and build weapons of mass destruction, and this is why I believe Iran was attacked. Iran was attacked for standing up a program to develop a nuclear bomb even though the delivery date is years off. The Iranians lied about their intentions, of that there can be no doubt. They did have a viable nuclear weapons program, dozens of sites, fissionable material, centrifuges, et cetera, and would have eventually got the Bomb, so the powers that be in DC and Tel Aviv decided to take out their nuclear capabilities now rather than wait a couple of years. Who's to say? Maybe it was the best of all possible decisions. Anyway, they'll be plenty of turmoil and dying in the Middle East, at least for the next six months or so, but that's the Middle East—they keep playing that same old tune over and over. Anyway, Jason, come to my office when you return. Aubrey's been sniffing around Susan again—apparently talked to her more than an hour last night, or so she says. Woke her out of a sound sleep Frightened the lass with that phone ringing so late. I thought you had a chat with Aubrey. I guess I'll have to weigh in."

Later that day Jason and Aubrey touched down at London's Heathrow Airport and proceeded to MI-9 as directed by Pettigrew. Jason could hear Pettigrew lecturing Susan to the tune of words, words, words. Jason knew that Pettigrew would cut Aubrey more slack; his contributions in Ibiza were monumental, and as for Susan, well, Susan would just have to learn to cope with men like Aubrey, insincere but amusing, or get hurt over and over, but over time she'd eventually learn—and probably learn the hard way, again.

After meeting with Pettigrew, Jason returned to his office; he sat peering out the back window, hoping Clara would put in an appearance. It had been some time since he had last seen her. His heart ached, but he knew someday he'd have to let her go and move on. If she could have somehow known how he'd been carrying on the last few years, she'd have been very annoyed and very disappointed.

Wait. Hold on, he said to himself. *There she is.* It was Clara, walking toward him, smiling and waving, right hand held high. As she got closer, he realized she was saying something. She was mouthing something, and, yes, he could make out what she was saying.

"Jason, I love you, but please get on with your life, darling. Enjoy it. Have some fun. I won't be coming to see you again. Please, dearest, be happy and live your life to the fullest, and when you do finally cross over, I'll be waiting."

Pettigrew had quietly sidled up behind Jason, as had Susan and Aubrey.

"Well, Jason, did you see her? Did she say anything? Come on, man—out with it."

"Yes, Chief, I saw her. She said she won't be coming back and I was to get on with my life and enjoy it, have a bit of fun."

"Well, Jason, and what do you intend to do?" the chief quietly asked.

"I guess I intend to enjoy the rest of my days, but I'm kind of out of practice. Don't know where to start—a bit on the rusty side."

"Yes, Jason, I get the message. Susan, come here." With that, the chief put Jason's hand in Susan's and told them to go out together and have a good time, and they both were to take tomorrow off. With that, they nearly skipped out the door, smiling broadly and chatting, chatting, chatting.

"But I thought you said no fraternization. I'm confused."

"Get over it, Aubrey."

The End

EPILOGUE

(One Year Later)

Ahmet and Ernna

Upon returning to Israel, Ahmet did in fact submit his resignation. Getting through that window proved to be easy once he realized what the window represented. Once his mind was irrevocably made up, the window cooperated; no contortions were required. The only thing that was required was a leap from the ladder to Ernna. She had won. The game was over; she not only caught but overwhelmed him with unrequited attention and affection. Ahmet's retirement papers listed medical conditions requiring rest and relaxation as the documented justification for his early retirement, but Ernna was the primary, undocumented reason, and they both knew it. If it came to choosing between his job and her peace of mind, well, that was a no-brainer for Ernna. After all, she reasoned, Ahmet had been on the go for almost three decades, and it was time for him to pack it in and enjoy. Ahmet's pension was prorated at 65 percent of his base pay, better than anticipated, enough for a small holding on the outskirts of town with ample space to farm chickens and sell eggs. Caring for the chickens became one of the many duties Ernna gleefully assumed. She was busier now than ever. Between routine housework, farming, and looking after Ahmet, who actually required no looking after at all, she kept busy from dawn to dusk. She was deliriously happy, she drank in moderation, and her bouts of depression and outbursts of unbridled hate evaporated like a morning mist in the fall. This new state of affairs was due to one thing, and that one thing was that Ahmet was home permanently, 24-7:

no more travel, no more risks, and no more worry and isolation. She could see him and talk to him whenever she wished, and for that she was grateful beyond words.

Ahmet, on the other hand, was bone idle. He had nothing to keep him busy or tax his brain, and as the Mask had dematerialized since his retirement, he was as fit as a man half his age. But in reality, fit or not fit, he was quite miserable and bored to death. He became morose and ill-tempered, but Ernna wasn't sympathetic or understanding in the least. *I've been to hell and back because of you*, she thought. *Now it's your turn.* Ahmet tried ballroom dancing, but that turned out to be too expensive, and he could see that Ernna wasn't very happy with him dancing with other women, most much younger and quite good-looking. Farming was not in his blood, and sport was out of the question; he was just too lazy, and he even managed to convince himself that he was too old for sport of any kind, even fishing, which, in his younger years, he'd quite enjoyed. While his wife was as busy as a bee, relaxed and cheerful, he spent hours each day daydreaming, wishing for the old days, wishing for that next op that he knew would never come. He had no friends, no interests worth mentioning; even collecting stamps or coins proved to be too tedious, too tiresome. He tried golf but always managed to bump into former colleagues still in Service. The conversations were forced, strained to the point of being embarrassing even though Ahmet had helped train many of them, so golfing also proved to be a nonstarter. Over several months he came to the realization that he was on a downhill slope to oblivion, a one-way ticket with no transfers. He knew the old days were gone forever. Even the infrequent calls to Mamet were uninteresting, for upon retirement all of Ahmet's accesses were terminated and Mamet had to be coy about what he said, as Ahmet was no longer part of the team—he was out of the loop, as they say. Soon the calls stopped altogether, and except for the occasional birthday or funeral Ahmet never saw or spoke to his once best friend. Ahmet became quite the whiner, complaining about one thing and then another. Nothing made him happy or even content; occasionally he even yearned for the peace of the grave. He even went so far as to speculate about his own death, how it would affect Ernna. *At least she'd know where I am, all the time, and she'd most likely visit me daily and chat. So much better than not knowing where I am or what*

I'm up to. Anyway, she'd adjust, even convince herself she's better off now than when I served.

Ahmet had managed to keep his sidearm in retirement, claiming it had been lost some time ago, locale unknown. Mamet backed him; after all, it was only a gun and Mossad had thousands. For now Plan B was out of the question, back-burner material. Ernna was just too happy, but later Plan B would prove to be his best exit strategy, a way for Ahmet to finally and unconditionally escape the insanity and madness of a meaningless life full of misery and woe.

Roger and the Missus

Roger was making plans, plans for becoming British. He'd talked it over with the missus, and his plan was to take an early retirement, grow the clock shop, and in future sell new clocks and maybe even learn to fix watches. Between timepieces and his Agency pension, he and the missus should be able to get by handsomely, and if the missus took a part-time job, maybe hairdressing, for which she had been trained, they'd be on easy street. Of course, retirement was some years off, yet to be determined, but as soon as Roger got word that Al or another polygrapher was on his way to the south of England, his papers would be submitted pronto-like and he'd be on civvy street within sixty days. Hopefully retiring was some time off, but he wanted to be prepared just in case.

How the Agency decided when an individual was to be reinvestigated for top secret clearance was serious business, and the algorithm used was unclear but many things were probably considered, including financial stability, travel, security violations, associations with foreign nationals, exposure to certain types of classified material, seeing a psychiatrist for a whole range of emotional issues, and, of course, run-ins with the law, which could include anything from a DWI to spousal assault. Being convicted of crimes of a more serious nature like robbery would result in an automatic termination of one's tickets, as individuals in prison had no need for tickets. Anyway, Roger figured he had at a minimum four years to grow the clock shop, and he'd need all four to make his little shop of clocks more profitable, profitable enough to sustain himself and the missus in style—not elegant style as the missus would have preferred, but more than comfortable, comfortable enough to make the neighbors envious and the missus gloat, and she wasn't shy about gloating. They had the neighbors over for drinks regularly and, as Roger was American, had a barbeque two or three time a year—no mince and hot dogs but steak, all prime cuts, usually rump.

In the interim, up to retirement, it was Agency business as usual: broken clocks in, packets of money in, a short TDY, fixed clocks out, intel out. Roger had gotten used to this rhythm, and no one was the wiser, not even the neighbors who spent a great deal of time peering out from behind closed curtains trying to figure out how a clock repair shop could generate enough money for Roger and the missus to live in such luxury and afford two cars with petrol costing close to seven quid a gallon and her car, a fairly new Range Rover, getting only ten miles to the gallon.

Roger convinced the missus that his next posting would most certainly be stateside, which was probably true, time frame unclear. She disliked the States—didn't want to live there or even visit—so Roger informed the missus he'd retire rather than relocate. Yes, giving up a job he dearly loved and never returning to the country of his birth were significant sacrifices, and hopefully she appreciated what he would do. She did, up to a point, but no way would she ever emigrate, and she wouldn't spend the rest of her days being overly appreciative of her husband. Yes, if a stateside posting seemed imminent, they'd retire and remain in England in their lovely home with a substantial annual income, income enough for two cars and an annual, super holiday, but in reality what Roger was planning was not how to avoid leaving England but how to avoid any and all future polygraphs. He'd lucked out with Al, God knew how, but he wouldn't tempt fate a second time. He was sure any future polys would result in imprisonment, divorce, and financial ruination. Roger still had nightmares about the death of his brother-in-law, how it had all happened, who was really driving. In weaker moments he tried to convince himself that he was the passenger. He also had thoughts of giving himself up—confess to the truth and take his medicine—but what would that accomplish? Nothing, so Roger was prepared to live with the guilt and lies. After all, lies were the fabric of any intelligence agency, and if one could not credibly lie, one would never succeed at the CIA. Roger mused: *If lying for one's country is honorable because it serves a greater purpose, then me lying also serves a greater purpose—to wit, keeping my family happy and safe and together.* After that flawed analysis, Roger seldom thought of that fateful crash and the death of his happy-go-lucky brother-in-law. He focused instead on eventually extricating himself from the Agency, family intact.

Pettigrew

The chief seldom thought about retirement and what she might or might not do, but one day about six months after the Ibiza op she got out of bed, called Susan, signed her papers, and packed it in. She did relocate to Hull in the northeast of England and did watch the breakers roll in, crash on the rocky shoreline, and drench the careless. While one wouldn't describe her as happy, she was content. She worked part time, pro bono, at the local animal shelter, working relentlessly at enforcing RSPCA guidelines for the care of pets, pets of any kind: four legged, two legged, or no legs at all. Each was to be treated kindly, and if you crossed that line between discipline and cruelty, she'd be all over you with a clenched fist and a warrant. With her two cats, Socks and Muffin, who she read to on a regular basis, she whiled away day after day in her third-floor flat overlooking the North Sea; she even purchased a pair of binoculars for people watching. She accomplished little, but accomplishing little was at the top of her bucket list. A life full of achievements and an MBE to be handed out by the Queen in the upcoming New Year were sufficiently rewarding for this lady.

She made no effort at contacting Jason or Susan or anyone else at MI-9. That was history, in the past, and this final chapter of her life would be devoted to helping the less fortunate, particularly those with a bark or meow. She did, however, have a limited social life with some of the other residents of the Metropole Hotel, a large Victorian hotel converted to flats about a hundred years earlier. There were early drinks Friday and Wednesday, and every Sunday evening there was a gathering down in the basement where a conga line was formed and, to the sound of 78 rpm records, the Funky Chicken was danced. As the conga line moved first this way and then that, everyone would periodically lock hands at the chest and flap their arms in unison like a chicken. While the chief performed admirably, she came in second to Mrs. Cod and Lobster, who usually led the line. Mrs. Cod and Lobster got her nickname from a pub she used to own in Runswick Bay. So while the chief did have some kind of life after MI-9, did manage to keep herself occupied, and did not pick up any truly bad habits, she was lonely and missed her MI days—or was it her youth that she really missed?—days that came and went like a spark in the dark. Now the only thing she had to look forward to was the Funky Chicken and eventually a grave on a hill overlooking the sea.

Mamet and Isule

Word had gotten around: Isule was not only an amateur but a dangerous amateur who put self-aggrandizement and pomp above the op and his colleague's safety. Upon returning back to Israel, Isule had been in such hot water because of his shabby tradecraft that he was grateful to only be demoted two pay grades. If it weren't for the fact that the op in Ibiza was technically a success, he would have been drummed out of Mossad in a heartbeat and probably sent to work as a clerk in an Israeli embassy in darkest Africa, where he would have most certainly bragged about his exploits as an agent of Mossad and claimed to be just waiting to get back into the clandestine game of undercover ops, underhanded chicanery, and hush-hush affairs of the heart. While Isule could tolerate the demotion, what really irked him was that he was to be Mamet's new partner, and Mamet was to be senior—something Mamet never failed to remind him of. Apparently, upper echelon thinking was that Isule could learn from Mamet, or perhaps someone up the chain just had an evil sense of humor, knowing full well the pair had nothing but contempt for each other and that the better man would eventually prevail. Mamet reveled in his new seniority and watched with masked glee as Isule moved himself from his corner office with a lovely view to a crammed cubicle with little natural light. "And what about your African violets? How will they fare? Not very well, I'm sure—the lighting is so bad. They'll all die in this cubicle, one at a time, and you can be certain of that."

Mamet sat, feet on desk, staring at the back of Isule's head. *After twelve months of sharing an office with this person I know nothing at all about him. No good morning, no good night; he just comes and goes like a mute. He's so taciturn it's eerie, and it's not like he's an enigma—he's as transparent as a millpond. All he wants is personal success, and I suppose he's sulking and will continue to sulk until he's got the biggest desk in all of Mossad, and then he'll start yakking a mile a minute.* Isule's present desk, a smallish one of blemished white plastic veneer, was tucked away in a corner so that Isule sat with his back to Mamet, the entrance, and any and all windows. He definitely didn't have an unobstructed view of anything except for a framed portrait of Moshe Dayan, patch and all, about three feet away, directly above. Between his monitor, phones, and keyboard Isule had very little space, even for a coffee mug, so a dozen or so of his precious plants were scattered here and there round the office.

As Mamet studied Isule, he wondered for a second time what made the man tick, if anything. *Maybe he's just like his plants—only reacts to external stimuli. He has no real inclinations one way or the other, just wants to get birthday cards by the dozens and be top banana, and just can't understand why he's not top banana already.* To compare Ahmet and Isule would be like comparing an owl to a squirrel. Isule and Ahmet were like chalk and cheese. While Ahmet was of a quiet nature—a loner, pensive, methodical, and maybe even a plodder—Isule was flamboyant, quick to laugh, and temperamental. He loved people—any kind of people would do in a pinch—so this self-imposed silence was most likely killing him one atom at a time.

Mamet rose, looked out the window, and then surreptitiously sprinkled a pinch of something onto the nearest plant. It was Roundup, a recent American import, and after a few more pinches over the next week or so the plant would wither, linger on, but eventually die, much to the annoyance of Isule, who could never quite figure why his plants were dying and at such a steady pace. Mamet always had an explanation: poor light, the heating, not enough water, too much water, fertilizer. "Yes, fertilizer—you know you're overfertilizing, my friend. I'm sure that's it." When one plant died, all the rest were relocated and repotted but to no avail. In a few more months a second would follow the first into the mulch pile, and then a third, until Isule restocked the office with a different variety of African violets, a more hearty variety, almost indestructible per the nursery, but Mamet knew better.

Aubrey

Aubrey's performance in Ibiza did garner him a bonus, a thousand pounds, but when Mrs. Aubrey found out about it, she insisted that they spend it all and then some on a holiday to the south of Spain, preferably some seaside town on the Mediterranean Sea with plenty of nightlife, loud music, red wine, and tapas. At first Aubrey objected, but he eventually came round to her way of thinking, knowing full well that after a couple of glasses of wine she'd head straight to her bed, leaving him opportunities to get to know the local women better. The more these locals drank, especially if he were paying, the friendlier they became and the closer they danced. Aubrey had a ball every night but failed to reach even second base with the local ladies, most feigning poor English, so the week progressed from one boring day to a night full of expectations that somehow never materialized. Before one knew it, they were back at the local airport, boarding pass in hand. When boarding the flight back to England, Mrs. Aubrey, knowing full well her husband's fear of flying, immediately ordered two large whiskeys, both for Aubrey; she'd be the designated driver. Aubrey really appreciated this act of kindness and even went so far as to clutch his wife's hand during takeoff, though more out of fear than affection.

"We'll have to do that again. I had a jolly good one, and that was rather decent of you."

"Yes, Aubrey, quite nice, and I expect you to carry through and book another hol back to Spain or Portugal before it gets too hot, and when we get back home my back needs rubbing. A nice massage from you, and then we'll get all dressed up and go to your local together. Such fun, and remember to tell your cronies I'm your wife, not some hussy."

All Aubrey could think was *Bloody hell. Thank God I'm back tomorrow. I wonder how he's getting on—probably shagging her by now. Why do these old farts get all the luck? Mind you, if anyone deserves a break, he does.*

Regardless of his wife's sometime cloying behavior, Aubrey had to admit to himself that the two of them did have a fairly nice holiday, and while the days were unimaginably long and uninteresting at least they were hot, uninteresting days full of sunshine, happy people, and the seaside. In fact the time they had together plus his guy time was more than he expected. *Maybe I should just be content with her, learn to overlook her faults, and get on with the drudgery of it. She's not a bad one, just so bloody annoying and possessive, but when she's in the right frame of mind a pretty good one, though I'm hardly an expert on that good one, bad one thing. I strike out one after the other, so why keep trying? I'm in my forties, and he cut me out of my last attempt with her, and he's in his fifties so maybe I should give them a wide berth and focus on mine and her. I'll have to sleep on that, but I've plenty of time regardless. I'm young, so maybe I'll settle down in a year or two or never.*

For a year or so Aubrey kept trying, kept striking out, and kept thinking that one day he just might hit a grand slam, but in his heart of hearts he knew that would never happen. He began feeling guilty about neglecting her and continuously pushing her away—in a nice, gentle way, but pushing her back nonetheless, as if to say, "not now, later." But later seldom came, and deep down he wondered if his aloofness might also be hurting her, but he was still young, had plenty of time to mend fences and still be actively engaged in the chase.

Then shortly thereafter, while on a shop up on Oxford Street looking for a sheepskin coat for her birthday, just off Oxford Circle, he experienced an epiphany. A portly gentleman about his own age, standing next to him queuing up to catch the number 9, clutched his chest, turned blue in the face, and fell straight to the ground. No wavering or swaying, not a word, just down like a falling tree. Several individuals who appeared to know what they were doing took charge, tried this and then that, but to no avail. Soon an ambulance appeared and picked him up like so much litter—didn't want the holidaymakers to be disturbed. Aubrey saw it all, covered the remains with his overcoat, and thought, *Who am I kidding? I've no idea how much I've left—maybe now, maybe later—and I'm wasting most evenings out looking for mince when I've steak back there. What a fool.*

With that, Aubrey's mobile flew into action.

"Yes, tonight's the one. I know it's not for a fortnight, but tonight we're out to the Mayfair—shrimp cocktail, lobster au gratin, and cherries jubilee, and I'm keeping these toasty warm for you, and before you ask, no, I'm not drunk, and, yes, I am deliriously in love with you."

Aubrey couldn't believe what he'd just said but was glad he'd said what he said, and he meant it.

Jason and Susan

Jason and Susan gently walked through Hyde Park, arm in arm, rather quiet and rather subdued, even pensive to a fault, almost as if they were strangers seeking some sort of common ground for conversation; any excuse would do. They'd been a couple for the last year or so—well, for at least most of the last year. Every two or three months there was a row, and they'd separate, but between Pettigrew and Aubrey's coaching they'd reunite and try again, and this afternoon they were on the first day of reuniting for the fourth time. The object of, or perhaps more accurately the reason for, these rows was Clara. Jason, no matter how hard he tried, couldn't shake Clara, though he wanted to and wanted to very much. Whenever the pair had an unusually fine day, a brilliant day full of passion and laughter, Jason would unexplainably grow sad and morose and wind up weeping. Understandably, this reaction not only upset Susan but annoyed her to distraction; there'd be an exchange of unkind words, and Susan would leave, holding back a mountain of tears, while Jason, being the gentle soul that he was, just paced, sometime for hours. For days they'd avoid each other, and then there'd be a reconciliation, a date, a patch-up, and like today both would try to figure out options, what to do next.

"Well, Jason, what do you think? Are we worth all this fuss, or should we just throw in the towel?"

"I'd like to think we're worth it. Just give me a bit more time. I do love you, Susan, and want to be with you for the rest of my life—even marry you, if you'll have me."

"Jason, Jason, Jason, you've had years to get over Clara; she's gone. She even gave you 'permission' to live your life to the fullest and have some fun, but you just can't manage to give her up and focus on me, me, Susan, and as far as marrying you, that'll never, never, never happen, not in a gazillion years, and why? Because you're still married to Clara. Look, Jason, let's sit on this bench. Give me your left hand. What's this?"

"My wedding band."

"And you talk of marrying me. Will you put our band on top of Clara's, or what? Jason, maybe you need to talk to someone, a specialist, a counselor of some kind. You've got to shake Clara before you and I can truly be a couple. Sometime I think you feel guilty about being with me, like you're cheating on Clara or somehow disrespecting her, a dead women, and how do you think that makes me feel?"

"I understand. You're right, but, bloody hell, I'm doing my best, Susan. And like I just said, I do love you."

"Jason, I appreciate those words, but that's it—they're just words. Over time those three words have become a crutch, a way for you to avoid reality. What we need is action, and the sooner the better. Tell you what, let's visit Clara's grave today, now, together. Maybe that'll give me some insight into what you're going through, or should I say putting us through."

"Sure, okay. No problem, Susan. Let's get going before it gets dark. Supposed to be freezing fog tonight."

Within fifteen minutes the cab pulled up to the Chelsea Memorial Cemetery, and within another ten they stood gazing at Clara's tombstone with its simple, unambiguous epitaph: name, dates, and the simple but profound inscription "Victim, London Bus Bombing." Adjacent to the grave was a small white marble flowerpot containing one red rose in mint condition, probably put in place that morning.

"It's lovely, Jason. She must have been a wonderful woman. Like they say in the pictures, 'it's hard to compete with a dead woman'—no matter what I do, Clara will have done it in half the time and twice as good."

"Please, Susan, you don't have to compete with anyone. It's you I love and you I want to be with, not … not Clara … she's gone. I know that, and I don't want to ever risk losing you. I do want to marry you and soon—yes, very soon."

"Jason, you talk of marriage, but I'm not even sure I want to continue seeing you. You're so complex, so deep, so screwed up. Really, you are screwed up, Jason, and only a madwoman would want to tie the knot with you. I know your heart's in the right place, but you are really, really screwed up, so screwed up."

With that they both burst out laughing uncontrollably, hugging and kissing till sanity prevailed.

"We better get going, but hold on. Let your screwed-up friend clean up the grave a bit, get rid of these twigs and such."

In less than thirty seconds they were off hand in hand, laughing. First he, then she, back and forth, a giggle, a laugh. They were hysterically happy, and it felt good.

"Hold on, boyo. Let's have a look at that hand again. The ring—where is it?"

"Where it should have been years ago. I buried it when I tided up the grave, and there it'll stay, forever."

"You're a good man, Jason. Maybe there's hope for us after all." And there was: twenty-five years of happiness.

Al and Margaret

Margaret's in the kitchen at the Duke, doing what she does best, preparing for evening meals, while Al's in the bar doing what he does best, drinking ale by the pint. The past year had been hectic. The improving economy brought more trade, more trade meant more staff and more work, and Margaret thrived on it. Like her mother, when all the work was done she'd slip out into the bar for a few drinks with Al, both always sitting on the settle.

"Hold on, hold on, Mr. Narrator. I assume you are a man and hopefully not a little man."

"Who's this interrupting my narration? Oh, it's you, Margaret. Yes, Margaret, I am a man. You do know its bad form to interrupt the narrator. You're becoming more and more like your mother—so abrupt, pushy-like. If you work at it, you may even become a martinet someday."

"Thank you for the compliment. I will work on it, but not now. Besides, I have a favor to ask."

"And how may I be of service to you, Margaret?"

"I hope you won't find my request too bold, but I would like to narrate this final segment, the one about me and Al, myself in first person. Would that be okay?"

"Why? Have you been unhappy with my narration?"

"Well, to be quite honest, there have been times where I questioned your depiction of certain characters in certain chapters, but overall you did a good job, quite reliable and accurate."

"That sounds to me like a left-handed compliment, Margaret. Are you accusing me of being an unreliable narrator? My word, if that were the case, we might have a sticky wicket on our hands, and where would that leave our dear readers? But after all, this is fiction. An example of my transgressions would be very helpful, if you don't mind."

"Certainly. I question your depiction of Roger as a buffoon, but I suppose like any caricature you take the obvious and exaggerate it for effect—make the character more interesting, less lifelike. Is that the case?"

"Yes, what you say is true. Roger is a very uninteresting man, very dull, so I chose to give him a makeover, though not necessarily a good makeover. Do you have another example?"

"Yes, Ernna. Surely she wasn't as disturbed as you picture in your narration, emptying her husband's suitcase and throwing and kicking his clothes about like she's some sort of madwoman."

"Yes, yes, another exaggeration, for effect as you say. You know, I take the uninteresting and morph it, make it more interesting, but after all, this is fiction, as I've already said. We in the narration business call it creative license like when a reader adds emotion to a drab paragraph when reading it aloud, makes it more alluring. Ernna's over-the-top behavior makes her a more interesting personality. Anyway, Margaret, if you would like to narrate, please do. Proceed, but don't make a habit of it."

"Thank you."

* * *

Well, it's like this: I never asked Al where he got the money. Didn't want to know; I figured knowing too much might get me into hot water some day so I never asked and Al never volunteered. A perfect arrangement for the pair of us.

Anyway, Al's in the bar drinking. Surprise. No, Al's a good drinker—has several pints and then goes over to lager, seldom goes legless, and is never awkward or stroppy. The Duke is doing well, very well, thank you very much. All that money is just sitting in our Swiss bank account earning 5 percent per annum, and up to now we seldom tap into it. In fact, if the truth be known, we don't even need it. No, I tell a lie—we did buy a small cottage just down the road, cash. Al and I head home every night about eleven. Doug closes up; he's a full partner now, does all the heavy lifting, and has all the rooms above the kitchen for himself and Daisy. It works out swimmingly.

A few months ago I wrote out a check for a hundred thousand to the Marie Curie Nurses Society; they care for the dying. They cared for Father—enough said about that. I got Al to sign it after a darts match. He'd had a wee too much to drink. Well, I didn't say the man was a saint, but there was little or no grumbling the next day, though he did ask me what I thought about adding a few pence to our bar snacks—as if a few pence would offset a hundred thousand. I just smiled. Al can be real funny about a few coppers, but he soon accepted it. Enough said about money; back to the kitchen. As you all know, the UK is noted for its fish and chips, and these islands do have some excellent cold-water fish, especially cod, plaice, and haddock. Actually, though, the most popular fast food is Indian—anything from chicken or beef tandoori to chicken tikka masala to vindaloo. All are lovely, but you have to like spicy foods, which I do very much.

One spicy food that's not very popular here is Mexican. Just hasn't caught on, and I can't figure out why, as it's quite tasty, so this evening, with Christmas not too far off, I'm going to see what I can do to turn things about for Mexico. I'm preparing a huge pot of Mexican medley as we speak, and just prior to official closing I'll set it out for everyone in the pub and see their reaction. The ingredients are pretty basic and inexpensive: a large pack of mince, chili powder to taste, a green pepper chopped, an onion diced. Right now I'm slowly browning the ingredients on the AGA in my biggest pot. Okay, looking good. Now, two tins of beef consommé and a large tin of tomato soup. Stir well. Finally, several cups of precooked noodles, corn, and minced mushrooms, and, voilà, we're done. I seldom salt—let everyone salt to taste. I'd put some salsa out, but most of the locals wouldn't know what to do with it—have to take things a step at a time.

I do love cooking. If you've been paying attention, you'll know I inherited my love of cooking and cookery books from Mother. I stare in the direction of the AGA, imagining Mother. Last orders are out, and she's smoking a fag and sipping a gin; the smoke curls up and over her forehead, threatening to set her hair alight. She's smiling in my direction …

I look up, snap out of my daydreaming. There's Bob, looking like a wet week.

"What's up, Bob? Something's wrong? Come on out with it, man!"

"Well, Margret, it's like this."

The fact that he called me Margret, not Margaret as is his usual manner, clues me in. Good news is not coming to town this Christmas.

"Mr. Steed was knocked down in front of the White House, walking home, not so long ago. He died in hospital. Just heard—thought I'd let you know."

I sigh; the fact that he was nearly ninety doesn't help, and Christmas is less than a week away. There's always some sort of drama or sadness at Christmas, without fail. From the other room comes the sound of silence; the bar's dead quiet. Mr. Steed was well liked.

"Well, as Mother would have said, life's for the living. You're a long time dead."

I force a smile, grab the pot of Mexican medley, and head for the bar.

Printed in the United States
By Bookmasters